EYE OF THE BEHOLDER

Shari Shattuck

A SIGNET BOOK

SIGNET
Published by New American Library, a division of
Penguin Group (USA) Inc., 375 Hudson Street,
New York, New York 10014, USA
Penguin Group (Canada), 90 Eglinton Avenue East, Suite 700, Toronto,
Ontario M4P 2Y3, Canada (a division of Pearson Penguin Canada Inc.)
Penguin Books Ltd., 80 Strand, London WC2R 0RL, England
Penguin Ireland, 25 St. Stephen's Green, Dublin 2,
Ireland (a division of Penguin Books Ltd.)
Penguin Group (Australia), 250 Camberwell Road, Camberwell, Victoria 3124,
Australia (a division of Pearson Australia Group Pty. Ltd.)
Penguin Books India Pvt. Ltd., 11 Community Centre, Panchsheel Park,
New Delhi - 110 017, India
Penguin Group (NZ), 67 Apollo Drive, Rosedale, North Shore 0745,
Auckland, New Zealand (a division of Pearson New Zealand Ltd.)
Penguin Books (South Africa) (Pty.) Ltd., 24 Sturdee Avenue,
Rosebank, Johannesburg 2196, South Africa

Penguin Books Ltd., Registered Offices:
80 Strand, London WC2R 0RL, England

First published by Signet, an imprint of New American Library,
a division of Penguin Group (USA) Inc.

First Printing, September 2007
10 9 8 7 6 5 4 3 2 1

Copyright © Shari Shattuck, 2007
All rights reserved

 REGISTERED TRADEMARK—MARCA REGISTRADA

Printed in the United States of America

PUBLISHER'S NOTE
This is a work of fiction. Names, characters, places, and incidents either are
the product of the author's imagination or are used fictitiously, and any resemblance to actual persons, living or dead, business establishments, events, or
locales is entirely coincidental.

The publisher does not have any control over and does not assume any
responsibility for author or third-party Web sites or their content.

This one's for Joseph, who inspires, encourages, and loves me. I can't say "thank you" enough, so this says it for always.

ACKNOWLEDGMENTS

My heartfelt thanks go to Laura Cifelli for her enthusiasm and support on this book. My gratitude goes as always to Paul Fedorko for his constant cheerfulness and encouragement, which mean so much. To my daughters, who love that I write and what I write, and who give me the time and space to write, even when they need me to come watch them jump on the trampoline, make them a sandwich, or help them save the world, I love you with all my heart. And to the two best girlfriends on the planet, Karesa McElheny and Michelle Echols, for standing by me through everything and holding me up a little bit higher so that I can see a little bit farther, I want to say thank you. My world is a far lighter place because of you.

Chapter 1

The Eye of the Beholder Beauty Salon and Day Spa opened for business on an ominous Thursday in January. Since the day after Christmas a roof of clouds had loomed over Shadow Hills. For seventeen days the strongest rains in a century had pelted the wealthy horse suburb of Los Angeles, and at last, on this particular Thursday, the valley's ceiling was showing small cracks. Blots of liquid blue sky were seeping through. The cerulean stains were widening and leaking clumsy shafts of sunlight that stabbed small, greedy portions of the drenched, forest green hills. The effect was glorious, luminous swatches of color surrounded by hungry shadows that hovered, eager to swallow up the vibrant outbreaks.

Greer Sands passed through the glass doors of her salon, looked up to the less threatening sky and the promising hills, and took in all the beauty of the two combined. The effect was so huge and dangerous that it made her tremble.

She stood for a moment overwhelmed by the pull of crackling storm energy surging in her. She felt the force of the weather as an insistent thrumming, as though her torso were strung with cords that nature plucked with skilled fingers, playing her like a musical six-string barometer.

She did not turn when her partner, Dario, came out and lit a cigarette as he settled next to her.

From his impressive six-foot-four-inch frame, Dario smiled down at his friend with handsome, watchful eyes. "Feeling like a guitar in a mariachi band?" He had known Greer, and her special sensitivities, for over fifteen years.

Her face, which was smooth in repose, revealed her forty-three years when she turned and smiled at him. Soft lines crinkled around her amazingly green eyes and the corners of her mouth. "Something's coming," she said to him through lips so full they almost seemed to get in the way of her words, lips made for pouting mischievously but not for conversation. And then she turned her eyes back up at the play of light as though whatever she sensed was coming was written up there like an archangel's sprawling footnote.

Dario nodded, his thick, black, glossy curls brushing his shoulders, and he watched her with eyes that had been compared to a night sky in the desert: deeply dark, but spattered with stars.

Greer went on, "Changes, and that's always good, and the number three for me—three new friends, I think—but there's something"—she tilted her head to one side, pursed out her luxurious lips, placed a hand flat on her chest, and shuddered—"something else, something black."

After their twenty years of friendship, Dario was accustomed to these bouts of psychic revelation, and though he had learned to trust them from experience, he'd never grown particularly comfortable with them, especially not when they pained Greer.

He shifted his weight and felt a surge of protectiveness. Time for a distraction technique, he thought.

"Something black?" he asked in feigned exasperation. "I certainly hope not! I've got enough peroxide on Mrs. Lawless to bleach Mickey Mouse! It had damn well better not come out black."

To Dario's relief, it worked. Greer laughed, and with a last glance over her shoulder at the magnificent panorama of water and light, she turned and walked back inside.

Dario watched her, admiring the way he had cut her thick auburn hair. He admired—in a purely objective way—her full and womanly form, but mostly he admired himself for having the good sense to have a woman like Greer as a best friend. Gratitude filled him like the warm burn after a shot of good whiskey as he watched her walk back to the reception desk. He sighed and glanced at his watch; minibreak was over. Crushing out his cigarette on the bottom of his shoe, he put it carefully into the trash can, scanning to see that there were no other butts or trash on the sidewalk in front of their brand-new salon.

Greer watched Dario survey the busy salon as he walked back to his station, and when she caught his eye they shared a proud wink. The Eye of the Beholder was off to a roaring start, even considering the weather. Or perhaps because of it, Greer thought. She and Dario had done their research well. This wealthy area was ripe for a luxury salon, and because of the mudslides and flooding limiting their routes to Los Angeles proper, the locals were eager to get out and be steamed, soaked, prodded, cut, trimmed, buffed, shellacked, blown dry, and thrust back out into their Expeditions and their five-bedroom ranch homes.

Greer turned to the pretty teenager standing next to her. Celia had a body that seemed capable of growing in only one direction at a time, and so far it had been up. Her hair was stick straight, blue-black and hung so flat that it gave the impression that her pale face was peeking through a velvet curtain. She was wearing a short black tube-like dress and clunky black Mary Jane shoes. The overall effect was that of an exclamation point.

"Celia," Greer addressed her, "I've got an appointment coming in now, so you'll have to mind the front. Remember what I told you about the appointment book?"

"Double-check the date before I write it in and only use pencil?" the punctuation mark of a girl asked as though unsure of the correct response.

"And?" Greer prompted.

"Get the phone number?" Celia added.

"And?"

The brown eyes flicked left and then back, widening slightly in fear. She couldn't remember anything else. "And . . ." She bit her lip.

"And relax." Greer smiled at her, feeling the girl's nervousness bristling a foot away from her body and smoothing it down with caressing words and a warm hand on Celia's arm. "If something goes wrong, we'll fix it. It's not the end of the world, or the salon. Okay?"

Celia smiled sheepishly. "Okay," she agreed.

Greer left the girl to worry her way through her first day. She entered the small treatment room and lit a candle; the cleansing scent of rosemary permeated the small room. Sensing a presence outside, Greer went to the door, opening it just as the woman was raising her hand to knock.

"Hello . . . Leah?" Greer asked, extending her hand in introduction. "I'm Greer. Come right in and get comfortable on the table, facedown. We're doing reflexology today, right?"

Greer wasn't surprised when Leah's nod seemed a bit reluctant; she was used to people who were hesitant their first time. So she asked a question she knew the answer to. "Anything in particular you want to work on?" Even without her special sensitivity Greer would have been able to read the signs of stress in this woman. Even after a sauna and a shower, Leah had her hair combed back so neatly that it looked more like it had been mowed, and there wasn't a trace of mascara smudged below her eyes.

"Just stress." Leah had the face of an Italian aristocrat, beautiful, with sienna brown eyes that appeared specially designed to veil any true sign of her inner life. "General stress." The way she held herself perfectly upright spoke of relentless self-consciousness that never took a day off.

To give Leah privacy while she took off her robe and climbed up onto the massage table, Greer stepped out into the hall. Standing quietly, with her hands on her chest and her head bowed, Greer closed her eyes. She found and focused her mind and intuition on Leah's energy.

It had the usual amount of city smut all over it, and a large dose of anxiety, things that were so prevalent these days that, sadly, most people had come to think of them as acceptable. There was damage too, though—abuse. Greer sensed a man with a violent temper and the woman's fear, both all too common as well. Sighing, she reentered the room after a soft knock and moved to the side of the table. Then she placed one hand between Leah's shoulder blades and the other on the small of her back. Greer held still and took a deep breath to sense the flow of energy through Leah's taut and toned body.

Immediately Greer's hands began to heat up, and the dark blockages showed themselves to her clearly. One thing in particular leaped up and stung her.

Before she could block it, into Greer's mind rushed one of the two worst memories of her life. Since she was a child Greer had known things about people, little things, like who was on the phone when it rang. She had sensed only small things until one night when she was fifteen.

She had been getting ready to go meet her best friend, Sarah, for a movie at the local mall, and David Bowie's "Changes" blared from her record player. As she had leaned toward her mirror to dab on some sparkling lip gloss that Sarah had loaned her, the reflection before her had suddenly faded out of focus. Her face had still been there in the mirror, but suddenly and sharply a sensation had overcome her that was so enveloping that she had been incapable of using her senses to experience anything else.

The phenomenon had removed her completely to another place, a place where time was bent, impossible to track; she had been aware only of utter and absolute terror. She had known without words or question that Sarah was in mortal danger. Greer had stumbled, unseeing, to the phone, still holding Sarah's lip gloss in her hand, to try to call her friend, to warn her. Then the room before her had disappeared and the vision had begun.

The fifteen-year-old Greer could see Sarah; she was walking along a dark sidewalk, and coming the other way was a man—a man whose face Greer couldn't make out. In her vision the man was surrounded by jagged shapes, like shards of darkness that moved with him but were visually impenetrable. She could feel Sarah getting closer to him; she could sense the man's egregious intent as he stalked toward her friend. Alone in her room, Greer dropped to her knees in despair and cried out loud, "No! Sarah, run!" But of course Sarah couldn't hear her. Desperately Greer struggled to focus on the numbers on the phone, but she could see nothing but the phantom figures, the night, and the strange, jagged black shadows.

The two figures came closer and closer to each other

until, paralyzed with fear, Greer watched as the man passed Sarah, turned, and struck her on the back of the head; then he dragged her into the bushes of an empty lot that bordered the sidewalk.

Then, as abruptly as the vision had begun, it ended. Greer found herself lying on the floor of her room, the green shag carpet distorted as it came in view inches from her face. She was sobbing and sweating. With trembling hands she gathered the phone and dialed Sarah's number.

Sarah answered the phone in her usual bright, eager voice. Greer almost fainted with relief. She made an excuse for the call, then went to her bathroom to vomit up the bile of fear. Greer was so shaken by the force and depth of what she had seen and felt that she was afraid to tell anyone, afraid to be thought a freak. Even Sarah, who had always treated Greer's talent with enthusiasm, couldn't always conceal that she was vaguely uncomfortable with the oddness of it. This vision, Greer worried, would have both repelled and frightened her friend. So Greer didn't tell Sarah; she convinced herself that it had been a fantasy or an anxiety attack. She briefly considered telling her mother, but decided against it. It was a choice she was to regret until the day she died.

The two friends went to the movie that night. They had ice cream afterward, and laughed and flirted with a group of boys they knew from school. Greer reveled in the familiarity and acceptance of her friend, but being unable to tell Sarah about her eerie experience made her feel distanced, different, and lonely. And, no matter how hard she tried to deny it, she couldn't shake the uneasy apprehensiveness.

In the days that followed, she'd tried to put it out of her mind. She had been afraid that she was crazy, that people would think she was some kind of bizarre mental case. That she *was* some kind of mental case.

And Sarah was fine, wasn't she? The whole thing had been the product of an overactive imagination coupled with teenage angst, she told herself. As the days went by, the convincing reality of the vision faded.

But two months after the vision, just after midnight on a cold Saturday night, the doorbell woke Greer from a sleep riddled with ugly dreams. She could hear her father's muffled voice and that of another man conversing through the closed door, and then the sound of the locks being unlatched, the door opening, and her name being called.

Confused, frightened, and sleepy, Greer was summoned to speak to the visitor, a police officer, in the kitchen. He wanted to know what she'd done earlier that evening. She told him that she'd gone to a coffee shop with her friend Sarah, that they had stayed until about nine and then said good-bye and gone their separate ways.

The officer shuffled his feet, sighed, rubbed his eyes as though they pained him—or maybe he was trying not to cry—and then he told them.

Sarah had been assaulted on the way home. She'd been knocked unconscious, sexually assaulted, brutally beaten, and left for dead in an empty lot. After a neighbor had heard moaning and called the police, she'd been taken to a hospital, where she was in critical condition. All they could do now, he had told them, was pray that she would pull through.

Greer blamed herself, prayed until her knees were raw that Sarah would pull through. She had not.

On the day of her best friend's funeral, Greer sobbed out the story to her mother, and her mother took her by the shoulders and looked into her eyes. Greer had never forgotten what had been said to her on that dismal day.

"Listen to me. You have a gift. One woman in every generation of our family has had this gift for as long as anyone can remember. My sister had it. There's nothing wrong with you, there's nothing to be ashamed of or even afraid of, *but you cannot run from it and you cannot make it go away.* You have to use it, embrace it, and welcome it as best you can."

Greer also remembered what she had said in response. "So, if I had told you before, I could have saved Sarah's life?"

And her mother's quick reply: "No." Then she had paused, looking troubled, and Greer knew that her mother had told her a lie and couldn't live with it, so she changed her answer. "Maybe. Some things you *can* change; some things you can only let go of."

That was it. Some things she could only let go of.

Like Sarah.

The forty-three-year-old Greer looked down at the woman on the massage table in front of her and knew exactly why she was remembering so vividly right now the feeling of terror that she'd had for Sarah so long ago.

She was having it again.

Chapter 2

To reach the house, you turned off the twisting two-lane highway onto a patchily paved road and drove around a canyon shoulder and through a narrow track, then cut between the side of the hill and a thick cluster of pine trees until you came to an open gravel parking area. The house was grand: two-story mission style with thick stone supports holding up a large wooden porch. There was a cluster of four other cabinlike houses, smaller than Greer's, just visible here and there through the trees; the group of five homes was hidden by canyon walls and oak and pine trees nestled within the national forest land. The tiny neighborhood was as isolated and quiet as you could get and still be only thirty minutes from downtown Los Angeles. Greer loved it, and she counted herself lucky to have found it. Today—Sunday—the salon was closed, and she was taking the rare opportunity to get her new house in order.

The rain spattered, softly now, on the roof of the porch outside the kitchen window, and Greer was feeling a liberating relief that could come only from breaking down the last cardboard moving box marked

KITCHEN when she heard a blast of music from one of the two upstairs bedrooms. Smiling, she walked down the hall, up the stairs, and stood in the half-open doorway. On the floor, teetering away from universally awkward pubescence and toward comfortable manhood, her seventeen-year-old son, Joshua, sat adjusting the controls of his CD player. The rest of his things were still mostly lying in piles on the floor or packed in boxes.

"Now you can have some background music to get everything else unpacked," Greer said to him.

"Mom!"

"The sooner you do it, the sooner it'll be done."

"I know. But I was hoping to go hike up the trail first."

Greer looked at her offspring. Just as his father had been, he was handsome, and although he'd inherited, to a lesser degree, the fullness of her mouth, the striking green eyes were a strictly female trait in her family; his, also like his father's, were hazel. His wavy blond hair was worn a little too long and unkempt, and his strong, tall, lanky frame was just beginning to solidify. As she always did when she noticed the physical similarity, she missed Geoffrey, Joshua's father.

"You'll have to wait a little bit before you go hiking; we have a visitor coming over."

"Who?" Joshua asked, his eyes looking doubtful.

"I think it's a neighbor."

Joshua looked at his unusual mother and, cocking his head to one side, he asked bemusedly, "How do you know these things?"

"I can just feel her focused on us." The gift came so naturally to Greer that she still sometimes found it surprising that everyone didn't have it.

Joshua grinned impishly and said with a familiar, teasing cadence, "You are so weird."

"And you," she finished the well-worn exchange with affection, "are such a teenager. Clean up your room."

As she went back to the kitchen, a crease deepened in her brow. She was thinking of her session with Leah and the prescience of danger that had come to her. She still felt the loss of Sarah, still suffered the wound of so many years ago and the desperate regret that she might have done something to prevent it. She must do something to at least warn Leah. But what?

That was the problem. She sighed and shook her head, putting on a kettle for tea. This wasn't the first time she had felt a powerful negative force in someone's future, though it was only the second time she had felt this particular strain of danger. And you couldn't just go up to someone and say, "Hi, I'm clairvoyant, and I'm pretty sure that some psychopath is going to attack you. Probably sometime in the next two months." Not unless you wanted to be investigated by child services first and later by the local detective force.

She would have to think about it. She sighed, reached for the china, and then paused. A new feeling came to her, also about Leah: Leah's face flashed into her vision and then the number one. She smiled; that was good. Leah was meant to be the first of three new friends. More hopeful, she busied herself again and had just placed two cups with saucers on the wide oak table when the knock came on the door.

"Hello, there!" said a friendly, plump-faced woman when the door was opened; her pitch was a bit unnaturally high, as though the visitor were wary that her overture might be perceived as an intrusion. Raindrops slid from her umbrella and splattered on the wide plank boards of the porch.

Greer smiled her welcome and could see the woman relax. "I hope it's not a bad time. I'm Whitney; my

husband, Luke, and I live in the house right there."
She pointed with the dripping umbrella to a much
smaller but charmingly neat and cozy home about
twenty yards to the right. "I just wanted to stop by
and say, 'Welcome to Silver Line Creek.' And, of
course, find out who our new neighbor would be," she
added with a wry drop in her tone to a confessional
note. Her comment was almost obliterated by the
sound of a large pickup truck as it rumbled down the
soggy road and stopped at the locked gate. Both
women turned and watched through a silver veil of
rain as a tall man got out wearing a long oilskin coat
and a cowboy hat. He waved a hand at the two ladies
and then went on with the business of unlocking one
of the many padlocks that secured the fire road for
the exclusive access of the forest service and residents.

As the man climbed back in the car, he shouted
over the loud growling of his giant engine, "Welcome
to the neighborhood!" to Greer, then added, "Hey,
Whitney, tell Luke he owes me five bucks on the
game!" before climbing back up into the raised cab
and pulling through the gate.

Turning back to Greer, Whitney said, "That's Mike;
he lives up the road. If you need any of your motors
made bigger, louder, and more obnoxious, he's got the
best garage in town." They both looked again as the
truck revved its massive engine and pulled easily
through the thick mud. "Actually, I shouldn't be so
antimale. He's really good at fixing just about anything, and he's helped me out plenty of times. Still, I
never really understood that need to turbocharge
everything."

Greer smiled, recognizing Whitney instantly as a
woman who would be in easy sympathy with her, and
she thought, *Friend number two.* What she said was,
"Come in. How nice of you to come by; I'm making
tea for us."

If Whitney noticed the presumption she didn't register it as anything unusual. Instead she leaned the umbrella against the side of the house and held out a freshly baked loaf of banana bread as she stepped over the threshold. "That sounds great, thank you. Here's something to go with it."

Greer took the bread, still warm and smelling deliciously of tropical comfort, into her arms and cradled it like a baby. She was watching Whitney's face. The woman's race was hard to read. She was dark-haired with olive skin that shone like her eyes. She could have been Asian or Hispanic or American Indian, or a blend of several races. Her body gave no distinct ethnic clues; she was well shaped, neither thin nor fat, but strong and smooth with rather more rounded hips and bottom than was generally celebrated by the beauty industry, but which Greer and so many men found far more attractive than the popular alternative. Whatever her origin, she stood there radiating a friendly glow, and Greer was warmed all the way through as completely as the bread in her arms. She took a deep breath, savoring the impending friendship before she introduced herself.

"I'm Greer Sands. I'm sorry I haven't been over to introduce myself, but between moving in and opening a new business, you'll have to forgive me. Sit down, please. I want you to meet my son."

Joshua had come into the room and was hanging back with the slight uncertainty of a foal around a new mare. But when Whitney turned to him he saw a face without fences, a person whose manner was as open as the Montana sky. "Hi, I'm Joshua," he said, and gladly extended his hand.

"Welcome to Silver Line Creek," Whitney countered, taking the offered hand and shaking it warmly. And then she added, laughing, "Well, it's more like a river right now, with all this rain. Did you hear we

broke the record for recorded rainfall? Luckily we
both live on this side of the creek. Bill and Debra live
across the creek bed, and they haven't been able to
get their truck out for a week. The road's under three
feet of water; it's usually just a few inches deep at
the crossing and they drive through it. They had the
footbridge, which is farther down that way"—she gestured downstream to a place hidden behind the pines,
where the banks were steep and high—"until last
week. The trees keep getting uprooted and one of
them smashed into it. Wiped it out."

"There goes my hike," said Joshua.

"How scary," exclaimed Greer. "Are they all
right?" She gestured to the table and Whitney sat
down.

"Oh, sure." Whitney's voice changed, sinking to a
more comfortable place, naturally deeper, with a constant hint of humor around the edges of the words,
and she waved one hand dismissively. "I went to the
store for them on Tuesday and picked up emergency
rations. Luke put the two cartons of cigarettes in a
bag with a stone and threw the care package across
to them, so they'll be fine for a week or so. Then
maybe they'll need another drop. They might even
want food next time." She turned to Joshua, asking,
"Are you going to Franklin High?"

"Yes, ma'am, I transferred last week," he answered politely.

"You transferred? That's got to be tough."

Joshua shrugged. "It's high school."

"How do you like it?"

"It's big," was his simple answer.

"Luke's daughter, Joy, goes there. She's fifteen; you
must be a little older than that."

"I'm seventeen, yes, ma'am."

Whitney fixed him with comically serious eyes.
"Okay," she said, "Now, I know that it's polite to say

'ma'am' and 'sir' and all that, and I really appreciate it, but it makes me feel old, so you can call me Whitney."

"Can I call you 'babe'?" asked Joshua so casually that they all laughed.

"No," Whitney said succinctly.

"You have a daughter?" Greer asked Whitney, backtracking.

"I inherited one. She's with us half the week. It's such a pleasure having a teenager around the house." Her voice was heavily tinged with sarcasm.

Greer smiled at her son. "I think so."

"Well, yours doesn't seem to be in the I'm-the-angriest-most-deeply-wronged-person-in-the-universe-no-one-has-ever-suffered-as-much-as-me   stage. He also doesn't have Pam for a mother."

In spite of Whitney's cavalier delivery, Greer could sense the change in her tension. It was the way with so many of her friends with teenagers. She shared a warm, grateful look with her son, and poured hot water into a pot filled with loose tea leaves before saying, "That must be especially hard on you. How's your relationship with her mother?"

"The witch of Winona Boulevard?"

"Not exactly copacetic, I'm guessing."

"Well, I mean, I just met you and I don't want you to think I'm exaggerating, so let me just simply say . . . she's the most vile, evil, insecure, bitter shrew that ever left a fat footprint on the North American continent." Whitney smiled, all innocent sweetness. "Not that I don't wish her well."

Joshua had eased into a chair across the table from Whitney, and he said, "So I take it you don't make *her* banana bread?"

Both of the women looked at him for a moment in surprise and then burst out laughing. "No, not any-more. Thank you," Whitney said as Greer set a steaming teacup and saucer down on the table in front of her, and followed it with the warm, pungent loaf of bread, butter, and a knife. "I did try at first, for Joy's sake, to get along with Pam, even though Luke warned me that it was a waste of time. And for a little while it seemed like I was making a difference in Joy's life, but oh, no, that wasn't allowed."

"Joy is your stepdaughter's name?"

Whitney looked up from the grain of the wood in which she had become intensely interested. "Yes, the light of my life," she said, and into her voice dropped a dose of sadness that seemed not to belong there, as if a teaspoon of sorrow were an alien ingredient in a batter of constant cheerfulness. "It's such a shame; really, she's a great kid, but she's not allowed to do anything but hate me."

Greer and Joshua both watched Whitney and waited. Finally Joshua said, "Ouch." They all nodded, and then he said, "Could you pass me that knife?"

"You want a piece of banana bread?" Whitney asked him.

"No," Joshua said with mischief in his voice, "I just think it would be safer if you weren't sitting near anything sharp." They all laughed again, and then he said, "Actually, that does smell really good. Can I trust you to cut me a piece?"

Whitney cast him a wry look. "Sure, babe."

Greer was sipping her tea and watching the exchange. Her son had such an amazing way of setting people at ease. Perhaps it was because he had already suffered a life-shattering change and learned that life went on. He often reminded her that the anxiety she put herself through didn't change a damn thing except to steal her happiness.

He'd lost his father so young, and borne it so well. At first he had asked, "Why can't Daddy come to see me?" And she had told him because he was sick. And then she had to tell him that his father wasn't going to get better, and finally that he wasn't ever coming back. "But he's watching over you," she had told him. "He will always be there." And her wise, eight-year-old little boy had held her tearful face in his hands and said, "I know, Mommy; don't cry. I won't forget him."

And there was Dario. Thank God for Dario and the void he had filled in Joshua's life, and vice versa. She knew that Dario missed Geoffrey as much as she did. Their relationship had been so close, so rare.

"I'm sorry," Whitney said pertly. "As usual, I'm running my mouth about myself and I haven't asked a thing about you. Are you married?"

"No." Greer smiled softly. "I was once." She remembered him fondly.

"So, where's your dad?" Whitney asked Joshua.

Joshua shared a look and the bittersweetness of his mom's memory before he responded. "He passed away when I was eight," he explained, and then provided the disclaimer before Whitney could express her sympathy: "It's okay; I got over it, and my mom's partner became a second dad to me even before my real dad passed away."

Whitney looked questioningly to Greer, who filled in, "My partner, as in business partner. We own a salon together; in fact, we just opened a second one up here in Shadow Hills, on the High Street."

"Oh, my gosh, is that you? Cool. You're right next to Jenny Sanchez's place. She's got the coffee shop next door to you. Have you met her?"

"No, not yet. I've been so busy. Is she a friend of yours?"

"Yeah, more like mutual customers so far. I like her salads and she buys my jewelry, but we keep threatening to get together socially. So, you're a hairdresser?"

Greer laughed. "Oh, God, no. Dario is the impresario in that department. I do reflexology, skin care, and Reiki healing. I don't think I'd care for hairdressing, but I love what I do."

"Excellent," said Whitney. "I don't know much about Reiki. I've heard of it; it has to do with energy flow, right?" Greer nodded. Whitney finished her tea and set down her cup but kept her fingers wrapped around it.

"And you make jewelry?" Greer asked.

"Mostly. I work in silver and semiprecious stones. Luke is an artist; he's a jeweler and a painter."

"A very creative couple. You must enjoy what you do."

Greer was watching the cup in Whitney's hands, which she turned by increments as she responded. "I love what I do; hell, I love everything about my life now, finally." Her face clouded even as the rain outside ceased to fall. "Except for Joy. I just wish I knew how to help her." She stared down at the soggy tea leaves undulating in the last few drops of moisture in the bottom of her cup.

Slowly Greer reached across the table and pulled the cup from Whitney's hands. Holding the china in her right hand, she swirled it three times counterclockwise, and then turned it upside down on the saucer. "Shall we ask the cup?"

Whitney's eyes lit up with delight. "You read tea leaves? Cool."

"Keep thinking of your question," Greer told her.

Whitney nodded and closed her eyes. Joshua recognized this as his moment to make a quiet escape. Smiling at his mom, he whispered, "Exit, stage left," before hurrying back to his bedroom.

After she had waited for the remaining liquid to drain and Whitney to focus her question, Greer said, "Now, let's see." Whitney opened her eyes, and Greer turned the cup upright. "Tea leaves are imprecise, to say the least, but sometimes I can get a feeling from them." She angled the cup this way and that, and then with a sharp intake of breath she said, "She's in trouble."

"She's always in trouble," Whitney said.

"No, I mean, there's a very bad influence around her. And it's not her mother," Greer added quickly before Whitney could chime in. "It's male. She's drawn to him because she thinks he understands her. But you've got to stop this."

Greer's face had gone white, and a sheen of sweat was showing on it. Whitney had thought this would be fun, but she felt a squirming in her chest. She watched Greer with a growing sense of unease.

"It's someone you know, but you don't know. Like a . . ." Greer's eyes squinted as though straining to see a face in the cup. "Like, not a friend, but someone she comes in contact with regularly. You have to . . ." She stared intently and then seemed to catch herself. "You need to keep her close to you, keep a constant eye on her." Greer set the cup down and wiped her brow, trying to ward off the evil-tinged shakiness that had grabbed hold of her with the vision. She hadn't expected anything so clear and intense, and she hadn't meant to frighten Whitney. Looking up at Whitney, she saw that her eyes had grown large with trepidation.

Greer was always careful to keep her readings optimistic and helpful. She knew the power of suggestion well enough to be careful not to reveal anything negative in case belief helped to bring it on, but she was at a loss for a way to put a positive spin on this one.

"I'm sorry." Greer tried to lighten the mood, at a loss for other words. "Hell, she's a teenager. Like you said, it's not an easy time for anyone. Just . . . keep a close eye on her, talk to her. It's probably nothing—I get these little senses about things; I always have."

"How accurate are your 'little senses'?" Whitney asked dead seriously. She was thinking that this woman looked like the real thing, and as the daughter of a full-blooded Cree medicine man, she'd seen the real thing before. Greer was clearly shaken, and it scared the hell out of Whitney.

Greer couldn't lie to her. "Pretty damn accurate. But you have to understand that anything I see is just one possibility."

"What did you see?"

"That she needs guidance. Look," Greer said, reaching across the table to touch the other woman's hand. "We just met, and I didn't mean to scare you." She sat back and tried to detour the conversation. "Why don't you bring your husband and Joy over to have dinner with us on Friday? Will you have Joy then?"

"Yes," Whitney answered slowly, watching Greer suspiciously to see if she was trying to distract her. But the truth was, while Whitney *was* curious to know what Greer had seen, she knew better than to ask for bad news, so she let it go.

She said, "That is, Joy will be with us if she deigns to honor us with her presence less than four or five hours past when she's supposed to show up. And I'm sure Luke would love to come. I do desserts, but I'm not much of a cook. Can I bring something?"

"Dessert," Greer said, still feeling slightly dizzy. "Just come on over. I get back from the salon around seven; is that too late?"

"Not on a Friday." Whitney rose from her chair and held out her hand again. "Thank you for the tea. I hope you'll be happy here. I'll have to come to your salon and see what your magician can do with this mop of rags." She indicated her lusciously thick black hair, cut in a messy bob.

"I don't think he'd change a thing," Greer said, feeling immensely relieved that the other woman had been astute enough not to push her.

Whitney went to the door and then turned back and asked, "Are you all right?"

"I'll be fine, thank you."

Greer closed the door behind Whitney, leaned against it, and, covering her face with her hands, sobbed once before gathering herself together.

What the hell was going on? There was something or someone in this small suburb that was watching, ready to prey, and she had walked right into the middle of a grisly hunting season. Maybe that was why she had come. Maybe the gift was given to her for this reason, to try to stop it.

But what if . . . She remembered her last and only visit to the unconscious Sarah, and her throat clenched up.

She had crept into the darkened room filled with the rasping hiss of assisted breathing, and seen a monstrous creature propped on a sterile bed, a purple and swollen thing that bore no resemblance to her pretty, laughing, lively friend.

No. She could not stay silent this time. She would not stand helplessly by, fearing and waiting for some horrible turn of events.

But what could she do? And what would she say to this young woman, Joy, when she met her? Greer already knew exactly what the girl would look like. She had seen her face imposed over the soggy leaves in the bottom of the teacup: a pretty girl with a bow-shaped mouth on face that might once have looked angry or animated or smiling. But Greer had not seen any of those things; she had seen the face and would know it again, indeed, would never forget it. Never forget those wide-open eyes.

Eyes open but unseeing. Staring in horror. Surrounded by portents of death.

Chapter 3

He sat on his porch—a nice porch, with a pretty view, well cared for—and thought, *I want a woman, and I want one tonight.*

The thought of what he'd do to her made his jeans tighten, and he reached down to adjust himself. He felt hungry, but not for food. He needed a female, preferably one who was both young and inexperienced. He liked it when they were afraid. The thought of their look of fear and the small screams brought him to his feet, his black boots hitting the ground heavily as he swung them off the railing and planted them firmly on the wooden deck. Next to him, his dog raised his massive head from the planks, growling at an imaginary movement in the trees.

Twilight. Good, he liked the dark. He'd go hunting. He could almost smell the distinctive odor of the cold sweat of fear as he entered a woman forcefully and banged her hard, and it sent a tingling through his nostrils and into his mouth. He licked his lips. Wound up, he began to prowl, first around the outside of his house, through his groomed yard, and then into his den to pace the house, adjusting a pad of paper that was crooked on his clean desk, straightening a book that had fallen slightly to one side amongst the rows of leather-bound volumes standing with militant uniformity on the dust-free shelves.

Then into the bathroom, gleamingly clean, to primp for the night's activity. He considered his reflection, attractive in a rough way that he knew women liked. Many women had told him that. Some of them had even told him they liked dangerous men. He smiled, satisfied, at that thought. They'd found out what being with a dangerous man meant. But none of them had talked about it later; he'd made sure of that.

Choosing a cologne from an orderly row, he applied it, careful not to overdo, and winked rakishly at his reflection. Yes, tonight he'd get a young one, and he'd enjoy himself.

He reminded himself to be especially careful with the teenagers, to leave the bruises only where they wouldn't show. He'd gotten good at it, holding them by a fistful of hair on the back of their heads while he twisted or slapped, hard and openhanded, until the skin was red and raised in little welts that would slowly turn to shades of purple and green. He always found out first where they lived, early on, when they thought he was charming and were flattered by his attention. Then afterward, he'd let them know what he'd do to them and their families if they talked.

But even the thought of a girl screaming as he smacked her and used whatever part of her didn't seem quite enough. It sated him for shorter and shorter periods—hardly at all if they liked it or came back, which sometimes they did. He was hungry for more, to go further. He combed his hair and considered his new idea. He'd need to be careful, but it could be done.

The hunger drove him out of his house. He'd start at the bar on the corner of Foothill and see what was there; it was close to the high school and a burger joint, and sometimes the kids hung around. It was easy to fraternize with them on the sidewalk without drawing too much attention. Most parents up this way didn't notice that a kid was missing until at least midnight, and he could usually have them back by then.

But as he climbed on his motorcycle and pressed the starter, he mused on his formulating plan, liking it more and more as the vibration of the bike massaged his thighs and his crotch, adding to the tingling warmth of rushing blood. He ground himself against the leather seat, increasing the pleasure of the fantasy, liking the allure of making it a reality. It would save a lot of trouble, and he was filled with a sense of power and excitement by the nastiness of his new idea.

Maybe this time he wouldn't hold back; he'd go as far as he wanted.

And maybe next time he'd keep one.

Chapter 4

"Yeah, the coffee shop next to you is in trouble."

Greer regarded the speaker, her mailman. Although he wore the traditional uniform of the U.S. Postal Service, his lower face was hidden behind the tangled shrubbery of a graying beard. In spite of his attempt to conceal at least half of it, the mailman had a handsome face and a strong brow that would have suited a professor of philosophy. He possessed that slightly-wild-with-pretty-eyes look that college girls found so seductive in anarchists and poets. And he was a talker. Since the first day he had come in and introduced himself as "Pete P. Pistalane, your personal postal representative, but you can call me Pistol," she invariably had to spend at least ten minutes listening to the man gossip.

"The coffee shop? Now, why would you think that?" Greer asked, just to be polite.

"I've been delivering too many notices from the bank," he said conspiratorially. "And," he added, "I'm not real sure her marriage is going so great. They were engaged for years, and that's never a good sign. Yep, and your other neighbor, the architect, he's working on a big project for somebody overseas; lots of correspondence from Italy. Looks like we might have some I-talians moving into the area." Pistol seemed pleased with himself, as though his gossip were little gifts he knew she would really like.

Greer wondered what her mail was prompting him to tell everyone about her private affairs. She handed him a stack of letters that were going out; a few of them were personal, and the return address was her new home.

Pistol sorted through and read the destinations unabashedly right in front of her. "You live out off Silver Line—nice places out there. I go riding with Mike; he lives in the last house at the end."

"Horses?" Greer asked playfully.

"Harleys," Pistol corrected.

"Oh, you ride a motorcycle?" Greer asked in mock surprise. "I would never have guessed." She smiled. Pistol could have been the poster boy for Harley-Davidson, less the gray-blue uniform, of course.

The comment went over Pistol's head. "Have you met him yet?"

"Only through the pouring rain. I've heard his bike, though." Greer grimaced. She'd moved somewhere remote for the quiet and the sounds of nature. Discovering she had a neighbor who purposely removed the muffler from his motorcycle to "impress" people had not pleased her. She just didn't understand the need to disturb everyone in a five-mile radius. She had always assumed that these men were desperately in need of some attention and that was the only way they could get it.

"Hard to miss it. Nice guy, though." Pistol nodded. "Always helping people out at his shop even when they can't afford it. He'll even take trades. Hell, I once saw him take a stack of old *Playboy*s for a new drive chain."

A woman had come in the door and was standing behind Pistol waiting a bit impatiently. Greer let her eyes go to the woman very deliberately, and Pistol seemed to notice. "May I help you?" she asked the woman. It worked; Pistol was out of his element when the woman started asking about pedicures and highlights. He waved and left.

When she had finished making appointments for the new customer she glanced up at the clock: eleven twenty-five, fifteen minutes until her next treatment. She thought about Pistol saying that the woman next door might be having trouble, and even though the salon had a full kitchen in the back, complete with gourmet coffeemaker, she decided to buy a coffee next door. She knew what it was to struggle to get a new business going.

The shop was charming and smelled deliciously of brewing coffee and baked goods, the latter of which were displayed in a glass cabinet and on covered cake stands on the counter. A bulletin board was covered in snapshot pictures of customers. The place was painted cheerfully, and homey furniture was covered in floral fabric; it was very welcoming.

A man with skin like lustrous brown velvet stood alone at the counter. His arm looked so smooth and inviting that Greer longed to run her fingers down the taut bicep that emerged from a fashionable short-sleeved shirt. He turned as Greer came up next to him and she was surprised to see vibrant green eyes, lighted windows in a dark frame. "Hello," the handsome man said in a distinctly upper-class London accent.

"Hi." Greer connected with his eyes, and then, feeling that she was enjoying looking at him so much that he might think she was staring, she dropped her gaze to the selection of pastries. "What's good?" she asked.

"All of it. I haven't tried the quiche of the day, but if you'll wait about thirty more seconds, I'll have an educated opinion on that too."

Something about the man's voice tickled her ear in a pleasant way, and she wanted to hear more of it, to keep that regal attention directed at her. But before she could think of anything to say, a woman came from the back carrying a plate with a generous slice of quiche and a mixed green salad.

"Here you go, Sterling," she said as she handed it over. "With the coffee, that'll be eight fifty." She turned her attention to Greer. "Hi, there, can I help you?"

As Sterling was getting out his wallet, Greer moved closer to the counter—and the man—and she could smell the lightest hint of subtle cologne. It smelled of fresh green things with a note of spice. Nice.

The face that beamed at her over the counter looked familiar to Greer. Not that she had ever seen it before, but she recognized her as a new friend at first glance. Greer didn't know about love at first sight, but she was a firm believer in friendship that happened upon you. She thought, *Here's new friend number three.*

"Hi." She beamed back. "I'm Greer Sands; I own the business next door, and I wanted to come in and introduce myself. And get some coffee," she added with a laugh.

"Oh, I'm Jenny Sanchez. I'm so glad to meet you," the pretty young woman gushed. "And this is Sterling Fincher. He's got the office next to you on the other side."

"Oh," Greer was slightly taken aback at how pleased she felt by this little tidbit of info. "You're the architect?"

Sterling laughed, a quick, deep, booming sound that filled the room. "Well, *landscape* architect. It's very nice to meet you." His eye contact was as strong and warm as his handshake, which made Greer's whole arm feel as though she'd plunged it into a bubble bath.

"Thank God you moved in," Jenny was saying. "My business has quadrupled in the last three days and nine out of ten people who come in here are from Eye of the Beholder." The cinnamon eyes looked radiantly into Greer's.

Laughing, Greer shook the smaller woman's hand and wondered if it was a Hispanic trait to have larger breasts—that were obviously real—on a slighter frame. Not that Jenny was skinny; she was . . . well, *sexy,* in stretch jeans and a T-shirt that ended about four inches shy of the low-riding pants, revealing baby-smooth skin over the ever-so-slightly rounded tummy. Jenny's mane-thick dark brown hair was pulled up in a high ponytail, and at about thirty she was effervescently pretty. In short, Greer thought without any sense of competition, she was a pleasure to look at.

Sterling picked up his plate and mug and made a move for the door, waving his coffee in lieu of a free hand. "Thanks, Sterling, see you later," Jenny called after him.

"Bye. Nice meeting you," he said to Greer. "Stop by and say hello anytime."

"Okay," Greer responded, wondering if she could work up the courage—or an excuse—to do that. She turned back to Jenny after the two of them had enjoyed watching the man's well-shaped back move out the door and shared a smile about it. "How do you know that they're my customers?" Greer asked her.

"Because they are in one of three various stages of beautification." She held up a single forefinger with a long acrylic nail finished with a lightning bolt. "One: There's the previsit look, chipped nail polish, dull, rodentlike hair, and a distinct lack of confidence." A second, equally decorated digit shot up to stand beside the first one. "Group two would be the ones who have to have me take the money out of their wallet because their nail polish isn't dry, have enough foil in their hair to get cell phone service, and they are somewhat conspicuous because they're wearing a black plastic bib."

Greer laughed.

"And then there's stage three"—Jenny leaned against the counter as she spoke—"the finished, polished, shiny-haired, lip-glossed, born again beauties who come to give me first approval."

"Maybe they're just women who always look that way who dropped in for a coffee."

Jenny shook her head. "Uh-uh," she said, "because they keep on patting their hair and looking at me hopefully until I tell them how gorgeous they look." Jenny winked. "Which I do. Completely unsolicited, of course."

"Of course," Greer agreed. "Sounds like we should be giving you a kickback for making us look good."

"Girl, I'm getting it!" She slapped her thigh as she spoke. "Speaking of which, what can I get you?"

Greer looked around. The menu was up on a chalkboard. She ordered a flavored coffee and a vegetarian sandwich. When Jenny turned to make them, Greer resumed the conversation.

"I'm so glad to hear that your business is picking up. Our mailman had me worried."

Jenny, knife in hand as she sliced a tomato, turned and threw a worried look over her shoulder. "Pistol." The way she said it made it sound more like toxic waste than a person. She sighed. "Yes, Pistol is our bearer of news. I've heard all about you and your forwarded mail from Old Town Pasadena, and the fact that your husband's name is Joshua."

Greer laughed again. "Joshua is my seventeen-year-old son. I don't have a husband."

Jenny sighed deeply. "Lucky you," she said.

Greer cocked her head to one side and asked, "Husband troubles?"

"No, yes, no, yes, no." Jenny swayed her shapely hips from side to side with each contradiction. "I've only been married for six months—"

"Congratulations!" Greer cut in.

"Thank you. But we lived together for five years before that. Some days Lewis is the most wonderful, mature grown-up, and some days . . ."

"He's twelve?" Greer asked knowingly. There was a reason she wasn't in a relationship. Sometimes it was just plain more trouble than it was worth.

"No, not twelve," Jenny said dismissively. "More like seven. You know, when you play, 'Nuh-uh, *I'm* not stupid; *you* are!' on the playground. That's about seven, right?"

"Or eight." Greer nodded. "Today's one of those days?"

"Today," Jenny said, placing a slice of whole grain bread on the top of layers of fresh vegetables and sprouts and slicing the whole thing diagonally with a flourish, "I want to take his head and push it into a gallon vat of mayonnaise and then agitate it up and down until he admits he's wrong." She turned and placed the sandwich on the counter, next to a huge, steaming mug of vanilla coffee.

Greer suggested gently, "They say it doesn't really matter who's right or wrong."

"And as long as *that's* true," Jenny retorted emphatically, "then why can't *I* be right and *Lewis* be wrong?"

"Well, maybe we should ask Pistol," Greer teased, pulling some cash out of her pocket. "I'm sure he'd have an opinion."

Jenny's face clouded a little. "Let's not. He's not my favorite person in the neighborhood. Do you ever just get a *feeling* about somebody?"

Greer looked at Jenny and experienced an over-whelming sensation of warmth and affection com-pletely inappropriate for the connection created by a five-minute conversation. She nodded slowly. "Yeah," she said, "sometimes I do."

Chapter 5

From Leah's desk at State National Bank, she could see all the tellers and the door to the manager's office. Behind that door lay the den of a snake, the despised, arrogant bastard of a bank manager: her ex-husband, Vince.

Nervously, Leah tried to focus on the loan application in front of her, but she kept glancing compulsively at Vince's door. He was in there with the regional supervisor, and part of the meeting was to go over a new practice policy that had been written by Leah. She had thrown herself into it, invested it with her hopes, and—driven by her venom for Vince—she had honed it till it was perfect. Leah was a woman who drove herself hard and was seldom satisfied with her work, but this report was really good. She sat staring at the entrance to the den with what she wished were X-ray eyes. If the regional manager was smart enough to see *how* good, it could mean a promotion. Maybe a promotion out of this office, away from "the Rattler," as she called him, and just possibly help her achieve the revenge she wanted so badly: to outrank the Rattler.

The floor was quiet this morning. Three tellers tried

to look busy at their stations, chatting with the occasional customer to prolong the exchange. The nine-o'clock weekday rush was past, and there would be the regular midmorning lull until lunchtime. Normally Leah enjoyed this part of the day—got herself a third cup of coffee and buckled down to do twice as much paperwork as any other loan officer—but not today. Her hand was shaking slightly as she reached for the coffee mug, and the taste in her mouth was bitter.

"Focus," she commanded, taking a deep breath and willing herself to read and understand the words on the paper in front of her. Leah managed half a paragraph before the sound of an opening door pulled her head up with a snap. But it was the street entrance, not the office, and the woman who had come in paused just inside to look around, as though she were unfamiliar with the place.

Some mom who wants to start a twenty dollar savings account for her kid, Leah thought, scowling. Not wanting to be bothered, she buried her head quickly in her work again. But from the corner of her eye she could see the woman coming toward her desk. "Shit," she cursed under her breath, and turned deliberately away, swiveling her chair and pretending to search through some papers on a counter behind her.

"Hi!" The woman had reached her.

Leah sighed and put on her professionally helpful face before turning back, patting her styled hair to discipline any forbidden strays. She looked up at the woman and squinted against the glare from the glass front of the bank behind her. It was impossible for Leah to make out more than a silhouette. Straining the sinews of her professional patience, Leah managed to ask politely, "May I help you?"

"Oh, I'm sorry, Leah," said Greer, realizing that Leah was at a disadvantage, and moved to sit in the chair across from her. "Yes, I hope you can. I want to establish a payroll account. It's nice to see you. How are you?" Greer looked unguardedly at Leah.

The woman seemed to know her. A panicked moment of impending ineptitude throttled Leah, but she maintained the slightly aloof smile, while her brain swung around desperately searching for a face/name connection. She was somewhat hampered by her inner voice berating her for being so stupid. It was almost two full seconds before she could connect the woman to the reflexology treatment she'd had at the new salon last Thursday. The voice in her head cursed her slow, preoccupied brain. "I'm, uh, fine. Nice to see you again." She was searching her mind for the woman's name—it was something very different—while at the same time trying to sort out the request and re-evaluating the value of the woman whose hand she was now shaking. Payroll account? A therapist? She covered her confusion by turning to rummage in a drawer for the forms. "Have a seat," she invited.

"My partner and I decided to move our banking for this salon to a local bank, and I remembered that you said you worked here, and you're local. Right down the street!"

Leah could handle this part. "Well, you came to the right place. Where do you have your business loan?" she fished.

"We don't have a loan on this salon; we were fortunate enough to be able to turn our profits from our other salon in Pasadena. But we were banking with National City there."

"No loan?" Leah stopped being busy to be unabashedly surprised. It was expensive to set up a new business, and having an intimate knowledge of the local real estate market, she knew that they had bought the space and spent a considerable sum fixing it up. She felt impressed—and belittled. This woman was more successful than she was, and Leah both admired and despised that.

"We've been very lucky. And my partner, Dario, whom I think you met, is kind of a celebrity in hairstyling circles; that helps quite a bit. We're not exactly starting from scratch, if you know what I mean."

"That's true. I'd heard of his—that is, *your*—other salon. That's why I called to book the appointment with you."

"But you just got a massage and reflexology." Greer was thinking about her session with Leah and the sense of impending danger that she'd been left with. "Did it help with the stress?"

"Oh, yes, it was wonderful!" Leah said enthusiastically, before embarrassment washed over her. "I have to apologize again for getting so emotional," she said tightly.

It was Greer's turn to look surprised. "Apologize? Oh, you mean for crying. For God's sake, a little releasing is the healthiest thing you can do in that situation." She smiled at Leah as though it had been a real treat for her. "It's like this: You put so much stress in a container, more than it can hold, so you pack it down hard and put the lid on it. What I do is make a tiny hole in the side of the container, just a little opening so that the compacted stress can start to leak out. That's what you were reacting to. It's scary at first—it just seems like so much—but it gets easier as the pressure in the container goes down."

Leah felt the truth of what the woman—*what was her name?*—was saying, but at the same time she was ashamed for having shown weakness. She asked sarcastically, "Why don't you just turn the container over and dump it out?"

If she expected a laugh, she didn't get it. Instead of

looking amused, Greer looked sadly resigned. "Because that would probably kill you."

Feeling very unstable that this woman knew something both intensely personal and unflattering about her, Leah tried to get the upper hand back by being dubious and slightly superior. "Why would getting rid of my stress kill me?"

"Because it's all that's holding you up right now."

This was so true that Leah felt a lump form in her throat like a saturated sponge that might leak tears if she squeezed it. With a quick little exhale to relieve the unwelcome pressure of emotion rearing its ugly head in her carefully controlled environment, she looked questioningly at the woman across from her.

As Greer explained, Leah watched the plump lips and noticed the way they seemed slightly behind the words that were spoken, as though they were too comfortably full of a good dinner and couldn't really rouse the energy to get up off the sofa. And her eyes. Leah had never seen anything so green except for sunlight on new grass.

"Of course, we all want to get rid of our stress, but since we've practiced it so diligently, and we believe that we can't live our lives without it, then if we don't have something to replace it with we'd just deflate and collapse. You know, it's not real, the stress. You just believe it is, so you make it true for you."

"Oh, isn't it?" Leah snorted in disbelief, her handsome face twisting slightly with disdain. "I don't know about you, but my life is just a *tiny bit* stressful." Leah glanced at the door to the manager's office. "*Believe* me."

But Greer's eyes glinted as she leaned in and whispered conspiratorially, "It's what he wants, you know—for you to be afraid."

Leah stiffened. The conversation had crossed uncomfortably out of her limited realm of normality.

"I'm sorry; I don't know what you're talking about," she said in an attempt to regain control by implying that she was the sane one sitting across from a wacko. *Why could she not remember the woman's name?*

But she was foiled once again. Greer shrugged and said, "Don't worry; you'll get it eventually. You do really want to replace those beliefs, you know. *And* it would be much easier to just ask me my name, like everybody else, instead of beating yourself up for forgetting it. It's Greer. Unusual, but you'll get that too. We're going to be friends."

Leah's mouth hung open. Was this woman nuts? They were going to be *friends*? She couldn't have been less like any of Leah's friends, who were all very anxiety-ridden, type-A, uptight yuppies with exclusive gym memberships and big-ass car-lease payments who made deals on their cell phones as they were reviewing contracts while fixing gourmet dinners for chic, mandatory dinner parties. This woman, in spite of running more than one highly profitable business, was disconcertingly, to Leah, *at ease.*

But before Leah could assimilate the swirl of her feelings and decide whether to dismiss Greer as a hippie relic or pursue her as a potential ally, the door to the snake's den opened. Two men appeared in the doorway: one was the Rattler. Tall and far too perfect, he was holding a large, thick manila envelope in one hand and resting the other on the shoulder of a shorter, balding man. This was Steve Kenner, the bank chain's regional manager, whom Leah's friend Towler had once described as a beach ball that was losing air.

"Excuse me a minute," Leah said without a glance at Greer, and, rising from her chair, she crossed over to one of the tellers with a form in her hand, so that she could eavesdrop on what the two men were saying.

Towler, a slight young man with a nervous smile

and a perpetually crooked tie, greeted her casually. "Hey, Leah, what's up?"

"Do me a favor, Towler. Just pretend I'm showing you something for a minute. Okay?" Her eyes darted to Vince and the regional manager and then back to him.

"Got it." Towler nodded intelligently. He pulled the blank form she was offering across the counter, and, taking up a pen, pretended to be reviewing the sheet, occasionally making a meaningless mark. Leah pointed her face toward the paper too, but both of them were entirely focused on the conversation taking place behind Towler.

Steve Kenner was speaking in a low growl to Vince, and though Vince's smile was plastered in place, Leah was pleased to sense a nervous twitch at the edge of it.

"We'll be keeping an eye on this branch," Kenner was telling Vince.

Vince's smarmy, pseudo-sincere voice jarred Leah's ears. She'd heard it lying to her far too many times, and she'd bought it once too often. "Thank you, Steve. I can't tell you how much help you've been."

Leah could see him behind Towler, but even if she hadn't she would have known exactly what he was doing. It was his I'm-overcome-with-gratitude routine. He'd put the hand holding the envelope down by his side while the other reached up to scratch his head, and then he let it rest, open palmed, on his chest. His voice sounded solid and confident, but just on the edge of being overcome with emotion, as he said, "Without you, I don't think I would be where I am."

"Mmm," Kenner grunted dismissively. "Listen, the truth is, your performance is off, and you need to show some improvement to *stay* where you are. Understand?"

Vince nodded his head. "I'm on it," he said definitively. "And having your support means everything to me."

Leah glanced up at Towler, who pretended to gag. She suppressed a smile by grimacing as though at a difficult part of their important work.

"Come on." Vince made the transition back to Perfect Confident Man. "I'll walk you to the door. How's the beautiful Susan?" he asked, his voice overflowing with intense and sincere-sounding interest as the two men started for the exit. The reply was lost when Vince pressed a button to buzz them out onto the floor.

Vince held the front door open for Kenner, and the two shook hands as a preamble to saying good-bye.

But Vince wasn't finished. "Did you see my new toy?" he asked, pointing to a bright yellow Ducati motorcycle in the parking space marked BANK MANAGER.

But instead of looking impressed, Kenner frowned, and it seemed all Vince could do to keep his facade up as the shorter man turned a narrowed eye back at him. Leah strained to hear what he said to Vince, but all she caught was something that sounded derogatory about hours and Vince's commitment to work instead of fun.

Just then Pistol came into the bank carrying a white plastic laundry-basket-size box marked U.S. POSTAL SERVICE, which was full with the day's correspondence. Vince held the door open for him and he nodded his thanks without looking up. Leah had to stand to one side as he walked to the counter and handed the box over to Towler, who took it and traded him for an exact replica of the mail crate with the outgoing mail. For a moment she lost her view of the drama in the doorway.

When Pistol moved away, she could see that Vince had opened the glass door for Kenner, who exited without looking back. "Tell little Bobby he owes me a game of catch!" Vince called after the retreating regional manager. He let the door close and his smile disappeared as a look of disgusted anger swept across his face. With an impatient gesture he stopped Pistol, who was just exiting. "Hold on; this is going out too." He put the thick envelope into the crate and started across the floor for his office, but Leah intercepted him.

"Well?" she asked, angry with herself for seeming too eager, for feeling afraid of him.

"Well what?" he asked mockingly, tilting his head to one side as though he just couldn't think of what it was she might want to know, and giving her body an insulting up-and-down sliding look.

She could have stamped her foot and snorted, she hated him so much. She allowed herself the pleasant visual of running him through with something sharp before she smiled with a fake sweetness to make fun of his own. "Why, the report. You know the one, Vince—the one I *just couldn't* have done without you."

She saw the flare in his eyes and knew she'd pissed him off. *Good*, she told herself, but a flicker of fear lapped at her belly, and she was relieved when he let it pass and smirked at her. "Oh. *That* report. He liked it. He congratulated me on it." He turned and started to the security door that separated the customers from the tellers. "Good job, by the way," he called out loudly enough for most of the bank's employees to hear.

It was all Leah could do to keep her voice down as she pursued him, though it cost her her pride to do it. "Wait a minute," she said, anger shaking her incredulous voice. "Are you saying you took credit for *my* report?"

At the desk a few feet away, Greer watched the

exchange. She couldn't hear all the hushed words, but she could see the auras around the two of them as colored clashing energy, and she could sense Leah's frustration and fury. She shifted uncomfortably and tried to create an appropriate boundary between herself and the hostility.

"Of course not," Vince oozed, pretending to be deeply offended. "Your name is right there in big capital letters, on the cover, where you put it. *Desperate* for someone to notice," he finished with a nasty dig.

"Then . . ." Leah was thrown, and she hated being off balance, especially in front of this bastard. *When would he stop having this effect on her?* Hadn't she had just seen Kenner admonish Vince? Yet he was behaving as though the man had given him a gold star. Suddenly shaky and unsure, she asked, "Why would he congratulate you?"

Vince smiled and shrugged his shoulders in an infuriating mockery of disinterest. "Oh," he said, inspecting his perfect manicure, "he understands that a good manager inspires his employees to do outstanding work. Delegating is a great talent." Then he dropped his hand and the polite pretense, and leaning forward, hissed under his breath, "So get the fuck back to work." Spittle had formed in the corners of his mouth, and Leah recognized the edgy fear in his irises. She knew better than to touch that.

He began to turn away again; then he spotted Greer. "Hello," he said, mostly to himself, taking in the full breasts and lips. "What have we here?" He crossed the three yards to Leah's desk and said with his most disarming boyish charm, "I'm Vince Slater, the bank manager. Could I be of service?"

Greer looked up at the mid-forties man and thought what a sad little boy he seemed to be, but she shook the hand offered to her, though it sent a frosty tingling up her arm that she quickly blocked before it reached her heart. "No, thank you. I'm being very well taken care of by an extremely competent individual." She leaned forward and looked into his handsome eyes without being impressed in the least. "And this part is important." She fixed him with a hard eye and said in a friendly but pointed way, "I prefer to work with someone I can trust."

"I'd be glad to help you *personally*." He stressed the last word as though this would be a huge and rare favor.

"No, thank you," Greer said very clearly, and turned to Leah, who was watching the exchange, shell-shocked. "Leah, I'm sorry to rush you, but I do need to get back to the salon. So if we could get my paperwork done . . ."

"Of course," Leah said, collecting her wits and grabbing the advantage that Greer was offering her. "If you'd excuse us, Vince, I've got some new business accounts to open." Both women dismissed him utterly.

He didn't leave immediately; instead he stood looking down at the two of them for a few seconds, thinking with bitter arrogance that it would snow in the Sahara before he'd let a fucking *woman* get the better of him. Then he looked Greer up and down and thought about what he'd like to do to her and how he'd make her like it. He knew just what he'd use on her, too.

Fingering his belt and imagining the snapping sound of thick leather on flesh and the red welt it would leave, he turned away with a satisfied smile and retreated to sulk in his den.

Chapter 6

Each blow dryer had its own resonant vibrato, and together with the animated chatter of the stylists and clientele, they filled the salon with a syncopated rhythm that rose and fell with the sweet unpredictability of a fusion jazz ensemble.

Lulled by the sound, Dario fell into a meditation on Greer. She'd been alone for too long, and, Dario decided, she needed a romance. He was so deeply into his musings that it took him a moment to notice that Celia, the receptionist, was standing beside him, wearing a shiny silver jacket on her toothpick frame and occasionally waving a nervous scrawny hand to get his attention. He shut off the dryer and turned to her.

"Yes, sweetie?"

"Um, I'm sorry to interrupt you, but the plumber is here."

"The old one or the new one?" Dario asked her.

"I think it's the new one?" She winced as though she expected that to be the wrong answer. "He said he'd never met you before?" She raised her voice at the end of every sentence so that it sounded like a question.

"The new one." Dario set the dryer down and said to his client in his deep baritone, "I'll be right back, gorgeous. Don't you dare leave until I've had a chance to revel in how fabulous you look." Leaning down, he asked the older woman's reflection in the mirror, "Do you love it?"

"Oh, yes," she gushed, and then giggled. "My husband is going to be surprised."

Dario straightened up and said in a loud, not-so-secret whisper, "He won't let you out of bed for a week!"

The woman laughed outright with scandalized delight, and Dario spun on his heel and marched to the front with the pencil-thin Celia in her retro disco jacket trailing closely behind.

He spotted two men standing at the front who would be hard to confuse with anyone who might have come in for a pedicure. They were obviously brothers and shared the sun-leathered good looks of the working class. The elder brother's age was hard to guess—maybe forty, Dario estimated—his long hair hanging in a straggly blond braid down his back. His clothes, which were none too stylish but certainly appropriate for a foray into a dank crawl space, were splattered with goodness knew what, but Dario noted with approval that the man's fingernails were clean and his face was unguardedly friendly as he shook Dario's hand. He was the only one of the two who made eye contact, even if it was somewhat tentative. The younger brother, who seemed to wear a permanent defensive scowl, glanced in Dario's general direction and nodded. Dario did not offer his hand, but he noticed the rough tattoos on the younger man's forearms and hands. "Hello, I'm Dario," he addressed the elder. "Can I help you?"

"Hi. I'm Paul," said the plumber with friendly pale

blue eyes. His words were simple and slow, as though his mouth relished making the sounds and refused to hurry through such an enjoyable sensation.

Celia had caught up to them, and she contributed, "Paul Newman."

"What about him, other than the fact that he makes a surprisingly good spaghetti sauce?" asked Dario, slightly annoyed. He had three appointments in various stages and didn't like keeping anyone waiting.

But it was the older plumber who replied. "That's my name," he said with a self-deprecating laugh that seemed to bubble up as though it were always on simmer, ready to move into a rolling boil with the slightest pinch of salt. "Paul Newman."

Dario looked back at the man and decided not to make the obvious blue-eyes comparison and opted for, "Well, won't the ladies be all excited to hear that Paul Newman is going to work on their plumbing."

Paul's face reddened slightly, but he seemed pleased with the association. "Yeah. And this is my brother, Army." The surly youth with the prison tattoos nodded again, then resumed scowling at the floor.

"Delighted, I'm sure," Dario said drolly. "Let me show you where the last plumber was working when he vanished into thin air."

They started to walk through the long, open salon toward the back. Paul walked the same way he spoke, like a lazy two-foot surf on a sunny day in Malibu, and Dario found himself breaking his decisive stride to match the other man's comfortable way of moving through the space and life. Army followed stiffly, holding his thick arms rigidly at his sides.

"Nice place," commented Paul with a rhythmic, smiling nod that continued far beyond the simple compliment.

"Thank you. And thanks again for actually showing

up. The old plumber just stopped returning calls and disappeared."

Paul nodded, his sky blues twinkling, and said, "Yeah, that happens," with the laugh rolling up from underneath the words again, but not quite boiling over. He was an ever-simmering Crock-Pot of self-amusement.

"Does it happen to you?" asked Dario pointedly.

"Sometimes," came the easy confession. "If people have emergencies I have to get to them first. Otherwise somebody's house might float away." He did it again—carried the end of his statement away on a rising current of glee. Dario found himself liking the man. His brother, Army, on the other hand, continued giving the rebellious impression of having seceded from the human race.

Dario showed Paul the shampoo area and the three sinks that were still in boxes with capped plumbing jutting out from the walls. Paul looked the situation over and proclaimed that he and Army could finish it up tomorrow.

"How much do you think it will be?" asked Dario as he signaled to his assistant, Jonathan, to get a pretty young pregnant woman shampooed and into his chair.

"Oh . . ." Paul's eyes glanced around as he calculated and considered the price of the job before he pronounced his verdict with an amused shrug. "Not much." The low laugh played in his throat.

Dario smiled. "That was *exactly* the price I was thinking. See you tomorrow at . . . ?"

The eyes roved around again and then fixed on Dario with an amused twinkle. The top of Paul's head swung from left to right in a playful arc, as though any answer he was going to give was more or less just hopeful speculation. "Mm . . . probably about maybe . . . ten?"

Dario laughed. Usually a stickler for punctuality, he couldn't help forgiving this man even *before* he was late for work. "Okay. We'll just say that you'll be here sometime after the sun is warm, if it's not raining again, of course."

Paul nodded in a funny, chin-jutting way, with a knowing smile that showed he was pleased that Dario was so intuitive, and sauntered out with his loping downbeat of a gait, his brother following in a sulking, silent, heavy walk. But as Dario watched Paul go, he said to Jonathan, "There's a rare creature—a happy man."

Jonathan's thick brown lashes, the envy of all who saw them, followed Dario's gaze; then he said, "*I'm* happy."

"Not like him."

"Why not?"

"You want to be my assistant for the rest of your life?"

"I want to own a chain of salons named after me, become the stylist to the stars, and die rich and famous in a suspicious boating accident on my extravagant yacht."

"You've given this some thought," Dario said. He was watching Paul, who was half out the door, saying something to Celia.

Greer emerged from her treatment room and followed Dario's glance to the figure in the doorway.

Dario turned to her. "What's your feeling about our new plumber?"

Greer raised one eyebrow. "You know I don't read men very well," she reminded him. "I mean, with women I seem to just *know* things. With men it's sketchy and always more of a guess, if I get any sense at all. I suppose it's because I have something to go on, being a woman."

The tall, perfectly groomed Dario turned his sharp,

dark goatee to face her and whispered, "Bullshit."
And then he proclaimed in full volume, "You know
men as well as I do."

Greer laughed. "Dario, darling, I don't think anybody knows men as well as you do."

He narrowed his handsome black eyes at her. "I'm
just more *interested* in men than you are; that's all,"
he quipped. Then he added sotto voce, "And we need
to work on that."

Greer waved him off and turned again to see the
plumber going out the door at the end of the long
salon. She saw his good-looking, boyish face for a moment, and then, as the sunlight hit him, the color of
his aura. It was a lovely bluish gold. The joy of it
warmed her. But just then another man joined him, a
younger version of the plumber himself, also nice-
enough-looking, but there was no boyishness in his
tough countenance. The murky rust color of his energy
jarred Greer, blocking the bright day behind him. And
then the door swung closed and the snapshot of a
vision was over.

A rusty brown. A man with trouble in his past and
more trouble up ahead.

Chapter 7

Joshua had hiked about an hour up the trail and then back. The water was still raging fast, and the trail ran through a narrow canyon for almost three miles at one point, crossing back and forth across the swollen creek. He had tried to find ways over it, but eventually had to make the iffy choice of plunging in. It was tricky, and probably not too smart, he had thought on the last crossing as he felt the water throw its shoulder against his calves and shove in an effort to knock him off his feet and send him rushing downstream. His hiking shoes and jeans were wet up past his knees.

He sat down on a boulder in the shade of some cottonwood trees and took off one boot and then the sock. He rubbed his numb toes to revive his circulation and then squeezed the water out of the sock before putting it back on. It was as he was repeating the motion with the second sock that he saw her.

There were nine houses total on Silver Line Creek. Five, including Joshua's, were grouped together near the parking area, and four beyond the locked gate. Two of those required turning off the fire road and crossing the creek bed, which was impassable now, and two more lay farther up the narrow drivable track.

As Joshua watched the girl, she reached the last house, which sat at the end of the road where it became the trailhead, and went up the path to a gate in a wooden fence. She stood on tiptoe to try to look over. A vicious barking that sounded to Joshua as if it could come only from the three-headed dog that guarded the gates of hell broke out, and the girl backed away quickly. Then she took what seemed to be a white envelope from her pocket and, approaching cautiously, slipped it into the mail slot.

Since Joshua was sitting about twenty yards up the trail, in the shelter of a grove, she still hadn't noticed him. She walked quickly, fearfully, back to the road and then stood there, looking despondent.

The girl wore an affected slouch, a Goth look, too much heavy eye makeup, purple streaks in her hair, and grungy clothes. Yet, even at this distance, Joshua could see that she was pretty.

She stooped and picked up a good-size rock, weighing it in her hand. Then suddenly she let it fly with a vicious force. "Shut up, you fucking nasty, piece-of-shit dog!" she howled. The rock crashed against the wooden fencing, sending the unseen mythological monster into a fresh frenzy of verbal attack.

Witnessing the outburst, Joshua felt that he'd crossed the line into spying. He didn't want to frighten her, or become the object of that wrath and the well-hurled rock that might second that emotion. So he laced his boots up quickly and then, pretending to be just coming along, he started out, whistling.

He didn't make eye contact until he was about ten feet away; then he stopped and said, "Hi."

She didn't bother to return the greeting. Instead she snorted slightly and said, under her breath but loud enough for him to hear it, "Fucking day hikers."

Joshua could imagine her fear of meeting a stranger in an isolated spot, but he smiled. "You must be Joy."

She shot a look at him, her eyes wary as those of a sly wild thing. "How do you know my name? What are you, fucking psychic?"

"No." He shrugged and said conversationally, "That would be my mom, Greer. I'm just your new fucking neighbor."

That made her smile—not the neighbor part. "Yeah?" she asked, looking at him with a slight challenging smile. "You got a name, fucking neighbor?"

"Fucking Joshua." He nodded.

She laughed, pulled out a pack of cigarettes, and lit one. They started to walk together down the strip of road. As they walked in and out of the speckled light from the oak trees overhanging it, Joshua noticed that her hair looked streaked with purple only in direct sunlight. In the shade it looked uniformly dark brown. He noticed quite a bit more without seeming to. Her face was heart shaped, and her nose was long and sharpish, but it suited her overall look and the shape of her eyes. She was obviously wearing contacts that made her eyes a fake, flat light brown. He wondered what color they really were. Her body was slim, and though she tried to conceal them, her chest was thrusting out breasts, small but full. He looked quickly away from them and all the thoughts that they sent flooding into him. Her mouth was best; it looked fresh, pink, and inviting, like it would taste good. Every time she raised the cigarette to her lips and sucked he winced slightly. It was as though someone were painting graffiti on a Botticelli; it just shouldn't be allowed.

"So who lives in the house? Friend of yours?" Joshua asked to make conversation.

A small smile twisted her pretty mouth. "More a friend of my dad's. We accidentally got one of his letters delivered to our house. I feed his monster dog when he goes out of town. I won't go in there. I just slide the food through the space under the gate."

"Wise move," Joshua agreed. "Sounds like a nice animal. Do you have to feed all of its heads?"

She smiled again in a less twisted way, letting her lips part to show her amusement and a row of nice teeth, slightly buck in a sexy way. "How'd you get stuck out in this godforsaken backwater?" she asked him.

"My mom opened a shop up here. We were both tired of living in Hollywood."

"You lived in Hollywood?" Her eyes had come to life, even veiled by the lenses that shielded them. "What was it like?"

"Oh, traffic and anger, and people all desperately wanting to be something that somebody else made up."

She narrowed her eyes and blew a stream of smoke at him. "Where did you live in Hollywood?"

"The Hills. It was okay, but I like it better here." She snorted again, so he repeated his shrug and added, "Sorry."

"Here," she spit angrily, "the middle of fucking nowhere."

"It's only thirty minutes from where I used to live," Joshua said.

"You got a car?" Joy looked at him with a hungry, greedy interest that lasted until he gave his answer.

"Nope." He wished that he did; he would have liked to impress her. "I've got a motorcycle . . . well, a dirt bike, really."

"Can you drive that down?" She was watching him sideways as they walked.

"I could try, but it would probably burst into flames after a mile or two on the highway; it's only a Yamaha two-fifty. Mostly I just ride it around the neighborhood, and sometimes to school. If I keep my grades up, I'll get a car next year."

Joy stopped and threw away her cigarette. "That's

so fucked! Adults love to do that shit—hold something over your head that you really have to have, like it's this terrific prize, and make you jump through fucking hoops for it."

Joshua looked at the cigarette. It was still smoking and lying in a leaf-littered dirt road in the middle of a national forest. He walked toward it as he spoke. "I don't know about that," he said as he crushed out the miniature torch with the toe of his hiking boot. "I think it's a good thing to earn something in life. I like that feeling." He leaned down and picked up the butt of her cigarette. Without comment he put it into a pocket in his backpack.

She watched him as if he were insane. "What the fuck are you doing?"

He looked steadily back at her. "Picking up trash. You like that word, *fuck*," he said easily.

Shaking her head to show that she was filled with disdain for him, she said, "It works on a lot of levels, you know?"

"Yeah," he agreed, "I know. But when people use it as much as you, it kind of makes me wonder." He started to walk quickly away down the road, and she followed.

When she came level with him, she asked, "Wonder what?" in a voice that clearly proclaimed that she was pretending not to really care, but did.

"Oh," Joshua said, as though he didn't care one way or the other either. "It makes me wonder if they know any other words. And the reason I picked up the cigarette butt is because . . . I don't know, it's litter, and they don't decompose for over two hundred years, and the birds gather them and use them when they build their nests."

Being reprimanded was so expected and resented by Joy that she snapped, "So I'm providing a fucking service for the birds. Free construction materials."

"I don't know about free," Joshua said. "There are

so many abrasive chemicals in the filters that when the baby birds hatch and sit against them in the nest, the chemicals actually burn through their bare skin and kill them."

"How the fuck do you know *that*?"

"My dad. He used to be a scientist; he studied wildlife and forest ecosystems."

She snorted derisively. "So your dad's a fucking forest ranger."

"No," Joshua corrected, "ecological scientist. He was."

"What does he do now?"

"Well," said Joshua thoughtfully, "that depends on your philosophical point of view. Maybe nothing; maybe he's a young goatherd in India; maybe he plays the harp in the Holy Philharmonic."

"What the fuck are you talking about?"

"He's dead."

"Oh." Joy nodded and mumbled, "Sorry," but she didn't look at him when she said it.

They had reached the clearing where both their houses sat, and, feeling both uncomfortable and stupid again, Joy lashed out at Joshua one more time. "So I'm supposed to care about some baby birds that do nothing but grow up to fly around and eat and shit all day?"

Joshua stopped and turned to her. "You mean eat and shit all day like, say, humans?" He raised his eyebrows and his face cracked into a playful expression. "And as for caring . . . the fact is, you didn't know." He hoped he didn't show it, but he was hoping desperately that she would like him, that he could get to know her. He could use a friend, and she was obviously in need of one. And then with a widening grin he winked and walked toward his house. "See you later!" he called over his shoulder.

"Don't count on it," Joy said sourly, expressing her self-inflicted sense of isolation.

Joshua stopped and turned back. "Oh, I think I can. You're coming to dinner tonight," he informed her, and then without waiting for any more bitter attempts to alienate him—which would fail—he went up the steps to the wide wooden porch and through his front door.

Joy stared after him, wondering what fucking planet he had dropped from, so clean-cut and fucking *nice.* Definitely not her type. Still, he was good-looking, but she hated people who thought they were better than her, and that was pretty much everybody. She started toward her own house, kicking at the sparse gravel.

Upstairs in the large open great room, Greer heard the door slam and was grateful her son was home, but she didn't let it break her concentration.

She was kneeling on a large, flat purple cushion. In front of her was a small brazier with a single round charcoal burning inside of it. Three candles burned in silver holders, placed around her on the floor to make a large triangle. On the ground in front of the smoking charcoal were several objects laid out on a bright orange cloth.

An unsheathed knife lay perpendicular to the other objects, as though underlining them. It had a simple wooden handle, but in the glinting sunlight through the large windows the blade shone gold. A small pile of dried herbs was there also, as well as a vial of oil and three strips of colored cording, green, gold, and black.

Reaching out, Greer took a pinch of the herbs and sprinkled it on the charcoal, where it began to smoke. She followed that with three drops of oil from the vial, and a strong, sweet, earthy aroma filled the room, a rich, wet, humid smell, like a river swollen with rain and silt. Next she took the knife in her left hand and, separating out three of her own longest hairs with her right hand, cut them off with the gold blade. Then, taking up the cords with the hairs, she knotted the six strands together at one end.

Using one hair with each of the colors, Greer began to braid the cords, and while she worked she chanted softly:

> *I call upon the powers that be.*
> *Bind her to me, let me see.*
> *Help me keep her safe from harm.*
> *Make it stronger, three by three.*
> *Put your life into this charm.*

Three times she repeated the chant, and when she had finished braiding the three strands, she picked up the last item on the orange silk, a shining, faceted green stone with a hole drilled through it. It sparkled as she strung both ends of the braid through it and fashioned a knot. To test her handiwork, she pulled it on and slid the stone up to fix the bracelet firmly on her wrist. Then, taking it off again, she held the pretty trinket loosely between her fingers out over the smoking brazier until it was saturated with the smoke scent and energy of the herbs. Finally, taking a few deep breaths, she closed her eyes and held the talisman between her palms to her heart in a prayer position.

A few moments later Greer opened her eyes and seemed to remember herself. She put the bracelet in her pocket, blew out the candles, and left the room.

The small stream of smoke from the brazier continued to rise through a diagonal shaft of late-afternoon sunlight. It curled and flickered and shone in glimmering white shapes that, had anyone been there to see it, looked very much like two small graceful forms dancing and flitting first apart and then back together to merge again into one flowing, living stream.

Chapter 8

It was all Joy couldn't do to pretend that she couldn't care less about the bracelet. She sullenly let Greer slip it onto her left wrist, tighten the green stone firmly, and fix it in place with a knot. Then she pretended that it annoyed her. But Greer watched her sneak looks at it throughout dinner, and the young woman wasn't skillful enough to hide the delight in her eyes.

Luke turned out to be a large, handsome Native American man with long, dark hair graying elegantly at the temples, an easy manner, and a quick wit. Greer and Joshua both liked him right away. He brought them a housewarming gift: a painting of a Native American on a running horse decorated for the hunt, holding a bow and arrow. There were several fluffy animals running in front of the horse. The style was basic, like a colorful line drawing.

"Wow," Joshua said, smiling. "What are these?" he asked, pointing to the small four-legged animals at which the Indian was shooting his arrows.

"The title of that one is, *When Poodles Roamed Free in Beverly Hills*," Luke said, nodding seriously. Both Greer and Joshua laughed. "I like to be as authentic as possible," Luke told them, winking.

"I love it." Greer thanked him. "And it's perfect for our new home."

Outside, the guttural throbbing of an illegally altered motorcycle coming from the highway interrupted the stillness of the evening. In the natural chamber created by the steep canyon walls, the sound carried from far off, reverberated, and bounced back again, magnified. Joshua watched Joy straighten up from her slump, and she leaned back in her chair to watch out the window. His mother caught his frown. When the motorcycle passed the house, the sound was so loud that conversation was impossible until it had passed a good way up the dirt road.

"You know," Luke said when it was possible to say anything, "I just don't get that."

Greer's gaze shifted to Joy, who seemed to bristle at the sarcastic comment. She said, "You're, like, the only people in the universe who don't get it."

Joshua tried to back her up and keep the peace at the same time by adding, "It *is* loud. I mean, you have to admit. But I'd like to have a Harley. I think it's cool." He was rewarded by a look from Joy, who seemed to be regarding him in a slightly different light.

"I thought you liked Mike," Whitney said almost accusingly to her husband, ignoring the teenager's comments. "You lost money to him. Five bucks. Mm-hmm, didn't think I knew about that, did you?"

"Oh, like I don't know you have a drawer filled with losing lottery tickets. Mike found me a part for my truck at cost and helped me put it in. He's a good guy, even if he did goad me into betting on the Steelers. I just don't understand thinking it's cool to be deliberately obnoxious," Luke said, his dark, wide face cracking pleasantly as he unveiled his white teeth. "I don't much care if people want to make a lot of noise; I'd just prefer it if they all got together in a closed room at the same time and made a lot of noise until their ears bled, and left the rest of us in peace and quiet." He looked pleasantly around. "Mike's okay.

Loud, but he'll always help you out if you need something."

They ate salmon cooked on the grill and wild rice, then settled in for tea and lemon icebox pie that Whitney had made. Joy participated in the conversation only when she was called upon, and then with the utmost of disdain. After a while, Joshua couldn't bear any more of her discomfort and asked her if she wanted to go sit outside. She muttered that she was dying for a smoke. Her father called after her, "It'd better be a cigarette."

When the screen door had swung shut with a creak behind them, Luke turned to the two ladies with his wise grin and said, "You know you're in bad shape when you're glad your fifteen-year-old is smoking cigarettes."

Greer nodded. "You're right; I guess it could be pot."

"Or crack," Luke said, both dismissing the suggestion as humorous and condemning it as contemptible with his easy delivery.

When they got to the big boulder at the foot of the canyon wall and Joy had lit up a smoke, Joshua said, "Your dad seems pretty cool to me."

"Oh, please!" Joy spit. "You heard them; somebody rides by on a motorcycle and they act like it's a federal offense."

Joshua shrugged. "I guess they don't like the noise."

"They think they're better than everyone else, especially me," she muttered angrily.

"They don't seem *that* bad."

"No? You try living with the spiritually perfect."

Joshua laughed. "Aren't we all? I thought that was one of the main themes of the new spirituality: 'Each moment is as it should be.' "

In the semidarkness Joshua could just make out Joy's face. The tip of her cigarette glowed as she inhaled, her breath fanning the tiny ember; she was smiling. "That's good. I think I can use that." The smoke curled out around the bow of her upper lip as she spoke, and Joshua envied it.

"Go for it." Joshua waved a hand as though he were strewing largesse to the masses. "The next time they try to get on your case for breaking curfew you can just say, 'It's all part of the great web.'"

She laughed and choked a little on the smoke. "Good one—you think that up by yourself?"

"No, that was this other guy. Marcus Aurelius, I think." Joshua considered. "He goes on to say that all of our suffering is preordained and we can take comfort in that."

"Oh, he does, huh? Well, you can tell him for me that he's a fucking ass."

Joshua laughed too. "Next time I see him," he reassured her, "I will."

She finished her cigarette and stubbed it out on the rock. Then, turning away from Joshua to partially conceal the movement, she awkwardly stuck the butt into her pocket. He said nothing.

"You got any liquor?" Joy asked him.

"No. And I wouldn't give it to you if I did." He was feeling proud of how he'd affected her behavior, and it made him cocky. "That's the last thing you need."

Joy snorted in the darkness and asked him how the fuck he knew what she needed.

He responded casually, "I mean, no offense, and call me crazy, but anger and liquor sound like a bad Happy Meal combo. I mean, what's the toy surprise? A hangover?" He tried to keep his voice conversational and joking, but he knew it was an iffy thing to say.

The response was immediate and far more vicious than he had anticipated.

Her body went rigid and she practically spit at him. "Fuck off. What do you know, you goody-goody little mama's boy?" She turned and shot for her house.

"C'mon, Joy," Joshua called after her, his heart sinking. "I shouldn't have said that; I'm sorry."

But the only response other than the crunch of her heavy black boots on the gravel was the silhouette of a solitary middle finger raised on a fist in defiance as she stormed away. He cursed himself for being so stupid, realizing that he should have known that because something was so obvious made it all the more taboo to say it out loud.

Because of the light on the porch beyond her, Joshua could make out her shape quite clearly as she stalked away, haloed in the saffron glow from the yellow bug bulbs. For a fraction of a moment it seemed to Joshua, as he watched her, that the light and darkness played a trick on his eyes. In the rim of light around her he thought he saw the figure of a person above and to her right. It was hazy, blackish, and seemed almost to flutter in and out, but the figure appeared to be extending one arm toward Joy and the other toward Joshua.

It lasted only a second but it unnerved him; Joshua shook his head and rubbed his eyes. He headed back to his house quickly, trying to escape the jittery anxiety that had gripped him. Halfway to the porch something swooped by his face, a black, fluttering shape, and he reeled back before realizing it was a bat. That must have been what he'd seen crossing between him and the light. Though the conclusion didn't satisfy the feeling the image had left, he was able to dismiss it as a flying mammal by the time he reached the steps, turning instead to feelings of disappointment about Joy and scowling to himself. *Great, Joshua,* he thought bitterly.

That was stupid. Good thing I didn't sound too much like an insufferable know-it-all. He stopped and kicked the first stone stair; as he did so a light went on in an upstairs window of Luke and Whitney's house.

Joy moved into the middle of her room, and then sat down hard on the edge of the bed. Through the window Joshua could see her, slumped motionless in a posture of total depression.

And then she rose, went to a drawer, and pulled something out. It looked like a cell phone, but instead of holding it to her ear she held it to her mouth and spoke into it.

He watched, wondering what it could be, until she suddenly stopped and tossed whatever it was onto the bed and came to the window. She seemed to have spotted him watching her. He turned away quickly, but he heard the window slide open and she called out to him.

"Hey, fucking neighbor!"

"That would be me," he answered, and turned to look up at her through the sparse pine branches.

"Tell my dad I'm going to bed."

"Sure." He waited, but she said nothing, so he asked, "Anything else?"

"No, just that." There was the noisy silence of a forest at night while they both waited, but neither spoke.

"I'm sorry," he said at last, "if I upset you. I didn't mean to. Sometimes stupid shit comes into my head and leaks out through my mouth."

He couldn't see her very well—she wasn't close and the light was behind her—but her body seemed to relax a little.

"Don't sweat it," she said. "But if you want to be friends, you gotta mind your own business. Got it?"

Joshua hesitated only a moment before the need to be liked overwhelmed him. "Got it," he said firmly.

"I'll hold you to that. Bye." The window closed.

                              *   *   *

Much later that night, Joshua was startled awake by a scrabbling noise. He went to his window, expecting to see a raccoon, but it was an altogether different animal that was climbing down the tree next to Whitney's house.

Joy pretty much fell the last few feet onto the soft pine straw underneath, and through his cracked-open window Joshua heard her utilize her favorite word to express pain. He started to open the window and ask if she needed help, but she was up on her feet in a second, and with a nervous glance up at her own house she disappeared around the front of it, and then reappeared briefly on the dirt road that led to the highway before disappearing behind the trees.

Joshua sighed and let his head thunk against the cold, hard glass. He was torn. Where the hell was she going in the total darkness at this hour? Should he wake up Luke and tell him that his daughter was probably hitchhiking to God knew where on a dark highway? Then he remembered Joy's words, first about minding his own business and then about being a goody-goody. Was he? Lots of his friends sneaked out and did things in Hollywood. Hell, he'd even done it once, but he was a guy. That was different, right?

One thing he knew for sure: If he ratted on her, she would never trust him. And he wanted her to trust him, to like him. He wanted it very much.

Joshua crawled miserably back into his bed and lay there, his eyes open and his heart beating in a guilty tempo in his chest, praying that he wouldn't regret this.

Chapter 9

Several customers were already milling around on the sidewalk when Leah rapped smartly on the glass of the bank door and Towler came to let her in. She was glad Saturdays were only half days for her; they were always so busy. She was balancing a stack of paperwork she had taken home, and her thermal travel mug was clasped in a precarious hold. As she fumbled to set the papers down on her desk, the cup tipped and the coffee sloshed out through the crescent-shaped hole, ran down across the top of a loan request, and saturated the front of her gray silk blouse.

"Oh, f-f-fabulous." Leah dropped the papers unceremoniously in a heap and headed quickly for the ladies' room. One of the cleaning staff was mopping in the doorway, so she detoured and went to the janitor's closet, where she knew there was a sink and paper towels.

She slipped around the corner into a short hallway, which ended in a grilled doorway behind which lay the vault and safety-deposit boxes. Halfway down the hall, the door to the storeroom was standing partially open. The light flickered when she snapped it on and then shone dimly with all its feeble forty watts. Some genius had laid out the room so that the sink was right behind the door. She had to go all the way in and close the door to be able to use it. Working in a bank had made her wary of doors that locked behind her, so she left this one cracked slightly, just shy of latched. Pulling a roll of paper towels off a shelf, she wet one and had started dabbing at the stain when she heard someone pass down the hallway, and keys jingling as the grate was unlocked.

At first she thought nothing of it, and then, glancing at her watch, she realized it was only seven forty. The vault wasn't usually opened until eight thirty. Curious, she leaned forward and peered through the crack in the door. It was Vince; she could tell from his tall, wide back. Something about his manner, a glance over his shoulder as though checking to see if anyone was watching, made her suspicious. Leah reached over and switched off the light so that she could see him better through the crack in the doorway.

Seeming satisfied that no one was there, Vince went through the grating and into the safety-deposit box area. From her vantage point, Leah could see almost the whole wall of units through the bars. Taking the master key from the work desk, he went quickly to one of the larger boxes, took out his key, and opened the six-by-eight-inch door. He slid out the long drawer and then busied himself with his back to Leah. She couldn't see what was in the box, but when Vince slid it back in, secured it, and turned to leave, he was holding a padded, legal-sized manila envelope. He came quickly away, relocking the gate and pocketing the keys. On his face as he came near her, a thin veneer of sweat shone in the fluorescent light. With a thrill of discovery, Leah realized that he was afraid.

As he came level to the supply room door, he stopped. Leah shrank back against the sink. She could see him through the crack, and she was glad she had

had the intuition to switch off the bulb. And then the door started to swing open and the light from the hallway fanned slowly across floor of the tiny room. Leah held her breath and shrank into the ten-inch space between the sink and the wall. The door stopped a finger's width from her face and she waited, every nerve in her body on alert. She knew the Rattler was looking in at the buckets and mops and gigantic packages of toilet paper; would he look behind the door? Then he grunted slightly and pulled the door closed behind him. Leah heard the tumbler click as the door was closed. She remained still in absolute darkness until she was sure he was long gone, and then tried the door.

It was locked.

She struggled to keep panic from rising. If she knocked and raised a ruckus, he would know she'd been in there. If she wasn't back at her desk when the bank opened in fifteen minutes someone would go looking for her. And she couldn't just stay in here! She was starting to breathe in short, shallow gasps, gulping for oxygen. She switched on the light again and tried to find a lock on the doorknob, but it was smooth and solid. She grabbed at it and pulled, but nothing happened. Her lungs felt as though she were breathing through a dripping sponge. She yanked hard on the doorknob, feeling a scream rushing up inside of her. Once, twice—then it opened.

Standing in front of Leah, with her key still in her hand, was the woman who had been mopping the ladies' room floor; she looked mildly surprised. Leah muttered something about her blouse and accidentally closing the door, but the woman, who seemed to have grown up from the floor a couple hundred years ago and would be perfectly content to stand there converting carbon dioxide into oxygen for another brace of centuries, only stared at her. Turning sideways,

Leah slipped around the immobile woman and her mop.

Leah hurried to the corner, glanced around it, and saw no sign of Vince. His office door was closed. With a deep breath she walked calmly back to her desk and started straightening the papers. She wondered if she should tell anyone what she'd seen. And what *had* she seen? So Vince had a safety-deposit box at his own bank. Big deal. But why did he look so nervous about going into it?

Leah felt a thrill of pleasure that caused her chest to swell and her pulse to quicken. There was something about Vince's manner that told her he was up to something he shouldn't be. It was his look, his furtive manner. It was his *fear*.

She smiled to herself, pulling out the payroll account paperwork for Eye of the Beholder and putting it into a clean envelope. She'd take it over to Greer herself when the bank closed at noon today.

It felt good to get a nice, big new client.

It would feel even better to get something on the Rattler.

Chapter 10

Joshua had walked his dirt bike around to the front of the house and brought out his toolbox as an excuse to sit where he could see both Joy's window and the front of their house. When he had woken with a start early that morning and peered out from his bedroom, he had been met with only the impenetrable curtain of Joy's open bedroom window. He had no idea if she had returned and, bound by his promise, he couldn't very well go over and ask.

So he tinkered unnecessarily with the mixture valve on his carburetor as he glanced repeatedly up at the window. The curtain was doing its bit as the impenetrable veil, occasionally trembling slightly in the soft breeze, increasing Joshua's anticipation, only to settle again and hang, limp and still, having revealed nothing. After a short time he heard the crunch of wheels coming down the dirt road from the trailhead. A large silver pickup truck pulled up to the gate that kept hikers from driving past the parking area. Joshua watched with slight interest as a man got out and unchained the gate. He waved a hand at Joshua and then got back in the truck and drove over to where Joshua was working.

Cutting the engine, he climbed down from the high

door and strode toward Joshua with a smile and his hand extended. "Hi, there, I'm Mike. You must be the new neighbor."

Joshua rose and shook the man's hand. He had a look about him that would have suited a fireman or an astronaut. He had a deep cleft in his chin and light brown eyes, the color of which reminded Joshua of fool's gold. He was good-looking, but in a real work-ingman way. Incongruously for a mechanic, his jeans were pressed and his T-shirt was spanking white. Joshua wondered how he looked at the end of his day. "Hi, yeah, I'm Joshua. My mom's Greer. She already left for work."

"Oh, well, hell, I'm sorry I missed her." He looked honestly disappointed. Then he turned and regarded Joshua's bike. "Whatcha got here?"

Joshua told him lamely that it was a Yamaha two-fifty—seemed pretty obvious to him—and Mike bent down to take a look at the engine of the motorcycle. "Start it up," he said. Joshua did, and Mike picked up the flathead screwdriver that Joshua had left lying on the ground. In a couple of minutes the mixture was right and the motor was purring like a leopard cub.

"Looks okay to me," Mike said as he straightened up and wiped his hands on a clean rag from Joshua's toolbox. "Listen, if you'd like, I could come by and we could trick this little boy out. I got a couple of spare parts sitting around the garage that would al-most double the power on this engine. I might have some time next weekend."

Joshua's interest in his motorcycle was mainly as a mode of transportation—it wasn't exactly the dream machine—but he did enjoy working on the engine, taking it apart and getting to know it. "That would be great." He smiled up at the taller man as he cut the engine and the quiet of the clearing resumed. "That's really nice of you."

"Oh, no problem." The man waved a clean but calloused hand and flashed a surprisingly boyish smile at Joshua. "It's my job, but it's my hobby too, if you know what I mean." He winked.

"I guess so. Sounds like you love your work."

"It's a little tough cleaning the grease out from under my nails, but"—he turned and regarded his gleaming four-by-four—"it pays well. Especially up here, people are really into their bikes."

"Yeah," Joshua agreed with him. "I noticed that."

"Well, tell your mom I'm sorry I missed meeting her, and if you guys need anything give me a call."

"Thanks, I'll tell her." Joshua was wondering if his mom could overlook Mike's loud motorcycle. She hadn't dated anyone for a long time.

"No, really, I mean it. Anything at all. I'm real handy." He pulled a white card out of a black leather wallet and handed it to Joshua. It had a picture of a Harley-Davidson, and a phone number. "Mike," he reminded Joshua, pointing to himself. "Bike," he said, pointing to the card. "It's easy to remember that way."

"Thanks, see ya," Joshua said as Mike climbed onto the running board and then up into the supersize truck. He waved as the truck hit the dirt road, headed back to the highway, and left a thick track in the wet ground, the giant tires rolling over the deep ruts in the pitted road from the recent rains as though they were no more of an obstacle than garden hoses on smooth pavement.

Joshua had just sat down on the ground and was trying to find something else to tinker with when the door of Luke and Whitney's house opened and he saw Luke coming toward him. His heart rate quickened.

"Morning," he called out.

"Good morning," Luke said, sounding more serious. "Is your mom in?"

"No, she left for the salon early. She had paperwork to do before her first customer."

"Well, Whitney is out running errands, and she was going to get her hair done at your mom's salon. I need to get her a message, and the woman left her cell phone at home again."

Joshua's mouth felt a little dry. He hoped that he didn't look too nervous or eager as he asked, "Message? I'm gonna go by the salon in a little while; you want me to tell her something?"

Luke sighed. "Just tell her that we won't be going to the movies tonight. Joy's grounded."

Joshua felt a small sense of relief, but it was incomplete. He still didn't know if she was home safe.

Trying to sound only vaguely interested, he asked, "What for?"

"She snuck out last night and came home drunk."

Joshua hadn't realized he'd been holding his breath until he exhaled. "Oh, did she wake you up when she came in or something?"

Luke laughed a little and shook his head. "No," he said. "I sleep like a hibernating grizzly, and Whitney wears earplugs, plus Joy didn't come in. In fact, she would have gotten away with it if I hadn't found her passed out on one of the deck chairs out back this morning."

"How do you know she was drinking?" Joshua asked.

Luke smiled, and an amused twinkle lit his eye. "You know us Cherokees: We don't hold our firewater too well. She was so hungover she could barely raise her head."

Joshua nodded, smiling in spite of himself. "She sleeping it off now?"

Luke's mischievous smile extended until it was

stretched across his rugged face. "Hell, no. I made her get up and vacuum the house." He raised his brows at Joshua and then turned away.

Through the open door before it closed behind Luke, Joshua could hear the high, penetrating, torturous whine of a Hoover.

Chapter 11

Leah had finished the paperwork on a home loan just before noon, and she needed Vince's signature. Towler buzzed her in to the back, and, reminding herself to stay calm and businesslike no matter what a dick Vince was, she knocked on his office door.

He didn't answer. In fact, he didn't acknowledge her at all. She puffed out her cheeks and blew out slowly, trying to calm herself, but a spark of anger at his infuriating disregard for anyone else—especially her—combusted, and she recklessly opened the door without an invitation.

"So sorry to interrupt your . . ." She stopped in her tracks; the room was empty.

Turning around, she surveyed the bank floor, but she didn't see him there either.

"Josie?" she addressed a teller who was at the file cabinet. "Did you see where Vince went?"

The older woman with the pinched face of a long-time smoker looked up from her paper search. "Uh, I think he went out to get something to eat. Anyway, he said he'd be back in fifteen." Josie turned back to the cabinet, her huge hoop earrings swinging.

"Oh. When did he go?"

"Just now."

Leah sighed. Now she'd have to wait for him before she could leave, which would mean staying past closing. Typical. Maybe she'd just leave the papers and tell the clients that Vince had made them wait until Monday. It was a shallow thought of a threat; she was too professional to let it wait and she knew it. Sighing, she went in and laid the papers right on top of his other work so that he'd have to sign them first when he got back.

She'd started to turn away when something caught her eye: The right-hand drawer of his desk was open about two inches, and in a small compartment she could see a single small key alone on a key chain with a heavy, dangling charm. His safety-deposit box key.

A thrill went through Leah. This was a chance she might never get again. It would mean her job at least if she were caught, but she was sure he was up to something. Making a snap decision based more on her raging need for revenge than on any kind of cool deduction, she snatched up the key and her papers, folding them with the key concealed inside. She exited quickly, glancing at the front door, wondering if she could really get away with this.

She waited for Towler to buzz her out and went straight to her desk to pick up her own keys. Leah kept a safety-deposit box at the bank as well. It would give her an excuse for being in the vault. Then she headed down the hallway.

As she reached the iron-gated door, she smiled in what she hoped was a casual, friendly way at the young man who headed up that department.

"Hi, Jerry!" she said, in what sounded like an overly bright voice to her.

"Hi, Leah. What's up?" Jerry had the translucent appearance of a man who was basically attractive but fluorescently pale from spending his entire working life in artificial light and, Leah guessed, his free time in front of a computer screen playing online games and ordering collectible action figures.

"I need to get something out of my box."

"Okay." His face was drawn back to the cold green glow of his screen, and he looked reluctant to have to break away. "I'll be right with you," he said without looking up again.

Perfect, thought Leah. "No, don't worry about it; just give me your key and I'll do it. It won't take a minute. That way you can finish up and get out of here on time for a change." She was careful to use a conspiratorial, commiserating tone. It worked. He glanced up to see if anyone would see him do it, but there was nothing behind Leah except an empty hallway. Then, with a grateful little smile, he handed over the master key and returned to the vortex of cyberland.

Leah made sure she was past him before she looked back to check the hall. Nothing. She'd have to hurry. Her box was one of the smaller upper ones over to the far left. The one she had seen Vince go into had been one of the larger drawers lower down to the right.

She looked again. Jerry was nothing but an eerie silhouette rimmed in blue, hunched forward as though pulled by some invisible sucking force. As long as she was quiet he would not be a problem, and if anyone else came in she would hear them speak to Jerry. The only person she needed to fear was the Rattler. Just like old times.

Old times. It had started out so perfectly. They'd made such a beautiful couple, and both of them were devoted to their careers. But then the drinking had begun, and a man she didn't know had emerged who was very different from the man she thought she'd married. He was supposed to be moving out; he was supposed to leave her alone. She had promised not to press charges and in return he had agreed to keep his distance. But the promise of a violent drinker was nothing more than a gust of wind with the stench of something dead in it.

Unsure of the box number, she took three tries to find the right one. With a deep inhalation she tensed as first the master and then Vince's key turned in the lock. Just before she slid it open she almost lost her nerve, convincing herself it was none of her business.

And then it overwhelmed her: a night two years ago that no amount of effort or logic could block or erase from her memory.

She was sleeping when he came in drunk. She heard him run into something in the living room and then swear as though it were the something's fault. She sat up in bed, tense, knowing that drunk and angry were a dangerous combination in her estranged husband—dangerous for her. Closing her eyes, she prayed that he would go to the guest room, pass out, and be in a bad mood at breakfast, but she heard him coming noisily down the hall, stopping at the bedroom door.

He tried the lock, cursed, and then called out to her in a mocking tone, "Oh, cupcake, my little yummy girl."

Leah clutched the sheets and looked at the phone. The house was up a long, twisting road from the main street; it would take the police a long time to respond, too long. He banged loudly on the door. "Open up! I've got a little something for you, you nasty little bitch!"

She flew out of bed and reached for her jeans with shaking hands. The thought of facing him in a night-gown horrified her. Not that she was any match for him fully dressed. She put the pants and a T-shirt on quickly and then listened. She heard nothing; maybe he'd gone and passed out. Hoping fervently that it was so, she backed up against the wall.

The window next to her shattered as a lawn chair came flying through it. Leah screamed and tried to flatten herself against the closet door. There was glass everywhere, and she was terrified that if she took even one step in the dark her feet would be cut to shreds.

The shadow of Vince's tall figure was climbing through the window. He stepped onto the glass wearing his motorcycle boots without any fear of injury and looked at the empty bed. Whimpering, Leah cowered as far into the corner and the dark as she could, like a lizard hiding from a snake.

But snakes don't need to see their victims; they can sense them. Vince turned slowly and moved toward her. She could hear his breath coming fast; she could smell the tequila on it. As he came toward her he unbuckled his belt and pulled it off, opening his fly.

"Get on the bed," he ordered.

"Vince, please, you're drunk. Let's talk about this tomorrow. C'mon, you don't want to do this." Leah could hear the pleading and the fear in her own voice, and she despised herself for it.

He laughed. He liked it when she was afraid, and she knew it. It turned him on; she was only feeding his sickness. She hated him with every terrified fiber of her being—she hated the bastard, and he laughed.

"Get on the bed."

"No," Leah said through gritted teeth.

The belt lashed out, striking her across her chest, the thin T-shirt offering only the pretense of protection. He grabbed her by the hair with his left hand and half lifted her across to the bed. Leah could hear the glass crunch under her feet, but the pain of her hair being squeezed into a tight fist and wrenched away from her head distracted her. She landed facedown and he held her there, pressing her face into the sheets. With the chunk of her hair still in his left hand, she felt him use his other hand to pull down his pants. Tears of pain and anger stung her eyes but were absorbed by the linens. She tried to cry out, but the mattress muffled the sound. He grappled roughly with her jeans and with three yanks had them off. Next he grabbed her thin shirt at the back of the neck and ripped at it. The collar caught at her throat and choked her, but he kept ripping until it came away. She felt as though her thorax had been crushed.

"Open up," Vince ordered, and Leah automatically pulled her legs together and crossed her ankles, fighting back the only way she could. Both of her hands were holding the wrist of his hand on her head, trying to lessen the intense pain of her hair being pulled out at the roots.

"Do it!" he growled, and she felt the lash of his belt across her back, the loud smacking sound accentuating the stinging pain. He struck her again and again until finally, willing to do anything to stop the pain, she had spread her legs and sobbed while he climbed behind her and forced his way unnaturally into her, using her in a way that she would never—could never—tell anyone about while she wept and raged impotently. The thought of pressing charges and making this shame public was unimaginable.

That distant night wavered in her memory as Leah looked down at the box in front of her. With hope and hatred in her heart, she opened the door and slid out the drawer.

It was filled with cash and several hundred small bags of white powder.

All the breath went out of Leah's body. She had to lean both hands flat against the counter to keep from swaying visibly. Taking one of the small bags, she stuffed it into the top of her bra and quickly closed the box, turning both keys. Then she retreated hurriedly from the room, praying that the bloodless state of her face didn't show too badly. She went rapidly back down the hall.

"Hey! Hold on, there!" Jerry's voice called out sharply.

Leah froze and turned back to face him.

"What do you think you're doing?" He held out his hand. "My key?"

"Oh," Leah stammered, and crossed back to him, holding out his master key with a shaky hand. "Sorry."

Jerry was watching her—was it suspiciously? Had he seen her go to a box that wasn't her own? Could he even possibly know that it had been Vince's? "Are you okay? You look pale," he told her.

Leah exhaled, relieved. His voice sounded nothing more than politely concerned. "Oh, I'm fine. I am getting over a little bit of a bug. You know, all the rain and stuff," she blabbed pointlessly.

"I hope you feel better," Jerry said, taking the key and returning to the pool of green light.

"Thanks. I do."

Leah hurried back to her desk, checking around surreptitiously. No sign of Vince. She walked back to the teller's door, and as Towler buzzed her in she asked, "Is Vince back?"

Towler looked up from his customer and shrugged. "I don't know. I didn't know he went out."

The small hairs on Leah's arms stood up. But she smiled as though it were all for the best and crossed to his door, clutching the contracts, and forced herself to knock casually.

No answer.

She opened the door. "Vince?" He wasn't there. She went in and put the contract down on his desk again, pulling his heavy key chain and its single small charm out from behind it. She returned the key to the desk drawer and was just sliding it closed when she heard someone behind her.

"What are you doing?" Vince's voice was cold and hard.

"Oh." Leah jumped and turned around to face him, pushing the drawer closed the rest of the way with the back of her leg. For the first time in her life she hoped her hips were wide enough to block out the view behind her. "I was just bringing in these loans for you to sign off on. I was leaving them on your desk."

Vince's eyes had narrowed; they darted from her face to the drawer and then back again.

She tried to distract him by collecting up the papers. "Here, if you could just sign them. It's a standard home loan; you've already seen the approvals."

Vince ignored the offered papers, crossed around her, and slid the drawer open an inch or two, just enough to see that his key was there. Then he turned a look on her that was almost pleasant. She didn't like it. Had he seen her put it back?

"Of course I can." He took the papers from her, sat down in his chair, and signed off with a flourish. "Nice work, by the way." He smiled as he handed the papers back to her.

"Thanks," she muttered, and turned to leave.

"You know"—he stopped her—"there really isn't any need for us to be so uncomfortable with each other. We were married; it didn't work out. You got the house; I got the account. Everybody's happy. We should just let bygones be bygones, don't you think?" He leaned back and put his hands behind his head. As he did, a glint from his silver belt buckle caught Leah's eye.

She looked into his smiling face and said coldly, "Yeah, Vince. No hard feelings."

Chapter 12

"Am I good?" asked Dario as he pulled the black smock off of Whitney and flourished it as though it were a matador's cape.

"You are a hairdressing god," Whitney told him, her dry wit easily rising to his flamboyant level. She fluffed for a minute and then added, "I lay my laurel wreath at your feet. I canonize you the patron saint of styling." She made the sign of the cross in his direction regally, like the pope giving his holy blessing.

"Stop right there!" Dario held up one strong, masculine hand. "I draw the line at the requirements for sainthood. The miracles I can do, but dying a martyr's death just doesn't appeal to me." He turned to Jonathan, who was standing next to him nodding his head, and handed him the smock. "Besides, you're Catholic, aren't you, Jonathan?"

"Uh . . . yeah." His wicked assistant playfully smiled.

"Are there any gay saints?"

"None that the nuns told me about in Catholic school. I did hear somewhere that there was a cross-dressing pope."

"I heard that too!" said Whitney enthusiastically. "And they didn't find out she was a woman until she died and they were preparing her body for burial."

Jonathan balled up the smock and shot it into the laundry bin. "Bit of a shock, that."

Greer came out of the hallway from the treatment rooms and clapped her hands together in delight at the sight of Whitney's new shorter, more flattering haircut. "I didn't think it could get much better, but it did!"

"Hmph," Dario voiced in a mock-hurt tone.

Greer smiled at him, amused. "I was just going to get a sandwich next door; would you like to join me?" she asked Whitney.

"Great, that was all part of my master plan."

"Dario?"

"I've got two more clients, but I'll come over and get something to go in a few minutes, thanks."

Without waiting to be asked, Jonathan patted his perfectly flat tummy and said, "I'm on the South Beach."

The two women were going out the door when they ran into Leah coming in with the paperwork in her hand.

"Oh, hi." Leah looked surprised. "I was just bringing you the papers to sign. But if you're on your way out, I can come back, or you can come by the bank on Monday."

"Perfect timing. Do you know Whitney Whitehorse?" Greer asked.

"No, I don't think we've met. Hi, I'm Leah Falconer." The two women shook hands warmly.

"Nice to meet you. Why don't you join us for lunch?" Whitney invited.

Leah looked unsure. "I don't want to intrude."

"Don't be silly; you'll be great company." Greer laid her hand on Leah's arm and steered her to the shop next door. "Besides, I want you to meet Jenny Sanchez. She's terrific, and her shop is so darling."

The bells on the door jangled as the trio entered.

Several other customers were scattered about on the living room–style sofas and tables. Jenny stood in intent conversation with a handsome young man at the counter. Greer assumed from her frustrated body language that this would be her husband. The women approached the marital spat warily, but when Jenny saw them she broke quickly away, waved a big hello, and then came out from around the counter to meet Leah and kiss both Greer and Whitney on their cheeks before extending a hand toward the handsome young man.

"This is my husband, Lewis."

Lewis muttered hellos, said he was just leaving, and kissed Jenny's cheek. She watched him go, shaking her head, and then effortlessly switched to another channel.

"You," she said to Whitney, who kept unconsciously reaching up to pat her shorter hair, "look fabulous. Is that a new cut?"

"Why, yes, thank you for noticing." Whitney pretended to be only slightly pleased. Greer and Jenny shared a quick, knowing look.

Jenny turned her effervescence on Leah. "I've seen you at the bank; you always look good."

Taken aback at the unsolicited compliment, but pleased, Leah said, "Thank you."

"Okay, what can I get you?"

They all placed their orders and took a cozy table by the window. Greer signed the papers after giving them a perfunctory once-over.

"Don't you want to read them though?" Leah asked.

"I know what they say. We already discussed the terms, and I have faith in you." She winked and then rose to help Jenny when she saw her balancing several plates on her way to the table.

"Can you join us for a few minutes?" Greer asked her. There were no customers waiting now.

Jenny looked around. "You know what? That sounds good. I've been on my feet since six a.m." She pulled a chair over from nearby and sank gratefully into it, relaxing by degrees like a stop-motion picture show.

Greer frowned at her. "Now that your business is picking up, why don't you get someone to help you? You can't drive yourself this hard; you need to take a break."

Jenny shook her head. "Can't afford it yet." She sighed. "You'd think my husband could help me out when he's not working. I mean, if I ask him to come fix the disposal or lay tile, he'll eventually get to it, but as far as making coffee and change, no way. The concept of my needing a break is beyond him. After all the time I spent helping him build up his contracting business, now, when things are light for him, instead of helping me he stresses about the fact that he's not making tons of money. They just don't get it."

Whitney nodded. "I know; some men just can't get past that caveman mentality."

Leah looked at her curiously. "Meaning?"

"Meaning that once they've clubbed the meat and brought it home, they think their obligation to the relationship is over. It's not really their fault; it's how our society brainwashed them."

Greer watched them all flow into easy conversation and felt warm inside.

Jenny smacked her hand on the table. "Exactly," she said emphatically. "It's not that he's a bad guy. He means well, but sometimes I just want to pick up his little brain and squash it to see if it really is hollow."

The door opened and Joshua came in, his helmet under his arm. Greer beamed proudly. "Hi, sweetie."

"Hi, Mom." He leaned down and kissed her. Whitney sighed wistfully as she watched the gesture of affection. Joshua said to her, "I've got a message for you, babe."

She shook a finger at him. "I told you not to call me that." Then, out of the side of her mouth, she added, "Not in public. What is it?"

"Um, Luke told me to tell you that you're not going out tonight. Joy's grounded."

Whitney sighed, and, placing her elbows upon the table, she let her face fall into her hands and rubbed hard on her temples. "What now?"

Joshua fumbled a bit over the next wording. "I guess she, uh, snuck out last night."

Whitney didn't even look up. She nodded her face-hand combo and groaned. "And?"

"And, uh, had a few cocktails."

"And?"

"And fell asleep out back on one of the deck chairs, where Luke found her this morning when he made her get up and vacuum the house."

Jenny grimaced. "Ooh. That's harsh."

Greer bit her lip to keep from laughing. Leah felt too out of the kid loop to comment.

Whitney looked up at Joshua. There was a moment's silence. "Vacuum the house? With a hangover?"

Joshua nodded solemnly and then said, "I might be betraying my fellow teenagers, but I thought it was really good parenting."

Their laughter was still shaking the shop when the bells jangled again and the handsome landscape architect, Sterling, came in. Jenny jumped up, wiping tears of amusement from her eyes, and went to wait on him.

Greer couldn't help thinking that his eyes lingered on her longer than was casually friendly when he said hello. She wondered if she was hopefully imagining it, and decided that she wasn't. But it gave her a thrill of insecurity—and possibility. Could he be attracted to her? She'd had relationships since her marriage to Geoff, but they'd all fizzled out. Eventually she had gotten to like being on her own and just stopped looking for someone else. For the first time she realized that she'd probably chosen to stay a single mom because it was just less trouble. The revelation surprised her; she didn't remember planning to be alone. Now, to consider flirting and mating an option again felt slightly alien. She glanced surreptitiously over at Sterling. He was laughing with Jenny at the counter, but he glanced back over his shoulder at her, as though checking that she was still there. Greer blushed and looked away.

Whitney was watching her. She asked pointedly, "So, what's the dating situation for you two?" She looked from Leah to Greer.

"Oh, pretty nonexistent," Leah said glumly. "I'm recently divorced from a real son of a bitch, and I guess I'm just a little gun-shy."

"What happened?" Whitney asked, as though she were inquiring how Leah had gotten a dent in her fender.

Leah didn't answer immediately. Jenny's return to the table eased her hesitation and discomfort. Sterling took a table close by, and Greer wished she had the nerve to invite him to join them. Whitney was still looking questioningly at Leah.

"He had a bad temper," Leah said at last.

"Oh, boy. One of *those*," Whitney said, and then added reassuringly, "I'm sure you're better off without him."

"I wish I were," Leah said, surprising herself with the confession. "Without him, I mean. He's still my boss."

"Ow. That sucks," Jenny commiserated.

Greer guessed from her reading that it was far more than a bad temper, but she didn't know anything specific and she revealed nothing. That would be up to Leah to share when and if she chose. Nonetheless, her interest was piqued. She wondered if this man, still so predominant in Leah's life, could be the future threat as well. She remembered meeting Vince, and the chill that had crept up her arm when he shook her hand.

Jenny asked bluntly, "Did he hit you?"

"What?" Leah jerked, and her coffee sloshed on the table.

"Did he hit you?" Jenny repeated, unabashed. "Usually when a man's got a temper they aren't too emotionally mature, and they look around for a punching bag." Her face darkened. "I should know. My family was a regular fight club."

Leah grabbed at the opportunity to take the embarrassing focus off of her. "What do you mean?"

Jenny sighed and looked around the table at Greer, Whitney, Leah, and finally Joshua. "Some other time I'll go into all that. Let's just say for now that I had to make a choice not to be a victim. And I'm sticking to it."

"Okay, how about you?" Whitney's sharp, dark eyes cut to Greer. "Men?"

"I'm leaving." Joshua rose from the table. "Not that I don't enjoy girl talk. I just have some guy stuff to do: poker playing, cigar smoking, bear hunting with a blunt bowie knife, that kind of thing." He collected his helmet. "I'm gonna go next door and see Dad."

"Okay, honey, I love you. See you tonight?

"Sure. Bye."

Greer watched Joshua leave and then was surprised

to find all three women staring at her. "Dad?" asked Jenny.

Greer sighed. "It's a long story."

Whitney leaned comfortably back in her chair, taking her coffee mug into her lap. "I've got all afternoon."

Looking around at the three remaining women, Greer saw nothing there but loving interest. She took a deep breath and began. "Dario's been a second father to Joshua since he was four years old. I fell in love with my husband, Geoffrey, when we met hiking up in Joshua Tree. He was working in the area; I was vacationing. Anyway, we got married and had Joshua. Geoffrey was always honest with me, and when he came and told me he'd met someone else, I was upset but I understood. I'd always known it was a possibility, and frankly, Geoffrey and I were always better friends than lovers. Joshua was three at the time, so I won't say that the next year was easy, but we got through it, made the transition. Geoffrey didn't desert Joshua or me, but he'd met the love of his life. It was just meant to be. Even I could see that."

Whitney nodded. "So Dario was your partner, and he became like a father to Joshua when Geoffrey died?"

"Long before that, actually." Greer smiled gently and looked at each woman's face wondering what she would see next. "Dario and I didn't open the first salon until two years *after* Geoffrey's death."

"So, I don't get it. When did he come into Joshua's life?" asked Jenny.

"When Dario married Geoffrey, and Joshua got two dads."

There was absolute silence. None of the women looked away or wavered. Leah took a sip of her coffee.

Then, as Greer watched, the corner of Whitney's

eyes crinkled, and Greer could tell that a joke was coming.

"No wonder you don't date," she said dryly.

The moment was broken, the mirror of shocked silence shattered with a tinkling musical giggle into a thousand tiny pieces, each reflecting a few seconds of pain, time, a life, dissolving and falling into the women's laughter.

"You know," Jenny said when they'd recovered, "I read somewhere that if you ask a man what part of a building he relates to, it'll tell you what kind of man he is. Like, say he says 'roof.' That would mean he's very protective. What was Geoffrey?"

Greer thought. "A sliding glass door; he never hid anything."

"I asked my husband and he said he was a wall." Jenny sighed. "I could have told you that, after having to break through it with a sledgehammer." She turned to Leah. "What was your delightful ex?"

"The septic tank," Leah said, surprised at her quickness in responding. They all laughed again.

Jenny turned and looked over at Sterling, who was looking through some superglossy design magazine as he ate his salad. "Sterling?" Jenny called out. "If you were to describe yourself as any part of a building, what would it be?"

Without missing a single beat, Sterling said in his crisp British accent, "A flying buttress."

They all laughed again. "Well, at least you're honest," Leah said. "And that's good."

"Honesty's good," Greer echoed as she felt his eyes watching her. She glanced up at the clock on the wall and stood. "I've got to get going; I've got a client at one."

She said her round of good-byes and, turning to the door, almost collided with Sterling, who was on his way out. She glanced at his lunch; his salad was only half-eaten.

"Oh, sorry," Greer breathed, a kind of girlish excitement flushing her face.

"Not a problem. Here, let me get the door."

She mumbled her thanks, hoping that the other women hadn't seen the rush of color in her cheeks. Sterling fell into step beside her.

"Well, business looks good," he said, and Greer was surprised to find that he sounded ever so slightly nervous.

"Very good." They had reached her door, and she paused with her hand on the handle but didn't push it. Searching awkwardly for something to say, she was reminded of why she had stopped dating. "Uh, how's yours?"

"Great, actually. There's a lot of turnover in the neighborhood right now, and people want to remodel the landscaping as well as the house."

"Oh," Greer said, slightly surprised. "I thought you were doing quite a bit of business in Europe?"

For two seconds Sterling's noble brow drew down into a concentrated frown. Then, like water restored to lucid clarity as the ripples of a skipped stone flowed away, his face cleared and he laughed, a sound that reminded Greer of sunlight streaming through a dense forest, of ferns glistening with drops of dew, of the rumble of distant thunder.

All of the things she liked best.

"You've been listening to Pistol," he said when his eyes rested on her again. "I *have* been getting some correspondence from Italy, but that would be my final divorce documents, from my Italian marital mistake."

Greer felt her smile widen as her heart opened a small door. "Well, we all have one of those. A marital mistake, I mean, not necessarily an Italian one."

He frowned slightly again with sensitive concern. "I thought that your husband had died."

It was Greer's turn to laugh, and in the sound of it Sterling felt the warmth of a fire crackling while silent snow fell all around. He heard a soft breeze rustle the leaves of a poplar tree, and the silvery tinkle of water flowing over a thousand tiny falls in a mountain stream. His heart took on a wrinkle as hope made a dent in the smooth hardness of his hurt. "I'm sorry; I didn't realize that was a funny thing to say."

"It's not." Greer kept the smile, but her eyes saddened. "But what I meant was that I was divorced before Geoffrey died, and you've been listening to Pistol too."

Sterling mock pouted. "Guilty," he said.

"And besides," Greer continued, "there's no such thing as a marital mistake, really, only a learning experience. Mine wasn't a mistake anyway; we always knew it was borrowed time. We just loved each other as people so much. Do you understand?"

Sterling nodded solemnly. "Yes. I do." He sounded envious. "Unfortunately, I have no such defense. It would be a bit of an exaggeration to say that we like each other very much at all right now."

Tilting her head curiously to one side, Greer noted, "You must have once."

"Yes, once. But then reality set in and there were just too many cultural differences."

"Like what?" Greer didn't know if she was crossing a line, but she liked talking to Sterling, and she wanted to sustain the conversation.

She needn't have worried. With a deep sigh and a sad shake of his head, Sterling said morosely, "Though I loved her lasagna, she could never learn to make steak-and-kidney pie. Alas that it should be so."

Greer laughed again. "Well, I couldn't even learn

to make my own traditional dishes. I'm Greek, and I never learned to make spanakopita."

"Ah, those little wedding appetizers that flake all over your suit. Never cared for those, and I have a deeply held belief that you should never eat triangular food."

"That's an interesting belief."

"Everybody's got to believe in something."

"I believe I've got a client." In addition to amusement, there was more honest reluctance in Greer's voice than apology. "I've got to get going."

Sterling took hold of the door handle, and as he swept it open for her he bowed slightly and said, "We shall meet again at Philippi."

"Or at the coffee shop, anyway." Greer beamed warmly at Sterling as she started past him, and the grin was bounced right back at her.

From his station halfway back down the salon floor, Dario watched the exchange, nudging Jonathan and gesturing for him to observe as well.

At the last moment Sterling placed a hand softly on Greer's shoulder in a familiar way, and Greer turned back to sustain the contact before smiling a good-bye and entering the salon with an added lightness in her graceful, swaying step.

The two men raised delighted eyebrows at each other. "Well, well," mused Dario. "What have we here?"

"Flirtation at the gates," Jonathan confirmed. "She's under friendly fire."

"And from a worthy adversary, from everything I've seen and heard." Dario watched Greer disappear into the hallway. "I think we might need to help this along. Just a little nudge in the ribs."

"Oh, please." Jonathan half snorted. "It'll take a hard shove between the shoulder blades for that girl.

You need to *launch* her off the edge. We're talking about damaged heterosexuals in their forties."

The two men grimaced conspiratorially at each other.

Then Dario showed his teeth as he said, "Man the battle stations."

Chapter 13

"Not to be too nosy, but what's with your brother's prison tattoos?" Dario asked nosily.

Paul smiled in his usual way, but his eyes saddened. "Oh, something bad happened, and he spent a few years working out in a small yard surrounded by barbed wire."

"Is it a family secret?" Dario was watching Paul as he finished putting in the last of the tile on the ledge above the sinks he had installed. He was good at it. Dario had found that Paul was one of those people who could do numerous things well, once you actually got him to show up.

Paul shrugged automatically in response to the direct query, but his ruddy face had reddened slightly. "I guess not. I kinda got him into a bad situation." The laugh surged up again, as though even this, his brother's prison sentence, were an unavoidable situation that had to be taken with a grain of salt and a sense of humor. Which, thought Dario, of course it was.

Paul glanced up at Dario and saw nothing but intelligent interest on the taller man's face. "See, I was married for a while and she had a few kids before." He paused, his smile pushing his cheeks up into rosy mounds.

"A few?" Dario asked.

"Four."

"Oh, my."

To his credit, Paul laughed. "She had four more with me. I've got custody of them all now."

"Eight?" Dario was thunderstruck. "You have eight kids? For God's sake, man, that's a litter!"

The chuckle bubbled up. "No, I've got my four. The other ones were older. But the father of her oldest boy was . . . well." Paul looked up with a sheepish grin. "Let's just say he was a loser, and he was making threats and stuff."

Paul went back to spackling, and Dario stood casually with his arms crossed, waiting. He had a few minutes before his client's weave was done baking.

"Anyway, I went over there with the boy, who was thirteen, to try to talk to his father and get him to stop being so aggressive, and Army came with us. When we got there the guy was drunk and just wanted to pick a fight. He got out a gun and shot at us." Paul made it sound as though shooting were an everyday occurrence in his life.

Stunned, Dario asked, "He shot at his own kid?"

Now Paul turned a full-on grin toward Dario, and with a tremolo of humor under the words he said, "He missed!"

"Jesus," Dario swore. "Nice dad."

"So Army runs to his truck and gets out his gun and shoots back at the guy."

"And he *didn't* miss?"

"He winged the guy."

"Self-defense, right?" Dario asked, trying to stay as conversational as Paul, but with difficulty.

"Well, that's not the way the police saw it." Paul shrugged again as though, fair or unfair, the flow of events was a force of nature and we were all jetsam on the tide. "It might not have been so bad if Army hadn't run off. But he was scared. The guy was pissed at me for being with his ex and his kid, so he said I was the one who shot at him, and I was arrested."

"But he shot at all of you first! The kid was a witness!" Dario could feel a sense of outrage surging up in him. That wasn't fair.

The shrug again, the acceptance. "I didn't want the boy to testify against his own father; it was his word against his dad's anyway. And by the time the cops came, the guy had gotten rid of the gun, cleaned up, and his bullets had missed us." Paul paused to laugh. "Bad luck."

"Did they catch Army later or what?" Dario asked, trying to piece it all together.

"No," Paul said slowly, shaking his head as though to knock the grin off, but it stayed put. "He turned himself in when he found out I'd been arrested."

"And he spent six years in prison." Dario was impressed. Good brother.

"It would have been seven, but I cut a deal with the DA and took part of the blame. I spent a year in jail. Not the big house, but the county lockup."

"Was it horrible?"

The shoulders did their little jig and the smile deepened as the laugh came up again. "It wasn't great." Paul turned and wiped some white Spackle off of the deep blue tile. "The worst thing was that it was a big dorm kinda room, and they never turned off the lights or the television."

Dario shuddered. "The depths of hell," he commented.

"Not as bad as what Army went through." For the first time, Paul looked as though his story disturbed him in spite of all his efforts to remain jovial. "It changed him. I'm just glad he lived through it."

"He must be very bitter," Dario said.

The indefatigable laugh rose in the words again as Paul said, "It didn't do much for his sense of humor."

Dario watched the wave of amusement pass through Paul and saw the disturbed concern that returned after it. "Hell, I'd go back and kill the son of a bitch." Then quietly he asked, "Are you worried about him?"

Paul finished, wiped his hands, and turned full-face to Dario. The warmth that radiated from the plumber didn't cease, but the simple honesty in his eyes almost made Dario turn away.

He asked, "Wouldn't you be?"

Dario held his look for a long moment without smiling back before he nodded. "Yes," he said. "Deeply."

Paul cleaned up his things, and the two men walked together to the front. Dario stopped at the counter to get a check for Paul and a cigarette for himself, and they both went outside.

Parked just off to the left was Paul's truck, a large, rusty affair. Tied in the back of it was an enormous German shepherd. Dario lit his cigarette as he walked toward the truck. "Nice dog," he said, and extended a hand.

The dog went for it, snapping and lunging, Dario only just managed to pull back in time. Paul had gone to the far side to put his toolbox away; he shouted a command and the animal quieted.

"Oh, sorry about that." He chuckled a bit. "That's my brother's dog, and a tree limb fell last night, broke part of his fence. He lives out, kind of remote, but still. You can't really let a dog like that wander."

"No," Dario agreed wholeheartedly, "not a good wandering dog."

"I'm gonna help him fix the fence tonight. So, don't worry; I won't have to bring him again." Paul's laugh rumbled along under his reassurance, as though the whole idea of a man-eating dog were a funny concept.

"Well, your truck is safe; that's for sure."

"Yeah. Kind of funny—my convict brother picked a police dog."

Dario nodded and backed up onto the sidewalk. "People get used to things."

Paul laughed again. "I'll just be glad to have somebody else watching him."

As Paul drove away, Dario wondered if he had meant that Army was watching the dog, or the other way around.

Chapter 14

The light in the room softened as the direct gaze of the sun disappeared over the edge of the high canyon walls outside to look down on other places. Greer liked the twilight; it was a strong time for romantic magic.

On the little brazier, a small dried rosebud and drops of magnolia oil sizzled as they evaporated into a sweet scent that altered the feeling as well as the smell of the air. In Greer's hand two acorns rested while she bathed them in the thin white smoke rising in front of her. When she was satisfied that every exposed place on the seeds had been touched, she wrapped embroidery floss around them like belts, one in blue and one in pink, knotting the strands tightly so they resembled sashes on two fat little gnomes, and left a long strand hanging from each one.

She smiled and hummed as she worked, thinking of Jenny and her husband and imagining them together. Immediately she sensed a rosy, golden cord traveling from one to the other, a strong connection of love, but there were other things around the couple as well, dark ropes that had attached themselves to one or the other and strained to pull them apart. These lines were links to the past, baggage. Still holding the acorns snuggly in the palm of her left hand, Greer focused on each of the dark cords one at a time and snapped the fingers of her right hand as she pictured the ropes being cut and then dissolving away.

Last, she took an end of the floss from each acorn and began to knot them together in a complex but beautiful design, and while she did this she chanted:

> *"Unbind the past and weave together,*
> *Flower, moon, and owl feather.*
> *Build upon the love that's there,*
> *Earth, fire, water, air."*

Three times she repeated the chant and three times she made the same knot.

Satisfied, she held it up by the knotted string and let it swing for a minute, regarding it hopefully.

As she went to the door of her sanctuary, she mused on the nature of love spells. Impossible to create love, of course—it had to already be there—but you could help things along. Love could be strengthened, healed, nurtured. Her charm was just a little energy focused in that direction.

As she passed by the door of Joshua's room, she saw him seated at his desk with his back to the door, concentrating on his homework. She paused and watched him affectionately for a moment until he was distracted by the sound of the loud Harley coming down the road from the trailhead. Through the window she could see as it paused while Mike got off at the gate and unlocked it, passed through, and then dismounted to lock the gate again. Greer waited until the bike had driven off toward the highway before she commented. "Saturday night. I guess our neighbor is going out."

Joshua turned and looked at his mom, surprised that she was there. "Oh, yeah, I forgot to tell you. That's Mike; he stopped by the other day after you left and offered to help out if we needed anything. He seemed like a pretty nice guy. I put his card on the bulletin board."

Greer shook her head dubiously. "A nice guy with no consideration of anyone around him?"

Joshua looked a little taken back. He thought the bike was loud, but cool. As casually as possible he said, "He's not bad-looking either, and I think he makes really good money with his shop."

Greer raised her eyebrows at her son. "Are you trying to fix me up?"

"No," Joshua lied. "It's just that . . . well, I'll be going off to college soon, and I think it would nice if you had somebody around."

Crossing the room as she laughed, Greer laid a hand on her son's cheek and beamed down at him. "I don't have a boyfriend because I like it that way. If I meet someone really special, that might change, but I'm not afraid to be alone." She stroked the cheek and added in a softer voice, "You don't need to be afraid for me."

"I know, Mom." Joshua shifted away from his mom's hand, feeling awkwardly too old for such a gesture. "It's just that I know you compare everybody to Dad, and . . . well, he loved you, I'm sure, but he ended up with somebody else." There was an accusatory note in his voice.

Greer sighed and sank down on the bed. "What are you trying to say?"

Joshua felt befuddled and out of his league. He hadn't planned to bring this up and didn't really know what he wanted to say. "I guess I just think . . . I don't know . . . maybe you picked Dad because he was safer, in a way." Joshua fumbled and couldn't recover. "In a *very* weird way, and you know what? This is none of my business. I have no idea what I'm talking about."

He looked apologetically at his mom, expecting her to look angry or, at the very least, annoyed, but he was surprised to see that she was looking out the window with an expression of melancholy.

"Oh, Mom, I'm sorry. I shouldn't have said that about Dad—"

"No," Greer interrupted him. She turned her sylvan eyes on her son. "You are very intuitive; you always have been. Of course, you are right." She smiled wryly and said, "Intuition runs in the family, but unfortunately it seldom extends to self."

She stood and walked to the door, where she paused, turning back. "Don't feel bad; you've given me something to really think about. Well, *reminded* me, more like." Then a grin creased her face and she winked. "And it might be excellent timing."

Joshua's relief at seeing his mom look excited about something—or someone—released him from any guilt about bringing it up. He extended a hand in a blocking gesture. "I don't want to know any details."

She left, laughing.

Joshua had positioned his desk just under the window for the view, which included Joy's bedroom. As he turned back to his work, he glanced across the ten yards or so of space between the two windows, which included a few pine trees. The branches were spaced in a way so that if he leaned this way or that he could see part or all of her window.

He had cracked his window open, and even from here he could hear the distorted booming of loud music playing in Joy's room, but he hadn't seen Joy all evening. Just at that moment, though, a figure passed in the gloom on the far side of her room, and the reverb from the overamplified bass ended abruptly. Joshua sat up and watched. Nothing for a moment, and then Joy moved into the failing light from the window. He could see her with something in her hand that might have been a cell phone or maybe a small tape recorder; he couldn't make it out. She spoke into it several times and then threw it across the room.

It happened so suddenly that Joshua thought clouds had obliterated what little was left of the daylight. Everything in Joshua's vision went dark except Joy, and she was a shadowy outline, illuminated solely by the soft glow cast by the image of an eye, cartoonish yet menacing, that had appeared above her head.

Joshua watched Joy, feeling a complete loss of control and sanity, before he noticed something else: the figure of another girl, just over Joy's left shoulder. It was too dim to see clearly, but he felt sure it was a girl around Joy's age. She kept pointing at the eye and then holding her hands out to Joshua. Then both images faded and his vision returned to normal.

Joshua's skin felt hot and prickly, but when he put a hand to his brow the thin layer of sweat was cold to the touch. *Not again!* What the hell was happening to him? Was this what happened when his mother would "see" things? She had always said that the gift was passed to women in the family, and he had felt comfortably exonerated from the responsibility. It couldn't be, there must be another explanation.

But with a growing sense of horror Joshua realized he could not logic away what had just happened to him as a trick of the light or give it any other reasonable explanation. Afraid, he looked back toward Joy's room, but Joy had moved away from the window.

An overwhelming sense of panic engulfed him. He didn't understand why he was seeing things, and he couldn't seem to stop it. He'd never felt so out of control, and the sensation left him dizzy and baffled. But somewhere inside of him another, stronger fear was making its presence known, pecking away at him like a woodpecker smashing holes in his brain.

Someone was trying to tell him something. He was supposed to act, to help, and he was the only one who could. The symbol and girl had been meant for him to see. He had to figure out what they meant.

Thinking that he might have to face being abnormal was horrifying. But denying what he'd seen and fighting it might mean that something unthinkable would happen to Joy that he might be able to prevent.

And that seared his soul with terror.

Chapter 15

"Nervous?" he asked the teenager. He had found one who was just what the doctor ordered, a ripe little thing, slightly plump, with a tattoo on the small of her back. He imagined her trussed up with an apple in her mouth, his private feast. He wouldn't keep this one; he thought she'd be better for a short ride. So he'd brought her to a motel in the next town over, where they took cash and asked no questions.

She was sitting awkwardly, their knees almost touching, trying to look as if she weren't frightened, but her eyes darted around the shabby motel room, and her voice was high when she answered, "No."

"Here." He handed her a fifth of Southern Comfort—the young ones liked the sweet stuff—and watched, amused and excited by the inexperienced fear he could see and smell in her body. He put his hand on his crotch and straightened his stiffening cock. Her eyes tracked the move and then looked away quickly. "I got something else for you too." Her breathing quickened, and she began to look a little panicked. The heat in his jeans increased. "You liked that ride over here, didn't you? Feel that bike vibrating between your legs—makes you all wet and ready, doesn't it?"

Her pupils, already big from fear, jumped a size

larger. He'd been polite until now, the perfect gentleman, but now that they were in the room—away from
prying eyes and any chance for her to back out—he
started to play with his prey.

"How do you feel?" he asked her, eager to hear
her fear, to feel the thrill of dominance, of having the
power to do whatever he pleased with her. He was
staring at her nipples through her thin T-shirt.

"I think maybe I'd like to go outside for a minute.
Maybe we could go for another ride." Her voice was
trembling; as she lifted the bottle to her mouth, it
shook visibly.

He smiled and reached out, taking the bottle and
pressing his forefinger forcefully into her mouth. She
whimpered. "I think not," he told her. "I think you're
gonna be busy for a while. You want another drink?"

She looked at him, paralyzed with fear, his finger
still stuck in her mouth up past his knuckle. She pulled
away and he slapped her quickly across the face, took
the back of her hair in one hand, and reinserted his
finger. Both her hands had flown up to cover the red-
dening spot on her cheek. He didn't care if he left a
mark on this one. Tonight he wasn't going to hold
back.

"Do you want another drink?" he asked, as though
nothing had happened. She closed her eyes, tears
starting in the corners, but she nodded.

"Then suck," he ordered. "And let's remember that
I know where you live. Hell, I know where everybody
lives." He laughed.

She did as she was told. He enjoyed the sensation
for a moment, watching the tears that trickled from
her closed eyes and ran down her face. This was sweet,
so sweet. With his other hand he unfastened his belt,
pulling it free of his pants, and then opened his fly
and extracted his growing member. Her eyes fluttered
enough to see what he was doing, but then closed to

try to block the vision out. With a wide grin and a cavalier flair he carefully poured a small amount of the liquor onto his cock, and then, crooking the finger in her mouth into a hook, he pulled her sharply forward off her chair and onto her knees in front of him. "Suck," he ordered again.

She started to cry hard now, the sobs gagging her slightly as she obeyed him. He imagined that she thought she'd finish him off and that would be it. He let her work at it for a few minutes, occasionally taking a swig from the bottle as he watched her. Then he pushed her back roughly. She sprawled onto the floor and he stood over her.

"Get up."

He was hoping she would plead; he liked it when they begged. He wasn't disappointed. "Please, I'll do anything you want, but don't hurt me, please."

He reached down and grabbed the front of her shirt, yanking her up onto her feet. She yelped and struggled. "But *that's* what I want—to hurt you." He pulled her face right up to him and licked it wetly, from the chin to the forehead. "That's what I like."

She opened her mouth to scream, but he had his hand on her throat fast enough to cut off the sound.

"Now, now, none of that." He squeezed tighter. Both her hands clawed at his wrists, and her eyes popped. He watched, applying pressure, until he thought it was just the right amount, a few seconds before she lost consciousness. Enough to control her easily, steal her voice for a while, and then he let go. Her hands went to her throat as she staggered backward, and small rasping noises came from her throat.

He laughed with the exhilaration of it. Then he grabbed her and pulled her up against him, rubbing and grinding on her first from the front and then spinning her around and rubbing his exposed skin on the back on her super-low-cut jeans—so low that he could see the crack of her ass when she'd leaned over to push her hair up under the helmet he'd given her to wear on the ride over, the one with the dark face mask. He forced one hand down the back of the jeans, and a finger found the place he was looking for. She gasped almost soundlessly, and her body went rigid. He enjoyed himself there for a minute before spinning her again and grabbing roughly at her plump breasts. He squeezed hard and then, grasping the fabric of her T-shirt, he ripped it away.

She was quivering with fear now, and his excitement was building to a new place, a high he'd never had before. This time he wouldn't hold back. This time she was his, and he'd use her. He retrieved his belt from the table and lashed it across her body. She cowered and tried to cover herself with her arms. "Take off the pants," he said in a singsong voice that dripped with malice.

She was weeping, sobbing in a strange, terrified parody of a horror film without sound. He threw the belt aside and hit her with his fist. The brutal contact shocked her out of crying, and she sank to her knees, holding her jaw and staring wordlessly at the floor.

"Take off the pants!" he said more forcefully, grabbing her by the hair and pulling her to her feet. She grabbed for his wrists, but he released her with a shove and she fumbled with the fastener of her jeans, her hands shaking so badly she could barely manage it. When she got the pants off she stood there trembling, her knees and her forearms locked tightly together in front of her.

He let her wait, taking his time as he reached down and unhooked his key chain from a loop on his belt. Casually, as though he were having a copy made, he took a dangling charm off of the loop. Then he pulled a lighter from his pocket and, flicking on the flame, he held the metal charm directly in the fire.

The girl moaned slightly, but he ignored her until he was ready. Then he went to her and, using his foot, he pushed her back on the bed and kept his heavy black boot firmly on her chest to hold her there.

"And now," he said, "the fun begins."

As he breathed in deeply the smell of burning flesh, he calmly watched her face. Her mouth opened and her head shook from side to side in a long, excruciating, silent scream.

Chapter 16

"That's not the point, and you know it!" Jenny snapped at her husband, Lewis. She tried to keep her voice down, but it wouldn't have mattered if she had yelled it out in the noisy bar. It was almost midnight on Saturday night, and most of the customers in the sports bar had had enough liquor to think they were speaking normally as they shouted over the din of the football game and the video machines. The place was packed, and they were huddled together at the end of the bar, where they had come for a snack and a beer after a movie.

"Well, then, what is the point?" Lewis retorted just as sharply. There was a natural petulance in his full mouth and a lazy prettiness in his eyes, two features that were misleading, as he was both hardworking and masculine. He loved his wife very much, but she still baffled him by sometimes behaving as though he just didn't get it. He supposed she was right, because he wasn't getting it now.

"The point is that you could come in and help me—" Jenny began again.

"I spent hours fixing that place up for you!" Lewis cut her off.

"And I spent a lot *more* hours helping you build your business. Who answered the phone, placed your ads, called in your orders? Sure, now you've got a secretary, but before you did, I did it all."

"I know; I never said you didn't help me out." He felt as if she were sapping his strength.

"Well, why can't you help me now?"

"Because I need to be out there making more money doing contracting. No offense, honey, but the coffee shop isn't exactly showing a gigantic profit." Lewis held his hands out as though this were the most obvious thing in the world.

"But you don't work every day. Lots of times you have subcontractors in, or you're between jobs."

Lewis leveled a quick warning look at her over his beer. Being "between jobs" was a sore point for him.

Jenny's temper flared again. "What you're really saying is that it's beneath you to work in the coffee shop. It was fine for me, a woman, to do the grunge work for you when you couldn't afford help. But you're a *man*."

What she was saying was far too close to the truth for him to accept it with anything other than a strong offensive attack. "Oh, bullshit. And fine, you know everything I think and feel, so you just go ahead and talk—you know it all."

Jenny reined in her next cutting remark by finishing off the last of her draft beer and turning out to face the room. "You know what?" She felt drained. She was so tired of the same argument and no forward motion. "Let's just go."

"Fine," said Lewis, and finished the last swallow. He threw down some money and followed Jenny to the front.

When she opened the door the blast of noise from multiple Harley engines made Jenny put her free hand up to cover one ear. The parking lot was a sea of bikes, and four or five more were pulling in off the street now, revving their engines.

Jenny held the door open for Lewis without looking back at him. He took his time getting to it, making her wait—small slights that did so much damage. She looked instead at the bikers, who were now either dismounting or sitting on their parked bikes opening the throttles to display the throaty mating calls of their penis extensions.

Jenny realized with a vague sense of being out of place that she recognized one of the bikers. It was her mailman, Pistol, his wiry beard notably visible as he removed a black half helmet. He crossed to another one of the bikers, who was standing next to a particularly large, tricked-out bike. Jenny turned away; she didn't want him to recognize her.

Near the door, in the light from the windows, Jenny noticed another man squatting as he tried to get a wrench on something in an awkward spot up inside his bike's engine. He cursed loudly just as the last Harley was silenced, and the wrench clattered onto the black asphalt. Jenny could see the tattoos on his forearms. Unlike the elaborate, colorful illustrations worn by so many people, his were rough and blue.

Lewis came out the door and glanced down at him. "Hey, Army. How's it going?"

Army grunted in reply with an exasperated wave at his bike. As Lewis and Jenny started across the lot, he said by way of explanation, "Plumber. He and his brother worked on the Maser house with me."

Then, with a screaming whine, a group of Ducati motorcycles started up from the stoplight on the street, popped wheelies, and veered, leaning at dangerous angles, into the parking lot. Jenny and Lewis were forced to halt suddenly and back up a few steps as the bikes passed a foot in front of them. Lewis put an arm out protectively in front of Jenny, who muttered, "Assholes." Most of these drivers were wearing full body suits of leather with helmets that matched their bikes. The Harley guys turned and shook their heads disdainfully as the hotshots screeched to a halt and started to debike. They locked up their helmets carefully and started toward the bar.

Jenny and Lewis crossed the narrow lot to their car, and he came to her side to unlock the door for her. Both of them were surreptitiously keeping an eye on the dynamics between the two vastly different groups of men.

Jenny watched as Pistol's friend flicked his cigarette into the air, watched as it arched and landed at the feet of one of the newcomers, a tall, handsome man wearing jeans and a black leather jacket with yellow lettering to match his motorcycle that declared the make of his bike from every angle. She'd seen him somewhere, but she couldn't place him. Maybe he'd come in the coffee shop. All of his friends wore the same type of leathers with similar advertising, some from head to toe, with their brand name on every part of their bodies.

"Are you guys on some kind of a team," asked the Harley rider mockingly, "or do you and your girl-friends just like to dress alike?" His buddies hooted and made kissing noises.

Jenny watched as the tall man stopped and turned toward Pistol. "Tell your friend to keep his redneck mouth shut or I'll shut it for him."

Pistol said nothing at first, but the edges of his beard moved upward as a slow smile spread over his face. "*You* tell him. I think he'll like that." He turned to his companion. "Mike, this young lady wants to talk to you."

Jenny felt increasingly unsafe with the burgeoning testosterone level. She'd seen enough fights in her life to know when one was coming, and she had developed a keen distaste for bar brawls and domestic violence.

She got into the car and closed the door quickly behind her, shutting out the confrontation. Lewis started the car, and they eased their way out of the parking lot through the multitude of motorcycles.

On one of those motorcycles Mike leaned back, crossed his ankles at the heavy black boots, and continued antagonizing Vince. "Listen, fancy boy, I wouldn't want you to break a nail, and I'm in a good mood tonight, so you go on in and get yourself and your softball team there a round of wine spritzers."

Vince took a step forward, but one of his buddies put out a restraining arm and said, "Forget it. They're just cheap trailer trash." A glance around told Vince that, whereas the Harley riders were clustering forward, eager to rumble, his Ducati boys were backing away, and fear flickered in his eyes. After pointing a threatening finger at Mike, who laughed, Vince turned and walked toward the bar.

Mike called after him, "Bye-bye, princess."

Vince stopped and turned back, but his friends urged him forward. Vince's eyes met with Army's. Obviously solo, he was watching Vince from his seated position on the pavement.

Seeing a safer outlet for his rage, Vince snapped at him, "What the fuck are you looking at?"

Army regarded him coldly, his hands forming into fists before he muttered, "Nothing," and turned away, ignoring Vince utterly.

"Let's go. I need a drink," one of Vince's friends said nervously, and they hustled him through the glass door.

The Harley riders burst into catcalls and jeers.

Mike lit another cigarette, and he, Pistol, and the others sat on their bikes or stood around talking and smoking. Army, who had watched the conflict with bland detachment, cursed his bike again. Mike, his smoke dangling from his mouth, crossed over and leaned down to peer at the broken-down Honda seven-fifty.

"What seems to be the problem?" he asked, deliberately not making eye contact with Army.

"I wish to fuck I knew," Army grumbled.

"Well, maybe I can help you out." Now he turned a handsome grin on the younger man. "I'm Mike. I own a garage." He extended his hand.

"I'm Army." He took the hand in a hesitant manner and shook too hard, the kind of shake that a man who acts tough to cover insecurity gives. "Thanks, but I can't pay you," he said gruffly, as though that were no big deal and the end of it, and turned back to his work.

"Well, Army, I didn't ask you for money, did I? I mean, it seems like an awful waste of talent for me to sit here watching you dick around when I could do this." He reached two long fingers up inside the bike and there was a clicking sound. "And that should do it. Why don't you give it a try?"

Army stood up and tried the ignition key. It sputtered.

"Throttle," Mike ordered.

Army followed his directions and the ignition caught, coughed, and held. He chanced a glance up at Mike. "Thanks," he muttered. Then he started to shake his left hand, waving it back and forth as he held his right arm stiffly down by his side.

"No problem." Mike smiled at the younger man's reluctant acceptance of help. The tattoos told him most of the story. Prison was no place to be needy. "Did you burn your fingers?"

Army's eye's shot up at Mike and he curled his left hand into a fist as though to hide it. "Uh, yeah," he said hesitantly. "On the muffler."

Mike dismissed it. "Done it a million times." He smiled. "Still hurts like a son of a bitch every time."

"Thanks again." Army climbed onto his bike and put on his helmet.

"Why don't you come in and have a beer with us?" Mike invited.

"Oh, I can't. I, uh, got a curfew." Army mumbled the last words and turned his face away, pretending to check out something down by his leg on the bike.

"Yeah," Mike said kindly. "The State of California is a jealous bitch of a wife." He smiled and nodded.

Army turned and looked at the other man directly for the first time, and for a fraction of a second a smile flickered on his mouth. But then his eyes went dead again, as though returning to a habitual state. Dead to caring anymore.

"See you around." Mike made to punch Army's shoulder, thought better of it, and turned abruptly away as the backfiring bike sped out of the parking lot.

Chapter 17

Sunday

Overnight the sky had filled again with thick clouds, and soft, plump raindrops had begun to fall. The rain and wind loosened the ripe acorns of an oak and a few fell, knocking intermittently on the tiles of the roof below it. The rain kept up a constant background tempo.

The sound thrummed through the bedroom where Jenny and Lewis lay on opposite sides of the bed, sleeping. The moisture increased the chill in the January air. Without waking, they moved closer to each other in the bed, seeking the warmth and the comfort of the other's body.

Lewis heard the music of the rain and the light, sporadic tapping of the acorns before he opened his eyes to the bare gray dawn. He found that he was nestled against Jenny, his arm curled over her chest, his face in her hair, and he smiled. He loved the soft warmth of her body against his, and he pressed ever so subtly against her. On her way to wakefulness, she responded.

They rocked slowly and gently against each other as she pulled his arm tighter up against her chest, and, opening the front of her flannel pajamas donned in defense the night before, she placed his hand snugly on her breast.

It felt so soft and firm and comfortable, so female. He pressed harder against the roundness of her backside, and she equaled the pressure. Reaching down with his free hand, he pulled at the elastic waistband of her pants; she rolled onto her back and lifted her hips to free them. Ah, permission granted.

Unbuttoning the last few buttons of her shirt, Lewis ran the flat of his hand over her stomach and down between her legs. He kissed her neck, and then, when the moisture below equaled the moistness outside, he lifted himself up on top of her, and with a sigh of pleasure lowered the heated skin of his chest against hers.

Jenny pulled up her knees and received him with the supreme satisfaction of having a man who fit. They moved slowly against and with each other until the friction increased and the pace mounted. The rain fell harder outside and thunder rumbled. As the rain became increasingly frantic, the sounds of quickened breath and small cries of effort and pleasure filled the warming room.

And then came the quiet, soft kisses, apologies. Defenses were abandoned. Forgiveness was gracefully granted. They listened honestly, spoke without filters, and, reaching out beyond their fears and insecurities, did the bravest thing: They compromised.

Chapter 18

It was late afternoon, and Sherry Jackson's feet ached, and it was raining again, which always made her bones hurt. At least it wasn't pissing down, the way it had for three weeks in a row right after Christmas. This rainfall had lightened to an on-and-off smattering. She'd been up at dawn doing the motel's laundry and cleaning out the rooms. Some of the things these people did were disgusting. A couple of the cheap rooms rented out weekly, and those guys usually weren't too bad, or if they were, they didn't expect her to deal with it every day; in fact, they preferred she stay out. That was just fine by her. Sometimes it was families who had no place else to go, too many people crammed into a small room with a double bed, and a bathroom with an upright shower. Those rooms had so much stuff on the floor that she couldn't do much except change towels.

The worst were the meth smokers. Those rooms were sticky with spilled liquor, the tang of chemical smoke, and she didn't even want to think about the blood and vomit in the bathrooms. Cleaning toilets on this job was as disgusting as scraping out a toxic shit-house. Sherry had become a real detective in her years of cleaning rooms. She used to make a game of guessing things about the people who had stayed there and their distasteful habits, until she'd become too sickened and jaded to care anymore. *I could write a book,* she had thought, and then the next thought had been that no one could bear to read it.

There was only one room she hadn't done today, fourteen. The broken DO NOT DISTURB sign hung crookedly from the knob, oddly mimicking the reflective number four, which dangled askew from a single tack. Whoever it was had paid for two nights in advance, but she was still supposed to at least check and see if they needed towels. She'd been around all day and she hadn't seen anyone go in or out. Most likely that meant they'd stayed up all night doing methamphetamine or crack and were either crashed or hiding from the light in a dangerous state of vampirelike paranoia. *Great.*

Glancing at her watch, she saw that it was almost four o'clock. She wanted to get back to her studio apartment and start drinking in earnest. She kept a small bottle hidden in the laundry room, but it had run out a couple of hours ago, and she was down to her last couple of smokes.

Screw 'em, she thought, and she shuffled painfully up to the door, her Rite Aid slippers making a scuffling sound on the rough pavement. She rapped loudly. "Housekeeping!" she called out brusquely. There was no answer. She tried again, but there was still no response. She put her ear to the flimsy, hollow door and listened; you could hear through these doors like cardboard.

Nothing.

Great. One more jerk who'd left the sign on the door and gone out; now she'd have to clean the room and that would take another fifteen minutes. She pulled her master key from the cord around her neck and put it in the keyhole, hoping that the chain lock would be on and she could get out of this hellhole and go to the one she lived in. At least she could put her feet up and watch TV there.

But the door met no resistance. She opened it about a foot and peered into the darkened room. The lights were off, the curtains were drawn, and the rain-darkened afternoon afforded little illumination through the partially opened door.

"Hello? Housekeeping," she called again, but there was no response. She sighed and, leaving the door open, went to retrieve her cart, which she rattled noisily down the cement until she was outside the room. Then she swung the door open the rest of the way and gathered an armful of towels. She surveyed the dim room, waiting for her eyes to adjust as she stepped in. It wasn't the worst; there was a bottle of Southern Comfort lying on the floor, empty, of course. Damn, she could have used a drink. All the sheets were off the bed except for the bottom one, and it had a large yellowish stain and was smudged with something else—she didn't know what and she didn't care. She'd stuff them in the laundry with enough bleach to kill the Great Barrier Reef and forget about it. The rest of the sheets were piled in a heap in the corner. There was the normal musty, moldy smell of carpet that never really dried out after the rain had seeped through the roof, mixed with years of human body odor, but something else was in the air: the lingering smell of burned meat.

Sherry looked around. It wouldn't be the first time someone had barbecued inside the hotel room. She'd caught one Korean family with a little brazier happily grilling up chicken skewers and some god-awful thing that looked like the tongue of a large bovine. *Yuck.*

She turned back and switched on the light. Steeling herself for the worst, she started for the bathroom, glancing again at the pile of sheets in the corner, and then froze.

From the jumble of dirty linen jutted a human foot—a female foot with chipped dark green polish on the toes. The rest of whoever it was was completely covered.

The hairs on Sherry's arms shot up as though they were trying to get the hell out of there, but something else—an excited curiosity—thrilled through her as well.

"Hello?" she tested again, but the feeling of speaking to an empty room remained. Her mouth, already sour from cigarettes and whiskey, went dry and rancid. Breathing shallowly and clutching the towels in front of her like protective padding, she took a few steps closer to the foot. "Hey!" she shouted, and then she reached out a slipper and nudged the heel. The foot moved a little, but then stopped again.

With a trembling hand, Sherry reached out and took hold of the piled sheets about where she guessed the head would be, and pulled.

A convulsive shudder rattled her whole body, and she ran, screaming and retching, from number fourteen.

Chapter 19

Luke and Whitney looked at each other when Joy came into the kitchen. She looked like hell; her eyes were sunken, and her skin was more pallid than usual. She did not acknowledge them in any way. She got herself a large glass of tap water from the sink and gulped it down, then turned to shuffle out, deliberately snubbing her father and his wife.

"Joy," Luke said in a voice that made it clear he would not be refused or ignored.

A huge exasperated sigh was forced out by Joy as she turned toward them and crossed her arms. "What?" she asked sharply.

"Well, first of all you can lose that attitude with me if you ever want to leave this house again." She exhaled belaboredly and rolled her eyes slightly, but the gesture was quieter and less emphatic this time. "Second, you might want to sit down, 'cause this could take a minute."

"I'll stand," Joy said, but she looked as though bolting would be far more preferable.

"Fine. Now listen. Yesterday morning you weren't just drunk, were you?"

"Whatever." Her eyes floated around the room, resting on anything except Luke and Whitney. Whitney watched her, feeling anger and pity in equal parts.

"I'm not really asking," Luke cut in sharply. "I'm telling you, I know it was either cocaine or speed, because you were too jumpy and paranoid to just have been hungover. You think you're the first person to use drugs? Baby, I snorted my weight in cocaine in my late twenties." He paused for a moment to make sure that sank in. Joy tried to look completely unconcerned, but for the first time her eyes shot to her father and then away. Luke went on: "I'm going to ask you a question in a minute, but I'm gonna say something first."

The girl mumbled an inaudible response and crossed her arms more tightly. Luke ignored it.

"You think you know everything. You think nobody understands you but this older crowd I know you've been hanging with. I'm gonna give it to you straight: You're pretty, and you've got a body that's a lot more grown-up than you are. There's gonna be men who play on that. Who treat you like an adult because they know that's what you want. They'll offer you freedom and drugs and anything else, and all they want is to fuck you."

The statement shocked Joy; that much was obvious to Whitney. Joy's body went rigid and she looked panicked.

Luke went on: "They'll use you up and spit you out. You will end up strung out, used, and very possibly hurt or dead."

Whitney looked down at her hands, remembering Greer's warning. She had said nothing to Luke, and she could certainly see the need to keep a close watch on Joy, but the frustrating fact was that it wasn't really in their control. Joy spent too much time with an incompetent mother who thought of nothing but herself.

"Do you have anything to say?" Luke asked his daughter.

"Is it too much to think that people might actually

like me?" Joy asked. The hurt in her voice was ill disguised by the sarcastic contempt.

Luke took a moment to pretend he was considering it. "Yes," he said definitively, "it is." Joy opened her mouth but he went on: "If we're talking about men, not teenage boys, and they are paying a lot of attention to a fifteen-year-old girl, filling her head with bullshit about what a grown-up she is, then my answer is yes. Because no *man* is gonna hang out with a fifteen-year-old unless he's twisted enough to try to take advantage of her." Before she could say anything, Luke leaned in and told her, "I'm telling you this because I *know* these kinds of men."

Joy looked as though she'd been lashed with a whip, but she had no response. Her mother let her do what she wanted; why couldn't he just leave her alone?

"How about you?" Luke asked Whitney. "Do you have anything to add?" Joy narrowed her eyes resentfully at her stepmother.

"Yeah, I think I do," Whitney said softly. She turned to the teenager and fixed her with a hard stare. "Joy, I know you hate me, and you don't want to hear anything I have to say, but I don't care. Your father is right. Keep it up and it's only a matter of time before something very bad happens to you. The odds of your getting raped are excellent."

Joy snorted again and rolled her eyes to express that Whitney was full of shit and didn't know what she was talking about.

"I don't know where you go when you run off or when you're with your mom, but if you think these people have your best interests at heart, think again. You're being used, and if you don't want to see that, then you're just plain stupid." Whitney was surprised at herself for saying these things, but she was afraid for Joy, and nothing else had worked.

Luke was nodding. "That pretty well sums it up.

Now, my question." He waited until the sheer fearful curiosity of it brought Joy's eyes to his. "Is your mother doing drugs with you?"

Joy's jaw almost dropped; she was able to catch it only by gnashing her teeth together. How the hell did he know that? She covered as best as she could. "No! What are you talking about?"

"Your mom was in pretty bad shape for a while when you were little. I had custody of you from the time you were a year old until you were two and a half. But she seemed to get her shit together and I figured you needed a mom, so I agreed to split custody later. But I know she's been having trouble lately, and it wouldn't take much to push her back over the edge. I need you to tell me the truth."

Joy looked away. She thought about scoring crystal meth for her mom and then going out to do whatever she wanted while her mom stayed home and got high. The truth was, she had smoked with her mom once, but it had been too weird. She preferred to go off with her friends and not see her mom strung out and talking shit. Her mother was embarrassing enough sober.

"No," she said. Her mouth and her heart both felt dry and scratchy.

Luke watched her until she squirmed, but he said nothing.

"Can I go now?" Joy asked finally, in an impertinent voice.

"Yes, but remember what we told you," her father said with finality. Joy hurried from the room, trying desperately to look put out. When she was gone Luke turned to Whitney.

"She's lying," he said simply.

"Obviously, but what can we do when she's with us only half the week?"

Luke sighed, and, reaching out, he put one hand on

the back of Whitney's neck and rubbed. "I can talk to Pam—or try, anyway." Whitney made a little snorting noise. "I know, but if she is doing drugs again she might let us keep Joy for most of the week, and then we can have a little more consistency on the discipline."

"Oh, please," Whitney said irritably. "The minute you ask Pam for anything she'll demand the opposite just to be a bitch. She fights us on everything because she hates that you're with me instead of with her. She's never thought for a minute about what's best for Joy; you know that. She fought us about getting Joy a health plan, for God's sake! You know the energy she puts into trying to undermine us. What a waste," Whitney finished limply.

"I know, but remember, she might see this as a way to help herself." He sighed and raised his other hand palm up in a questioning way. "And I have only one other choice: wait until the police call, or she gets violated and comes home to Daddy."

Whitney took his hand and pressed it. "That's not a choice."

"No, I know."

Back upstairs, Joy threw herself on her bed and cried in confused hurt and fury. They didn't get it! They didn't know anything. Her older friends were the only ones who understood.

She had to take care of something else, though. She sat up and wiped her face, brushing the tears angrily away, then went to her door and listened. At the bottom of the stairs in the kitchen she could hear the murmur of voices. *Good.*

Glancing out her window, she looked down and could see Joshua sitting on his porch. He was such a goody-goody; they'd trust him. Yes. That was perfect.

Going to her dresser, she pulled open the bottom

drawer, stopped to listen again, and then reached underneath it, peeling off the thin cardboard that she'd duct-taped to the bottom. Sandwiched between the board and base of the drawer were several small, triangular plastic bags filled with white powder. She stuffed them quickly into the bottom of her shoe.

She moved down the stairs as quietly as possible and didn't speak until she got to the kitchen. Then she flashed her cigarettes and a lighter. "Would it be acceptable for me to walk outside?"

"Don't leave the yard," Luke told her firmly.

"Fine," she said sarcastically. "I'll just shout at Joshua across the driveways." She started to move toward the door.

Whitney glanced at Luke, and both of them shared the same thought: Joshua would be a good influence for a change, a nice kid who was closer to her own age. Luke nodded slightly at Whitney's questioning look.

"You can go to Joshua's house if you want, but no farther." Whitney fell slightly short of sounding as authoritative as Luke, but she was feeling sorry for Joy. It was tough enough being a teenager, and having a mother like Pam made an already difficult time into a tour of duty in a foreign country riddled with land mines.

The lighter flared the minute she stepped onto the porch and she inhaled deeply, filling her lungs with the calming toxins of nicotine. Doing something everyone told her she shouldn't gave her some kind of relief from the other oppressive directives. She waved a limp hand at Joshua and he waved back.

When he spotted her coming through the door, Joshua sat up quickly. He tried not to look too eager as he returned her greeting.

"Hi!" he called out. "What's up?"

Joy crossed her arms, blew out a long, slow trail of smoke, exaggerated by the moist, chilly air, and then started to scuff her way down her porch steps and through the damp pine straw toward him. "Oh, not much. What are you doing out here?"

"Enjoying the weather."

Joy looked deliberately around at the dismally cold, misty day, and then back at him.

"I happen to like it," he told her before she said anything. "And this thing I'm wearing is called a coat," he added. "You should get one."

"So that I can sit around by myself in the rain?"

Joshua felt a blush warm his numb cheeks. He couldn't say that he'd been waiting there in the hope of seeing her. So instead he asked, "How's it going?" trying to be upbeat but not a geek.

"It couldn't get much worse, so at least there's that." She had reached the bottom of his stairs, and she stopped and wrapped her arms tightly around herself. Although the rain had taken a break, there was a kind of mist hanging in the air.

"C'mon, it can't be that bad."

"You know that thing you said about 'it's all part of the web'?" She looked at him and took a long draw. He nodded and she went on: "Well, I'm the fly that's stuck in the web, trapped in sticky shit with all the blood sucked out of me."

Joshua laughed. "Listen, it *is* kind of chilly out here. You want to come in and . . . I don't know . . . have something warm to drink or"—he felt crippled, inept—"something?"

She shrugged, "Sure. I'd like to see your room."

"Really?"

"Why do you sound so surprised? Wait, don't tell me—is it all decorated with Britney Spears posters or something?"

Joshua fixed his face into an air of innocence and said, "Never heard of him."

Joy suppressed a smile. In spite of her efforts at

disdain, she was beginning to like him. There was something about him she couldn't put her finger on. With the older crowd she hung with, she often felt like a fraud, someone who was just pretending to fit in. With Joshua, she never felt like she was about to be found out.

They walked through the kitchen, where Greer was standing chopping onions at the large butcher block in the center of the room. A wonderful smell of browning meat came from a large, heavy casserole on the stove. She greeted Joy kindly and said, "I'm making you guys hot chocolate; it'll be ready in a minute. You want marshmallow crème?"

Joy looked at her, surprised. It was such a kid thing to drink, but she loved it. "Uh, yeah, sure."

"Me too," Joshua said. "Thanks, Mom. We're going up to my room for a few minutes."

Greer smiled, happy that Joy was here and safe. "Fine. But, Joshua?"

"Yeah?"

"I need you to pick up a few things at the grocery store later." She pointed at a short handwritten list on the bulletin board where they kept people's cards and phone numbers.

"Okay, no problem."

The pair of teenagers tromped up the stairs, Joshua chatting happily about his CD collection, completely aware that he was talking way too much but unable to shut up, until they got to his room.

Joy paused in the doorway and looked around. It wasn't what she had been expecting; it was nice, actually, very comfortable. The bed was made, covered in some kind of really soft-looking comforter in dark green. The walls were a tan color, and there was a large black-and-white photo framed on the wall of a moon over a village in what looked like the Southwest. Joshua saw her looking at it.

"Do you like it?"

"It's okay," was all Joy would admit to, but her voice betrayed that she was a little more impressed than that.

"Do you like Ansel Adams?"

The name meant nothing to Joy, but instead of admitting it she echoed Joshua's joke: "Never heard of him." Then she added, "Nice moon."

Joshua stood awkwardly in the center of his room. "Uh, do you want to sit down?"

"Sure." Joy circled around him, then chose the chair at his desk. She looked out the window. "You can see my bedroom from here," she commented, and turned to look at him with her eyebrows raised.

"Can you?" Joshua asked, but his voice was too high.

Joy laughed again. It was fun to see his confidence a little shaken. "It's cool. I'll just keep my curtains closed at night now." She pretended to look through his CDs, which were in a standing rack next to the desk. She tried to be casual. "You know what? Would your mom mind if we had the hot chocolate up here and listened to some music?"

Joshua could think of nothing better, but he forced himself to move at a normal speed toward his door. "Sure. You pick something and I'll go get it."

"Thanks." Joy smiled at him and then pretended to study the titles again. She heard him hit the top of the stairs and run down.

She stood up and swept the room with her eyes. She had only a little time, and it had to be good.

Where in the hell could she hide this stuff?

Chapter 20

Detective Sheridan watched as the girl was loaded into the back of the ambulance. Her face was so swollen and distorted that it would have been impossible to tell it was a girl if she hadn't been naked when the maid had found her.

The siren wailed and the emergency vehicle pulled away, headed for the hospital, the flashes from the red and white lights falling strangely short and blunted in air that felt as heavy as a wet gray sweater. After all his years on the force, he didn't have much hope for her pulling through. Whoever had done that to her was one disturbed monster, and he felt a sick, acidic gnawing in his gut that this was no isolated incident.

It was the mark that made it different. The marking was the twisted indicator of a serial freak. He sighed, wondering who the girl was and what she was like. Had she gone with this guy willingly or had he forced her? Was she from around here, somewhere nearby, or another state? Los Angeles County had a surplus of runaway teenagers, and there were far too many Jane Does in his unsolved murder files.

Turning, he surveyed the depressing roadside motel whose rooms made a horseshoe-shaped semicircle around a barren parking lot in Chatsworth. The whole layout sloped slowly down toward the street side. *Bad luck,* thought Detective Sheridan. *You've got to turn a horseshoe up, or all the luck runs out.*

His stomach churned and twisted. He didn't have much hope of finding a reliable witness here. This was the kind of place where they made it a point *not* to know anybody else's business. He'd already talked to the clerk who'd rented the room. She was the owner's wife, a puckered skeleton of a woman who had the loose-toothed look of a crack smoker. She claimed she'd been busy watching her favorite TV show when the guy came in and she didn't notice anything. She couldn't remember if it was this one guy with a beard or this other guy who she thought might have had a mustache; she couldn't recall which one had taken which room. Neither one of the two men, who had come in about the same time the night before, had shown ID, and Sheridan doubted the name and address on the registration card of number fourteen would be worth the pencil it was scribbled in. From the smell of the woman's breath and the bottle of Wild Turkey he had seen in the office, he doubted she would be in any condition to notice, much less remember, anything useful past eight o'clock on any given night. She did say she was pretty sure that both of the men who had come in and gotten rooms the previous night had been on motorcycles; what kind of motorcycle, she had no idea.

That narrowed it right down to a couple of million suspects. Sheridan swore and kicked at the curb as he walked back toward the room. He hated the crime and the abuse he saw every day, lived for the few times he could actually get one of these degenerates off the street. But more than anything he despised the psychopaths, the ones who did what they did because they enjoyed it. No, that wasn't right, exactly. It wasn't only that he despised them; he feared them. There was no logic, no predictability to how and when they would strike, leaving him helpless.

He stood in the room and watched the white-coated officer gathering up any material evidence he could find. They'd get a sperm sample from the girl; that he was sure of. The blood and excrement were most likely all hers. Any hair they found would be useless, as even an idiot public defender could argue that the hotel room was used by hundreds of people every year.

Yet, there was the mark. That was something different. Sheridan turned and looked out at the traffic in the failing half-light. Did it mean something? Lead somewhere? His stomach flared into action again. He pulled a roll of Tums from his pocket and popped six in his mouth, crunching them expertly. This was his third pack today. He looked again at the stains on the sheets and tried to tell himself that it wasn't his fault, that maybe this was just a onetime thing.

But the burning in his gut told him differently. Like a power line in the rain, the pain crackled and sizzled with a message for him, a warning sign that every fiber in his body had learned not to ignore.

There was a monster loose out there, someone with an appetite for sadistic pain. A monster who was sated for the moment, but soon he would be hungry, eager to feed again.

Chapter 21

"Mom?" Joshua called out softly at the door of Greer's bedroom.

"Yes?" She turned from where she was sunk into the down pillows of an overstuffed armchair, with a large picture book of runes propped up on her lap. He recognized the book as one that Dario had given her on her last birthday.

"Can I talk to you about something?"

She put the book down and sat up higher in her chair. "Sure, come on in."

Joshua perched across from her on the edge of her bed and wondered where to begin. "It's about Joy," he started, and then corrected himself. "Actually, it's about me, but it concerns Joy. At least, I think it does."

Greer smiled knowingly, but there was worry in her eyes.

"It's not what you think," Joshua hastened to add upon seeing the smile. "I mean, I like her okay, I guess, but . . . it's not that."

Not knowing what to expect now, and not wanting to rush or press her son, Greer said nothing, just waited quizzically.

"I, uh, *saw* something." Joshua stared at the carpet. There was a strange pattern woven into it, almost like one of the runes in the book now resting on the thick arm of his mom's chair. "I don't know what it was— maybe just a trick of the light or a bird or a branch or something." Joshua took a deep breath and forced the worst of it out. "Or maybe I'm just seeing things." He pretended to laugh a little, but his mother could hear the fear in it.

"Maybe you should tell me what it was you saw and then we can take a guess?" Greer suggested.

Joshua nodded. "Okay. First, the night Joy came over for dinner, when we went outside, I thought I saw a figure-ish thing, like a person kind of"—he searched for an appropriate description—"floating over Joy's shoulder. And then a few days later I could see her in her window, and I saw a different figure over her, and then I saw a . . . a shape." He trailed off, afraid to look at his mother, afraid she would be looking back at him with fear in her eyes. Fear for him.

But he needn't have been alarmed. In reality she was watching her son with a growing wonder. "Joshua," she said softly, "did you *feel* something when you saw these things?"

He looked up and saw to his amazement that her eyes were moist and glowing. "Uh, yeah, as a matter of fact. Different things."

He described both of his disturbing bouts. "The first time I thought it was man's figure, kind of"—Joshua raised his right hand and waved it in the air beside his head over his right shoulder—"here. She was walking away from me, outside, and I thought it might have been a bat."

"Was the figure doing anything?" Greer asked.

"Um, holding out his arms, one to Joy and one toward me. At least, that's what it kind of looked or *felt* like." Joshua laughed again self-consciously.

Greer smiled with him, but she did not laugh. She

was getting a feeling herself, and it was mostly one of surprise that she had never considered the possibility before. What Joshua was describing was not what she saw or experienced, but that didn't mean it wasn't something similar. The gift had always come to women in the family, yet she had no daughters. Of course, her mother hadn't had it. Greer had always thought that maybe if Joshua got married and had a girl . . .

"Tell me about the second time," she prodded gently.

"The second time was when Joy was in her room." Joshua's face reddened a little, but he braved on. "I can see a little bit into her window from my room, and she was talking on a phone, I think. Anyway, I saw a . . . like a symbol above her head. An eye, or more like just a drawing of an eye. And then another figure, only this time on the other side, and I thought it was a girl. It . . . she was pointing at the eye and then holding out her arms toward me."

He fell silent and waited for his mom's reaction. He knew she often made uncanny predictions and seemed just to know things, but that was different. Wasn't it? She didn't see people waving their arms at her in thin air.

His mother's hand reached out and took one of his. "Joshua." He looked up at her, and she was searching his face so intensely that he would have been afraid if there hadn't been so much love in her eyes. "What did you *feel* when you saw these things? I mean, I know that you were scared to see something you couldn't control. I don't mean that. I mean, what did the figures and the eye . . . what did they seem to be telling you?"

Joshua's eyes filled quickly with tears that he tried to blink back while he waited for his throat to un- clench. He had thought about this again and again, and he didn't know what to do about it. It frightened him more than anything.

"They were telling me to help her. That something bad is happening to her and I am the only one who can stop it." Joshua's hands clenched into fists with the effort of refusing to succumb to a girlish emotion. "But I don't know what they want me to do," he finished desperately.

Unlike her son, Greer let her tears come freely. "Joshua," she whispered, "you have the gift. It's different from mine, I think. Mine is always future; yours seems like it might also be present. I don't know. I don't know what each of those things you saw means, but I know that you will figure them out as time goes on. When you stop fighting it and fearing it, then you'll be able to interpret what you see. Joshua, you can help people."

Joshua was on his feet. "I don't know *how* to help anyone!" he shouted in frustration. "I don't want that responsibility! I just want to be normal; I don't want to be a freak!" The moment it was out of his mouth he regretted it. "I'm sorry. I didn't mean . . ."

Though she felt the hit, Greer was smiling wisely. "It's all right, Joshua. I understand why you say that. People are afraid of anything they don't understand or don't have proof of. It *is* unusual, and so it's something that some people will define as freakish, but sit down," she told him firmly.

He composed himself back on the edge of the bed and she went on. "Let me tell you something. I saw danger all around Joy before I ever met her—the first day, in the tea leaves. But my gift is only one of prediction and possibility. I see nothing but the person, and maybe some indicator, like darkness around them or colors that over the years have come to represent things to me. Sometimes I see a whole event or scene,

with those indications in it. But I only see people who
exist, who are alive now. This sounds like you have . . .
well, other entities who are informing and guiding you.''

Joshua was not finding this comforting. "Great, so
you're saying that I see *dead* people?''

"I didn't say they were dead. Maybe they *are* spirits
from the other side.'' He shook his head and rocked
uncomfortably, so she hurried on. "You wouldn't be
the first; that is a possibility. Or maybe they are just
manifestations of need or representative of what the
person, in this case Joy, is creating. It will be up to
you to figure that out.''

"What if I don't want to figure it out? What if I
don't want to see this stuff?'' Joshua's voice sounded
tortured.

Greer sighed. She knew the pain of that all too well—
and the consequences. "Let me ask you one thing.'' She
spoke soothingly. "If you thought that Joy was in
danger—say you knew that there was a fire in her house
and you could get her out—would you do it?''

Joshua tried to take a deep breath, found he
couldn't, and swallowed hard instead. "Yes.''

His mother said nothing. She raised her eyebrows
just slightly and watched him.

A cold hand had gripped Joshua's heart. He felt as
though someone had snatched away his future. One
minute his teenage life had been filled with options,
and now every door had closed except one. He stood
up quickly again. "I don't want this. I'm not the right
one. What can I do?''

Greer nodded. "I absolutely understand how you
feel, and I'm sorry.'' Her eyes went distant for a moment, and she said much more softly, "I remember.''
Then she seemed to shake off the mistiness and
looked at her son again. "But I don't think it will go
away. It's a gift you've been given for a reason.''

Joshua shook his head. "I don't want it,'' he told

her. "I don't want this 'gift.' I'm giving it back. I just want to be normal." He leaned down and kissed his mom on the top of the head and then walked out of the room. In a few minutes she heard music, loud and distracting, coming from behind his closed door.

Restless, Greer made her way downstairs, her feelings for her son tumbling up and down like a child rolling down a hill, high excitement and sympathy going around and around until she was dizzy from the spinning.

She pulled a bottle of good red wine out of the rack on the counter and opened it with a corkscrew to let it breathe, placing a glass next to it. Then she busied herself making a salad to accompany the beef stew that was simmering on the stove, all the while sifting through her thoughts.

If Joshua did have a gift and he was seeing indications of a way to help Joy, then that was encouraging. It seemed to signify that she could be helped. But what was the eye? What did that mean? To keep an eye on her? She'd made Joy the bracelet to try to offer her some small degree of protection by weaving in watchfulness and a spell to ward off bad energy, but it would do next to nothing against real evil. It was imbued with positive thought and protective prayer strengthened by energies from the flow of nature that Greer had learned to draw on and concentrate into an object. Those were powerful forces, but if Joy was courting something stronger without knowing it, they would be like a paper shield.

She heard the crunch of wheels on gravel and looked out the window. Dario was getting out of his hybrid SUV and starting toward the door. *Good.* She could use his support.

He stuck his head in the door and said, "Boo. I thought I'd drop by and see how the move-in was coming along."

"Hi! There's a bottle of wine open for you, and I need your advice," Greer told him, glancing at the bottle with her eyes to direct him.

"Can't you even act surprised?" Dario muttered.

Greer laughed. "I hope you're hungry too, because I cooked beef stew."

He poured some wine and sipped at it while Greer set the table and told him in a quiet voice about what had happened to Joshua. Dario took it all in as though he had expected as much. When she'd finished he sighed and said, "So maybe he'll get his own TV show."

Greer frowned. "I'm worried about him adjusting. It's very scary at first." She reflected on her recent readings for both Joy and Leah, how they filled her with fear and apprehension, and revised her statement. "Hell, not just at first."

"I'll talk to him. But what are you doing tomorrow night?"

Greer looked up, surprised. "On a Monday night? What do you think I'm doing? I'll be here." She regarded him warily. "Why?"

"Well, everybody has told me that the steakhouse, Al Wright's, is really excellent, and I thought maybe you and I could go have dinner there. Maybe celebrate our success by returning the favor of supporting the local businesses. Plus, it'd be nice to check out your new neighborhood."

Feigning shock, Greer said, "Are you serious? You'd be willing to leave Pasadena or Hollywood for a social evening?"

"Oh, I'm not saying I'll drink the water," Dario quipped. "But I did happen to see that it was rated as one of the best out-of-the-way steakhouses in *Los Angeles* magazine."

"Aha! It passed the hip requirement!"

"By the skin of its buckteeth. Come on; it'll be fun."

"Well, I'll ask Joshua if he wants to go."

"If I want to go where?" Joshua had come down the stairs into the kitchen, and he crossed to give Dario a hug.

"I think," Dario interrupted before Greer could ask him, "that your seventeen-year-old son would be just fine at home alone for an evening. In fact"—he looked at Joshua—"if I'm not mistaken, he might really like to have some time alone."

Greer looked at Joshua questioningly.

Joshua's face had the roseate hue of a revealing blush, and he was wearing a sly smile. "Nothing personal," he muttered.

"You two have been scheming," Greer accused with a hand on her hip, but she was amused and pleased. It was such a lifesaver to have Dario's masculine input while raising a boy to a man.

"Done," Dario exclaimed. "I'll meet you there tomorrow at seven o'clock. Supposedly there's one of those great, dark oak bars with red upholstered booths, and they make martinis the old-fashioned way."

"What's the old-fashioned way?" Joshua asked.

"With *gin* and a bottle of vermouth waved over the top. These days people have confused martinis with a noxious mixture containing apple flavoring or the color pink, both of which are just wrong." Dario saluted his odd extended family and took a sip of his wine, feeling deep affection for both of them. In his eyes was the glitter of a man who was up to something.

Chapter 22

Leah was woken from an uneasy sleep by the sound of glass breaking. She sat up in bed and listened, but all she could hear was the wind blowing hard through the branches of the large pine trees surrounding her house. They creaked and complained at being pushed beyond their upright limitations.

After a few moments she decided it must have been a dream, or maybe the glass cover of the porch light had been knocked loose by the wind again and had smashed on the tiles below. Knowing she wouldn't sleep until she made sure, she slipped out of bed and into a plush robe, stepping into her slippers. The thick carpet beneath her feet made almost no sound as she went down the hallway, checking doors and windows as she went. Everything seemed fine. She switched on a small table lamp in the dark living room. As her eyes adjusted to the dimness, she looked around. All the windows were intact; no errant branch had disturbed them. She went into the kitchen and almost stepped onto the broken wineglass on the floor. The heavy base of the crystal glass must have toppled it from where she had set it upside down to dry, and it lay in small fragments on the slate.

She released a relieved breath, but the wind had given her an eerie angst that was hard to shake off.

She put some water in the kettle and cleaned the glass off the floor as she waited for it to boil; then she took her mug of tea into the living room, settling herself into the corner of the sofa near the small pool of light from the lamp.

Her brain was busily churning out questions. What was Vince up to? And more important, what should— or could—she do about it?

Going to the police seemed out of the question. The source of her information was shaky at best. It wasn't exactly legal to open someone else's private safety-deposit box. The fact also remained that she feared Vince; she knew what he was capable of. The thought of testifying against him was as inviting as kissing a venomous snake. She'd been bitten before, and the puncture wounds still bled their poison into her, rendering her incapable of facing the Rattler without incapacitating fear. Thinking of the violence he'd shown during their brief marriage chilled her, and she reached out for the lap blanket on the back of the sofa, as much for comfort as for warmth.

A branch scraped against the dark window, and Leah started. Tomorrow when she got home from work she would trim that tree back, even if it were still pouring rain. The sound was too spooky.

An anonymous call might be the best thing. Anyone could have tipped the police off, she reasoned. As much as part of her would have liked for him to know she was the one who nailed him, it made her shudder to imagine his reaction. Of course, she could wait and watch, hope that he gave himself away, but then she might miss the chance. No, the best thing would be to call the police tomorrow, maybe from a pay phone, and give a tip without leaving her name. She wondered nervously if that was something you could do in real life or just on television.

The thought that Vince might find out that it *was*

her made her almost catatonic with fear. Her face burned with the disgrace and indignity of the things he had done to her, and worse—much worse—the fact that she had never lifted a finger to make him pay. Well, this would make him suffer. The thought pleased her, but a wad of dread still ricocheted around her torso and couldn't get out.

Leah wanted the warm, purring presence of her cat; where was she? "Kate?" she called out. "Here, Katie." She made a kissing sound with her lips while thinking that her cat could sleep through absolutely anything except the sound of the can opener.

She listened, but she heard nothing but the rickety skeletal branches popping and creaking outside. Rain drummed against the roof.

"Katie!" she called again. Her voice in the void made the empty house seem vacant, uninhabited. She thought about whether she'd seen the cat after she'd come home. Yes, she'd fed her, but she hadn't seen her since then. Could she have gotten outside? She called out again, and this time she heard an answering meow from out back somewhere. It sounded distant and pitiable.

Oh, no, poor Kate—she was outside. She'd probably been sheltering somewhere, feeling miserable. Leah got up quickly and went toward the back porch. She unlatched the door and opened it. "Katie!" she called, looking out into the blackness. She could make out nothing except the vague shapes of the shrubs and the trees. But she heard no answering call.

With her right hand, Leah fumbled for the light switch, found it, and pressed it on. The yellow porch light flooded the darkness, falling on the speckled sheets of rain beyond the covered veranda like a flickering motion picture screen.

It fell on the figure of a man three feet in front of her. She gasped and tried to back into the house, but

he moved forward and blocked the door with his foot
before her numbed system could react and close the
door.

"Time for a little chat," Vince said as he came in,
rain dripping from his leather jacket onto her carpet.

"You can't be here," Leah said lamely. "What are
you doing here?"

"Relax." Vince clamped a strong hand painfully
onto her upper arm and pulled her to the sofa. "Sit
down. We're just going to have a little heart-to-heart."
He smiled, and Leah felt as though she'd been
drenched in icy water.

She sat, more to get free of his grip than anything
else, and looked up at him, trying to arrange her features into something resembling contempt, but knowing that she was failing by a long shot.

"So"—Vince was looking around—"I like what
you've done with the place," he said. "Very . . . female, busy and cluttered. But then, I always did like
everything just so."

"What do you want?" Leah asked.

"Not feeling very conversational?" Vince was still
standing right over her. "Well, no, I suppose it's late,
so let's get to the point." He fingered a ring of keys
hooked onto his belt as he spoke.

"It has come to my attention that you may have
noticed certain things that do not exist, and I can't
have anyone saying untrue and libelous things about
me. In fact, if anyone were to wrongly accuse me of
anything, I would be very upset." Vince looked down
and placed the heel of his large wet boot over Leah's
toes in their soft slipper, effectively pinning her foot
painfully to the floor. As he continued speaking he
applied more and more weight. "Now, you have a
little bit of experience with me when I'm not happy.
I like to be happy." He ground his heel down hard,
and Leah cried out in pain. Reaching out with both

hands to his leg, she tried pointlessly to push him off, but his thigh felt like a solid fence post and he didn't budge. "And I'd like to *stay* happy. So, let's agree." He took one of her straining arms by the wrist and pushed back the sleeve of the robe. Leah was whimpering from the unrelenting force on her foot, and now, placing his fingers skillfully on a point about halfway between her hand and her elbow, Vince squeezed hard, and unbearable pain shot up her arm.

"No, God, please stop," Leah begged. But he didn't.

"Let's agree," he continued, ignoring her exclamations, "that if you ever say *anything,* I will first take you down with me, and second get out on bail and end your miserable, worthless, little bitch life."

He ground his heel down harder, pressed his thumb into the pain point with crushing accuracy, and then released both. Leah recoiled into the cushions of the sofa, pulling her foot up and holding it, tears streaming down her face, hatred and fear burning in her heart. Pain radiated from both injuries like heat from the glowing red metal of hand-forged steel.

"Do you understand?" Vince asked, as though he were speaking to a naughty three-year-old.

Without looking up, Leah nodded and then cringed as Vince lowered his face suddenly to her level.

"Good. I'm so glad we had this little chat." He walked to the door, which had remained open, and added, "By the way, your cat is taped up inside a box. It's probably getting soggy. I thought about bringing my pit bull, Rex, over and letting him do a little cat hunting. It's kind of isolated at my new place, and Rex has eaten most of the local wildlife, so he's probably hungry."

Kate's pitiful meow came from the backyard again. Vince made a *tsk*ing sound. "Really, I should call the SPCA. It's just abominable how some people treat their animals." With a hateful laugh, he went out into the night.

Leah leaped up and, limping painfully to the door, she closed and locked it.

Then she remembered Kate and wondered how she would find the courage to go out into the night and retrieve her cat, meowing, wet, and suffering, from the box by the back wall.

Still thinking she didn't have the guts, she opened the door, crossed the patio, and hurried, terrified, into the darkness and the rain.

Chapter 23

The uniformed policeman with the crew cut asked Celia's permission to put the flyer up on the window. Celia asked Greer, who said, "Yes, of course."

The young officer took the black-and-white notices and taped them to window, one facing out and one facing in. It was simple, a single sheet, slightly blurry, like a bad school photo reproduced too many times, and a few words handwritten underneath it that read, *Missing, Zoe Caldwell. Last seen Saturday, January 25, in the vicinity of Foothill Boulevard and Mount Gleason. If you have any information please call the Foothill Precinct.* It then gave a brief physical description as well as a phone and case number.

When the officer had thanked them and gone, Greer moved in to look at the picture more carefully, feeling a wave of old emotion. Sarah. This girl was maybe Sarah's age, and she was missing. She regarded the photo. In it the girl was smiling, but she didn't look happy. Her short dark hair looked limp and dirty, pulled back on one side with a single bobby pin.

And then over the girl's picture was suddenly superimposed the figure of an eye. Greer gasped and reeled back. The eye in her vision was drawn in fire.

She saw the girl's face surrounded by blackness, and knew that she would die soon. She gasped and pulled her hands up to her mouth and then felt a hand on her shoulder.

"Are you all right?" It was Sterling, and as she turned to look at him, horror-struck, tears filled her eyes. Sterling glanced at the photo and scanned it quickly. He pulled her into an awkward, first-time hug. "Do you know her?"

"No," Greer said, grateful for his comfort, but unable to release the image of the burning eye over the girl. "But I know something about her." She pulled back and looked up at him. He seemed both curious and slightly nervous, as though he suspected she might have hysterical tendencies. Greer knew that it would be a long stretch for him to believe what she had seen, so she just said, "I had a best friend who was taken and killed when she was about that age. I've never really gotten over it."

"I guess not," Sterling said. "That's not the kind of thing you ever get over." He regarded the picture again and said, "Let's hope that she just ran off for a couple of days; teenagers do that kind of stuff sometimes. Maybe she's okay," he offered.

"She's not." Greer said it in a whisper.

"How do you know?" Sterling asked sharply.

"I can't really explain it. Sometimes I just know things."

She looked up at him and waited for the inevitable doubt and mockery to come into his eyes, for the change of tone in his voice, but they didn't. Instead he continued to look sadly at the girl's photo and said, "Well, I hope you're wrong this time."

Pistol walked in the front door, his mailbag slung over his shoulder and his keys jangling on his belt. He spotted the two of them looking at the flyer, and he jerked his head at it, his eyes glowing with pleasure.

"Know her," he said casually. "Her family's on my route."

"Seems like you know just about everyone," Sterling commented, and managed to make it sound like a neutral comment.

"Goes with the job," Pistol intoned, but as he handed Greer a stack of letters the glow in his eyes deepened, and he said. "She's bad news, that one. I'm not really surprised she ran off."

Greer bristled, but she stayed calm as she asked, "What do you mean, bad news?"

"Ran with a nasty crowd; her mother couldn't keep any kind of control over her. She was using drugs and sleeping around."

"You know all that from delivering her mail?" Sterling asked, his voice colder and harder than it had been before. Pistol didn't seem to notice.

"Sure, her mom would come out and chat with me sometimes. She was really at the end of her rope. Plus, I've seen her hanging out drinking and smoking with her bad-boy buddies out behind the school. It's hard to miss when you drive by every single day." He looked at the Xerox and then said lasciviously to Sterling, "Plus, she's got a body it's hard not to notice, if you know what I'm saying. And she didn't exactly hide it."

"It says here she's *sixteen*," Sterling said pointedly.

"Yeah, well, nobody told *her* that. She was headed for trouble."

Greer had heard enough of this ugly gossip. "I don't really think it's any of our business whether a young girl dressed sexy or smoked cigarettes. I'm just concerned about her safety."

"She wasn't just smoking cigarettes," Pistol continued, unchecked. "I'm talking about crank."

There was a resounding absence of comment until Sterling asked, "And how do you know *that*?"

For the first time Pistol didn't answer right away. He just smiled slightly and raised an amused eyebrow before saying, "Small town."

As if she'd touched an exposed electrical wire, the hairs on Greer's arms shot up.

Sterling sensed that their postman's inappropriateness had gone far enough, and he interceded. "I've got some outgoing mail for you. If you'll come with me I'll give it to you."

Much to Greer's relief, Sterling led Pistol out the door. As she watched him go, she remembered Jenny's discomfort with the man, and she couldn't have agreed more wholeheartedly. Moving quickly back to where Celia stood at the desk, she addressed her. "Celia?"

"Yeah?"

"Do me a favor. When Pistol comes in, don't talk to him alone, okay?"

"Why?" The young girl's eyes had gone all round and curious.

"Because . . ." Greer hesitated and then went on. "Because I don't think he's a very nice person." It sounded hopelessly lame, but she didn't want to frighten Celia. "Just promise me, okay?"

"Okay."

Still shaken, Greer went back to the flyer. The image of the burning eye did not repeat itself, but it remained lingering in Greer's memory. Was it the same eye that Joshua had seen over Joy? He had said nothing about fire. Yet she felt sure with all the power of her substantial intuition that it meant something, both to this poor girl and to Joy. She raked her mind and her feelings, but she couldn't find any answers. She was sure of only one thing: It meant something deeply evil.

Chapter 24

Franklin High was a big school, and even though Joshua had spotted Joy a couple of times in the last week, it had been only by chance and from a distance. Today, though, instead of eating his lunch in the cafeteria, he ignored the drizzling rain and went to sit out under the covered awning, where he knew the smokers hung out.

She was there, leaning against one of the posts, talking to a boy wearing a black longcoat over a black T-shirt and black jeans. The coat was so big on him it almost brushed the ground. He had the pale, sickly look of a bug that lived underground. His body was thick in the wrong places, and his yellowy eyes bulged slightly. He did not look healthy, and the badly dyed hair and eyebrows did little to complement his sallow complexion.

Joshua sat on the end of one of the long tables and took out his sandwich. When Joy glanced his way, he pretended to notice her for the first time.

"Hi!" he called out. "How's it going?"

She looked as though she might ignore him for a moment, but then, after muttering something to the potato-bug boy, she crossed over to him. "Kinda cold out here for a picnic, isn't it?"

"I don't see you huddled by the radiator," Joshua

told her, and took a big bite of his slightly soggy sandwich. "Who's your friend?"

"Oh, that's Joey, but he likes people to call him Elvis." She rolled her eyes a little.

"Okay. Anyway, it's not that cold, and I like dining al fresco."

She smiled, tight-lipped, in spite of herself. "Whatever that means. I'd rather be out here than hang out with the dweebs in the cafeteria." Her eyes kept darting to the far side of the football field. "At least I can steal a smoke if none of the Nazis are around."

"You want some chips?" Joshua offered, holding out an unopened bag.

Joy looked as though the idea were slightly nauseating. "No, thanks. But if you could lend me ten bucks, I'll give it back to you after I get home today."

Joshua was a little taken aback. Ten bucks? He was on the verge of asking her what she wanted it for when he realized he would sound like a parent asking her what she was up to. "Uh, let me see if I have that much." He grimaced as he reached into his pocket. He had exactly twelve dollars on him, but he handed over two fives and put the two ones back in his wallet.

Joy's eyes looked hungrily at the bills as she stashed them away. "Cool, thanks. See you at home."

Her whole demeanor had gone from listless and stagnant to motivated. She moved quickly back to Joey, and they resumed their conversation. Feeling stupid, Joshua finished his sandwich and was tossing the bag in the trash when he saw Joy and her friend start out across the soggy playing field. "Bye, see ya," he muttered under his breath. He sat morosely and watched the pair until they reached the far chain-link fence, Beyond it was a strip of sidewalk and then the street. He wished that he could be sauntering casually across the field with her, just hanging out.

A few cars were passing on the street; a mail truck

stopped at each mailbox on the opposite side. Joy and
Bug Boy had reached the fence, and they leaned
against it, looking out. The mailman got out of his
truck and waved at them. Before he could even see
it, Joshua heard the sound of a loud motorcycle coming up the street, and he wondered why someone
would be riding in the rain. He continued to watch
Joy and Joey—Elvis, whatever.

"Hi, you're Joshua, right?" An expressive voice
spoke so loudly to his right that Joshua actually
jumped a little as he turned to see the speaker. She
was one of those extremely animated girls who he had
assumed was a cheerleader only because everything
she said sounded enthusiastic. He'd seen her looking
at him in his chemistry class.

"Uh, yeah."

"Hi." The syllable sounded as though it were going
down a spiral slide on a playground and having a great
time doing it. "I'm Natalie; I'm Celia's sister," she
continued, as though this were fabulous news. Joshua's
face registered no comprehension, so she seemed delighted to expound on the subject. "Celia works for
your mom. She answers the phone and stuff at the
Eye of the Beholder. You know, the salon," she added
helpfully in case Joshua had forgotten the name of his
mother's business.

"Oh, right. Celia. Yeah, you look like her." This
was true in only the remotest of ways. While Celia
was dark, hesitant, and superthin, this girl was golden,
perfectly rounded, and perky to an inflated degree.
All Joshua could think was that it must drive Celia
crazy to have such a popular, outgoing sister when she
seemed to be so timid.

"Anyway, I wanted to introduce myself and let you
know that if there's anything you need to know about
the school, or the games or the"—she blushed slightly
but seemed completely unfazed by her own reaction—

"the dances, you could ask me." She left it at that, and Joshua wasn't sure if she meant for him to ask about the dances, or to ask her to one of them.

"Thanks, Natalie. That's really nice of you, but I seem to be figuring it all out pretty well."

"Not really." She shrugged apologetically and then explained: "Only the losers come out here for lunch in the rain. You should *really* come sit with me and my friends in the cafeteria."

Joshua glanced back across to Joy and Joey and was surprised to see the postman standing at the fence and talking to them.

The bell rang, and Joshua reached for his book bag. "Well, nice to meet you. See you in chemistry."

Natalie raised her well-shaped eyebrows and beamed at him. "Chemistry, right," she said, her tone thick with innuendo. Natalie was definitely not subtle.

She turned on her heel and pranced off, glancing back over her shoulder at the door with a bright smile. Joshua waved feebly.

He lingered, pretending to fuss with a buckle on his bag, until Joy and her buddy returned and passed him; then he fell in behind them, trying to think of something to say to her.

They had reached the door when he saw Joy reach into her pocket, start to pull something out, and then glance around. She looked startled to see him there, and she shoved the hand back, deeper into her pocket. "What do you want?" she asked accusingly.

Joshua shied back. "Nothing," he said quickly, feeling shunned and hurt. "I just want to get to history."

She seemed to relax a little. "Sorry," she mumbled, and then hurried away, the streaks in her hair looking garishly violet in the brightly lit hallway.

Crushed, Joshua shuffled toward his next class.

Chapter 25

The bar at Al Wright's looked as though it had been nice once and then a cheap restaurant had come and squatted around it, refusing to move away. Greer took a stool at the end of the bar and asked for a glass of white wine. She sensed immediately that it was the wrong thing to ask for, but the bartender, who seemed older than the wood, poured it without comment.

She took a tentative sip and settled against the back of the stool to look around. She could feel that Dario wasn't anywhere nearby. While she waited for him she entertained herself by observing people.

But she had just begun to enjoy watching an older couple cooing at each other like teenagers when the door to the bar opened, and, glancing up, she saw Sterling enter and look around. He spotted her, looked surprised but—she thought—pleased, and then came over to her.

"Hi! Well, this is kind of a coincidence," he said, and looked questioningly at the empty stool next to her.

She indicated that he should take it. "Yeah. Strange that you would come in the same night as Dario and me."

Sterling was trying to catch the bartender's eye, but he turned to her at these words. "Dario? Not really."

"Yes, really."

"I'm sorry, I don't mean to be rude, but he invited me to have dinner with him."

Greer felt confused, annoyed, suckered, and then begrudgingly amused in rapid succession. "That bastard," she said with a fond smile.

Sterling seemed to follow her train of thought, and though he looked slightly embarrassed he nodded and then asked, "So, I take it he's not coming?"

Greer shook her head. "Never meant to, I would guess."

"Ah." Sterling looked uncomfortable just long enough for Greer to doubt her previous impressions.

"You don't have to stay. It's not fair," she said to him.

"Oh, no! It's not that. I mean, I'd like to, if you'd like to. It's just that I hope you don't think I put him up to this. Not that I don't think it's a good idea, but I wouldn't want you to think I would trick you." His words rushed together.

His discomfort was so apparent that Greer laughed. "Don't worry; when you get to know Dario, you'll realize that this is small-time meddling for him."

"I see. Well, if we're staying, I guess I'll order a drink." He tried again in vain to subtly catch the bartender's eye. The older gentleman avoided it with practiced dedication and went on washing glasses.

With a smile, Greer focused her beautiful green eyes on the man. He seemed unable to resist looking back at them. She flicked her look toward Sterling, and the bartender followed the look. "Can I get you something?" he asked.

"I'll have a gin and tonic," Sterling answered gratefully.

"How very British of you," Greer said playfully.

"Good thing I'm not Russian; then we'd both be drinking potato vodka," Sterling told her. "You're Greek—aren't you supposed to be drinking ouzo?"

She laughed again. "I'm not really much of a drinker."

"Me neither anymore. I used to be a bouncer in a pub in one of London's less fashionable neighborhoods, and in England they don't tip; they buy you a pint. So, I saw—and lived through—enough drunken brawls to keep me to a two-drink limit, one if I'm driving." His glass arrived and he saluted her with it.

"So," he said with the inflection of one who was just beginning, "how do you like Shadow Hills?"

Greer frowned slightly; it was a tough question. The truth was that she liked it very much, especially Sterling and her new friends, but how could she tell him about the visions and her sense of impending dread?

"I love the place," she answered finally. "It's beautiful."

"It's pretty special. A combination of LA and rural living; I guess that's why I like it. Plus, being located where people have at least a couple acres for a yard instead of a couple hundred square feet is good for my business."

Greer nodded. "How did you pick landscape architecture?"

He shrugged and ran a finger down the condensation on the outside of his glass. The dark brown of his skin was a beautiful contrast to its opaque luminosity. Greer felt a little twinge and found herself thinking of that strong finger brushing her skin as softly as it did the tumbler.

"I love two things: spatial design and gardening. I couldn't find any other job that let me work with both of those."

"And you didn't see pub bouncing as a lifetime career?" Greer asked him.

"More of a means to get through university."

Another couple came into the bar and took seats at one of the booths. Glancing up, Greer recognized the bank manager who had been so upsetting to Leah. What was his name? *Vince, that's right.* He was with a young woman about college age. She looked pretty, but not very worldly. They were both dressed in leathers, the expensive kind.

"I've always loved gardening," Greer said, and gently introduced a topic that she knew could be a red flag to Sterling, but she had to get it in sometime. "I've spent some time studying the traditional magical properties of plants and herbs, and I always try to incorporate that into my gardens."

Instead of regarding her warily, Sterling perked up, his interest piqued. "Really? What a great idea. I mean, why not? I've already incorporated the aspects of feng shui that make sense to me. I absolutely believe in the energies of different plants. I see the effect that environments have on the people who live in them, so if nothing else they have that power." He was nodding and looking energized. "Yes, this is excellent. Can you recommend some good source-books?"

Greer was delighted, and she said so. "I'd love to. I have several you could borrow."

Their conversation was interrupted by a voice from the booth behind them. Vince called out loudly from his table, "Hello? Does anyone work here? Anyone?" The girl looked mortified. She touched his arm and murmured something.

Sterling turned and looked at Vince, annoyed, but he said nothing. The bartender stopped his washing, and without looking up he came around from the bar and went to their table. Sterling muttered, "Git."

"Do you know him?" Greer asked.

"I've seen him around. It always amazes me that someone can think so much of themselves and be so oblivious to the fact that no one else shares their opinion."

"Remember the pretty brunette you met the other day at the coffee shop" Greer asked him, then realized that that description could fit any of the three women who were with her. "The one dressed like a banker; she used to be married to him."

"Well, the operative words there are *used to be.* She's got to be glad to be away from him."

Greer looked across to Vince. Though he maintained a calm facade, it was fairly obvious that he was bullying his date. Apparently he didn't like the fact that she had tried to restrain him. "I just hope she is," Greer said to Sterling, and then in answer to his questioning look she added, "He's still her boss; he's the manager at the bank where she works."

Vince's restrained yet angry voice wafted up to them again, but only the words *don't you ever* cut through clearly. Sterling sighed. "I couldn't work for him. I'd have to kill the bastard." His dead-serious tone gave Greer a sense of what Sterling must have been like in a bar fight; there was a more brutal side to this man, one that had survived a world that had very different rules. He looked straight ahead, and for just a moment the red neon sign behind the bar reflected in his irises like flickering flames, as though his eyes were on fire.

"I'll get us a table so we don't have to listen to his 'courting.' " Sterling got up and went to the hostess, giving Greer a chance to study Vince and his date for a moment. He was leaning toward her, too close, and talking fast. His hand was holding her wrist, and she looked as though she'd much rather not be there. The bartender was studiously not noticing. Wondering if anyone else was witnessing this, Greer looked around. The only other person in the bar was at the far booth, seated alone with a beer in front of him. It was dim, but on his arms Greer could make out the crude tattoos that identified him as Paul's brother, Army. He was looking deliberately away, as though he was choosing to block out not only Vince but the rest of the human race as well. She thought about saying hello, but decided to respect his solitude.

"Okay, all set. Let me just pay for these." Sterling returned and had surprisingly little trouble getting the bartender's attention to take the money.

They had started to their table and were passing Vince's booth when the young woman with Vince stood up suddenly but was pulled back by Vince gripping her forearm.

"We're not going anywhere. Sit down," Vince told her curtly, leaning toward her and keeping his voice low and controlled, but threatening. She glanced around self-consciously, said something to him in a placating voice, and then tried to pull away. He stood and blocked the way out of the restaurant without releasing her arm. "Sit down!" he hissed at her.

It happened in a couple of seconds. Sterling had already turned to intervene when another voice beat him to it—a deadly serious voice, calm and low, but very audible in the sudden silence that had fallen over the bar.

"Let go of her arm." Army stood just beside Vince. He was shorter by a good five inches, but he was wider and obviously tougher, and there was something in his eyes that was bigger than the altercation in front of him.

Vince turned and looked mockingly down at Army. In a very quiet tone, he said, "Walk away, asshole; this has nothing to do with you." He twisted the girl's arm and thrust her slightly back toward her seat. She made a small crying sound and sat, staring down at the table. Her face was red with embarrassment and fear.

"She's leaving," Army said to Vince. "And you and I are taking this outside."

Vince looked at Army as though both slightly out

of his league and half-amused. "I know you," he said, softening his face and voice. He narrowed his eyes at Army and scoffed in a voice that only Army, Sterling, and Greer could hear, "You've got that little piece-of-shit, broken-down bike. You're nothing but crap on my boots. Fuck off."

Sterling had positioned himself just behind Army, placing one hand on the younger man's arm that was tense, ready to launch forward, and ended in a tight fist. He began speaking very quietly into Army's ear. Army seemed almost unconscious of his presence.

"Let's take it outside. You don't treat a lady like that," Army said steadily to Vince.

Vince laughed. "Oh, that's rich. *You* are going to tell me how to treat a woman, faggot? You couldn't get a piece of ass if they sold it at the grocery store."

Sterling kept up a steady stream of talk in Army's ear. The girl watched nervously. Vince continued to mouth off insults at Army in a quiet taunting voice that couldn't be overheard by any of the patrons in the restaurant nearby.

Finally Army looked down at the girl. "Do you want to stay?" he asked her flatly.

"It's okay," she said with a tremulous fake smile. "We just had a little argument."

Army turned back to Vince, who was smirking. "You're not worth it," he said to Vince, and started past him.

"Fucking faggot," Vince mocked him, his voice edgy and ragged but still low. "If I ever see you again I'll kick your bitch ass."

Sterling was unable to keep Army from stopping and turning back. "I hope you do see me again. I look forward to it." There was a flatlined deadness in his voice that finally shut Vince up.

The tension, though contained, was beginning to draw attention from the restaurant area, and the manager had hurried over from the front. She had stood meekly a couple yards away during the altercation, but now she stepped forward and said carefully to Army, Vince, and his date, "I think maybe you should go. I'll be glad to buy your drinks, but in the interest of our other customers, I'm going to have to ask you to leave." She looked terrified.

Vince switched on his rehearsed personality in the time it took him to turn his head toward her. He flashed a smile like headlights at the woman and said, "We were just leaving. My date had a sudden craving for Mexican food. Let's go, Terry." He put a firm arm around the girl's back.

Now Greer spoke up. "You don't have to go with him, Terry," she said to the girl, her voice clear and calm. "If you want I'll give you a ride home, or wherever else you want to go."

Terry looked at Greer with surprise. Greer did not look at Vince, but she could feel his hateful gaze on her.

"No, it's okay." Terry's voice trembled as she spoke. "Thanks. C'mon, honey; let's go."

With a reptilian smile Vince turned his back on the lot of them and stalked to the door, holding firmly to Terry's arm.

Army watched them go, and then, without comment, he threw down some money for his beer and went out the back way.

At their table, Greer found she was too keyed up to feel very hungry. But Sterling seemed to be completely unfazed.

She regarded him shyly. "That was impressive," she said. "What did you say to him?"

"Oh, it's an old trick for stopping a fight I perfected on Tooting High Street. Pick the one who's not the aggressor and then you keep talking in their ear. They're so hopped up they don't even know you're there, but it usually gets through, because they weren't looking for a fight to start out with."

"But what did you say?"

" 'Jail.' I just kept saying, 'Think about jail. He's not worth it. Bars. Think about bars.' " Sterling smiled grimly at her. "From the look of that guy, he's had a little firsthand knowledge of the big house."

Greer didn't comment on Army's story. Instead she sat thoughtfully for a moment. Finally she said, "I wonder why she went with him."

Sterling exhaled hard and shook his head. "I wish I knew."

Greer started to laugh. "Tooting High Street? That sounds more like something out of *Peter Pan* than a tough neighborhood."

"Trust me," Sterling said, leaning back as his steak was placed on the table in front of him, "the Fox and Forrester's was no never-never land. And I'm no Tinkerbell." He fixed her with a look that told her she wasn't the only one at the table who was afraid that something about them might scare the other person away.

Greer didn't know whether to be thrilled or afraid.

Chapter 26

Tuesday

The air in the windowless two-car garage was brutal: It was infused with a burning, lethal smell, a chemical-soup combination of pure ammonia with acetone stirred in.

The two men who worked there both wear cheap paper masks, the kind housepainters wear when they are spraying a ceiling. Their eyes were red, blood-shot, raw.

The boss finished weighing out the night's product and handed out cash to the men, who took it hungrily and counted it in front of him. He didn't mind their distrust. He didn't employ them because they were honest. He didn't even know their names, and they sure as shit didn't know his. They were both illegal aliens who lived in daily fear of being picked up and sent back to the stench of the poverty across the border. This man gave them plenty of money to send back to their families, and they asked no questions.

Wiping some of the white dust off of his jeans, the boss picked up his keys by the key chain, swinging them in a small circle, enjoying the weight and feel of the heavy, dangling charm in his hand before fastening them onto his belt loop. Then he cracked the door and looked out on the shabby neighborhood. It was just before dawn; the birds were on high alert, twittering and chattering frenetically, and somewhere on the next street over a dog barked.

Careful not be seen as he exited the garage, he walked down the dirty street to where he had parked. He was tired but energized. He would go home and get a couple of hours' sleep before his day job. As tempting as it was, he knew he couldn't blow it off because he needed the cover, if not the money. Besides, it afforded him both connections to maintain his more profitable business, and respect in the community.

He laughed quietly and deeply at the irony of that under his breath; the sentiment left wispy traces of moisture in the cold air that quickly dissipated. Yeah, he was making a real social contribution. He stopped for a moment and looked around at the sleeping, dilapidated houses around him and up at the looming hills behind them, and felt swelled with the license to do as he pleased. It was really so easy, once you realized there were no real rules.

The power of having a secret life, undetected and untraceable, was exhilarating. He felt intoxicated with his ability to create his own law, his own world. *This fucking place belongs to me,* he thought. *I can do anything I want and nobody can stop me.*

He thought again about the girl he'd had and how much he'd enjoyed it, but nothing further about her. Any thought of what had become of her, whether she had lived or died, did not enter his mind. She had been his property to do with as he chose. He had stolen her, used her, marked her, and disposed of her. In his mind he was finished; she was gone.

Now he was hungry for more. He had one in mind, one he could easily draw invisibly away, and once he had her hidden . . .

Yes, this time he would savor it, make it last.

And no one would ever suspect him, and no one could stop him.

He laughed again, louder, adding a kind of whoop on the end that set off a cacophony of barking junk-yard dogs.

Chapter 27

Joshua was about to turn onto the highway when he spotted Joy walking despondently toward the school bus stop. He pulled over and cut the whining engine.

"Morning. I'd offer you a ride, but I'm not supposed to have any passengers, and I've only got one helmet anyway." He shrugged apologetically.

She looked cold in her light jacket, but she smiled slightly anyway. "What makes you think I'm going to school?"

Joshua was surprised. "Aren't you?"

She looked disdainful and disgusted, with a rebellious glint in her eye, and then she snorted a little and laughed resignedly. "Of course I'm going. I've got a year and a half left on my mandatory high school sentence, and my dad won't let me drop out."

"Oh, well, I guess I'll see you in the cell block, then."

"Right. Let me know when you get your grown-up bike," she said sourly, but she couldn't hide her smile. Slightly encouraged, Joshua started the bike up again and pulled out, watching her as long as possible in the little round mirror on his right handlebar. She turned quickly away and walked back from the road toward the bus stop bench, and then he rounded the first curve and couldn't see her anymore.

* * *

At lunch Joshua went out to the chilly yard to see if he could spot Joy, but he didn't see her there. He saw Elvis/Joey and waved. The boy nodded sullenly and went on talking to another kid with a rainbow mohawk hairstyle. Both of them looked as though they hadn't slept the night before.

Joshua wanted to ask if they'd seen Joy, and was almost to them when he overheard Elvis say, "Man, I wish the mail would come."

"No shit, you got any money?" his friend asked, and then they noticed Joshua and both of their faces turned blankly to him as though he were something to be observed rather than related to.

"Hi, I, uh, was just wondering if you guys have seen Joy?" Joshua said, trying to find the balance between friendliness and disinterested teenage cool.

The faces remained impassive for a moment, and then Elvis said, "Why? Is it my day to watch her?" They both stared at Joshua.

"Oh, okay. Well, thanks."

Joshua sat down and opened his lunch. It was cold, and after another glance around the dismal playing field, he threw his sandwich back into the bag, muttering, "Screw it," and headed for the cafeteria.

There were a few open chairs at the end of one table, and with a nod that was not returned from the three Hispanic guys at the other end, he sat down and got his lunch out again.

"I told you, you can sit with us." Joshua knew from the chirpy voice that it was Natalie before he looked up.

"Uh, thanks," Joshua said, and fumbled for his book bag, "but I've got some studying to do for a test."

Natalie sat without waiting for an invitation. "Oh, take a few minutes off. Did you hear about Zoe Caldwell?"

"No." Joshua steeled himself to look interested that someone he didn't know had been nominated for homecoming queen or some such news.

Natalie's eyes glistened with excitement and genuine concern. "They found her! In a hospital over in Chatsworth." She looked as though she might cry. Joshua felt completely at a loss. What was she talking about? "She'd been beaten so badly that she might die. Isn't that just awful?"

Joshua felt the time had come to straighten the subject out. "I'm sorry, Natalie, but I'm new and I don't know, uh, Zoe? Can you tell me what happened?"

Natalie's face softened and she apologized quickly. "Oh, I'm sorry; of course you didn't know her. She's a senior here. I mean, I didn't really know her—she was one of the ones who, you know, hang out on their own—but I'm sure she's very nice. Anyway, she disappeared after last Friday and they've been looking for her." Natalie glanced around and then leaned forward and whispered, "Most people here thought she ran away. She was kind of, you know, trouble." She sat up again and resumed her normal tone. "I don't mean to be judgmental or mean, and I've been praying for her since I heard."

"Jesus," Joshua muttered, almost to himself. "How awful." His thoughts had gone immediately to Joy and his feelings of unease. She'd been labeled *trouble* as well. "Do they know who did it?"

Natalie shook her head, her glossy ponytail flipping from side to side as though she were whisking away flies. "No, but this is the scary part—they think it might be somebody she knew." Natalie's eyes widened. "That means it's probably somebody from around here."

Joshua's mind was whirling. He was thinking of the image of the girl he had seen over Joy's right shoulder. He needed to get away from the noise and think.

The bell rang, and Natalie stood up quickly. "Listen," she said as Joshua stowed his things, "the spring dance is coming up in about three weeks, and if you'd like, we could go together. It doesn't have to be a date." The look on her face said otherwise.

Joshua was incapable of processing the switch from missing girl to Spring Fling, and he answered lamely, "Yeah, sure, that'd be great, thanks," before walking away.

As he went down the hall to his next class, his eyes raked the teenagers, searching for Joy's dark, tinted hair. As usual he didn't spot her. He didn't know if he should be worried again. Even if she had cut classes, it didn't mean she was in any danger. He found himself shaking his head at her stupid behavior. He hadn't met her mom, so maybe she had a reason to be unhappy that he didn't understand, but how hard was it to go to school and come home at night?

Why would she go out looking for trouble?

Chapter 28

The door to the salon opened at about one o'clock, and Jenny danced in carrying a whole chocolate cake on a glass stand.

"Anybody feel like dessert?"

Greer laughed, and Celia eyed the sweet suspiciously. "I do?" she said hesitantly, as though she weren't sure whether she did, or if it was okay to want cake.

"C'mon, let's go to the kitchen and get some plates," Greer directed.

Humming, Jenny swept them into the back, offering slices to Dario, Jonathan, the other stylists, and anyone else in her wake as she went. The result was a small, informal party near the coffeemaker.

Dario watched Jenny's body sway with pleasure as she handed out servings. "What's the occasion?" he asked.

"It's Tuesday!" Jenny chirruped.

Dario accepted a plate from her and said knowingly, "You got some last night."

"Wrong," Jenny sang. "I got some last night and this morning and *twice* on Sunday!"

Jonathan sighed audibly, "My hero!" he exclaimed.

"And may I ask who's watching the shop while

you're over here spreading sweetness and light?" asked Greer.

"My love slave." Jenny laughed delightedly. "We had a really good talk, and he's agreed to come in and help me out until I can afford an employee. So today that means I get to thank my best customers and make a trip to the bank without closing up shop."

Greer felt the warm spread of gratitude in her chest. It delighted her to see her new friend happy. She noticed that Dario was watching her with one eyebrow raised.

"What?" Greer asked.

"I believe *you* may have something to report as well," he suggested.

A dozen eyes turned to Greer. Dario explained, "She had a date."

Greer laughed. "I was set up, more like!"

Jonathan and Jenny chorused each other with a single word: "And?"

Looking mischievously from face to face, Greer made them all wait while she took a large, deliberate bite of cake and savored the rich taste. Then she said, "I had a delightful evening."

"And?" Celia asked.

"And," Greer told them all firmly, "that's all I'm saying."

The bells on the front door jangled, and Dario leaned his head around the corner to see who it was. Sterling had come into the shop.

"Is it a customer?" Greer asked, setting down her plate and wiping her mouth on a napkin.

Dario's eyes glittered evilly. "Speak of the devil and he will appear."

"It's not that big a deal, Dario," Greer told him. Turning to Jenny, she asked, "Do I have chocolate on my teeth?"

"Clean," Jenny told the grinning Greer, who straightened her dress, checked her face in a small mirror, and, after composing herself with a deep breath, sauntered casually out onto the salon floor, where she registered surprise as she rounded the corner.

The Cake Eaters United looked at one another and tried not to laugh out loud.

"Hi, may I help you, sir?" Greer asked in her most professional voice as she reached the front, but the blush gave her away.

"Oh, yes. I was interested in getting a treatment." Sterling put an elbow up on the counter and leaned against it.

"Really, what kind of a treatment?"

"The special treatment comes to mind." His white teeth flashed, and Greer thought, *Wow, he's handsome.*

"Let me check and see if we have that on our menu of services." Greer picked up a trifolded flyer and pretended to peruse it. "Oh, yes, it seems that we're running a special on that special treatment. Lucky you."

Sterling looked into the magnificent green eyes that regarded him playfully, in which he read a great deal of desire for him, and with a purring smile he said, "Yes. Lucky me."

Jonathan pulled his head back around the corner and offered his hand, high in the air, to Dario, who slapped it with a sharp smack.

"Score!" Jonathan did a miniature victory dance.

Jenny's eyes narrowed. "You did not set them up."

"Oh, yes," said Dario, "we did."

Celia's gaze went reverently from Dario to Jonathan. She sidestepped to the hallway and peeked out at the couple at the front, who were flirting unabashedly. Turning back to the small group in the kitchen, she looked worshipfully up at Dario.

In a breathless, eager voice, she said, "Do me next."

Jenny threw her head back and laughed. "Girl, have another piece of cake."

Chapter 29

Jenny spotted Leah when she came into the bank and waved. Leah was so jittery she could only smile back tightly, and was relieved when Jenny went to get in the teller's line. She watched as Vince came out from his office and spoke to Josie. He glanced up and caught her watching him. His eyes glinted meanly at her before she could look away. He knew he had her, that she was afraid. *Damn him!*

The door opened again, and a young woman came in wearing dark glasses. She stopped and looked hesitantly around. All the tellers were busy, but no one was seated at Leah's desk. The woman in glasses came over.

"Hi. Is Vince in?" she asked Leah.

Leah perked up. Who was this? She glanced over at Vince's office; he'd gone in and shut the door. As Leah was wondering why the young woman didn't take the glasses off on an overcast day, she spotted bruises on the girl's wrist that she quickly tried to conceal by pulling down her sweater cuffs.

"Can I tell him who's asking for him?"

"Terry."

"And what is this regarding?"

The girl blanched visibly and reached up to readjust her glasses. She turned sideways as she did so, and

Leah saw the discoloring of a black eye. "It's, um . . . well, he'll know. It's personal."

Leah's heart twisted like a wet rag in a wringer. No, not again. She couldn't stand by and see the Rattler victimize someone else.

She didn't know exactly what to say, but she felt she had to make some connection, so, keeping her best business voice, she said, "If it's personal business with you two, I may be able to help you." She waited while the girl took that in.

"What?" she asked, obviously confused.

"I'm his ex-wife, and I'm very familiar with how Vince deals with women on a *personal* level."

The girl started back as though Leah had slapped her.

"Listen," Leah said hurriedly in a low voice, "if he did that to you, you need to talk to somebody. You might think it's none of my business, but, girl, that man is big trouble, and you can still walk away."

Over the girl's shoulder she saw Vince come out of his office again, spot Terry at her desk, and head purposefully to the buzzer door.

"Take one of my cards," Leah urged, picking one up and shoving it into the stunned girl's hand. "Call me."

Vince closed in on the pair, and without so much as a greeting he turned to Terry. "What are you doing here?" he said, a public smile on his face, but a very private anger in his tone.

Leah cut in. "She was just inquiring whether you were here. I told her you were busy, but that I would see if you had time to meet with her. That's as far as we got. Is there a problem?" Her heart was pounding. Would the girl be smart enough to pick up on this and keep her mouth shut?

Terry turned to Vince, and Leah watched as she slipped the business card deftly into her pocket, out of Vince's line of sight.

"Hi, I was in the neighborhood and I thought you might want to get a cup of coffee or something."

Vince took her arm, and Leah watched as the girl flinched. She could remember all too well that grip on already bruised skin.

"And why," asked Vince, turning his considerable contempt onto Leah, "is she asking *you*?"

Another memory cut into Leah's vision like a flash card: being tied to the bed by Vince, the cutting pain in her wrists, hiding the abrasions with long cuffs. She managed to shrug. "I was the only one who didn't have a customer, I suppose. Why shouldn't she ask me?"

He smiled slowly. It was a warning smile with all the warmth of an approaching tsunami, but before he could speak they were interrupted by Jenny. Her transaction finished, she had appeared beside Leah's desk.

"Hi, I just wanted to stop by and . . ." Jenny's friendly greeting died on her lips. It was apparent to the meanest intellect that there was a confrontation going on, and she instantly recognized Vince as the antagonistic Ducati rider the night outside the bar and realized why he'd seemed vaguely familiar then. She hadn't recognized him out of the bank and his fancy suit. But the look on his face now was the same as it had been then: angry and challenging. "Oh, sorry," she muttered.

Leah didn't look at her, but she was intensely grateful for the break as she said, "Don't be; we're almost done." She prayed that it was true, because she didn't think she could maintain the casual pretense for more than another ten seconds.

"No, no." Vince put on his charming-bank-manager face, but he couldn't stop his eyes from sliding licentiously up and down Jenny's body. "You two go right ahead. I'm going to walk Ms. Richards to her car.

Have a great afternoon." He gave Jenny a friendly wink and, still holding Terry firmly by the arm, walked her to the door.

Leah sank into her chair and found that no matter how hard she tried, she couldn't get enough oxygen into her lungs. She started to draw rapid, shallow breaths.

Jenny leaned over her. "Are you okay? Come on, come on, you're hyperventilating. Let's go to the ladies' room."

Leah nodded, snatched up her key to the employees' restroom, and half led, half followed Jenny to the narrow hallway. Once inside, Jenny grabbed at a section of paper towel and instructed Leah to hold it over her mouth and breathe through it. "Same principle as a paper bag," she reasoned. She placed her open palm on Leah's back between her shoulder blades and rubbed softly in a circle, the way a mother would to calm a sobbing child.

Within thirty seconds, the carbon dioxide and the comforting contact had done their work, and Leah's breathing had slowed to almost normal.

"Better?" Jenny asked her with concern in her pretty brown eyes. Leah nodded. "You want to tell me what *that* was all about?"

"That," said Leah, sucking in a big breath, "was my ex."

"Oh. And how about the girl?"

"Don't know her, but I think . . ." Leah stopped; she'd been on the verge of revealing that she'd been abused by saying that she suspected he was doing it *again*. "I think that he might have hit her. She had a black eye, and he's got a nasty temper. He drinks a lot. I left him when he started drinking. His personality changed." She hoped, lamely, that it sounded like she'd left before he'd turned violent.

"I see." Jenny waited for a moment, still rubbing

Leah's back in the rhythmic circular motion. When she spoke again it was with a quiet sense of impartiality.

"It's frustrating, but there isn't much you can do. Some women are ashamed that other people would find out about it, so they deny it." Leah had a knee-jerk response and shifted uncomfortably, as though her whole body had jumped suddenly a couple of inches to the right. Jenny did not comment on the reaction. "Or, for some fucked-up reason, they think they deserve to be treated badly." She fell quiet but kept the massaging contact. Leah was enchanted by the lull and the strength of this woman. It felt good just to sit with her and suck up her potency by osmosis; she felt safe for the first time in months.

Then Jenny began to speak again. Her voice was without extreme emotion, which, oddly, gave the story an even greater sense of being deeply intense and personal.

"And then some have nowhere else to go. I remember, from as early as I *can* remember, my father hitting my mother. He drank too, but he'd hit her even when he was sober. If she said something he didn't like, any excuse would do. He was a miserable bastard with a shitty life, and he took it out on her.

"He hit me a few times, but mostly he went after my older brother or my mom. I realize now that she would get in between us to keep him away from us."

"How awful," Leah said.

"Suffice to say I didn't exactly have a *Brady Bunch* childhood, and I don't want to drag you through my depressing memories, but there is one particular time that I want to tell you about."

Jenny sighed and leaned against the sink, staring straight ahead at the tile wall in front of her. "My dad had a friend who was always trying to feel me up and corner me when he and my dad had polished off a bottle of tequila. Well, one night, after my mom had died, my dad drank so much he passed out on the sidewalk outside our apartment building, and this guy, he came after me when I was asleep, thinking I'd be easy prey. I woke up and heard him taking his pants off. He was panting like a freight train, not real subtle."

Leah's breathing had gone from hyperventilation to almost nothing. She was fixated on the words that echoed softly through the bathroom from Jenny's past.

"It was a tiny room. I tried to get up and run around him, but he pinned me down on my bed." She paused as a shudder of revulsion crossed her face. "I can't tell this story without thinking I smell tequila and body odor. Anyway, I was terrified, of course, but something else. I remembered my mom and all the years that she suffered because of my father, and a kind of rage came up and gave me a strength that shocked the shit out of me—and him too, I can tell you. I only knew one thing." Jenny turned and looked at Leah, her eyes bright and fierce. "I would *not* be a victim. I would *not* make that choice, whatever else happened. I was going to fight."

Almost daring to speak, Leah asked softly, "What did you do?"

Jenny looked away again, as though that would make it easier to say. "I grabbed his dick in one hand and his balls in the other, and I twisted as hard as I could in opposite directions." Leah was too shocked to say anything, and Jenny went on. "He beat the shit out of my face, trying to get me to let go, but I wouldn't. He broke my nose, but I hung on. I don't know how; I was so angry that I didn't even feel it until afterward. I kept twisting until he was begging me stop. But I wouldn't; I made him stand up, walk out onto the street, and call for the police."

"Did they come?"

For the first time, Jenny smiled. "Them and the rest of the neighborhood. It was quite a visual, I'm sure: this fat, ugly, middle-aged fucker with an underage girl in a white nightgown trying to twist his dick off."

There was absolute silence, and then—she couldn't help it—Leah snorted with laughter. Both her hands flew up to clap tightly over her mouth, and she turned horrified eyes to Jenny. "I'm sorry. It's not funny. I didn't mean to laugh," she apologized.

But from Jenny's compressed lips a hooting laughter escaped, and like jumping from a plane at twenty thousand feet, they both launched into the free fall of helpless release, laughing until tears streamed down their faces and they snatched at paper towels to blot them away. Eventually the hysteria subsided and the parachutes came out; they drifted gently back to earth and a thoughtful calm came over them again, punctuated by an occasional gusty giggle while they both leaned against the sink with their shoulders touching lightly.

"The point is, I think," Jenny said, "that you have to *choose* to not be a victim. And that woman out there today—and every woman—has to make that choice for themselves. Sometimes that choice means asking for help." She glanced at Leah, then said wryly, "And sometimes it means trying to separate a man from his dearest possession."

The two women smiled at each other, having said everything they needed to say.

Chapter 30

"There's a Whitney Whitehorse on line one for you? Do you want me to take a message?" Celia had knocked tentatively on the door of Greer's room while she was changing the covering of her treatment table.

"Oh, okay, I'll take it. Thank you, Celia." The thin face slipped back out of the narrow opening, and as Greer turned her attention to the blinking light on the phone, a vague foreboding rose inside her like a tide turning.

"Hi, Whitney, is everything all right?"

"Probably. But the school called, and apparently Joy didn't show up today. I was wondering if Joshua was there and if he'd seen her, or if you guys had heard anything." Whitney tried to keep her voice light, but strands of worry were woven into it like an overly loud plaid.

The waves of premonition lapped higher in Greer's chest, salty and icy cold. "No, I haven't heard anything. Joshua went this morning on his bike. He doesn't have his cell phone on at school, so I can't call him, but I'll leave a message at home for him to call you as soon as he gets there. Okay?"

"Okay, I'm sure she's fine. It's not the first time she's cut classes to go hang out and smoke with those loser friends of hers." There was a pause, and then Whitney asked hesitantly, "What do you think?"

Greer didn't want to answer—or rather, she did, but she wanted to be reassuring, confidently cheerful. Instead she told Whitney the truth. "I don't know what to think yet. But I have a question. Was Joy wearing the bracelet I gave her when she left today?" Greer held her breath waiting for the answer. *Please say yes,* she was praying.

"I think so. I didn't really notice, but I don't think she's taken it off since you gave it to her." She waited for a response, but Greer was breathing her thanks, so she asked, "Why? Is it important?"

"Maybe," Greer told her. "It will help me find her energy and sense what's going on with her."

Whitney perked up, eager for an ounce of control in the situation. "Can you locate her from that?"

Greer felt sad. "No. I don't have that kind of ability. Only a sense of what forces are around a person, mostly future influences. But maybe it will help. Let me call you back in a little while. Call me if you hear anything?"

"Absolutely, of course. Greer?"

"Yes, honey?"

"Should I be afraid?"

"No. You should be as positive as you possibly can." Greer hung up the phone and wished she could take her own advice. She punched the intercom button on the phone and said, "Celia?"

Over the busy noise of the salon came the response: "Yes?"

"Can you please see that I'm not interrupted for about ten minutes, no calls, no questions?"

"Uh, sure. Do you have a client?" Celia asked, and Greer could hear her flipping through the appointment book.

"No, not until three. Just, please, I need ten minutes. Okay?"

"Sure."

The rustling noise of people and activity ceased when she cut the connection. Greer lit a candle and placed it on the floor; then she sat cross-legged in front of it and tried to clear her mind. Her anxiety was blocking the way, and it took a moment to settle the chatter and the waking-nightmare images that were not clairvoyant but products of her brain's frenetic busyness.

Finally, though, she settled, reached a place of vast emptiness and infinite possibility, and began to search around for the energy of Joy and the bracelet. Little traces of color, like wisps of scent, drew her mind in one direction, until finally an image of Joy appeared in her mind. She seemed safe for the moment in a circle of green light, light the color of sun through the peridot crystal on the bracelet, but wounded spaces, like angry welts of darkness, struck again and again at the circle, and it was growing thinner.

Joy wandered his house, reveling in the secret of being somewhere she wasn't supposed to be, somewhere that no one knew where to find her. Freedom. He had let her in and told her to do as she pleased, stay as long as she liked; he had to go to work and he'd be back later. She had amused herself going through his drawers and then fallen asleep for most of the morning on the sofa. When she'd woken she'd turned on the TV and made herself a sandwich, careful to put everything back just so and wipe away all the crumbs in his spotless kitchen.

Come afternoon the soap operas had bored her, so she turned off the television and started wandering again. It was quiet here. There were no other houses nearby, and she felt very mature. *He* trusted her with his home. She fantasized about making love to him when he came home and felt a swell of fear. He was not some kid; he was a man, and she wondered if she could please him. She wasn't a virgin, but the fumbling, embarrassed sex she'd had a few times hadn't left her feeling overly confident.

Sliding open a drawer on his superneat desk, she fingered the objects in different small compartments. Paper clips, nail cutters, staples, and a key on a key chain. She picked up the key and let the charm dangle in front of her face. It was an interesting-looking thing, maybe Egyptian? Almost playfully she reached out a finger and touched the heavy metal object to send it swinging.

Greer gasped and both of her hands flew to her forehead, where an intense burning was making her eyes water. She pressed two fingers of each hand to the spot, just above and between her eyes, and pressed until the momentary pain subsided. Breathing deeply, she got to her feet and looked in the mirror, but there was no sign of any injury. Greer knew this pain had something to do with Joy, but it was beyond her talent to know what it meant exactly, or how to help her. She had to do something; she couldn't let this happen again. Not twice in her life! She looked hopelessly at her reflection and began to cry. The images of Sarah in the hospital, of her casket swaying slightly as it was lowered into her gaping grave, of her empty desk at school, flooded Greer's mind.

"Sarah," she called out in a hoarse whisper. "Sarah, help me!"

But the only answer was a crackling sizzle as a speck of dust hit the burning candle and evaporated into an undetectable wisp of smoke.

*   *   *

Joshua was staring down at his textbook when it happened. The fluorescent light of the ugly, windowless cinder-block classroom disappeared and, as though through his own eyes, he saw a hand held up in front of his face, a girl's hand holding a dangling charm of some kind. Sunlight streamed through a window and glistened on a bracelet, causing the green stone to spark with light. Joy's bracelet. Joy's hand.

His whole body jolted with the shock of it. His right arm swung wildly, as if to wipe the unwanted image away, knocking his books off of his desk instead. A cry of alarm at the strangeness of it escaped him.

The room returned. Every face had turned to stare blankly at Joshua. He muttered something about being clumsy and reached down to retrieve his books and hide the burning redness of his face. He was shaking and sweaty. The teacher, a hip young man who seemed not long out of college, stopped the lesson and started over to Joshua.

"Everyone, please turn to the end of the chapter and answer questions one through five," the teacher commanded, kindly trying to pull the attention away from Joshua. It didn't work. Not one face bothered to do anything other than blatantly stare at the spectacle of Joshua's discomfort. He felt like an accident on the side of the highway.

"Are you not feeling well?" the teacher asked in a low voice when he reached Joshua's desk.

Joshua automatically started to say yes, and then shifted gears quickly. "No, I'm not feeling well. I think I might need to go home."

The teacher regarded his new pupil. The few days Joshua had been in his class had been enough to show him that this was a serious student who was both respectful and honest. He could see the slight glow of sweat on Joshua's brow and the flushed color.

"You look like you might have a fever. Why don't

you get your things and go by the office? Is there someone who can pick you up?"

"It's okay; I have a bike."

"All right. Go ahead, then; homework will be an essay on the causes of the French Revolution. We'll see you tomorrow. Feel better."

The other kids were still watching him voraciously, as though they were hungry for a full-scale seizure; some were snickering behind their hands to friends, and others were smiling with malicious delight. Joshua's face burned even darker as he rose, put his books away, and took the endless walk between the desks to the door. It was horrible standing out like this. He felt like a carnival sideshow, as though he'd grown horns or his skin had turned scaly and green. Furious and embarrassed, he forced himself not to make eye contact with any of the other teenagers. As he passed Natalie's desk, she whispered, "I hope you feel better." He glanced down at her, but even she had a guarded fear in her forced smile, as though she were being nice, but trying to put distance between them.

"Uh, thanks." Joshua hit the hallway and half ran to the front doors. He didn't stop at the office for a permission slip—he didn't even answer the teacher who called out to him, asking what he was doing out of class—he just kept moving until he was on his motorcycle, pushing it as fast as the tiny motor would tolerate.

Opening the throttle and punishing the little engine, he tried to outrun the whispering faces and the cruel smiles, to leave them behind him in the classroom, but he couldn't. The reality of his outburst and his vision wouldn't be blown off him by the chilly wind that stung his face and hands.

The cold wind blinded Joshua with tears, and he realized that he could never outrun the stares and the snickering, not as long as he *was* different and it

showed. And it wouldn't help Joy. He slowed the bike
to reasonable rpms and wiped his eyes with the back
of his jacket sleeve, but the tears continued to come.
He hadn't asked for the strange things that were happening to him, but running wouldn't stop the premonitions, if that was what they were. They didn't come
from outside of him, but from somewhere that was
connected to him somehow.

And what did it mean? The bracelet in his vision
had been the one his mom had given Joy, but so what?
How was that supposed to help her? And what had
she been holding? Some kind of key chain. He let out
a frustrated cry into the winter air as his fear for Joy—
and his inability to translate anything he had seen—
filled him with rage and frustration.

And how could he face school tomorrow? He would
have to learn to control what was happening to him;
he had to. But what if Joy was in danger, and what if
something he saw might save her?

Joshua tried to shake off the horrible heaviness of
that possible responsibility. He had zero faith in his
ability to help anyone with these disconcerting images.
As desperately as he wanted Joy to be safe, he
couldn't fathom that her well-being would be up to
him. He couldn't shake the feeling that if it was, to
use her own phrase . . .

She was fucked.

Chapter 31

Vince was returning from a late lunch when he spotted Army in line at the bank. He was with a slightly older man who was so similar in build and look that he must have been his brother. He sauntered over and held out his hand.

"Hi, there, I'm Vince Slater, the bank manager. How are you gentlemen doing today?"

The brother's face, which seemed to wear a perpetually amused smile, looked surprised, but he reached out to return the handshake. "Hi, I'm Paul."

Keeping his smile friendly, Vince extended his hand to Army. "And you are?"

Army kept his arms crossed. He looked once at Vince's hand and then away, ignoring him except for a tightening of the jaw. Paul seemed used to this. "This is my brother, Army. He's not real social."

"No? Oh, well." He raised his abandoned hand in a gesture of surrender and then placed it casually in his pocket. "So, what brings you in today?"

Paul looked around at the other people waiting in line and assumed a slightly embarrassed, guilty manner, as though he suspected he'd been called out of class for some kind of misbehavior. "Just depositing some checks."

"Oh, great." Vince laughed. "We love to *take* people's money. What do you do? If you don't mind my asking."

Vince's manner was so polite and friendly that Paul seemed to relax. Army continued to bristle in his rock-like stance. "We're plumbers."

"Oh, plumbers. Have you got a card?" As Paul fished out a stained card from a worn wallet swollen with receipts, Vince looked directly at Army and continued. "I mean, if my toilet ever gets clogged up, I might need to give you guys a call!" He laughed to show that this was just a lighthearted joke. The muscles on Army's biceps tightened and his nostrils flared, but he said nothing.

Paul's chin jutted forward, and his blue eyes twinkled. "Yeah, well, we're in the only business where a flush beats a full house." He laughed easily at his own old joke.

Vince smacked him on the shoulder, as if he'd told a good one. "That's funny, Paul. You mind if I use that?"

Paul shrugged, the constant smile mimicking his shoulders, rising quickly up into a more pronounced grin and then back into its fixed, pleasant position. "Help yourself."

"Well, I just wanted you to know that we appreciate your business."

From her desk, Leah watched Vince's routine, one hand on the chest, the other holding the manila envelope down by his side, and she wondered what he was really up to.

"And if there's ever anything I can personally do for you"—his eyes went again to Army, who glanced back at him briefly—"I certainly intend to do it." Army's body made a slight move toward Vince, but the motion was arrested and he went rigid again. "You gentlemen have a nice day." Vince turned and started across the floor.

Army muttered to Paul that he'd be in the truck and strode toward the door as though he were intending to smash through the glass instead of opening it.

Leah studied the two men whom Vince had made such a point of belittling. She recognized his fake friendliness for the cheap tactic it was; she'd seen it too many times. Who were they, and why was he behaving like that toward them? She watched the younger one stomp away and fling the door open just as Pistol reached it holding his mail carton.

Leah lifted her cold coffee cup and pretended to blow into it as she avidly watched the postal worker cross the room, his large collection of keys jangling on his belt, and place the carton upon the counter. Towler took it and replaced it with the outgoing mail. Vince crossed casually toward them and dropped his envelope into the new carton, glancing up at Leah as he did so. She was careful to be busy looking at something else.

She grabbed her car keys and made a point of calling out to Towler that she needed to get something out of her car and she'd be right back so that Vince could hear her. Pistol was still standing at the counter, sorting the envelopes by size, making them into neat, trim little bundles that he fastened with colored rubber bands before replacing them, like pressed laundry in orderly stacks, back into the carton.

Leah went out the door without looking back. If she timed this just right, she might get a look at the address on Vince's mysterious envelope, but she'd have to be careful. She'd come early this morning and parked just next to the red zone where the postal truck always pulled up. On the other side of her a large, beat-up pickup truck had squeezed into the space; on the side of it was painted PAUL'S PLUMBING in faded and chipped lettering. She opened her car door and leaned into the backseat, where she had deliberately left a folder, and pretended to look through it while she watched for Pistol to come out.

A crash next to her made her straighten up so fast she bumped her head hard against the doorjamb. Extracting herself from the BMW, she he looked over the roof and watched as the young man she had just seen Vince talking to sent a thick metal pipe smashing down onto the floor of the flatbed for the second time.

"Motherfucker," he swore. A third time he brought it up over his head and swung down viciously, as though smashing through the skull of an unseen foe.

A few people who had been making their way into the bank had halted, and were watching the naked display of rage in startled horror. The man's brother came out of the bank and rushed forward.

Leah watched, fascinated, as the older man placed a hand on his brother's arm and said smoothly. "It's okay; it's all right. Come on, get in the truck."

Breathing hard, the angry young man hurled the pipe into the bed of the truck with an furious clatter.

"Sorry, everybody!" The plumber, who Leah assumed was Paul, smiled sheepishly around at the onlookers. "Bad day; sorry." He hurried into the driver's seat and started the engine.

As the truck backed out, Leah turned just in time to see Pistol putting the mail carton in the back of the truck. Clutching a legal-size envelope in her hand she approached him, careful to keep the postal truck between herself and the bank.

"Excuse me, Pistol! Could I give you this?" She walked toward him, keeping the envelope near her body.

He jumped slightly, as though surprised at being addressed. When she'd first started at the bank he'd trapped her into several long conversations, and she'd learned to studiously avoid him. "Sure," he said, and held out his hand for the letter, but Leah kept it close to her and continued to advance. She couldn't see into the carton yet.

"Thanks, I forgot all about it. It's one of those crazy days. You know what I mean? Wow, look at all the mail!" She leaned forward, feigning interest in the contents of the truck.

"Busy day," Pistol said. He looked as though he would be happy to settle in for a nice long chat.

"Well, here you go." She held out the envelope, asking, "Shall I just put it in this with the others?" She moved up next to the carton and glanced down into it. The manila envelope was facedown.

"No!" Pistol's hand shot out and took the letter. "I've got to sort it all so it goes into the right place at the station."

Leah pretended to be impressed. "Wow, look how neat you are! So then you go by what, zip code?"

"Zip code, size, and postage. First-class, business, metered, mass mailings, all kinds." Pistol was enjoying the attention.

"What about, say, this one?" Leah plucked Vince's envelope out of the carton and tried to read the address before Pistol took it out of her hand with a possessive yank. It was the padded kind, thick, but surprisingly light.

His face, under his beard, had gone slightly gray. "I'm afraid I can't let you handle any mail after I've accepted it." He narrowed his eyes at her slightly. "You have a nice day now." He reached across in front of her to close the door, effectively blocking her from any further snooping. Her heart fell as she considered, for the first time, that the postman might not be ignorant of his baggage. How stupid could she be?

"Oh, okay, thanks. You too!" Leah called out with a cheerfulness she did not feel, turning back to the bank with a growing sense of dread. The chill of knowing she'd done something foolish seeped through her.

If Pistol *were* in on it, he would tell Vince about her snooping. The envelope had been addressed to a name and a business that she did not recognize.

And now, she suspected, that did not exist.

Chapter 32

"Mom?"

Greer turned in her chair, where she'd been staring into the fire. "Yes?"

"It, uh, it happened again." Joshua focused on the fire as well as he came in and sat in the chair next to hers to avoid the sudden hopefulness that came into her eyes. *Damn it.* What did she expect from him? He knew the answer, of course, and couldn't blame her. It wasn't expectation; it was hope. She hoped for the same thing he did: to find Joy.

"They still haven't heard from her?" he asked, glancing out the window at Luke and Whitney's house, which sat with its lights shining feebly in the gloomy evening.

"No, nothing."

"I suppose you didn't expect them to," Joshua said.

"No. I hoped." Greer's voice was soft with emotion. He knew she was waiting for him to speak, so he braced himself and started in.

"It was different this time. Instead of looking at a person and seeing a figure or a shape near them, I saw an image from somewhere else, not what was in front of me—like a film, as though I were looking through Joy's eyes." He hesitated in his explanation, aware that his mother had come to attention. "Why would that be?" he asked her, frustrated.

"The bracelet," Greer whispered. "I meant it to link her to me, but it seems that you have the stronger connection."

He nodded. "Yes. I saw the bracelet, and her hand—she was holding something up, a key chain, I think. It was very fast; I couldn't really make anything out." He shook his head disgustedly. "To tell the truth, I was so surprised to see Joy's hand in the middle of European History that I made a fool of myself and had to get the hell out of there." His face felt hot, and he didn't know if it was from his proximity to the fire or the memory of the malicious delight in his classmates' expressions.

Greer sighed deeply. "Joshua, I know this is hard for you. High school kids aren't exactly famous for being tolerant and embracing differences." They shared a rueful expression. Passing over that, she went on. "I've had that kind of image—and it's always been future—only a few times in my life, and only in the beginning. Now I've learned to see the signs instead of the scenes, if that makes sense. I don't know how your gift is different from mine, but I do know that, for me, the *feeling* I get from something I see is more important than *what* I see."

"I know; you told me that before." Joshua was nodding, staring at the flickering orange coals. "I keep thinking about that; that's what's killing me." He brought his hands up and raked them through his sandy hair. "Because the feeling I get is that I should be helping her."

Trying to steer him away from beating himself up, Greer asked, "Were the keys hers, do you think?"

"No, they were more like something a man would carry. They were clunky and heavy, and there was some kind of charm—silver, I think."

"Would you recognize it if you saw it again?" Greer asked gently, not wanting to pressure him.

Joshua turned and smiled at her wryly. "I think I might recognize the *feeling* of them, if you know what I mean."

She nodded.

They were both quiet for a few moments, listening to the crackling logs, and then Greer reached out and took Joshua's hand. She squeezed it softly, almost nostalgically, remembering when that hand had been far smaller and had fit in hers so willingly, when she could close her fingers around it protectively, kiss it without embarrassment or restraint. She thought to herself that things changed too quickly; life was so fragile. Nothing was as precious to her as this boy, this man, who sat beside her struggling with something bigger than either of them, and facing it with wisdom beyond his years.

She drew in a deep breath to ease the tightness that had come into her throat before beginning to speak quietly. "Your father is the only person who *never* questioned me. He always believed in the interconnectedness of all things. Some of that was because of his work and his love of nature. It's hard to spend a life studying the biology of the earth and not see the infinite number of ways that life communicates. He used to compare my gift to ducks migrating and a new generation of butterflies returning to the same tree that their parents had used. He always said that I was just listening on a different wavelength, like radio or television, something that other people weren't tuned in to." She laughed a fond little laugh and went on. "He used to joke that I had some kind of transmitter or tube built into me, the way other people might have a cowlick or a birthmark. Maybe he was right."

Joshua was watching his mother, and as always when she spoke of his father, he was struck by the love on her face. In spite of all his mother and father had been through, Joshua still got the strong impression that there had never been another man that she could love the way she'd loved him. That she had never let him go.

"I have to believe," Greer said, leaning toward Joshua and fixing moistened eyes on him, "that he's there to help you. There is no way that the connection between the two of you could be broken."

Joshua nodded and glanced uncomfortably away. He remembered his father as a laughing, happy face that regarded him with pride and joy. Though he'd always had Dario, he'd felt the loss of his father very much in his life until it had faded into nothing more than a pleasant, dreamlike memory. He did not feel a connection to a man he so sketchily remembered—something that he had never confessed to his mother. Instead of doing so now, he asked, "Why are you telling me this?"

She tilted her head to one side and spoke gently. "Because it's time to claim your gift. You won't suddenly understand it; you won't be perfect in your interpretations; you will make mistakes. But"—she took a deep breath and reached out her free hand to stroke back her son's hair—"you will not be alone."

"How can you be so sure?" Joshua asked, unsure of anything.

"Because I can see it." His mother's eyes were shining in a very different way from when he had come into the room. "There are others helping you. They are all around you."

Joshua stiffened. "You can see them?" he asked incredulously.

"Not the way you do. I sense light, several lights; each is a different color, and each one has a distinctively different energy, all good," she added quickly. She closed her eyes and breathed deeply in and then out. "They feel . . . wise and helpful. There is one—" she broke off, as though almost overwhelmed.

"What?" Joshua asked, concerned more for her than for himself.

Greer's breath had quickened, and her chest rose and fell under her thick sweater. "It's all right," she said. "It's very strong. I don't know who or what it is, but it's intensely positive. I get the sense that it— or *they*—will protect you." She opened her eyes and seemed to readjust to the room around her. She smiled almost sheepishly at her son. "It's all good," she murmured reassuringly.

Joshua wished he could share her faith in him and her simple sentiment. But when he thought of Joy and where she might be tonight, he felt that things were anything but good. He felt that things were as bad as they could possibly be.

Chapter 33

Wednesday

It was all Greer could do to pretend to be cheerful to the clients who came into Eye of the Beholder. Joy had not come home, and Greer had spent the hours from dawn until she'd left to open the shop waiting with Luke and Whitney, who had been up all night. Her sense of foreboding for Joy was growing stronger.

Oddly, though, the Shadow Hills day proceeded normally, as though nothing had changed. The community seemed both unaware and, it seemed to Greer, uncaring that a young girl was missing, that her parents were in a living hell, that something evil lurked in its midst. Greer caught herself resenting anyone who laughed, as though, despite their ignorance of the situation, they were being callous and apathetic. Of course, she knew that this wasn't true, and she wondered how many people in her lifetime had listened to her laugh while they suffered the way Luke and Whitney were suffering now.

The door to the shop opened and Sterling came in. Though he smiled at Greer, his face was drawn and concerned. He came directly to her and asked, "Have you heard?"

Greer's heart contracted. How did Sterling know?

Had she been wrong, and was Joy already hurt—or worse?

"Heard what?" She breathed the words.

He pointed to the flyer taped to her window. "They found that girl. She's in a hospital in Chatsworth. She was sexually assaulted and beaten to within an inch of her life. They don't think she's going to make it."

When her head stopped spinning, the prevalent facts sank in: It wasn't Joy, another girl had been assaulted and beaten, she was someone's daughter, her fear and pain must be horrible, it was what Sarah had felt. Greer leaned on the desk and moaned, "Oh, no, oh, my God."

Sterling came around the counter and put an arm around Greer. "It gets worse," he told her. "She was scarred. The sicko son of a bitch branded her with the shape of an eye." His voice rippled with anger and compassion.

The room swam before Greer, and she was slammed with connected images: the burning eye, Joshua telling her he had seen an eye over Joy, the impending danger signs around Joy's face in the tea leaves. She reached up and touched her forehead with one finger before turning her face up to Sterling's. "Where? Where did he brand her?"

Sterling looked taken aback, as though that were an odd question. "Does it make a difference?"

Greer pulled away from him, unfairly impatient. "Yes, it does. Did they say *where* she was branded?"

"On her cheek." He looked put out. "The paper said she'd been branded on her right cheek."

"That's wrong," Greer blurted out. She *knew* it was wrong. The girl had been branded on her forehead, almost right between her eyes. She knew now why Joshua had seen the eye hovering over Joy—because the same sicko had her friend's daughter. A wave of nausea raked her, and she turned and ran to the restroom, leaving Sterling standing, dumbstruck, at the counter.

Dario had seen Sterling come in and watched in his mirror as Greer ran, hand over her mouth, to the ladies' room. Excusing himself quickly from his client, he walked rapidly to the front. "What's going on?" he asked Sterling.

Sterling shook his head, bewildered. "I have no idea. I told her what I read about them finding that poor girl." He crooked a thumb at the picture. "Did you see it in the paper?"

Dario nodded, his handsome mouth tightening. "I didn't tell her because her friend's daughter didn't come home last night, so she was upset to start out with, plus the fact that she lost a best friend when she was a teenager . . ."

"Oh, how stupid of me; she told me that before." Sterling ran fingers through his short-cropped hair. "I guess I should have realized how it would affect her, but I was so upset. Right here! In our community! How can someone be that twisted and nobody notice?"

"I don't know," Dario said sadly.

Sterling looked to where Greer had disappeared. "When I told her about the branding, she said, 'That's wrong.' What the hell was she talking about?"

Dario's eyes narrowed. "She said that?"

"I mean, how does *she* know?" Sterling demanded.

"Don't ask me to explain it. I just know not to question it."

Sterling started to respond to this odd statement, but they both fell quiet as the ladies' room door opened and Greer came out, a wet cloth pressed to her mouth. She was pale and grim, and she looked very determined.

"Are you okay?" Dario asked her. She nodded.

"I understand now." She turned her eyes to Sterling

and took a deep breath, knowing this could be the last conversation she ever had with him, knowing how it would sound. "When the officer put up that poster, I saw a picture in my mind of a flaming eye. I didn't know what it meant, but now I do." She paused for breath and tried to calm her raging heart. Her blood was running like white-water rapids, and there was a roaring in her ears. "He has another girl; he has my neighbor's daughter." Greer's voice cracked, but she went on. "When I first met them, I 'saw' the girl; she was in trouble, surrounded by danger. Then my . . ." Greer hesitated; she didn't want to bring Joshua into it without his consent. "Then I saw Joy with the eye over her."

Sterling's face was incredulous—not disgusted or afraid, but utterly surprised. So Greer turned to Dario, who she knew would believe her, would understand. "Dario, he has Whitney's daughter; he has Joy. The man who branded that girl"—she pointed a finger at the flyer on the window—"has Joy."

Dario's face was frozen as well, but his was an expression of pathos. "Oh, Jesus Christ, no." He took two deep breaths and then seemed to pull himself together. Sterling was still frozen. "Okay, what do we do?"

Greer glanced at Sterling as if to have a last look at what happiness could have been like, and then she said, "I have to call the police."

Now Sterling spoke up. "And tell them *what* exactly? They're going to think you're insane!"

"Probably," Greer said, turning to look at him directly. Her chest felt spongy but resilient, as though anything that hit her now would both be absorbed and bounce away. "But what else can I do? Maybe I can help them in some way. I don't know. I just know that when I saw what was going to happen to Sarah, I didn't do anything, and she died. I can't let that happen again. I have to try!" The tears welled up in her voice as she spoke, the frustration and the pain imploding in her.

"Okay, okay," Dario soothed. "Let me turn my clients over to Jonathan, have Celia cancel all our afternoon appointments, and we'll go to the police."

"No, Dario!" Greer interjected. "Not you. There's nothing you can do, and there's no point in complicating things." Dario started to object, but she insisted. "Just me. You stay here and run things. I'll call you if I need you. Have Celia cancel my afternoon."

Dario nodded resignedly and hurried away, leaving Sterling standing awkwardly next to a distraught Greer.

She took a deep breath to steady herself and then said, "Thank you for telling me about the girl. I understand how weird this is, and I don't blame you for thinking what you think."

Sterling looked into those green eyes, made brighter with tears the way dewdrops on leaves intensified the color, and he saw nothing but sincere honesty there. She believed what she was saying. He smiled kindly. She thought it looked like the sort of smile you gave to a confused child. "Who knows?" he said. "Maybe you can help them. But may I offer one word of caution?"

She sighed, her tiny hope that he might understand rushing away from her with a sound in her ears like wind. "Of course."

"Talk to her parents first. If I were them, I wouldn't want to hear from a stranger that a psychic thought my child was in the hands of a killer." He stood looking at her for a moment, and then turned and walked away.

She looked after him, filled with a new, equally ghastly fear.

How would she tell Luke and Whitney?

Chapter 34

At school, Joshua was distracted and distant. It was almost impossible to concentrate. Finally, feigning continued illness, he left before his last class and headed for home, praying the whole way that Joy had returned while he was at school, that she had slept off another drunk on another lounge chair and awoken to a hangover and a hazy new day.

But when he rounded the shoulder of the canyon, the sight of multiple police cars in the shared parking area greeted him with a sobering dose of reality. Pulling the bike in between them and almost letting it drop to the ground, he ran up the stairs inside. "Mom?" he called out, not caring that his voice sounded high and girlish. "Mom, are you okay?"

Greer appeared in the doorway to the living room. "I'm fine, honey; I'm in here." Behind her he could see several uniformed officers and two men who were obviously detectives.

His voice rose to a broken croak. "Joy?"

Greer shook her head sadly. "No news. But, Joshua, I told the police what *I* saw." She stressed the *I*, and he immediately understood that she had taken on his visions. He was both deeply grateful and shaken. Even if they could help Joy, the police would think his mom was nuts. Or worse, suspect her.

"Mom, why?"

She came to him and put her arms around him. He was taller than her now, but it was comforting nonetheless. "Because I saw the figure of a flaming eye over the girl whose poster they put up in the shop, and it turned out that she was branded with an eye." Greer felt the shock wave go through Joshua as he put two and two together.

"*You* saw the figure of an eye?" He felt his mother nod succinctly. She wanted to be clear that she had *also* seen the shape, and was not just claiming his vision. The next thought made his stomach flip upside down. "Branded?" He whispered the question.

She pulled away enough to look straight at him. She didn't need to tell him what that news implied and how it related to the fact that he had seen the image of an eye over Joy. "I have to help them if I can. I'm sorry if this is hard for you." She turned to the men in the room, addressing one in particular. "Detective Sheridan, this is my son, Joshua. He and Joy Whitehorse are friends."

"Hello, Joshua, I'd like to talk to you in a little while, if that's okay."

Joshua felt the bottom drop out of his stomach. "Sure, whenever," he muttered. "I'll be up in my room." He moved quickly to the stairs, away from the prying eyes of the policemen. Something about the skepticism and suspicion he saw there made him feel creepy and naked, as though they knew something about him that he didn't. He closed the door and, for the first time, turned the brass key in the lock.

Greer turned back to the detective. "Now, I need to ask you something," she said to him.

Detective Sheridan was a short, stocky man. Too many years of eating junk food, and multiple unsuccessful attempts to quit smoking, had left his skin looking rough and unhealthy. His receding hairline made him look older than his forty-six years. The top of his bare head was discolored with light brown spots, variations in pigmentation that, because his pate was shiny, reminded Greer of oil on water, but the rest of him was hard—rocklike, in fact—and he sat so still that he might have been made of granite.

He was leaning forward with his elbows on his knees, waiting for her question with skepticism marbleized on his face.

"*Where* was the brand? The paper said it was on her cheek. That isn't right, is it?" she asked.

Sheridan's eyes dropped to his pad, and he flipped back and forth a couple of pages as though he were searching for something. The activity was completely pointless; the response was not written there. It was seared onto his memory, another in a long line of visuals that he would revisit again and again in the moment between sleep and waking, when he was unable to defend himself with practiced, well-constructed distractions. The eye wound, blistered and scabbed, right on the young woman's forehead, scarring her for life, if she lived, like a monstrous Cyclops.

"Why do you ask?"

"Because that's not right." Greer looked directly at him and prayed that she would be wrong, that this was all a product of her fear and imagination, that nothing meant that Joy was with this maniac, subject to his twisted whims. "It's on her forehead, isn't it?" Slowly she raised her right hand and placed her middle finger on the spot just above but directly between her eyebrows, where she had felt the burning. "Here."

Sheridan felt a strange thrill go through him, followed quickly by an overdose of suspicion. He had heard of psychics helping police before, but he had never thought it was real. This woman was either real or—his practical brain insisted loudly that his second instinct was far more probable—she was connected to the crime.

"How do you know that?" he asked, dropping the pretense.

Greer closed her eyes and swayed slightly as the reality of it rocked the room around her. She was right. "Because when I saw the image, I felt a burning here." She touched the spot again. "Sometimes that happens when I get a reading on an impending injury or future illness. I sense it in my body. Usually it's just a tingling sensation, but this . . ." She hesitated, searching for the words. "This was more . . . it was stronger than I've ever felt a physical sensation." She thought about the other things that made it stronger: that both she and Joshua had seen the eye, and the detail that she had connected herself to Joy with the bracelet, but she mentioned neither of these things to Detective Sheridan. She had something else to ask.

"Why was the article wrong? Was that a mistake?"

Sheridan sighed, thinking his answer out before he gave it. "Because, very often, a sociopath who leaves a mark does it to be showy. They want to read about it in the paper; they *want* it reported and want it to be reported *correctly*. The chances are this guy"—he paused and looked away from Greer deliberately—"had a reason for doing this. He'll be upset that the papers got it wrong. So, I give the wrong info to the papers, they publish it, and I hope to help flush the guy out by having him call in, to me or the reporters, and brag or insist that they get the details right. It's a long shot, but with no leads it's one worth taking."

The detective sat back slowly, like a boulder rolling into place, and clicked his pen twice. "And now you call me"—his eyes shifted back to her—"and tell me that I got it wrong." He let the statement hang, each word heavy as a large stone, ready to fall and obliterate everything below them.

It took Greer a minute to put it together. When she did she felt as though a fog had inundated her body, a thick, heavy haze. "Yes." Greer looked directly at him. "I assumed that you would have to suspect me."

Sheridan looked at her with unwavering eyes. "How long ago did you move into the community?"

"About a week and a half ago," Greer told him.

"And in that time two girls have disappeared."

"One of them is my neighbor's child."

"Exactly."

Greer waited, her body tingling with a million pin-points of apprehension.

"What was the name of your business again?" Sheridan asked, as though he'd forgotten.

"Eye of the Beholder," Greer answered by rote, and then heard the word *eye* come back at her. "But you can't think that has anything to do with this!"

"It's an awfully big coincidence."

"No!" Greer told him emphatically. "The eye that I saw was something like an eye-shaped talisman. The kind that superstitious people sometimes carry to ward off evil. Only this would be the opposite of warding it off, wouldn't it?"

"I'd say so." He was looking at her with one eyebrow a fraction of an inch higher than the other one.

Greer said pointedly, "I'm trying to help you. Why would I do that if I were somehow responsible?"

"Oh, you'd be surprised by what people do. And I don't think it was you," Detective Sheridan told her slowly, watching her hands, her shoulders, looking for a tic or an unconscious movement. "Not unless you can give me a sperm sample."

Greer was both relieved and revolted. The thought of Joy—or any woman—being sexually assaulted left her furious and weak. "Oh," was all she said, "I hadn't thought of that."

What the detective said next was the last thing that

Greer *had* thought of, the last thing she had even considered.

The hard man with smart, tired eyes looked at Greer and said in an even voice that would not be questioned, "Could you ask your son to come down here, please?"

Chapter 35

After Joshua turned the key in the lock, he leaned his back against the door. He was sweating, panicking. He realized that up until now he had hoped that it might all be unreal, hallucinations, a nightmare. But now there was proof.

His mother had said that the girl they found had been branded with an eye, and he had seen an eye hovering over Joy. There must be a connection.

He paced the room, finding it impossible to be still. Forcing himself to stop and try to calm down, he placed both hands on the back of his wooden desk chair, gripping the knobs until his knuckles were white, and looked out across to Joy's window.

Empty, dark, nothing.

The sound of a car driving up, moving too quickly on the rutted road, drew his glance away. A hatchback Toyota sporting a few rust stains pulled up behind the police cars and a woman got out. Hesitantly, as though she were afraid the black-and-white vehicles might bite her, the heavyset woman dressed all in black circumnavigated them and went to the door of Luke's house.

Joshua turned away, hearing only distantly the sound of the woman knocking. "I have to try to help them," his mother had said. He had to try too.

But how? He'd never done this before. The visions had come uninvited, and he had pushed them away. How would he go about calling them up? He thought about the girl—what had Natalie said her name was? Zoe? He tried to imagine how it would feel to be branded, and a halting half breath, half cry came from his parted lips. *Jesus Christ.*

He had to try.

Desperately his eyes scanned the room, finally fixing on the picture of the moon in the Ansel Adams photograph. With no other ideas, he placed the chair in the middle of the floor facing the picture and sat down. He watched the moon, trying to clear away anything but the image of it in his mind. He let his eyes trace the imperfect circle of its orb and he began to think, *Where are you?*

It happened just as suddenly as when it had come upon him unaware, but because he had been searching for it, it was less frightening. There was very little to see, really. Most of the room around him went darker. Joshua closed his eyes and entered into a feeling of being in a different place. It was dark there, and small. There was a line of light down low; Joshua could see very little, but he could feel fear, claustrophobia. At first he couldn't place it, and then he remembered hiding when he was small, playing with his father, playing hide-and-seek, and the light creeping under the closet door.

Joy was in a closet.

This was not a game; the door was locked, and Joy was trapped inside. Reeling back with the shock of it, Joshua almost pulled away, but something else was showing itself to him. Not in that place, not in any place that he could identify. It was more like a presence that was there with him, but not on the same plane as the room. It was the figure of a girl, not Joy, but a girl about Joy's age, with shorter, lighter hair and a smiling face. He could clearly make out her features this time. They were pleasant features, but intent, and as she looked at him she gestured continually, pointing up and to the left.

A sharp rapping at the door jerked Joshua's eyes open, and it took a few seconds for him to reconcile himself to the fact that he was in his room, and the figure of the girl was gone. He was sure that he had seen, almost as though through her own eyes, what Joy had been seeing and feeling in a dark closet, but it had given him no further clues.

The knocking came again, and someone tried the door. The lock held.

Joshua crossed to it, his equilibrium slightly askew, and rotated the key until the old lock clicked open.

Somehow, he was not surprised to see the detective.

Chapter 36

Joy had fallen into a fitful sleep with her head leaning into the corner of the tight space and her knees drawn up to her chest. The sound of a truck pulling up outside sent her bolt upright, her eyes open, but still seeing nothing in the dark closet except the line of dim daylight from the crack beneath it.

Please, God, she thought, *let it be someone, anyone, besides him.* But the sound of the heavy boots on the deck outside sent the hope spinning toward the ground like a songbird filled with buckshot. She cowered back farther into the darkness. He'd locked her in this morning, shortly after dawn, when he went to bed for a couple of hours. When she'd heard him leave she had tried everything she could think of to get out, but finally slumped back and sobbed into her hands. How could she have been so stupid?

Joy heard him move around the house as though completely unaware of her, the clinking of the keys at his belt always accompanying the heavy footsteps. She heard the microwave go on, and then a radio. She waited, listening furiously. Dishes clinked as they were washed, dried, and put away.

The leaden footfalls and mockingly mellifluous song of the keys approached the closet door and stopped on the other side. Joy's heartbeat pounded in her ears so loudly that she could hardly hear the keys jangle as one was inserted into the lock. She covered her eyes as the light from the room fell on her. He was a huge, black silhouette towering above her.

"Well, hello, there. Have you been a good little girl?" he asked her, as though she had spent the morning at kindergarten. Joy did not respond; she was shaking, and she couldn't look up at him.

"Why don't you come on out?" He reached in and pulled Joy, not unkindly, to her feet. With her pupils dilated from the extended unnatural darkness, the light was painful, but she looked up into his eyes. Maybe last night had been a nightmare. Maybe he would be different during the day.

"I, uh, need to go to the bathroom," she muttered.

"Of course you do. Come on; I'll walk you." They went down the short hall, Joy stumbling slightly as her legs cramped from being folded up for so long. She went in and, closing the door behind her, fumbled for a lock, but there was none. She heard a low laugh, as though he had known she would try that.

In spite of her embarrassment, she desperately needed to relieve herself, so she went to the toilet and, watching the door the whole time, lowered her pants and sat as quickly as she could. He didn't come in, and she hurriedly zipped herself up again. Going to the sink, she let water run into her cupped palm and gulped it greedily. Then she looked at herself in the mirror.

What she saw shocked her. One side of her face was bruised, slightly yellowish, and beginning to turn purple. That was the first place he had hit her. They'd stayed up most of the night doing drugs, and as the hours had gone on his personality had changed, sliding from pleasant and respectful down to base, crude. His musings had seemed directed at disconcerting her, and she had tried to act unaffected, until it had become impossible not to be disturbed at the depth of depravity he talked about so casually. This was a very different person from the one she had met before, the one who had flattered her and taken her for a ride on his bike. By dawn she'd known she was in trouble, worse trouble than anything she'd ever known. She'd said she needed to go home and he'd told her no, he wanted her to stay for a while. She'd tried to pretend he was joking, feigning a laugh, and that was when his hand had made contact with her face, sending her into the side of the sofa. After that she had sat cradling her head while he explained to her that things would be different now. That she couldn't go until he said so. She had expected him to rape her, but the drugs seemed to have rendered him incapable.

So it had been the closet. Glancing at the small, narrow window by the shower, she guessed it was early afternoon, but the overcast day made it hard to tell. The window was too small for her to fit through. The only thing she could think of was to try to talk her way out of this, or distract him somehow long enough to get away, to run back for help. But help, she remembered, was a good way off. She was still vibrating from amphetamines and fear, and her brain was addled with the residual effect of the drugs, the lack of sleep, and the terror of her situation. She needed to buy some time.

With a rasping breath, she turned the knob and opened the door. He was leaning against the wall of the hallway, as though he were waiting for her outside a public restroom.

"Better?" he asked.

"Uh, yeah. Thanks." He draped an arm around her shoulders and steered her back into the living room.

The closet door stood open the way he'd left it. Joy tried to avoid looking at the gaping dark hole and what it foreboded.

"Are you hungry?"

Her stomach felt sick, but it also burned from lack of food, and she knew eating would help clear her mind. "Yeah, kind of."

He sat her down in the kitchen chair farthest from the door. A surreptitious glance told her that the bolt was locked and there was no key in it, though she knew she wouldn't have made it very far. He made her a peanut butter sandwich and a glass of milk. She ate it slowly while he sat across from her, lit a cigarette, and smoked it leisurely, watching her with a kind of pleased power. She tried not to cry, but the peanut butter stuck on the lump in her throat, and she forced sips of the milk to wash it down. She could get through only about half of it. She wanted to ask for a cigarette to calm her nerves, but she doubted it would help much.

When she finished, he washed her plate and cup and put them carefully away, then came and stood in front of her.

"Now, I've got to go back to work for a few hours, and then I'll come home and we'll have a little more fun."

Joy's lids fluttered, blinking back tears at the malicious sound of the word *fun.* "I think I'd better go home. My dad will be really worried about me. Maybe I could come back later."

He laughed. "No, I don't think so. I told you, I'll let you know when it's time to go." He reached down and unbuckled his belt. "But before I leave, I think you need to show me what you can do. You've been wanting to show me you're a big girl."

Reaching behind Joy, he turned her chair so that she was directly facing his crotch, and then he unzipped his pants, grabbed Joy by the back of the hair, and forced her to face him.

"Time to play," he said. "And then the toy goes back in the closet, all neat and tidy."

Joy was frozen with fear. She could think only one thing.

Daddy, help me.

Chapter 37

Luke sat rigidly in the kitchen chair. Whitney kept one hand on his knee, but it was unresponsive. He was locked in a kind of anguished hell from which there would be no escape or relief until he got his daughter back. *And now,* Whitney thought, *he has to deal with this.*

"So she just disappeared? You have no idea where she went?" Pam asked accusingly. Joy's mother was a heavyset woman, with yellowed teeth and lines around her mouth from sucking on one cigarette after another. Her body looked as though it had been used up a long time ago, like a pillow in which the stuffing had pilled and separated into lumpy parts. She wore far too much makeup around her bloodshot eyes, and her voice was both shrill and taunting.

"We told you," Whitney offered again, struggling to keep her voice level. "She left for school, she went to the bus stop, and then she didn't show up in any of her classes. She's been late so often that they waited until about one o'clock to call me."

"Why didn't they call me?" Pam spit at Whitney. "*I'm* her mother."

A thousand responses flew through Whitney's head, the foremost being, *Because they know you don't care,* but she held her tongue.

Luke stirred himself enough to speak. "Listen, Pam, I know this is hard for you too, but the important thing is to get her back, not to accuse each other." He finished the line as though he would like very much to accuse her, but he was beyond that. "I need to know if you have any ideas about where she might have gone, or who she might have contacted."

Pam's eyes narrowed to rheumy slits. "Don't you dare try to put this on me. She ran away from you—and her." She threw a contemptuous look to Whitney, who took a deep breath and clenched her hands into fists to try to contain her outrage.

"The detective will be back over here in a moment, and he's going to ask you all these questions," Luke went on as though she hadn't spoken. The truth was, he didn't care how angry or spiteful the woman was, only that she might be of some use. "So maybe you could use this time constructively to make a list of who she's been hanging out with."

"I don't know!" Pam blew smoke out of both nostrils and sagged back in her chair like an old dragon with glutinous scales. "She's always off somewhere. I'm not a goddamned private eye."

"No," Whitney said coldly, mimicking Pam's earlier tone. "*You* are her mother."

Pam held up the hand with the cigarette, pointing a smoking finger at Whitney, and her voice rose viciously. "Don't fucking talk to me like that!"

"Stop it." Luke's voice was commanding and flat. "This is not about you, Pam; this is about our daughter." Pam fell silent in the wake of his cold strength and fury. She looked down and pretended to be disinterested, but his power was impossible to deny. "Now," Luke continued, "you think about everyone who might possibly be able to help us, especially any of the scum you let her hang around with."

Pam snorted, but there was admission in it. Not

guilt—she seemed unredeemable in terms of taking responsibility—but there was no denying that she knew Joy had been hanging out with a bad element.

"So tell me why"—she folded one arm under her hanging breasts and raised the one holding the cigarette up in front of her face—"are the detectives talking to the neighbors?"

Luke and Whitney exchanged a look. Whitney decided to field the question. "Because she's friends with them. She goes to school with the boy, and I'm sure they want to find out if they saw or heard anything."

Pam snorted, a thick, phlegmy sound, and said, "She fucking the boy?"

Whitney grabbed hold of Luke's shoulder as he started to rise, but she might have been a sweater draped casually across it for all the effect it had. "Luke, no!" she pleaded urgently.

But Luke had stopped himself, standing just over Pam, whose face, still half smirking, was frozen with fear.

"Listen to me," he said, his voice rumbling and dangerous. "If I find out you and your drugs had anything to do with this, if you've involved her with people who will hurt her . . ."

Pam's shaking fingers moved slowly toward her mouth, and she took a deliberate drag of nicotine as she looked up at her ex-husband. "You'll what? Take her away? Have me arrested?" A smile played at the edges of her nervous mouth.

"No," Luke said. He leaned forward, took the cigarette out of her hand, and crushed it, burning end and all, in his bare hand. "I'll kill you."

Chapter 38

The truck with the faded PAUL'S PLUMBING painted on both front doors pulled up noisily and parked in front of the shop. Dario watched it in his mirror and winced slightly. He wished that they would park that monster somewhere other than right in front, but he didn't think it would be very PC to mention it.

Only one of the brothers got out, the younger one. He pulled a large toolbox and a few pieces of miscellaneous chrome pipe connectors out of the back and headed for the door with his hands full.

Celia spotted him coming and rushed to open the door for him, her face flushing slightly. She'd noticed him when he was there before working with his brother; he was handsome enough to make her feel excited in a swirling, scary, roller-coaster way. There was also something about his quiet-outlaw reticence that made her curious and interested, challenged to break through the toughness and make him notice her. She smiled shyly, and he nodded his thanks as he passed her.

As he made his way down the salon floor, he kept his eyes focused on the back, where he was headed to work on the new sinks. Dario spoke to him as he grew level. "Hello, Army." There was no reply, only a slight shift in his eyes and head. "Where's Paul?"

Army stopped and stood awkwardly with his weight on one leg in an unsuccessful attempt at a cocky stance. He looked as though he had arrived late for class and while trying to sneak in unnoticed had been called out by the teacher.

"He's on another job. I'm going to finish this up so you don't have to wait anymore."

"Thank you. Do you need anything?"

Army shook his head, but glanced up to where Celia was watching him.

"You want a cup of coffee or tea? How about a sandwich?"

"No." Army looked embarrassed to be asked. "Nothing. I just had lunch."

"If you do, help yourself from the kitchen, or just ask Celia." Dario went back to his work and made a mental note to try to have a conversation with that boy. If ever someone needed socialization, he thought to himself, it was Army Newman.

Army strode to the back, his heavy work boots squeaking slightly as the rubber soles gripped the highly polished hardwood floor.

Jonathan was putting color on one of Dario's other clients in the next chair. Dario watched him check out the plumber as he headed to the back.

"Now, now," Dario scolded. "I don't think our young Mr. Newman plays with boys."

Jonathan sighed. "Oh, I know, but there's something about men with tight bodies who have been in prison that I find very distracting. And that work belt!"

Any other day Dario would have laughed and scolded him, but today his preoccupation and worry caused him to give only a scant recriminating look and turn back to his cut. "Do you want layers? Or just straight across the back?" he asked the young woman in his chair.

Outside, another truck pulled up and parked next to Army's. Pistol got out of the official postal vehicle and walked into the store. Dario watched warily as he handed over the mail to Celia and then seemed to settle himself in for a cozy chat. Excusing himself from his client, Dario strode purposefully to the front.

Pistol was in full swing. "Yeah, I always go home for lunch. It's on my route, so I can stop in and make myself something good. Real private too; you should see it," Pistol told her. To Dario his tone sounded far too suggestive.

"Is this all the mail today?" Dario asked, picking up the small stack and thumbing through it, making his presence felt.

"Yeah, light day." Pistol let his eyes sweep the salon. "Not for you, though—looks busy."

Dario leaned against the counter and crossed his arms pointedly. "We're *all* really very busy."

But Pistol was not one to take a hint, subtle or not. He seemed almost as happy to converse with Dario as with Celia. "Did you hear another girl's missing?" His eyes held a strange light, as though he were personally proud of having the information to impart.

"Yes, and I don't think it's an appropriate conversation," Dario said, deliberately glancing at Celia.

But Pistol rolled on. "I don't have her on my route, but she's the neighbor of a buddy of mine. He's all broken up about it, known her since she was a little girl. But if you ask me"—Pistol's voice dropped to a conspiratorial tone—"she was headed for trouble."

Dario bristled. He straightened up and was about to speak his mind when he heard Army behind him. "Excuse me; I'm going to have to shut the water off for about five minutes so I can hook up the sinks."

Dario's impressive bulk had blocked Pistol's view of Army's approach. As Dario opened up to include Army in the small circle, Pistol and Army got a look at each other. Pistol's icy smile and Army's cold stare of recognition were both so blatant that they smacked together and frosted the reception area, chilling both Celia and Dario.

"Well, well, well. Look who's here." Pistol's voice was an immature taunt.

Dario had no idea what was going on, but he wasn't going to put up with it—or subject Celia to it. "If you don't mind, Pistol, we all need to get back to work, and that means you, Celia," he told her pointedly. "Can you go to the back and show Army where the water shutoff is, please?" He waited until the two of them had walked away and then turned to the postal worker.

"Okay, listen. I like to be polite, but the time has come for me to be direct. From now on I would like you to drop off the mail, take the outgoing, and don't hang around. I'm sorry, but I don't want a lot of bad news dropped off with my bills. Do you understand?"

Pistol was not a small man, but he looked up at the six-four Dario with a look of surprise. "I didn't mean to offend you."

"You haven't offended me," Dario lied. "I would just prefer it if you would do your job, and let us—and my receptionist—do hers."

Looking completely thrown and offended, Pistol gathered the mail and continued to mutter. "Sorry. I don't know what the problem is if a guy can't just be friendly."

"I don't mind 'friendly,' " Dario told him. "But I'm very protective of my employees, and I think that Celia is a little young for some of the things you say to her."

Pistol looked legitimately affronted, and it immediately turned to the defensive. "I was just making conversation." His eyes flickered to the back, where Army and Celia were walking away. "And if you're worried about her, I'd keep an eye on *that* guy. I've seen him picking up a girl younger than her from the high school on the back of that piece-of-crap bike he rides."

"Thank you for the information." Dario filed the alarming revelation warily even as he acknowledged it. "But I need to point out that that is another example of your not being particularly discreet. And believe me"—Dario tried to soothe the wounded mailman with an attempt at humor—"being a hairdresser who hears things women won't tell their psychiatrists, discretion is something I know a little bit about."

The sentiment seemed lost on Pistol, who, Dario realized, probably didn't know the meaning of the word *discretion*, much less how to behave with it. Obviously offended, Pistol left the salon muttering under his breath something about people who thought they were better than everyone else.

Concerned, his chest churning with the aftereffects of the necessary confrontation, Dario returned to his client, who was treating Jonathan to a lengthy monologue about her loser boyfriend, who was cheating and drinking and living off of her income. Jonathan finally cut in ruthlessly, "Why don't you dump him?"

Dario watched the look of surprised shock on the client's face and gave Jonathan a tiny, resigned shake of the head. He, of course, had been thinking the same thing, but he found that people wanted to talk, not hear advice.

"You have your reasons to do what you do," Dario interjected smoothly to the shell-shocked young woman. "You know what's right in your heart." He paused and watched his client in the mirror. The look of dawn's awakening on her face told him that she was having an embarrassed epiphany. Dario swept her out of the chair and gave her a faux push.

"Remember"—he reached out and ruffled her new cut

with his fingers, giving it a sexy, tousled look, then softened his voice and said sincerely—"*you* are the prize."

She looked up at the handsome, masterful Dario
and her face lit up with an impish grin. If he thought
so, it must be true.

Dario didn't bother to reprimand Jonathan. Sometimes, in fact, he was grateful that Jonathan possessed
that sharp tongue of truth. Worried about Greer, he
looked up to the front. Celia wasn't there.

"Get Ms. Lender shampooed, if we have water.
Otherwise, let's go ahead and start mixing the color
for Susan's streaks," he told Jonathan, and walked
around the partition into the shampoo area.

Celia stood watching Army. With a glance, Dario
took in her enamored body language and Army's
seeming indifference.

"Celia, see if you can get Greer on the phone at
home for me, please."

The girl looked startled and caught, but she hurried
away. Dario went to stand where he could see what
Army was doing with a huge wrench, which was at-
taching a U-bend to the pipe jutting from the wall.

"How long do you think it'll be before the water's
back on?"

"Five minutes. I just have to put the faucets on, and
then you'll be set." He reached into his toolbox and
picked up a smaller-size wrench. Dario glanced down.
It was the cleanest tool kit he'd ever seen. Everything
was in its proper place; not a smudge of grease or a
spot of rust showed on anything.

"Wow, that's impressive." Dario gestured to the
box when Army glanced questioningly up at him.

"It's easier to find what you need if you keep it
neat."

"You could use those tools for surgery. Hell, I've
known gay men who would call that anal."

Army was either embarrassed or unaffected by the observation; he did not comment.

Dario decided that a direct approach would be the only one likely to produce results. "So, our Celia seems to be slightly enamored of you."

Army grunted slightly with the effort of tightening the connector piece. "She's too young for me."

"Really?" Dario said. "What about the girl at the high school?"

Army didn't respond or turn, but there was a slight delay in his movement, as though he were in a film that had stuck on one frame for a fraction of a second longer than it should. Then he continued to work as he asked, "Who told you that?"

"Our friendly postal worker. He seems to think that part of his job is delivering unwanted telegrams, along with the mail."

"Yeah," Army said, still not looking at Dario. "I noticed that."

"And I noticed that he doesn't seem to like you much."

Army replaced the wrench precisely into its holder between one slightly larger and one slightly smaller on either side. "Well, I don't like him either."

Dario leaned forward. "Why not?"

Army pulled the faucet and handles out of a box on the floor and began to connect them. "Let's just say he's not exactly Shadow Hills' leading citizen."

"What's wrong with him?" Dario asked.

Finally Army looked up at Dario and a thinly veiled exasperated sigh escaped him. "Listen," he said, "it's no secret that I did time. I met some real interesting people in there. One thing about prison is, it'll change your point of view. Things you thought were right, they aren't anymore. I don't talk about other people now, because it doesn't matter anyway, and the only thing worse than the people who do bad shit is the people who snitch on them."

Dario was watching him intently. "So, if you knew someone was up to something, you wouldn't say anything about it?"

Army's eyes flickered. A memory of another time, of believing in something better than what he had experienced in life, poked at the back of his consciousness like a sharp stick in his spine. But the inclination passed and he looked away.

"What's the point?" He shrugged. "If somebody's saying shit about me, it doesn't matter if I'm guilty or not; everybody just assumes I am. Fine. And who's going to care if I rat on somebody else? I'm not exactly your star character witness." He smiled, sadly at first, and then the smile and his eyes flattened out like vital statistics dying away on an ER monitor.

Dario gave Army a hard look in return, not sure how to interpret what Army had told him. Then finally, half in support and half as a fair warning, he said, "People do care, Army. *I* care."

Noting that Army did not look away or speak, Dario added, "And I think maybe you do too." He narrowed his eyes and regarded the younger man for a long moment, weighing the moral fiber of this man who'd been taught by experience to disregard what was right. Who, most likely, had learned that to survive he had to hurt people and feel nothing. Then, with his voice steeled with intent, Dario said, "But then again, maybe you don't."

From a distant, forgotten place in Army's soul, a voice, old and honest, told him that somewhere along the way he'd gone very wrong.

Chapter 39

The Rattler's obnoxious, taxi-yellow Hummer pulled into the manager's parking space outside the bank, overlapping the spaces on both sides enough to make it difficult if not impossible for anyone to get in or out of their cars. Leah watched as Vince stepped down out of the vehicle he now reserved for rainy or cold days, and thought for the ten thousandth time what an asshole he was. She glanced at her watch. He'd taken a long lunch. Remembering Steve Kenner's warning that Vince should spend more time working and less time off, she toyed with the idea of reporting him, but Vince would just find a way to use it to make her look bad.

So she sat seething with frustration as he sauntered in, a toothpick in his teeth, the ostrich leather of his cowboy boots peeking out from under his expensive suit. She knew now, of course, where he was getting all his luxury money from, but there was nothing she could do about it.

Not yet. But she noticed, as she watched him from the corner of her eye, that he looked tired, slightly used up. She guessed that the drinking and now probably the drugs were taking their toll. Good—that meant that sooner or later he'd make a mistake.

The phone on her desk rang. Distracted, she picked it up. "Leah Falconer," she intoned.

There was a long enough moment of hesitation to make Leah wonder if anyone was there, and then, "Hi, this is . . . uh, Terry. I met you the other day."

Leah's spine straightened up as though she were a marionette yanked suddenly into use by capable hands. "Yes, hello."

"Do you remember me?"

Leah thought of the sunglasses hiding the Technicolor skin around her eye, the bruised wrists. "Yes. I do." She glanced around; no one seemed to be taking any notice of her. Why should they? Nonetheless, she tried to keep her voice businesslike. "What can I do for you?"

"You said I could call." The tremulous voice dropped off.

"And I meant it." Leah hoped she sounded more confident than she felt.

"Do you think maybe we could meet sometime?"

"Of course. Um, how about tomorrow, on the High Street, there's a coffee shop next to the new salon."

"I know it. What time?"

"It'll have to be early, say, seven thirty?"

"Okay, I'll try to be there."

The line went dead and Leah placed the receiver carefully back in its cradle while her mind and her emotions were both screaming at her not to do this, to stay out of it. *Don't get involved! Let her screw up her own life!*

But she knew she couldn't do that. Even as she sat at her desk, trembling slightly with trepidation and doubt, an indignant rage surged up in her and filled her with blind, reckless intent. Her fury, fueled by the gross indignities and powerlessness she felt, grabbed hold of her controls and took off into a night sky with no maps or instruments. She might be too afraid to challenge Vince for herself; she might have been stupid not to see the kind of person he was when she got involved with him in the first place; but she'd be damned if she'd let someone else walk right into the same ugly, twisted trap.

Not if there was anything she could do about it.

Chapter 40

Fifteen bags of crystal methamphetamine had been found in a plastic CD case in Joshua Sands's room. Detective Sheridan noted uncomfortably that the boy's surprise was either very well acted or legitimate. When Sheridan questioned where he'd gotten the drugs, the boy had stammered out his ignorance, and then an odd look had come over him and he had refused to speak any more.

It all struck him as incongruous because both Greer and Joshua had invited the detective to search the boy's room and the house, saying that they had nothing to hide. Sheridan had opted to stick to procedure. Based on the mother's knowledge of the brand on Zoe Caldwell and the fact that the boy had been the last person to see Joy Whitehorse, it had taken him only an hour to get a search warrant.

The boy had been read his rights and then, because he was still a minor, his mother had been allowed to accompany him to the hospital for a blood test. Sheridan would have the blood tested for drug use and a type match on the sperm samples they had taken from Zoe Caldwell. The boy had an alibi for the night of her assault, but it was from his mother, who said he'd been alone in his room, and she could easily be lying to cover for him.

But why, if it was the boy, would she have called him? Sheridan shifted uncomfortably in the hard plastic chair outside the exam room. It was possible that she knew her son had done this and was trying to divert them away from him, but if she was making it up then she should have had a more substantial story, or at least someone to throw the suspicion on. Why bring the police into their house and call attention to the connections to the neighbor who was missing? She seemed smarter that that.

It just didn't add up. It couldn't be the boy; and while he sat here, the real maniac had another victim. If it wasn't the Whitehorse girl, if she had run away of her own accord, then Sheridan was sure that there would be another. He thought of the blistered and blackening mark on the first victim's forehead and felt the heat of the burn in his stomach.

She was here in the hospital—Zoe Caldwell, still in intensive care and not likely to leave it alive. He'd met the mother, a pale, tragic woman whose only hope had been that she would sneak through life unnoticed, transparent, without major incident or pain. Sheridan felt certain that this crime would kill her too. What mother could go on to live a normal life after this kind of horror? It didn't take a detective to answer that question.

He wanted the drug screen right away; the type match with the sperm sample would take a couple of weeks, and he didn't know if he had that much time. He squirmed to try to ease the pain in his gut and reached into his pocket for the package of antacid, but found only an empty wrapper. He stood, intending to go to the pharmacy and buy more, when the door to the lab opened and Greer and Joshua Sands both appeared.

The boy was holding his left arm crooked up tightly, and a wad of cotton peeked from the crease. Sheridan expected the mother to regard him with contempt, but she looked at him and smiled understandingly.

"All done," she said. "Now, do we go home or what?"

"We wait a little." Sheridan regarded the two of them, who both watched him calmly, without accusation, waiting to hear what they needed to do next, two people with the naive absolute confidence of innocence.

Sheridan had a thought. It was no more than a hunch, but then, he didn't have anything else. "Let's go down to the main waiting room. I want to get the initial results right away. We'll wait there."

They headed out of ER and down a long hallway, until they came to a set of double doors marked CRITICAL CARE, AUTHORIZED VISITORS AND HOSPITAL PERSONNEL ONLY. Flashing his badge at the dull-faced nurse behind the Plexiglas partition, he opened the door and he gestured for them to go through ahead of him. "We'll cut through this way."

Sheridan deliberately walked a few steps behind them, not speaking, but counting the ward numbers on his left. Two more, one more—suddenly Greer pulled up, stopping so abruptly that he almost walked into her. Raising both hands to her chest, she started to breathe quickly and shallowly. She spun to face him, almost accusingly.

"She's here," she whispered. "Zoe Caldwell is here." Swiveling slowly in place as though she were turning to face a ghost, she raised one hand toward the ward door. "In there."

Sheridan watched as she closed her eyes and tears started in the corners, streaming almost uncontrollably down her face. "Her mother is with her." Without warning or indication, the woman's almost eerily green eyes flew open, and she said. "She's going to try to kill herself."

Sheridan moved rapidly to the door and pushed it

open. A nurse looked up quickly from where she was fastening a drip bag over the patient. In a chair next to the bed, a woman with gray hair sat with her head bowed, immobile. She seemed to be beyond noticing anyone's presence.

Sheridan breathed a sigh of relief, then backed away from the personal pain, letting the door swing slowly shut on the sad scenario. The woman might very well try to kill herself, but she wasn't doing it now.

Greer was watching her son when the detective turned to her. Her tears were still wet on her cheeks, but there was awe in her eyes. Sheridan followed her look and found himself speechless again as it began to dawn on him that he was in the presence of something more than what he could see and perceive.

Joshua had positioned himself so that he could see through the glass in the door to the first bed in the ward. Zoe Caldwell's bed. He was staring, but not at the scene before him. It was as though he were looking at a double image, the bed and the patient, the mother, and something else superimposed over the picture on his retinas. He could see two places at once, or rather, the same place but in two different yet very real dimensions.

Over the white sheets and the bleeping monitors the figure of a girl hovered. She smiled down softly at the young woman on the hospital bed, and then looked up at Joshua and nodded, as though she were acknowledging him while she was patiently waiting, helping. As he watched, the girl no one else could see reached a hand down toward the patient and then scooped it toward her chest, smiling softly at Joshua, and somehow he understood. He nodded back and then turned away.

The detective was watching him intently. Joshua tried to recover himself, to look as though nothing unusual had happened.

Greer knew that her son had seen something she couldn't, something present, but with great strength of will she restrained herself from asking him. Instead she turned to Detective Sheridan and tried to deflect his attention.

"You have to try to help that woman. Please believe me; I've never been wrong about something like this," she pleaded.

But Detective Sheridan was far too steady a man to be distracted that easily. He didn't take his gaze off of Joshua. "What did you see?" he asked him.

Joshua felt a rising panic. He couldn't be drawn into this. It didn't matter what he saw; it would help nothing. He didn't want to be on display. "Nothing," he lied. "I mean, I saw that poor girl and her mother, and it's terrible. I'm really sorry for them." That much was true.

Sheridan's granite face regarded the boy without expression. His eyes flicked once to his mother and then back again.

"Come with me."

They walked quickly to the front waiting room and then to a door marked FOR POLICE USE ONLY. The room inside was small, white, glaringly bright, and held only a few folding chairs.

"Sit down," ordered the detective.

Greer and Joshua sat. She reached across to take her son's hand; it was clammy and cold.

"All right," said Sheridan, "maybe there is something to all this; I don't know. But just in case, I need to know *anything* you know. Any details, anything that could help me."

"I told you what I know—only that the burning eye was over the girl's picture, and then . . ." Greer hesitated before going on, and Sheridan knew that the truth was in that small pause. "Then I saw the eye over Joy Whitehorse."

Detective Sheridan said nothing, just sat, unmoving,

like a solid ton of rock until Joshua found himself wondering how the chair could possibly support him.

The detective watched Joshua without speaking until Joshua couldn't take it anymore. He fumbled for words. "Mom, remember you said something else? You said that you saw someone pointing up and to the left, and that it seemed like maybe Joy was somewhere dark and small, like a closet."

Greer was watching her son with both pride and empathy. She wanted so much to relieve the abrasive pain of discovery and guilt that she sensed he was feeling. She said slowly, "Yes, I did say that, but I didn't tell the detective because I wasn't sure that it would help." She wanted to let him know that he hadn't failed Joy—or her.

Sheridan didn't take his eyes off of Joshua. He got it now. It was the kid. Both of them, but the kid was the one who could help him if this whole thing wasn't some bullshit card trick that he was falling sucker to. His stomach felt seared at both possibilities, as though the serpents that writhed there had learned to breathe fire. "Is that all she saw?" he asked the boy.

Joshua looked down at his hands, busted. "That's all she told me."

The detective leaned back and tried to release some of the burning gas from his stomach with a long, toxic exhalation. "Go home," he said. "Your son is not to leave the neighborhood for a few days. But as long as his blood comes out clean, I'm not pressing any charges." A relieved cry escaped from Greer.

"Not now, anyway," the detective amended. "I've got work to do, and if *either* of you gets any other . . . ideas, you call me. Do you understand?"

Greer nodded. "Absolutely."

"I want one question answered in return." Sheridan rocked an inch closer to Joshua. "Who gave you the drugs?"

Joshua looked up and saw a man who was tired and jaded but still trying to make a difference. At least he could help him this much. Maybe it was something. "Nobody gave them to me. I think that Joy hid them in my room when she was visiting. I didn't want to say anything because I don't want her to be in any more trouble than she is."

Sheridan snorted slightly. "Great. For a teenager to have that amount of ice means she's either dealing drugs or at least scoring them for herself and some other people. But it's very likely that the drugs are involved in some way." He stared at the blank white wall—it offered exactly the same number of clues as he already had—before turning back to Joshua and Greer. "And if what you . . . 'sense' is true, then Joy Whitehorse couldn't be in worse trouble."

Chapter 41

Luke and Whitney heard Mike's pickup truck before it got to the parking area. The whole afternoon had been spent pacing and worrying, but no news had come. They heard the sound of the heavy door open and shut.

Luke opened the door of his house to a friend who was visibly riddled with pain and apology. "Ah, Jesus, Luke," Mike said, his eyes filling with tears as the two men embraced. "I didn't know if I should intrude, but I found out what was happening at the shop; everybody's talking about it. I'm so sorry. Is there anything I can do?"

"I wish there was," Luke told him, his lips pulling back into a thin, grim line. He stepped aside so that Mike could come into the kitchen. Mike gave Whitney a long, rocking hug and they both wiped tears away. "Sit down. You want some tea or a beer or something?" Luke asked.

"No, no, I'm fine. I'm just . . . well, I was working when a friend came in and told me about it, and I had to come over and see if you heard anything." Whitney shook her head and Mike sighed. "How are you doing?" Without waiting for a response he gave a sad, mirthless laugh. "What a stupid question. Obviously not very well."

Taking a minute to look first at Whitney and then at Luke, he seemed to come to a decision. "Listen, I've known you guys for a long time—hell, I've known Joy since she was what? Ten?" His voice choked up a moment, and then he went on. "And this is no time to mince words, so I'm just gonna come out and say it. I think Joy's been doing drugs. Now, I don't know for sure; most everything I hear is from my friend Pistol, who's a mail carrier, and he's a real gossip. I mean, frankly, he gets a tiny bit of information from a huge number of sources and draws a lot of conclusions based on an active imagination, if you know what I mean. But if what he's saying is true, he sees her at the high school talking with some pretty dubious characters, not all kids." Mike paused and shrugged almost apologetically. "I don't know if this is helpful or not—"

Luke cut him off. "We know she's been doing drugs. I searched her room but I didn't find any. I think she's been getting the money from her mother, and I think . . ." Luke swallowed and forced himself to go on. "I think she's been buying drugs for her."

Mike was shaking his head. "Jesus Christ."

Whitney made the leap to trying to find a connection. "Is there anyone in particular? Any leads that we could tell the detective about?" she asked.

"First thing I asked him." Mike was nodding. "Pistol doesn't know who the people he's seen are, but I told him today to try to get a license plate or a name, or anything that might be helpful."

Luke looked less than hopeful. "The detective already talked to most of the kids she hangs out with at school; they weren't much help. Of course, they wouldn't volunteer anything about a drug connection."

Mike nodded. "Scared shitless, I would guess. Hell, I would have been at that age." They all sat, silent

and sorry, as the kitchen clock fired off its ticking and
the refrigerator hollered its deafening hum into the
room. When the quiet became intolerable Mike stood.
"I should go back to work for a couple more hours.
If there's anything you want me to do . . . round up
some guys and go out looking, break into somebody's
house—I don't give a shit if it's legal or not, anything.
Please," he pleaded solemnly, "ask me."

"Thanks, Mike," Luke told him, and then added
gravely, "Believe me, if I can think of something, I
will."

Mike opened his mouth to ask them to let him know
if they heard anything, decided that it would sound
selfish to ask them to think of him at a time like this,
and, with a feeble smile, turned and left Luke and
Whitney to the interminable purgatory of ignorance.

Chapter 42

The darkness fell early, stretching the late afternoon into a limbo of twilight and gloom. *But maybe it's just me,* Dario thought as he glanced at the clock on wall. Five thirty—another hour and a half until he could close up and go to Greer's.

He walked to the front to check his appointment book. Three more, the last one scheduled at six thirty. He asked Celia to call and see if the woman could come in earlier; he'd work fast and try to cut out as soon as possible.

The absence of light outside turned the front windows to mirrors, and when the bells on the door jingled Dario looked up to see his own reflection, which morphed with a rapid swipe into Sterling making his way into the salon.

"Hi," he said to Dario, but his eyes swept the large room.

Dario spared him the trouble. "She's not back, but she called and said she's home. I'm going over there as soon as I can get off."

"Oh." The two men regarded each other, and then Sterling asked, "How did it go?"

Sliding a drawer open, Dario pulled out a pack of cigarettes and removed one of the long, perfect white cylinders from its neat packaging. He knew he shouldn't smoke, but the familiarity made the smokes seem like friends. Over the tough and lonely times they'd been there for him, more constant than a lover.

"Come on outside while I have a smoke and I'll tell you what I know." He offered the pack to Sterling, who shrugged a "Why not?" and took one.

They stepped into the cooling evening, shared a light, and Dario exhaled luxuriously.

"Well, you were right; they thought she was crazy," Dario said.

"What a surprise," Sterling commented dryly.

"It gets worse. They suspected Joshua. But"—Dario held up his artistic fingers to stop the expletive emerging from the other man's throat—"they don't seem to now. Apparently there was a little incident at the hospital that convinced the detective on the case that Greer might be for real."

Sterling said nothing, but he shifted his weight uncomfortably.

Dario took a slow drag on the cigarette and regarded the handsome man curiously. "You don't think she is," he observed without accusation. "For real."

Sterling looked even more uncomfortable. His tone was unconvincing as he responded, "It's not that. I mean, I don't really know her very well."

Dario's laugh opened up with a full-throttle release. "No, you don't. It would take a great deal more than one date to get to know that woman. Shit, I've known her for fifteen years and she *still* mystifies me. Of course"—he looked away, and his eyes twinkled as he regarded the mist hugging the hills in the last of the day's surrendering light—"all the good ones are like that."

"What makes you so sure?" In Sterling's voice was a plea to be convinced. Dario recognized it but didn't feel inclined to defend Greer. People either got it or they didn't.

But sometimes they needed a reason. Dario didn't mind telling his story; if Sterling believed him, fine. If he didn't, then there wasn't any point in his hanging around anyway.

"When Greer's husband left her to be with me, it was hard on all of us. They fought to keep valuing each other as people and have a good relationship for Joshua's sake. Geoffrey never doubted Greer's ability and deferred to it often. I . . . well, frankly I resented it. I felt threatened by her and their connection. I tried to be patient and understanding, but I'm sorry to say I pretty much sucked at both. So, I fought against believing in her; I even ridiculed her." He sighed. "I saw later how small and insecure I was acting. They were both doing something much harder, and they rose to the occasion.

"Geoffrey was a naturalist, a scientist who did field research. One day he bought a new truck, a four-wheel-drive monster, and joked that he could drive over mountains and through lakes with it. We went to pick up Joshua, and when Greer saw the truck she went all pale. Long story short, when Geoff took Joshua out for a ride, she pulled me aside and told me to get him chains for the tires. I laughed at her, but she put her hand on my arm, looked into my eyes, and said, 'Listen to me: He's going to get stuck in the snow, and without them he won't get out, and he won't survive.' That's all she said. I wanted to scoff at it, but when she had touched my arm a kind of kinetic heat had raced up into my chest, and I don't mind telling you it scared the shit out of me.

"So, feeling silly, I bought these monster chains for those big wheels, and Geoffrey thought I was paranoid, but he promised to keep them in the truck. Sure enough, that September he was up in the Sierras on a fire road, forty miles from pavement and three times that from any town, when he got trapped in a surprise snowstorm, slid off the road into a ditch, and only those chains kept him from freezing to death. He'd gone out without even a heavy coat, much less snowshoes or provisions. It would have been days before anyone would have found him, or even noticed that he was gone."

Sterling's eyes were laced through with fascinated interest. He finished his cigarette and put it out on the bottom of his shoe. "But did you ever think it might be a coincidence?"

"It was *not* a coincidence. Yes, it was a strong possibility that Geoff might get caught in a storm sooner or later, but it was very specific that he would need the chains when he already had four-wheel drive." Dario took the butt from Sterling and put it into the trash can with his own.

"So, you think she's psychic?"

"No. I know she is."

Sterling made a scuffing sound on the sidewalk as he twisted the ball of one foot slowly back and forth. "I don't mean to sound skeptical or rude, but that doesn't really prove it."

"No," agreed Dario. "And I might have thought it was a lucky guess too, except for one other thing: She told me the date that Geoffrey would die, months earlier than we expected to lose him."

Clearing his throat unnecessarily, Sterling said, "I know the odds are long, but she could have guessed that too. I mean, he was ill for a long time, wasn't he?"

Dario looked away, into the past, and treasured even those painful times when they had suffered the illness together—in very different ways—and had found surprisingly often that there were gifts hidden even in the hardest moments: strengths, almost unbearable love, laughter even. The moments shone like flickering lantern lights left far behind on a highway.

That's why we have memories, he thought, *so that when we look back, we don't see only darkness.* "Yes, that's true," he answered at last. "He was very ill for a long time. But Greer told me definitively which day, in advance, something she would normally never do."

"Then why did she? It seems like a terrible thing to tell someone."

"Because I was supposed to go away on that day." He stopped and cleared his throat before he continued. "I would not have been with him when he died, and I would never have forgiven myself for that. It was her gift to me—to us, really."

Sterling stared out into the gloomy, mottled night and tried to make out the vague shapes obscured by darkness and mist, feeling remarkably awake.

When he finally remembered himself and turned to Dario, he found that there was no longer anyone there.

Chapter 43

For several hours there had been nothing but the darkness of the closet and the faint, muffled sounds of wind, interrupted only by the occasional barking of a dog.

Then the sound of his truck returning sent frayed warnings through Joy's blunted nervous system.

The footsteps came into the house, and she heard him moving around in the kitchen. And then hope leaped into her heart as she heard more than one voice; the higher pitch of a woman's voice was mixed with his. Before she could call out, though, she felt and heard his solo footfalls as they came straight to the closet. The key turned; the door opened, mercifully, onto a darkened room.

He leaned down and grasped her firmly under one arm in a tight, clenching grip. "Don't make a sound," he whispered into her ear. "If you utter one word, I'll kill her. Do you hear me? And after I kill her, you'll be next." The lack of malice or emotion in his voice made the threat all the more real.

He jerked her arm, pulling her up against him, and she nodded her understanding. The cramping in her legs and back was so intense that she had to bite her lower lip hard to keep from crying out as he pulled her with him to the bedroom. "Now, you get in there, and you stay in there, and if I hear one peep out of you, you'll be responsible for two deaths."

He shoved her onto the bed and went out, closing the door. Joy massaged her legs and moved them tentatively until some of the blood returned. As soon as she could bear her own weight she moved to the window and pulled the curtain aside. Bars. She put her face up against the glass and was trying to see how the metal was connected when something on the other side of the window lunged at her, slavering and growling.

She fell backward onto the floor, petrified with fear, and a small cry escaped her, but the animal was throwing itself at the window and making so much noise that she was sure the sound she'd made wouldn't be heard from the living room. She climbed up onto the bed, as far away from the window as possible, and curled into a miserable ball. After a few more failed attempts to get through the bars, the dog disappeared into the night.

With the animal's barking gone, she could hear voices in the living room. She crept on all fours to the floor and pressed her ear to the wood, but it only distorted the sounds further. Did she dare open the door a crack? Noticing that there was about an inch of space between the bottom of the door and the floor, she lay down flat on the carpet and tilted her head as best she could to listen. Who was here? Was it someone who might help her? If she could find a way to let them know she was here without him knowing, then she might be saved.

She squeezed her eyes closed and concentrated on listening.

"You want a drink?" he was asking.

"Sure, I'll get it." There was rustling and quiet for a minute, and then they talked. She sounded nervous, but it seemed clear that they knew each other, that she had been here before, maybe frequently. Finally the conversation took a more serious tack.

She said, "You know, I really like you, but I don't think I'll be able to see you anymore."

He laughed. "What a shame. And here we were just making up."

"I . . . I think you need help." Her voice was shaking, and she cleared her throat too often.

Joy couldn't see him, but she could imagine the slow smile spreading over the face she'd once thought ruggedly attractive but that now repulsed her. "Do you?"

"Yes. Listen. I care about you. I want you to get better."

Glass clinked on glass, and Joy guessed that he was pouring another drink. "No, you don't."

"Yes, I do," she insisted, but even Joy could hear that she was lying, trying to appease him.

"No, you don't. You only came here tonight because you were afraid to refuse me. If I hadn't come around to your back door, you would have pretended not to be home. You know what will make me feel better? If you take those clothes off."

"No, I'm not staying. I know it starts off being a game, but you go too far; something's not right." There was an edge of hysterical panic in the woman's voice. "I have to go."

"Nope. You're staying."

"Let go. Come on, you're scaring me!"

There was the sound of a brief struggle and then a smack that Joy felt resound through her own head. "No, please," came the muffled pleading.

"That's right, beg me," he said in a taunting voice. "Beg me, and maybe you'll get what you're asking for."

The next sounds were the tearing of clothing, something fragile, whimpers and cries. And then a distinct repetitive sound that came over steady weeping interrupted by gasps of pain: the sound of leather striking flesh.

Joy retreated to the far corner, as far from both the window and the door as she could manage, and covered her ears, trying to block out the torturous sounds. She rocked and hummed, just a degree above inaudible, to try to block out the present and the future.

For a time there was nothing, and then the door to the bedroom opened.

"Where are you?" he sang out, as though he were playing hide-and-seek with a child.

She covered her head with her arms and rolled up tightly like a caterpillar sensing danger, keeping her eyes squeezed shut. *Please go away,* she prayed.

But when he spoke again he was standing right over her. "Tell you what, why don't you sleep in the bed tonight? That would be nice, wouldn't it?"

Slowly, like a fern, Joy unfurled just enough to look up at him. "Where is she?" she whispered fearfully.

"She left. But she'll be back. I'm sorry that I didn't pay much attention to you tonight, but something came up." He laughed at his joke, then said, "And now, seeing as how we didn't get a whole lot of sleep last night, I think it's time for beddy-bye."

He took her to the bathroom again, instructing her to take a shower because she stank. Instead she washed her underarms quickly with a soapy washcloth and put her shirt back on. When she came out, he took her to the bedroom and tied her wrists together, and then fastened the other end of the rope firmly to the headboard. She lay on her left side, as still and hard as if she were carved of stone, and waited as he undressed, brushed his teeth, and climbed into the bed next to her.

Her skin tingled with a nasty crawling as, pulling her shirt up enough to expose her waist and part of her rib cage, he lowered his mouth and nipped at her. She jerked away.

Laughing, he reached across her and turned out the light. "Good night, don't let the bedbugs bite." Then he turned away from her, and within minutes she felt the bed shake with his snores.

For a long time Joy lay staring into the darkness, wondering how long she would have to endure this before he killed her.

Chapter 44

In Joshua's dream, everyone was troubled. He was in a gray city of buildings so high that there was no sky. There were crowds of people, and all of them hurried with a frenzied desperation toward—or maybe it was away from—a frightening destination. Everyone was late. Everyone was harried. Everyone was afraid.

He was searching for someone who could help him, but he couldn't remember who it was. He walked on, trying to make out the faces of the passing strangers, but they sped by in blurry haste.

Joshua suddenly found himself in a barren field, looking back at the towering high-rises from far away. It was night, and there was nothing but an eerie silver glow from the lights of the buildings illuminating the clouds they pierced, disappearing like tall figures in a glowing shroud. Turning away from the distant civilization, he saw in front of him a single tree: a huge oak, twisted and scarred by fire. He walked toward it, and as he did he sensed a girl standing beneath it, her face hidden by the shadows of the branches. He came closer and heard a sound—the jingling of keys, almost musical, yet discordant.

He sensed that the girl was looking at him. She stepped forward out of the gloom and he saw her face in black and white, robbed of color by moonlight. He had seen her before, he knew it, but he couldn't remember where or what he was supposed to ask her. Frustrated, he held out his hands in a gesture of bafflement.

The girl smiled gently and shook her head. She turned and pointed up at the oak tree and then to the keys in her hand. Last she pointed to something that he hadn't noticed before: a motorcycle standing just under the tree.

"I don't understand," Joshua whispered to her. "What am I doing here?"

The girl pointed again—once to the tree, the bike beneath it, and then to the keys—and then she was gone, and Joshua found himself terrified and alone. He began to circle around the tree, first walking and then running out across the broken land, searching for her, searching for someone, anyone. His foot snagged on a root and he lurched forward, throwing his hands out to catch himself.

The movement jerked Joshua of his sleep, and he sat up in bed, sweat sticking his T-shirt to his chest. Looking out the window, he could see the pine tree that Joy had climbed down in the vague moonlight. It was still, unmoved by wind or weight.

From the hallway came a faint light. Joshua got out of bed and went to the doorway. The light was coming from downstairs, which meant his mother was probably in the kitchen. The illuminated clock on his dresser read 4:23.

Quietly he descended to find her looking toward him; of course she had sensed him coming.

"Can't sleep?" she asked softly.

"No . . . well, I was, but I had a nightmare." But even as he said the words, he wondered if it was true, for it suddenly came to him where he had seen the girl before. He stopped two feet from the table as the realization hit him.

"What is it?" Greer asked.

"I remember. I was dreaming about a girl; she was showing me three things: an oak tree, a motorcycle, and some keys." Joshua rubbed his eyes and sat down at the table. "There was more to the dream, people who were lost, and it was really, uh, disturbing, but then she was there, in an open place, and I kept wishing I could remember who she was or where I knew her from, and now I do." He stopped, gathering courage from the confident curiosity in his mother's eyes. "At the hospital, over Zoe Caldwell's bed, she was there. I recognized her, but I don't know her. I mean, I've never seen her before in, uh, life. You know what I mean?"

"Yes, I think I do. Sometimes when I see someone's future, I see an image of the person. I saw Joy in the tea leaves that day. It's not always so much distinct physical features—more often a sense of who and how they are."

Joshua shook his head. "No, this isn't like that," he said emphatically. "If I were an artist, I could draw you this girl perfectly. She has a nice face, kind of round, like someone who smiles all the time, and medium-length brown hair, and a few freckles, just light, across here." He raised his two fingers and drew a line from one cheek, across the bridge of his nose, to the other. "If I ever met her, I would know her," he said definitively.

Greer's breath had caught in her chest. She forced herself to keep her face calm, but she said, "Wait a minute." She rose and left the room, heading to the downstairs den. Joshua heard her rummaging through an unpacked box and then his mother returned, holding a high school yearbook. She sat next to him and slowly lowered the book onto the table to show him a page. With one finger she pointed to a photo.

Joshua leaned in to look, and then jolted back in

his seat. His mother put her arm around his shoulders. "That's Sarah," she whispered. "It's her, isn't it?"

Joshua was breathing shallowly, but he nodded.

"I asked her to help us." Greer brushed away a tear and then, drawing in a ragged breath, she said, "And she came."

Rising from the table, Joshua put some water on for tea with a hand that seemed not to be his own. He got a cup, the box of chamomile, and a spoon. Then, with his back still to his mother because he couldn't bear to see her tears, he started to intone in a soft voice what he had seen at the hospital.

"She was over Zoe Caldwell's bed, just waiting. She nodded at me, and I got the feeling that everything was all right, that she was there so that"—his voice threatened to crack, and he paused to draw a soothing breath before continuing on—"so that Zoe wouldn't be alone. Then she reached out one hand toward her so that a line of light connected them, and then she . . . uh, Sarah . . . pulled her hand back and laid it on her chest, and she looked at me again. What do you think that meant?"

"I don't know; what do you think?"

"That she was taking Zoe with her." Joshua gulped back a sob. "That she would be with her when it was time."

He heard his mother crying softly. After a moment she said, "That would be like her, to be there to help others through. She was always there for me." In the last words Joshua could hear and feel the pain that Greer felt she had not done the same for her best friend.

The kettle whistled. Joshua took it off and poured steaming water into the cup, covering the tears that came unbidden from his eyes. "But what was she showing me in the dream? Or maybe I just dreamed her and it doesn't mean anything?"

Greer waited until Joshua composed himself and came and sat back down. "It means something. But you are the only one who can interpret it. Maybe those objects aren't literal. Maybe they mean something special to you?"

Joshua sipped the hot tea, grateful for the scalding on his tongue that distracted him from his emotion. He considered it, but other than keys opening doors and a special fondness for oak trees, he couldn't think of any other meaning.

After a few moments he asked his mom, "Why are you up?"

She regarded him and bit her protruding lower lip. "It's getting close," she whispered. "And there's something else that you don't know about. The woman you met at the coffee shop, the one who came from the bank—Leah. She's in danger too, and I can't figure out what it is exactly, and I don't think she'll believe me if I try to warn her. I have to try to find a way to protect her, but I don't know how." Greer put her elbows on the table and sank her fingers into her thick auburn hair. "She needs a different kind of strength than mine."

Joshua watched her anxiety for a moment, and then, when she raised her luminous green eyes to him, he cracked a smile. "Maybe this was a bad move. Maybe we should move back into the inner city, where it's safer."

Greer laughed in spite of herself, and then it died away.

She looked seriously at her son and said, "Joshua, listen to me. If something bad does happen to Joy, there won't have been anything you could have done to prevent it."

He smiled sadly at his mother. "Is that how you feel about Sarah?"

A hush fell over the two of them like a blanket of cold, silent snow.

Chapter 45

Thursday

The first light bled through the window with the ghostly hue of tarnished metal. Joshua was sitting in the den, trying to read a book, trying to distract his mind enough to shut it down and, though he feared what it might bring, return to sleep.

But it was no use. He caught himself staring out the window at the emerging silhouette of Luke and Whitney's house. The house where Joy should be safely sleeping. His mind raced and his spirit felt irritable and unsettled. He stood up and paced, tried to sit and focus on the page, then popped up again, slapped the book shut, and tossed it onto another chair. "Forget this," he muttered out loud, and headed upstairs.

Yanking out drawers as though his anxiety were their fault, he pulled on jeans, a sweatshirt, and then his hiking boots. As he moved back through the hallway, he saw the light on under his mother's bedroom door, and he knocked softly.

Her voice sounded distant and slow as she responded, "Come in."

Cracking the door, he saw her seated cross-legged on the floor, her back straight and her head turned to him, but her eyes were slightly glazed. On the floor in front of her a candle burned, and smoke rose from the tiny metal brazier that she used to burn herbs and incense. A balsam pine fragrance met his senses; it was mixed with something that cleared his sinuses and head, something like camphor. It reminded him to take a deep breath and helped him to do it at the same time.

Uncomfortable with both the thought and the question, Joshua asked, "Are you trying to see something?"

She nodded.

"And, uh . . . ?"

Greer shook her head sadly. "Nothing useful. Remember I told you that I gave her the bracelet to try to bind myself to her?" It was Joshua's turn to nod. "It seemed to work for you, briefly at least, and all I can sense is that she's still in danger, and the death omens are growing stronger, closer. I don't mean to frighten you more than you already are, but since you seem to already . . ." She trailed off as though, sensing his distress, she thought better of what she was about to say, and then changed the subject. "You're going out?" she asked, seeing that he was dressed.

"I can't just sit here. I'm gonna go for a hike," he told her.

Concern was chased across her face by resignation and understanding. "All right. But be careful. There's still a lot of water in that creek."

"I know. I'll be back in an hour or so. If I just sit here I'll lose my mind." He muttered under his breath, "If I haven't already."

Desperate for solace, Joshua plunged out into the cold predawn. The light, though still shrouded, was growing steadily now, and he had no trouble finding his way along the first part of the access road. He went past the spot where the footbridge was washed out and paused to look at the two houses that sat, isolated and cut off, across the ten-foot-wide rushing water, then continued on, the chill air stinging his lungs as the road steepened slightly and he refused to slow his rapid pace. He passed the last house on the road, which sat on the dry side of the river, silent and still, then headed onto the trailhead, pushing himself fast and hard along the rocky path that was shadowed by the overhanging trees.

But it was only five minutes before he met the first crossing. Joshua stopped and regarded the angry water. In the absence of light its depth was incalculable, and its rippled, iridescent black surface surged purposefully over large rocks that would normally afford an easy crossing. Remembering the last time he had risked it, he felt a shiver slide up his spine, and he cursed softly, foiled by his own reluctance to pursue the small peace he might find in the depth of the woods.

Backtracking to look for another way to cross the river, he came to a break in the underbrush that led steeply up out of the canyon and away from the water. He stood at the base of it and peered up. It looked like a trail, maybe just an animal trail that switchbacked up an unremitting slope. Needing the punishment, he started up.

The trail went on for about ten minutes, almost straight up, bearing slightly left, back the way he had come, but high above it. The way was rutted and crumbling from the recent rain. He was sweating. His throat felt raw and his legs burned by the time he reached the top and looked back.

He was standing on one of the firebreak roads. The sun had not yet crested over the higher hills beyond him, but the night had lost its hold here, and the day was a few breaths away. It was that moment of promise in which Joshua could feel the unbounded possibilities of the unborn day. He remembered his mother

saying that his dad had always believed in the interconnectedness of all things. Today he did too. Anything could happen in this day. He felt that if he could
just find the thread he needed and grab hold of it,
then he could pick freely from the infinite possibilities
and instinctively choose the right path.

Looking down across the canyon, he saw the break
in the greenery where his house sat, and he could
make out the corner of the roof of the Whitehorses'.
Following the curve of the creek, he could tell where
the next houses were, and he guessed that almost directly below him was the spot where the road ended
and the trail began to snake its way up into the
deep canyon.

Throwing his head back, Joshua let out a long, audible sigh of exasperation. "Let me find her," he whispered to the first thin hint of blue tinting the sky. He
waited, but he felt nothing except a cold wind that
chilled the sweat against his body. And then with another, quieter sigh he started down the fire road
toward what he guessed would be the highway.

He had been walking on the wide, twisting road for
only a few minutes, and the black ribbon of highway
winding down from the hills had appeared ahead of
him when he saw her. Just the outline of the girl—at
first he thought it was someone else out hiking—but
even as his brain tried to force a rational explanation
he knew that there wasn't one.

The sun had come up, and Joshua was walking almost straight into it. The figure of the girl was not on
the ground, not far away or close by, just . . . there.
He stopped short and watched her. She held up one
finger and spun it, then pointed to her ear, as though
he should listen. At that moment a very loud motorcycle rounded a distant curve, and the sound carried
abrasively through the wind-brushed air, growing as it

came closer and passed, blocked from sight by trees.
He didn't understand. Was he supposed to listen to
the motorcycle or something else? Once again she
held up a finger and spun it. And then, moving directly
in front of the rising sun, she vanished.

Joshua rubbed his eyes; the sunspot burned brightly
behind his closed lids. He racked his brain. What did
that mean? He considered the motion she had made.
A spinning motion.

A freezing paralysis crept over Joshua's neck and
shoulders. And the hair on the back of his neck prickled like the hundred feet of a centipede. Slowly he
turned around and looked behind him.

He was facing a tree: an old and gnarled oak tree.
It had been through a fire; part of it was blackened,
and there was a large, gaping space where a huge branch
had fallen off years before. He had passed it looking at
the healthy side, and it had blended into the hundreds
of other oaks and shrubs that covered these miles of
park. But from this angle it was clearly the tree from
his dream.

Feeling as though he were trapped in a trance,
Joshua moved toward the tree and walked around underneath it. He could see nothing, no footprints, no
notes or scraps of fabric, nothing that might be helpful
to a detective trying to find a missing teenager.

Joshua felt suddenly very alone and vulnerable.
With a growing sense of unease, he moved away from
the tree and ran down the remaining part of the fire
road toward the highway, which curved and thinned
as he came toward the bottom. There was a chained
swing bar in front of it, just like the one near his
house. He climbed quickly over it and emerged onto
the lip of the highway. He looked around to determine
where he had come out and was surprised to see the
entrance to his road only a short distance away. It was

so seldom used that from the street he would never have known this was a road entrance. Joshua had thought it was some kind of forest service area.

He started toward the road that would take him easily back to his house and suddenly he stopped.

It was all rushing at him: the oak tree, this spot, that morning. He spun around in place and there it was: the bench, the school bus stop. Was that what Sarah was trying to show him? The place where Joy had disappeared? Because that, at least, made sense.

This was the last place he had seen Joy.

Chapter 46

Leah glanced at the clock on the wall in the coffee shop. Seven a.m. She was nervous; she'd arrived almost a half an hour early and spent the time chatting with Jenny when she hadn't been serving her early customers, a steady stream of men and women dressed in well-worn jeans and quilted flannel shirts, smelling sweetly of the hay and molasses in the oats that they had fed their horses before tending to their own needs.

She had selected a table that was away from the window but where she could still see out to the parking area. She had no idea what she might say to Terry when she came. All she knew was that she would do what she could.

Jenny seemed to sense her nervousness and suggested decaf when Leah requested a second cup of coffee. "You okay?" she asked.

"Yeah, I'm, uh, meeting somebody here. It's a little strange." She vacillated and then dove into an explanation. "Actually, it's my ex-husband's new girlfriend. She asked to talk to me, and I said I would."

Jenny cocked her head to one side. Leah felt uncomfortably as though the pretty cinnamon brown eyes understood far more than she had explained, and she was relieved when the door opened and Dario entered.

"Morning!" Jenny sang out. "You're here early."

"You're telling me." Dario's naturally deep, husky voice sounded an octave lower. "I had to come and let the plumber in; he's got to fix a leak in the main water line, and I want it done before we open." A smaller-model motorcycle that sounded as though it had contracted the flu sputtered and coughed its way into the parking lot, drawing his attention. "That would be him now. That's lucky."

"Yeah," Jenny agreed, "good timing."

"No, I mean it's lucky he's here on time or I would have had to kill him."

Jenny and Leah both looked out the picture window at Army climbing off his bike. "I don't think that would be a very good idea," Jenny said, raising her eyebrows. "From the looks of him, you might not be the first to try it."

"You're right; I wouldn't be," Dario said flatly, then turned to Leah. "Good morning."

"Morning," she returned, but could think of nothing else to say. She envied Jenny's easy, gregarious manner. "How's Greer?"

Dario and Jenny both stopped and looked at Leah. "Have you talked to her in the last couple of days?" Dario asked her.

"Uh, no."

"You should give her a call. I know she's been thinking about you." Dario smiled gently, turned to Jenny, and said, "Save me."

"Let me help you out." Jenny smiled at him. "How about a papa latte? Three shots of espresso."

While Dario eagerly agreed, Leah wondered to herself why Greer would have been thinking of her. She felt surprised, and oddly honored. She thought of Greer's unusual prediction that they would be friends and felt a quivering that it might be true.

Dario went out with his liquid jet fuel and met the

waiting Army; they disappeared into the salon next door. A couple of moments later, as Leah sat watching the passing traffic, she saw Vince's bright yellow Ducati rocket up the street, slow, and then pass. She suppressed a shiver that he might have come in and found her and Terry there together. Relieved that he hadn't stopped in, she leaned back.

The Ducati returned, cruising in from the opposite direction and parking across the lot from the shop. Leah looked around, wondering where she could go and hide. There was a restroom, but it was occupied. Shrinking back against the banquette, she held up her newspaper in front of her face and watched Vince outside. He sauntered forward without removing his helmet, and stopped by Army's bike. She saw him look around, then take something out of his pocket and slip it into the saddlebag on the side nearest her. Then he crossed back to his bike, started it, and pulled away. Leah exhaled. But what the hell was that? Had Vince planted something on Army's bike, or was it a delivery of some kind? Was the plumber involved with the drugs?

But before she had much time to muse on theories, a small Toyota pulled into the lot, and she recognized Terry getting out. Leah put down her paper, straightened her sweater, and tried to look casual and friendly as the young woman came in and approached her table.

"Hi, I'm glad you made it. Sit down." Terry looked so shaky that Leah decided not to tell her she had missed Vince by seconds. "You want coffee?"

"Thanks," Terry said. She seemed relieved to be able to answer a simple question.

Leah waited while the woman went up and got a cup, wincing as Terry mixed in a heavy dollop of cream and three artificial sweeteners. When Terry had sat back down and fidgeted herself through some awkward small talk, she fell quiet and stared down at the murky, mud-colored liquid in her cup. "I guess it must seem strange," she said at last, "my wanting to talk to you."

"Not at all," Leah told her. What *was* strange was how calm she felt now that the woman was here. It was somehow empowering to be the stronger one, if only by comparison. The other woman's extreme discomfort made her feel braver, more capable. She'd walked away; she'd survived a violent man. And maybe, just maybe, she could help Terry do the same. Leah felt oddly elated.

"He was different when we first met. Charming, you know?"

Leah nodded; she knew.

"But then he would drink too much, and something else would happen to him. Oh, he'd apologize the next day, cry even, and I'd think, 'He really feels bad.' " She looked up at Leah with eyes like a cornered deer. "I think he needs me. I'm sure I can help him."

Leah sighed and tried to contain her bubbling fury. "You can't," she said as blandly as she could manage. "He doesn't want to change; he enjoys it."

Terry pulled back from the table. "But he always feels so sorry later."

Leah wondered how far she could go. She knew that it would be difficult not to infuse her own experiences into Terry's; hers would be different. She knew that the other woman would not want to believe her, even if she knew that every word Leah spoke was the truth. "In my experience—which is extensive—that part, the being sorry, will go away." Leah watched Terry retreat from her emotionally and threw out a line to try to pull her back. "Why do you stay with him?" she asked gently.

"He's great when he's sober. I mean, he's handsome, and he's got money, and he's so smart, and he can be really sweet. And everybody—" She stopped, and a flush of color suffused her pale face.

"Everybody is impressed by him?" Leah asked softly.

"Well, yeah."

Leah took a good look at the young woman. She was maybe twenty-one; her clothes and hairstyle suggested that she hadn't been raised with money or class, much less any kind of sustaining self-image. It wasn't hard to guess at the reason this girl stayed with a man who abused her: She thought it was the best she could do—that he was above her and she didn't deserve more.

Leah leaned in and laid her hand on the back of Terry's. "Let me ask you something," she said. "If you had a child, a little girl, and Vince treated her the way he treats you, how would you feel?"

She could sense the tendons in Terry's hand tense as she pressed down hard on the tabletop. Her eyes flickered around the room, as though searching for an escape route, her breath quickening. "I . . . I don't know."

"Yes, you do," Leah insisted, but delicately. "You wouldn't allow it. So why are you allowing him to treat you that way? You need to take care of yourself the way you would a child. Wouldn't your mother want to protect you?"

Terry's face had hardened, as though suddenly all the elasticity had gone out of it. "I don't have a mother."

"Then you have to be your own mother."

The tears came with an almost violent force. Terry's face contracted into a silent grimace, and then she covered her mouth with her free hand as the first sob escaped her. Jenny's head jerked around from where she was steaming milk, and Leah shook her head slightly to let Jenny know that she should pretend not to notice.

"I . . . can't . . . get away," Terry managed to get out in a forced staccato. She took a deep breath in an effort to calm herself, and looked around to see if anyone was watching her. Jenny was feigning ignorance, and the coffee shop was experiencing a merciful momentary lull. "Every time I tell him he needs to change or I'll go, he laughs and says that he'll find me." She looked at Leah with her eyes flooded with tears. "And he does," she finished in a whisper.

It's gotten worse, thought Leah. She, at least, had fought back, had had the gumption to walk away in spite of the threats, had gone to stay with her parents, where she would be safe during the worst of it. This girl had nowhere to go, and no one to help her through it. "Can you tell me about the drugs?" Leah asked. Terry's eyes fluttered to hers; they were filled with terror.

"Okay, okay," Leah comforted, "I understand. You're afraid to talk about that, and you don't have to, but my question is this: Does he use the drugs, and does it get worse when he does?"

Terry looked around the coffeehouse again and then back to Leah. She nodded once in a jerky, secretive way. She seemed incapable of drawing breath.

"Okay. I understand. Just relax a minute, drink some coffee, breathe. We'll figure something out. The important thing is that you came to talk to me today; that's a huge step, Terry. I know how much courage it took, believe me," Leah told her with a smile.

"Because you had to do it?" Terry asked in a tearful voice.

That brought Leah up cold. She felt weak and small all of a sudden. But, drawing on a new kind of courage, she forced herself to say, barely audibly, "No.

Because I *couldn't* do it." And in those words she felt a kind of salvation, a release in speaking a truth, no matter how small.

Terry gazed at her for a moment in confusion, and then the understanding that Leah had shared something painful with her softened her eyes and, turning her palm up to meet Leah's, she squeezed her hand. "Thank you," she said.

The two of them turned away from the intimate moment to sip their coffee, gaze out at the brightening day, and compose themselves. As they watched, Army came out of the salon and went to his bike. He moved to one of the saddlebags, not the one Vince had fooled with, and took out what seemed to be some kind of tool. Leah was aware of Terry's body stiffening, much like a leopard sensing a movement in the underbrush.

"Do you know that guy?" Leah asked, curious to know whether Army was involved with Vince and the drug business. Though, based on the altercation she had seen at the bank, it didn't feel quite right.

"No, not really. But he kind of spoke up for me when Vince was being a dick at a restaurant. Vince was high and had too much to drink and started talking shit to me. That guy almost got into a fight with Vince over it. It was pretty cool, actually, but I was afraid Vince would hurt him, so I left with Vince and . . ." She looked away. "Well, it wasn't a good night."

Leah watched the rough and handsome young man, a man who bore the obvious marks of a convicted felon, a man without credibility, close up the saddlebag and disappear from her field of view.

And one word came to her mind.

Guilty.

Chapter 47

Greer was watching out the window for Whitney when she saw her come out of her house wrapped in a corduroy coat. As she held the door open she saw how haggard Whitney's normally vibrant face looked, and the smile she gave Greer was a shallow reflection of her usual. Even Whitney's thick, lustrous hair was dull and lifeless.

Greer didn't need to ask her friend if there had been any news; she knew that there wasn't. Without words the two sat down at the kitchen table and drank the tea that Greer had made. Occasionally Greer would reach across and pat Whitney's arm or rub her shoulder. Every so often a single tear would caress the roundness of Whitney's cheek and then slide silently down to her chin before she brushed it away stoically.

At one point Greer turned her head to the door, and the motion was followed by a light knock. She rose to let Luke in. He was holding something blue and plastic. It was a walkie-talkie.

Joshua came down the stairs into the kitchen and greeted Whitney and Luke.

"What's that?" Joshua asked him.

"It's a short-range walkie-talkie. I found it in Joy's room in a bottom drawer. But I only found one."

Feeling a wave of stupidity and guilt, Joshua nodded, but couldn't make eye contact with Luke or Whitney. How could he say he'd been watching her in her bedroom? Inside his head an angry voice snapped at him, *How could you not?* He spoke through the agonizing discomfort as though it were a chain-link fence around his own personal prison.

"I saw her using it," he blurted, and though he'd spoken softly, the words seemed to penetrate the room as though shouted through a bullhorn. All three adults looked at him in symphonic unison, on each of their faces a different note of interest and disbelief. "I can see into her bedroom window from mine. And I saw her talking into it twice."

Luke's astonishment had turned to hardened intensity. "And?" he asked.

"And the first time I though it was a cell phone or maybe a mini–tape recorder, but then I realized it must be something else. That was the night she snuck out." Joshua paused and felt his face redden. "I saw that too," he confessed. "She fell out of the tree on her way down, but she made me promise not to tell. I thought about it later and figured she must be talking to whoever picked her up on the highway. Those things don't have a very long range. But it would work that far."

"When was the second time?" Luke asked forcefully.

"The second time she didn't seem to get an answer. Anyway, she looked mad, disgusted with it; she threw it across the room."

"When was it?" Luke demanded, and Joshua recoiled at the anger in his voice, remonstrating himself for not telling anyone this before. But he hadn't thought about it; it hadn't seemed relevant. "It was, uh, a couple of days before she disappeared, I guess."

Luke's eyes flashed and his knuckles whitened on

the blue plastic object in his hand. He moved toward Joshua and no one spoke. The air in the room crackled like old paint. Joshua flinched slightly as Luke raised his hand, but it was only to lay it firmly on Joshua's shoulder.

Whitney's face had come to life again; a small amount of the shine it normally held had rekindled. "That means someone has the mate," she observed.

"Yes," Luke agreed. "I'll call Detective Sheridan. He said to let him know if there was anything at all . . ." His voice broke slightly, and he turned abruptly away to look out the window. Joshua and Greer exchanged a look.

"I'm sorry," Joshua said desperately. "I'm sorry I didn't tell you before."

Luke turned slowly back to face him. His gray eyes were rimmed in red; his handsome face was etched with deep lines. "It's all right," he said in a fractured voice.

Joshua felt the falsehood of this so strongly that it actually hit him in the stomach with a force like a fist, and he doubled forward, exhaling hard.

Greer was beside him instantly. "Are you all right?" she asked.

"Yeah," he gasped. "I think I'll go upstairs." He made his way to the base of the staircase, then turned back, feeling hopeless and frustrated. "Is there anything I can do?"

Luke smiled very softly. In his eyes was a wisdom that was far more knowing than Joshua could fathom. And then, with great clarity and purpose, as though making a simple suggestion that might save not only Joy's life but his own as well, he spoke two words.

"Find her."

Chapter 48

It was both a burden and a relief to walk into the salon. Greer entered the busy morning buzz and reveled in the normalcy of life, while at the same time she felt as though she were struggling to breathe in an alien, underwater atmosphere; she strained to give the appearance of being a happy part of it.

Dario excused himself from his client and crossed to her, but she shook her head. "Nothing," she told him when he reached her.

He sighed thickly, his whole chest taking the impact of the word. Nothing. "How are *you*?"

Greer shrugged. "Okay, I guess. Whitney made me come in. And I need to talk to Jenny about something."

"Is it Leah?" he asked. When she nodded, he told her, "I saw her this morning. She was in the coffee shop."

"Really?" Greer asked, surprised and feeling a tiny release of pressure. Maybe Jenny would already have some kind of idea of what was going on, and her request wouldn't sound so out-of-the-blue.

Dario smiled at her wryly. "Don't tell me you didn't *know* that," he teased, and headed back to his client.

Greer went over the day's appointments with Celia,

asked her to return a few phone calls, and then headed over to the coffee shop.

Jenny was sitting at a table with her feet up on the chair across from her. She had a piece of quiche and was eating it leisurely, as the only customer in the store sat near the window reading a paper.

"Hi!" Jenny greeted Greer. "I'm glad you came in; I want to talk to you."

"Ditto," Greer said. "No, no, don't get up. I'll get a cup for myself." She walked around the counter and picked up one of the comfortingly overlarge mugs, which made her feel as though she were a child drinking from a grown-up's glass. She filled it with cinnamon coffee from a thermal holder, all the while feeling deeply grateful for Jenny's potent support.

As the spicy aroma filled her senses, she was thinking how sometimes you had strength to spare for friends and sometimes you had to lean on them. Right now, Whitney and Leah needed all the support that she could muster, and Jenny was the only one who had strength in reserve.

Greer found that she didn't even need to broach the subject. "Listen," Jenny said the moment Greer sat down with her. "Leah was in here this morning with her ex-husband's new girlfriend, and something is not right. I think she might be getting involved where she shouldn't."

Greer smiled, pleased that her instinct about Jenny had been on the money. "She's *already* involved, albeit unwittingly. I sensed it when I worked on her. I'm sure that sounds strange to you, but the important thing now is that I'm afraid she's in danger."

"Me too." Jenny nodded and took a drink of water before she went on. "Okay, maybe I should let her tell you this—and it's only supposition anyway—but we had a little talk the other day at the bank. She didn't come out and say it, but I'm pretty sure that her ex-husband abused her—I think probably he beat the crap out of her—and she's never really dealt with it. Now she's watching it happen to someone else and it's eating her up inside."

"How could it not?" Greer said sadly. "But listen to me: I know this is hard to believe, but I get these . . . premonitions."

"I know; I heard," said Jenny casually. "Whitney told me you're pretty scary—in a good way, of course." She took a huge forkful of quiche and then patted her mouth with her napkin. There was a noticeable absence of cynicism and dubious apprehension on her face. When she could speak again she asked, "So, what's up for Leah?"

Greer was so taken aback by this absolute acceptance of her visions that she actually stuttered. "She, uh . . . well, she's . . . You mean you believe me? Just like that?"

"Sure," Jenny said. "Well, I went over and quizzed Dario for about forty-five minutes, and he's pretty eloquent on the subject. *And* I have a woman I've called for over ten years who's told me some pretty unfucking-believable stuff about my life. My theory is, it's all connected, and some people see more of the dotted lines than everybody else. So, yeah, I believe you. Plus, you're too smart and honest to make this stuff up. What would be the point of that?"

Greer had to concede that there would be no point. Why would anyone say things that would quickly be discovered to be wrong? Unless it was for money— and she didn't take money.

"Something violent is going to happen to her soon if she doesn't protect herself. I haven't told Leah this, because she's . . . well, she's not like you."

"You mean she's a *banker*," Jenny said, defining Greer's implication succinctly.

"Right," Greer agreed, feeling she couldn't have

summed up the mentality of a linear thinker any better. "And I knew she would have to doubt me. But the truth is, I've been so preoccupied with Joy"—Greer watched Jenny's eyes crease into sadness and concern at the sound of the name—"that I haven't been able to even think about helping Leah."

It was Jenny's turn to pat someone's arm reassuringly. "I got your back," she said. "I already told her this morning that if she needs a place to stay, or anything at all, she was to call me. I gave her my number, my address, wrote it all down on the back of a coffee shop card so she wouldn't forget who gave it to her."

A warm sense of relief, the first in days, flooded over Greer. "Thank you. But I should tell you that last night I had a sense that it would be soon."

"I'll invite her to dinner!" Jenny said. "Wanna come?"

Greer smiled at her sadly. "No," she told her. "I want to be nearby for Whitney."

"Mm, I'll have to think of another reason." Outside the window they watched as Army put his tools back in his saddlebags and then straddled the bike and prepared to start it. "I know!" Jenny said. "I'll hire that guy to go up and shut off her water main; then she'll have to come stay with me until he finds the problem."

Greer watched Army push the bike back out of the parking space and then start away. "No," she said. "He might not be the best choice of someone to involve in trying to *prevent* violence, if you know what I mean."

Jenny's eyes followed after him before she sighed and turned back to Greer. "Yeah, maybe we should ask someone who's *not* on parole for aggravated assault. In fact, let's just eliminate anyone who's been convicted of a federal offense."

"You think?" Greer asked, feigning a levity she didn't feel.

A strange smile played on Jenny's lips. "Yeah, let's go with someone who was, at least, never *convicted*." She put a sardonic spin on the last word and then turned one thumb up and pointed it in at herself.

Greer didn't ask.

Chapter 49

Detective Sheridan shifted in his seat. The vinyl caught at the back of his pant legs, and, using the steering wheel as a prop, he lifted his weight enough to pull the wrinkles in the fabric out from under his thighs. He'd been sitting in this position watching the high school yard and entrance for almost an hour and half. The tea in his thermos was cold and his ass was numb.

He was parked on the residential side of the street across from the dropoff zone. Twice now a woman had appeared at the door of her home and looked pointedly at him, so he wasn't surprised when the black-and-white pulled up behind him. "Great," he mumbled, and reached for his badge.

The enthusiastic youngster—a conspicuous rookie, from the buzz cut of his hair—rapped on his window. Sheridan lowered it and handed the man his badge. "I'm Chatsworth PD," he told the man, who was studying the badge as though he might have bought it from a specialty shop. "I'm working on the Whitehorse case."

The rookie's name tag said, WILLOUGHBY. He leaned down and said, "What case would that be?"

"High school kid, disappeared a couple of days ago; she's the second one in a week. The first one showed

up in a motel in my precinct and looks to end up
in the morgue. Please don't tell me you work this
neighborhood and you don't know about it." Sheridan
drew the words out, stringing them together
sarcastically.

"I know about it. I put up the flyers." The young
man sighed. "Just checking to see what you knew. So
you're the assigned detective?"

"Lucky me," Sheridan said dryly.

"Seen anything?" Willoughby asked.

"Just you guys, and you're not exactly making me
inconspicuous."

The officer straightened up and apologized.
"Sorry." He scanned the school field, which was surrounded by a ten-foot-high chain-link fence topped off
with a liberal dusting of barbed wire. "Not that it
would be easy to tell much; these kids know everybody from the guy who sells oranges on the corner to
the councilwoman. It's a tight community."

"Yeah," Sheridan agreed, thinking that it was pretty
clear that the barbed wire hadn't stopped whoever had
taken Joy Whitehorse and Zoe Caldwell. Whoever it
was had far more likely been known and trusted by
both girls.

"Good luck," said Officer Willoughby.

Sheridan fished out a card and passed it over. "Call
me if you see or hear anything?"

"You bet I will. Do me a favor?"

"What?"

"Catch this sick fucker." Willoughby's young face
stretched into a tight-lipped smile as he turned to survey the teenagers gathered around in groups outside
the school, and then he walked back to his car.

Sheridan sighed and decided it was time to move.
He started the car and drove it around the block until
he was parked at the far end of the school property,
putting the football field between himself and the

buildings; then he got out, leaned against his car, and lit a cigarette.

"Hey!" somebody called out to him. "You got another smoke?"

Detective Sheridan turned and was about to tell the underage kid to go ask his mommy when he noticed it was the kid he had talked to before, a pale-faced boy dressed all in black who he'd been told was a friend of Joy Whitehorse's. The kid—Joey, he remembered—recognized him at the same moment, and, if possible with skin already so white, blanched and turned away.

"Hold on," Detective Sheridan said. "Here." He walked forward and held out the pack so that it was up against the fence. The kid reached two long fingers through and extracted one of the Kools. "It's menthol," warned the detective.

"As long as it's got nicotine," the kid said.

Sheridan passed over a lighter and watched the teenager commit a misdemeanor, aided and abetted by him. "So, how's it going?" he asked as conversationally as possible. His sister had kids, but he wasn't much good at talking to them.

"It sucks," Joey answered, glancing over his shoulder back across the field to check for school personnel. In the chilly air the smoke made a stream of gray as they exhaled that disappeared quickly in the light wind.

"Haven't heard anything, have you?" Sheridan asked.

Joey tried to keep his face impassive, but the experienced detective could see the doubt and the fear cross it as though it were written in neon. The kid shrugged. "Nothing." He studied the burning end of his smoke for a minute, and then his eyes, painfully childlike, cut hopefully up to Sheridan's. "You?"

Sheridan shook his head, feeling an odd compassion

for this now and future lawbreaker. It was tough being a teenager, trying to act like you were never afraid, like you knew it all and didn't need anything or anybody, when, more than ever before, what you desperately needed was someone to tell you what to do, even if you would die before you'd admit it. All he said was, "Nope, not yet. I'm working on it, though."

As Sheridan and Joey stood there with nothing else to say, they watched the mail truck make its abbreviated trip up the street, stopping at every house on the far side momentarily before moving on. Sheridan didn't see Joey's eyes cut to him surreptitiously and then back to the truck. When it was almost directly across from them, a group of three other kids who were standing a few yards away spoke to the postman.

"Hey!" one of them called out. "Where's Pistol?"

The postal worker, who had gotten out to walk a large envelope up to the front door, was a woman, dressed in the bland gray of her office with a harried expression on her face. She looked surprised that they were speaking to her, and her response was slow in coming. "Called in sick today," she finally said in a voice loud enough to carry across the street.

"Shit," Joey swore under his breath, just loud enough for Detective Sheridan to hear.

"Friend of yours?" the detective asked.

"No," Joey mumbled. "He just likes to talk, so he usually comes over and shoots the shit for a few minutes." The kid finished his cigarette and threw it on the saturated ground, where it sizzled lightly in the dampness. "It breaks up the day."

Sheridan nodded. He remembered high school; he'd hated it with a passion, and any distraction had been welcome. But he also thought about what Officer Willoughby had said: "These kids know everybody." Glancing at his watch, he noted that it was almost twelve—time to go.

"So long. Let me know if you hear or see anything. You still got my card?"

Joey nodded sullenly, returned to his I-hate-the-world expression, and slouched away.

Sheridan thought to himself that if the youth of today was the hope of tomorrow, the world was in pretty bad shape.

And it wasn't their fault.

Chapter 50

Leah watched nervously for her chance. It came when Vince announced loudly that he was going home for lunch. She picked up her sweater and her courage, swallowed hard to force her heart back down out of her mouth, and followed him out to his parking space, wrapping the sweater over her shoulders.

It was important that she do this somewhere that they wouldn't be overheard, so it couldn't be in the bank, and somewhere they *could* be seen, so in full view of the bank's front windows was perfect.

"Vince!" she called out just as he was beginning to pull his helmet over his head. He turned, and that predatory, reptilian smile crept over his face. She noticed that his skin looked older, stretched out, and there were circles under his eyes. The drinking and the drugs were beginning to mar his good looks.

"Yeah?" He had paused, helmet in hand, to see what she had to say, and he looked genuinely curious. "If this is business, it can wait until tomorrow."

"Aren't you coming back this afternoon?" Leah asked.

"No, I'm taking the afternoon off for personal reasons." He smiled again gloatingly. "Which means because I feel like it."

"Fine by me," Leah said with genuine relief. "The

less I see of you the better. And by the way . . ." She took a breath, glanced around to be sure that no one was nearby, and then said, "I'm not the only one who feels that way."

"Really? You and the other coin counters been gossiping over by the water cooler? Am I supposed to feel threatened because somebody thinks I'm mean?"

"No," Leah said, her resolve thickening from liquid into a kind of thick mud as she spoke. "You're supposed to stop bothering Terry or I'll tell the police about the drugs."

Vince stopped smiling. His head spun quickly to both sides, checking to see if there was anyone nearby. His eyes studied her, and she was pleased to see a hint of fear in them. Then his smarmy self-confidence returned and he smiled again. "You're not serious," he sneered.

"I've never been more serious," Leah told him. "If you leave her alone I won't say a word, I swear, but if you hurt her again you leave me no choice."

"I'll waste you." Vince's voice was a snarled hiss.

Leah took a step back, stunned by the twisted hatred on his face. "Maybe," she said. "But there are people who know what to do if anything happens to me," she lied. "And that's a chance I'm willing to take." She could feel her own anger rising, turning her jelly legs firm, stiffening the tremor in her voice, solidifying her resolve. "You can't do that to me—or to anyone else—and get away with it anymore."

Vince looked completely shocked. His normally cool facade had melted down. He glanced around again and spotted several customers coming out of the bank, then visibly struggled to compose himself. "All right, all right. Fine." He laughed as though the whole thing were a joke. "Hey, she doesn't want to see me anymore? Fine. She's history." He turned back to his bike, and Leah saw his hand shake as he pulled his heavy key chain out of his jacket pocket. "But," he said, and the venom had returned to his voice, "the other part of our deal stands. You say one word, and I'll be seeing *you*."

Leah didn't wait to watch him pull away; she had turned and was fleeing back to the safety of the bank.

Once inside she searched though her bag until she found the card that Jenny had given her earlier that day. She knew that to go home alone tonight would be to flirt with Vince's unstable hold on his anger. She hesitated for only a moment before calling the number.

"Hi, Jenny? It's Leah. Listen, were you serious about letting me stay with you for a day or two? Because I think I might really need to take you up on it. I can stay at a hotel; it's no big deal—"

But Jenny cut her off with a warm welcome. "No, I was actually going to call and ask you to dinner tonight anyway, so why don't you plan on staying over?" After Leah had checked twice more to make sure she wasn't imposing, she wrote down the directions that Jenny gave her and then decided she'd better go to her house now during her lunch hour to collect a few things, rather than wait until after work. She slipped the directions into her pocket along with the card Jenny had given her. Then, keeping her head down to avoid questions, she slipped out, wondering how long it would be before she felt safe again.

Chapter 51

The darkness of the closet had begun to weigh on Joy as though it were made of iron—black, heavy metal that wrapped itself around her and pressed down with massive weight.

She knew that the time was coming closer, that it had been only an accident of fate that she was still breathing and thinking for herself, and inside a voice screamed at her to use what she had left. Forcing the numbing terror away, she concentrated on what she had. Her hands were tied, but in front of her, and that was a good thing. Her feet were loose—another plus. She was in a closet, a closet where things were stored; what things? Twisting herself around and fighting off the stabs of pain from the sleep in her legs, she began to feel blindly around on the floor of the closet, taking stock of what she could identify. A pair of cowboy boots, a box containing some kind of paper, possibly bills. That was it for the floor. Above her head hung coats, short coats that took up almost all the space across, but by pushing her body back and forth she managed to squirm her way up between them. First she checked the pockets, and came up with nothing more than a few loose coins and what felt like a movie stub.

Think, she told herself. When he had put her in

here she had seen a shelf above the coats. Straining and sweating from the claustrophobia and the tightness, she forced her arms up over her head like a belly dancer performing a snake dance until she could feel the ledge. More boxes, stacked in an orderly fashion, met her touch, and her fingers were becoming more and more educated as she used them to see with. She pulled one down and was showered by more paper. *Damn.* He'd see that if she didn't get out of here, and it would make him angry. She would have to put it all back. She'd never known anyone so compulsively neat.

The second box held what she assumed were office supplies: a stapler, a box of paper clips, and some packing tape. She knelt down and put the packing tape into a corner of the closet where she could find it again, and then resumed the laborious search. This time she hit on something with a handle and a long metal attachment: a screwdriver.

The beginning of hope stirred in her heart as she slipped the tool into the crack of the door and felt sightlessly for the catch of the lock.

Chapter 52

Leah told herself that the fear she was feeling as she opened her front door was unreasonable. Her driveway had been empty, and there were no cars parked on her street. She couldn't stop herself from pausing to listen as she came in through the kitchen door. Kate was crying loudly for food, making it impossible to hear much of anything else, so she grabbed a small handful of dried cat food and plopped it into the porcelain dish on the side table by the window.

Placing her keys in her raincoat pocket next to Jenny's card and the directions to her house, she hung the coat on the back of a kitchen chair. Trying not to succumb to the anxiety gnawing in her chest, she forced herself to walk into the living room. Everything looked normal, quiet, just as she had left it.

Even the back door to the porch. Wishing she could snatch the creepy feeling from the back of her neck and dash it to the ground, she crossed over and checked the lock; it was fastened tight.

The only audible sound came from behind her in the kitchen, where Kate was crunching the dried bits of food. But the uneasiness remained, and Leah decided to get in and out of there as quickly as she could, if for no other reason than to spare herself the imagined drama. She tried to tell herself that her anxiety was because she'd seen too many scary movies, but a small nervous laugh escaped her as she amended the thought to *No, I've been* in *too many scary movies.*

She went straight to her bedroom, grabbed a few clothes, and put them into a small bag. She stopped long enough to call her neighbor and ask her if she could watch her cat, saying that she was going out of town for a few days. She was in the bedroom when she heard a car door slam.

Her blood froze and her body stiffened. Straining to hear any small sound, she waited, trying to silence both her breathing and the beating of her heart. Had she locked the kitchen door when she came in? She moved to the hallway door on tiptoe and listened. At first she heard nothing except the faint, distant hum of the refrigerator, and then, distinctly, came the sound of a footfall. Just a soft *thump*, as though someone had lost their balance and put a foot down a bit too firmly, then nothing again for another lifelong moment, while Leah's eyes shot around the room looking for an alternate exit. The window, maybe, but it would take her precious seconds to get it open and slip outside, noisy seconds, and her car keys, she realized with a plunging drop of her heart, were in the kitchen.

She waited, listening, until the thin line of sweat that had formed on her breastbone chilled. Finally, unable to take the suspense anymore, she stepped out into the hall and called out, "Hello?"

Of course, no one answered. Leah retreated into her bedroom and picked up a heavy pewter candleholder. Its solid weight reassuring in her hand, she went slowly down the hall, looking into the spare bedroom as she went and pausing to survey the living room. Nothing.

Another sound came from the kitchen, the sound

of movement. A sharp breath escaped Leah, and she raised the makeshift weapon as the soft scraping approached the door.

"Meow." Kate rounded the corner, leaning against the molding to scratch her side as she came.

"Jesus Christ," Leah swore, and lowered the candleholder. She peeked her head around the doorjamb and she could see, through the kitchen window, her gardener beginning to unload his equipment. The thump she had heard, she now realized, had been Kate jumping from the table to the floor.

"Too many matinees," she said to Kate, bending to pet the cat. She retrieved her bag, put on her coat, and headed to the door. Kate leaped up onto the kitchen table and reprimanded her noisily.

Leah stopped and turned back. She was thinking of the night Vince had taped Kate up inside a box and then talked about how his pit bull liked to eat cats. "Too many movies," she repeated, looking down at the small ball of fluff. "Let's go." She scooped Kate up with one arm, threw the bag over the other shoulder, and retrieved her keys from the pocket of her raincoat. She would drop her cat off at the kennel before she headed back to work for the rest of the afternoon. That was one B-movie scenario she would not see played out.

Fortified by her planning and the presence of her yardman, Leah waved, locked the door behind her, and, juggling cat, bag, purse, and keys, started to her car.

Behind her, on the floor of the kitchen where it had fallen when Leah had pulled her keys out of the same pocket, lay the card with Jenny's name and address on it.

Chapter 53

Joy had spent the last forty minutes digging at the wood behind the lock of the closet door. Every few minutes she would feel around on the floor and collect any shavings she could detect in the darkness, dropping them into one of the boots that sat next to her. Since the door opened outward, she knew she either had to dig all the way around the metal bolt, which would be seen from the front, or that her other plan would have to work, and that would mean she would have to survive him at least one more time.

It had been hours, days, forever that she had scraped and dug away at the soft pine of the door molding. She slipped often and she could feel the nicks and scrapes on her knuckles, tasting blood more than once when she had sucked at each fresh wound.

The sound of the motorcycle and the frenzied barking of the dog greeting it sent her into a flurry of activity. She reached over her head and hid the screwdriver in a deep pocket of one of the jackets, hastily clawed at the floor of the closet where she guessed any shavings might lie, and then, most important, she felt for the triple thickness of packing tape that she had prepared and attached to the wall, just inside next to the lock. This would take luck, courage, and time. She prayed she had enough of each of them left.

He let the dog in this time. The monster animal came right to the crack of the closet door, and she heard his snuffling and growling just on the other side.

Shit, the dog. Was he going to let the dog attack her? She had spent hours imagining all the ways he would hurt her, how she might die, but she hadn't counted on this.

"Get away from there; get outside!" she heard him command, and she heard the dog whimper reluctantly, then trot out of the room. If she ever did get out she'd have to deal with the animal, and she had no idea how. She put it out of her mind for now. She'd have to cross that obstacle when and *if* she got to it.

After a few minutes he opened the door. From the light outside, Joy guessed that it must be late afternoon, but she was in no fit state to make an accurate assessment.

Her legs gave a little as she stood, and she fell against the side of the doorway, putting out both hands to stop herself from smacking into it, one hand cupped heavily over the other, as they were still tied together, and pressed herself back upright.

He pulled her out, untied her hands, and let her use the bathroom again. Then he settled himself on the sofa while he left her standing in the middle of the living room. He lit a cigarette and watched her, obviously enjoying her discomfort.

"Take off your shirt," he commanded.

Joy didn't move. She found an imperfection on the sofa fabric, a small pull that she focused on, trying to will herself away from this place. His voice came again, and she crossed her arms in front of her, closing her eyes against the assault that she knew would come.

But nothing touched her. She heard the jangle of his keys and the sound of his lighter flicking open again, and in a moment she cracked her eyes open to see what he doing.

He was holding the charm she had seen on his key chain in the flame from his lighter. The cigarette dangled from his lips, and his eyes squinted to keep out the smoke that curled up his face.

She whimpered. "What are you doing?" she asked in a tiny voice.

"Oh, I think it's time I made my mark."

The possibility of what might be happening was too horrific for her mind to hold. Seeing no other options, Joy took hold of the bottom of her shirt and pulled it quickly off over her head. She stood in her lace bra, the one she had chosen so carefully when she thought that this would be grown-up fun, and tried to focus on the floor through her tears.

She heard the lighter snap shut. She heard him stand, and felt him come near her.

"That's better," he said. "That's much better."

He dangled the charm inches in front of her face, and it swung back and forth, assaulting her senses with a familiar aroma. It took her a minute to place it, and then it came to her: It was the smell of a car engine after it had been on a long drive—the smell of hot metal.

Chapter 54

Joshua raised his head and looked quickly around his room. He could smell something—something hot. For a split second before it happened, Joshua recognized the feeling of an approaching unbidden vision.

Even as the room around him darkened, he thought, *Well, at least I'm starting to recognize it.*

When the image came it was the eye, but not the crude representation he had seen, rather the actual metal charm that held its shape. It moved in front of him, but this time the hand that held it was not a girl's; it was a man's.

The image faded as suddenly as it had appeared, leaving a metallic bitterness in Joshua's mouth.

Joshua knew now what the charm would be used for. He had seen Zoe's heavily bruised and bandaged face, and the smell of heat sent him racing for his door.

But he drew up suddenly at the top of the stairway. His mother wasn't here. She'd gone to work, and there was nothing he could do. He collapsed at the top stair and slumped against the wall. This was it? He was destined to watch as Joy was tortured, killed, to get little glimpses of the pain and horror she was enduring but be unable to help her in any way?

"No!" he shouted suddenly. "I will not see this!"

Tears started in his eyes, and he covered his face with his hands. "I don't want to see this," he screamed, his voice ragged with anguish. "Either let me help her, or leave me alone!"

Joshua's body slid onto the hard wooden floor of the landing as he succumbed to the desperation that had been held back by the fragile barrier of false hopes and denial he had constructed.

A fence made of brittle twigs that snapped like matchsticks as Joshua's sobs echoed through the empty house.

Chapter 55

Greer's head snapped up from the appointment book she had been staring at, trying to focus on. Something was wrong with Joshua.

Without even a word to the customer she'd been helping, she moved quickly through the salon, almost feeling her way as she went, until she came to her treatment room, where she closed the door on the noise and distractions. She cast around until she found his energy. No, he was safe—distraught, but safe.

Her breath was coming quickly, and she reached for her lighter to light a candle. She flicked the tiny wheel with her fingers, but even as the lighter sparked, she felt the burn on her forehead and called out, dropping the lighter to the floor as she pressed both hands to her face.

It was coming—it was almost here—and she knew that Joshua could feel it too. Greer reached out and snapped off the light in the windowless room. She sank quickly to her knees and tried to focus in the darkness on Joy, on what might be happening to her.

But all she could see was Joy's face with a ring of fire around it, with black slashes stabbing at the flames, not yet piercing through them, but striking them repeatedly.

With all her might Greer focused on the bracelet

that she prayed was still on Joy's wrist. She envisioned it filled with water, frozen water, icy cold. She directed the cold at the flames, and tried hard to focus on easing the heat, on forcing back the portents of violence and death.

But still they came.

Chapter 56

He ran his hand under the back of her bra and then grabbed it and twisted hard, ripping it. The girl cried out and lost her balance, falling forward onto the sofa.

He stood and looked impassively down at her. Something he hadn't expected came into his thoughts: He shouldn't do this quickly. She knew him—knew his name, where he lived; it wasn't like before. She knew him too well for him to let her go, and he might as well draw it out and enjoy it, because afterward, instead of him disappearing, he would have to make her go away.

He had intended to burn the mark onto her tonight, but a different sensation came over him now; his need to do it seemed to cool, and he felt that he could wait.

Looking down at her white skin and the small of her back, he felt a pleasing sense of proprietary power: She belonged to him. This body was his to do with as he pleased.

Until he was done with it. And what then? He would have to get rid of it. Glancing out the window as this thought passed through his mind, he almost laughed. This whole area was at the edge of a gigantic national park. He would drop it off somewhere that it wouldn't be found for a long while, maybe ever.

But first he needed a way to transport it that wouldn't cause any suspicion.

He laughed again. It was really so easy. On reflection he had all night—hell, all week, if he wanted it. Being a neat, efficient person, he decided that first he'd go get what he needed. Plus, he had an appointment to see someone else.

He put her back in the closet, where she slumped against the side of the wall as he closed the door. Then he checked himself in his hall mirror before he went out.

As he started the truck, he thought of the one other thing he wanted to do first, one other item that couldn't be ignored. He would attend to that, and then he'd be back.

Chapter 57

When Leah left the bank at four thirty it was already growing dark; as though to meet the evening's formal dress requirements, the sky was cloaked in clouds. She found the directions to Jenny's house in her coat pocket, but when she looked for the card with her home information, thinking to call and see if she could bring anything, it didn't seem to be there.

Oh, well, she must have put it in her purse or a different pocket. She'd stop and pick up a bottle of wine—she could use a drink herself.

She pulled into Burman's liquor store and bought the only two decent merlots she found nestled amongst the blackberry wines and Hennessy. She toyed with the idea of cheese and crackers, but the expiration dates were too far gone to make them an acceptable hostess gift.

When she pulled up in front of Jenny and Lewis's house, Leah experienced a fleeting moment of jealousy. The house was small, without much pretense or yard to speak of, but it was charming and warm and well kept. It was a home where two lovers lived.

Leah's sigh came out as a sustained melancholy note. She went to the front door and was surprised to find a note. *Come on in, I'm making dinner!* it read. Leah glanced around the tidy little neighborhood, feeling more and more comfortable. It must be nice to feel so safe that you could leave a note like that pinned to your door.

"Hello!" Leah called out as she came through the front door into a cozy living room. A fire burned in the small brick fireplace, and two mismatched but obviously comfortable armchairs shared the space around it with two rocking chairs.

"Hello?" Leah called again. Straight ahead she could see through an opening into the left side of the kitchen, and she heard what sounded like a radio playing some salsa music, and water running in the sink.

She set down her bag, pulled out the wine, and headed for the kitchen. "Hi! I brought some . . ." The words died on Leah's lips as she saw Jenny lying facedown on the linoleum floor of the kitchen.

Before she could scream or rush to Jenny, a hand clamped over her mouth and the bottles of wine fell with a crash to the floor. The neck of one of them broke, and the violet liquid made a *glug-glug* noise as it spread across the white floor.

"Don't worry; she's just taking a little nap. But don't you make a sound," the Rattler's hated voice whispered in her ear. "Or I'll kill her."

Chapter 58

The last customer had departed, and the only people left in the salon besides herself were Dario and Jonathan. Greer had pulled herself together enough to get through the rest of the day, though with a horrible sense of impotence. The fact was, there was nothing more she could do for Joy except hope and pray, and to sit doing only that would have driven her insane.

So she stayed as busy as possible, but her distraction had been evident, and Dario had kept a wary eye on her all afternoon.

As Dario was letting Jonathan out the front door, they shared a concerned look and a quick, back-slapping hug before Dario locked the door behind his assistant. He was about to turn away when Sterling appeared on the far side. Dario let him in, grateful for the interruption. He'd been planning on spending the evening trying to divert and comfort Greer, and he didn't have much hope for it being a night of light, entertaining repartee.

"Hi," Sterling said, looking almost apologetic. "Any news?"

"Nothing good, if that's what you mean," Dario told him, cutting his eyes meaningfully to where Greer was standing. She was staring toward the back of the salon with a look of utter distraction on her face. The two men approached her cautiously.

She started when they drew near her, and in answer to Sterling's gentle, "Hello," she turned and said, "Leah's in trouble. I've got to help her."

"Nice to see you too," Sterling half joked, but he could see that she was disturbed. The name Leah, however, was new to him.

"I thought the girl's name was Joy."

Greer's face tightened into a painful flash of a grimace. "It is, but there isn't anything I can do for her; or rather, I've already done everything I can. But Leah is another friend of mine, and she's in danger too. Possibly the same danger. It feels very similar, and"—she looked eagerly up to Dario—"I know where she is. I know where she's *supposed* to be anyway. If we can find Leah, maybe we can find Joy too." Her voice was very cautiously hopeful, as though she were afraid to entertain any of that emotion in case it might be too shy and leave the party.

"Can you call her?" Dario asked, while Sterling stood there feeling as though his head had come off and was spinning around somewhere about a foot and half above him.

Greer nodded, and with an empathetic glance to the obviously confounded Sterling, she pulled out her address book while summarizing her conversation with Jenny from that morning. First she called Leah's home number. There was no answer. The number listed as her cell phone produced the same lack of effect. Next she called Jenny's, hoping that Jenny would tell her that Leah was safe. This time she got an answering machine.

As each number rang and there was no response, the spooky feeling of imminent danger grew in Greer. She hung up the phone and looked up with a pale face at her partner.

"Okay," Dario said decisively, "here's what we're going to do. You've got both their addresses?" Greer nodded and handed the address book over to Dario. He reviewed them as he spoke. "Give me the Thomas Guide under the counter, would you?" He flipped through the map book to the page displaying the Shadow Hills area as he spoke. "We could call that pleasant detective and tell him to stop by." Greer's face told him all he needed to know about that suggestion; she had nothing to tell Sheridan except that she had a bad feeling about somebody else. "Okay, so that leaves us. I'll go to Leah's house," he said, tracing a street on the map with his finger to find the address number, "because that one seems more ominous, deserted, dangerous, that kind of thing, and I've always fancied I was a bit Bond. And you go to Jenny's, which is in the Golden Oaks subdivision on what is probably a nicely lit cul-de-sac and where her husband will most likely be home protecting her. Okay?"

"Nicely lit cul-de-sac, my ass," Sterling jumped in. "She's bloody well not going anywhere without me."

Dario and Greer turned to stare at him. He looked back, his determination turning ever so slightly into embarrassment. "What else am I going to do? Head over to the pub for a relaxing pint?"

"No," said Greer in a slightly awed voice. "I suppose not. I'd be glad of the company. Thanks."

"Right, then," Sterling said, shifting into his naturally commanding gear. "Get your mackintosh and get in the car."

Chapter 59

It was a full quarter of an hour before Joshua could find the strength to raise himself off the floor in the darkened hall. Unable to return to his room and its view of Joy's empty bedroom, he stumped heavily down the stairs and turned on all the lights in the kitchen.

He moved with a surreal, heavy-liquid feeling, as though he were made of mercury. Wondering if he'd be able to get up again, he sank into a chair and sat staring at the table.

Useless, he thought. *I'm useless.*

He might have remained there all night, or at least until his mother returned, but he was called out of his despondent reverie by the sound of raised voices outside. Summoning the superhuman strength it required to lift his leaden head, he looked out the window toward Joy's house, where the cars were parked in front of it.

Mostly he could see his own reflection, but the exterior lights on Luke's porch gave him a view of three people. Two were obviously Luke and Whitney, the former standing with his arms folded tightly over his chest, and Whitney with hers thrust deep into the pockets of a cardigan sweater. The third person was the chunky female he'd seen from his window before, and it was her voice that was doing the shouting. Puffs of steam—or maybe was it smoke—spit from her mouth and hung in the air to illustrate her verbal affronts.

From this distance, Joshua couldn't make out what she was saying, but the tone sounded harsh and accusatory. As he watched, the woman moved toward Whitney and got right in her face. Whitney diverted her head slightly but Luke placed a hand on the woman's shoulder and pushed her gently away, placing his body between his wife and the stranger.

Even from here, Joshua could make out the smooth, commanding timber of Luke's powerful voice. The woman was being told to keep her distance, to calm down.

Joshua's heart twisted like a wet rag as he watched Luke's noble stance. Erect, proud, even in his pain and his crippling situation, he remained stoic and strong enough to appear stable when others were snapping and lapsing into indulgent hysteria. As Joshua looked on, he acutely felt his own deficiencies. He had neither stoicism nor strength. He had nothing to offer anyone. Had his mother been here, he would have begged like a baby for her to support him in his need and pain.

Somewhere between his reflection and the image of the three discordant adults, a fifth figure materialized as though etched on the glass—or rather, as though the glass contained all the world outside, much like a snow globe, and she floated freely in its clear essence. Joshua knew her now. Sarah seemed more frantic than before as she gestured urgently. She pointed to the left, and Joshua saw three images: the oak tree, a set of keys, and a motorcycle. Sarah shook the keys and pointed at the other two objects, which flickered in and out before him, like a weak slide show on an uneven surface.

He sat forward and tried to study them. "I don't understand," he whispered to Sarah. "I found the tree, but I don't understand."

She beckoned to him, as though asking him to come with her. That was when he noticed that she appeared to be just over his own dirt bike. Then she was gone, and the trio's confrontation outside had subsided into low, murmured voices.

Was it *his* motorcycle she was referring to? What could that mean? That he was supposed to ride it somewhere? Joshua got up and paced the floor, his head so filled with churning thoughts that he felt his skull would crack open and spill its contents onto the kitchen floor.

Gradually one thought came to the front: He wanted to help Joy, and a blind, stumbling effort would be better than doing nothing, than not trying, and hating himself for the rest of his life.

Chapter 60

Vince kept one strong arm around Leah's neck with his hand clamped over her mouth as they drove in his Hummer the fifteen minutes to the dark road where he lived. She'd never been to this house, which he'd bought since the divorce—hadn't ever wanted to go— and she certainly didn't want to see it now.

The fact that he was making more money than he should was apparent the moment it came into view at the end of a long drive. As the electric gate closed behind them, a package of muscle and teeth shot at the truck, snarling and lunging at the tires.

Finally Vince released Leah, and she pulled away from him disgustedly.

"What did I tell you—is that a fine animal or what?" Vince flashed his own white fangs at Leah. "You might want to stay with me while we go into the house, and I don't really recommend stepping outside unless I get ahold of him."

"I'm not going anywhere with you," Leah said defiantly.

Vince reached into a compartment in his door and drew out what Leah recognized from her many movies as a Glock semiautomatic pistol. "Oh, I think you are."

He opened the door on his side and snapped a loud

"Hold!" to the pit bull, who stopped snarling, but seemed barely able to contain himself. Vince reached in and, grabbing Leah by the arm, dragged her down out of the Hummer and then walked her up onto the porch and into the house.

It was large, made of pine and stone, with a vaulted living room and lots of leather furniture. Everything was in its place; it had the look of a showroom ready to be photographed. He took Leah to the sofa and ordered her to sit. She looked around the room as inconspicuously as possible, checking for exits. There were two doors. She guessed that one led to a hallway; the other seemed to be a closet of some kind.

It had a lock on it. She could only guess what skeletons Vince kept locked up in his closet.

Chapter 61

Greer tried to call both Leah and Jenny several more times as Sterling drove toward Jenny's neighborhood, but they got no answer.

"Here it is," Greer said as she read off the address on the mailbox when they pulled up in front of the neat little Craftsman-style house.

The cell phone, still clutched in Greer's hand, rang, and she yanked it open. "Yes?"

"It's Dario. I'm at Leah's house, and there's nobody here. No cars, no pets, nothing. I walked around the house, shone my flashlight in windows, knocked. It's empty."

In spite of the fact that she'd expected it, Greer's heart sank. "Okay, thanks. Would you mind going to my house and staying with Joshua until I get back? I know this isn't easy for him either."

"Exactly what I was thinking. Have you guys seen anything?"

"We just pulled up, and there's two cars parked out front. I'll call you back in a little while."

Dario wished them luck and signed off.

Sterling had come around and opened Greer's car door. He took her hand as she climbed out and didn't let it go as they went up the walk.

They got to the front door and knocked. The house

was cheerily lit but silent. They knocked again and waited, but there was no reply.

Greer looked questioningly at Sterling, who tried the door. Locked.

"I'll go look around the side," he told her. "You stay here in case someone comes to the door."

Greer nodded, infinitely grateful to lean on his capable strength. She watched him disappear through a garden gate and then strained to see through the leaded glass inserts on the door, but could make out only a distorted image of furniture and a small fireplace.

"Greer!" The shouted cry came from the side of the house. Startled, she quickly traced Sterling's footsteps and found him struggling to force open a window. Leaning around him she saw Jenny on the floor. She was stirring, trying to sit up with one hand clutching her head.

"Hold on, hold on!" she said when she managed to focus on them. "Don't shout; my head's about to come off." She got to her knees, then her feet, and, supporting herself with the kitchen counter, she moved to the side door and unlocked it.

Sterling stood back for Greer, who rushed in and put an arm around Jenny's waist, taking her weight and helping her to a kitchen chair. "What happened?"

"I don't know, exactly. But I'm sure as shit gonna start locking the front door." Jenny groaned and put her head down. "Uh, I don't feel so good."

Sterling had gone to the freezer and filled a dish towel with ice. He pressed it gently to the place where she was holding her scalp. "Are you going to be sick?"

"Maybe. No. I don't think so." Jenny groaned again and then squinted up at them as though the light hurt her eyes. "Where's Leah?"

"Didn't she come here?" Greer asked, her blood temperature dropping suddenly.

"She was supposed to. I left the door open for her. Uh. Big mistake. Last thing I remember, I was in here making pasta sauce, and then I hear you guys trying to smash my new Pella windows." Jenny seemed to notice for the first time the broken wine bottle and the mess on the floor for the first time. "Where did that come from?"

Sterling exchanged glances with Greer and then slipped out of the kitchen. Greer held the ice gently against Jenny's head. "We've got to go get that head looked at. That's a nasty bump."

"Really? Ow!" Jenny exclaimed as she touched it gingerly. "Jesus, it's the size of an apple!"

Sterling reappeared in the doorway. "Are these yours?" He was holding a small overnight bag and a purse.

Jenny shook her head and instantly regretted it. "Ouch. No, that's Leah's purse; I recognize it from this morning."

Sterling was holding a piece of paper in one hand. "Did you write this?" It was the note that Leah had pulled off the door and set down on top of her bag, telling her to come on in.

Jenny looked as though she had trouble focusing on it, and then she sighed. "No, that's not my writing."

"It looks more like a man's writing, don't you think?" Sterling asked.

With a trembling hand Greer reached out. "Give it to me," she said. She took the torn sheet and looked down at it. But instead of seeing the ink and the paper, she saw a brownish black space, and inside of it was Leah's face.

"He's got her," Greer whispered.

Chapter 62

He sat down across from her in one of the leather armchairs, set the gun casually on the arm, and, extracting a cigarette from a box on a small table next to him, he lit it and regarded her with a pleased, ugly glint in his eye.

"Oh, how rude of me—I haven't offered you a drink."

Leah said nothing.

"Whiskey? You used to like Jack Daniel's, as I recall. A bit on the sweet side for me, so if you don't mind, I'll have a little Knob Creek."

Taking the gun, he moved to a built-in bar and poured two glasses of the brown bourbon. Crossing back, he offered one to Leah; she ignored him.

"Oh, well, can't say I never gave you anything." He laughed, downed first one and then both the drinks, and sat back down again. "Now, let's talk about why you're here."

"I know why I'm here, Vince," Leah said coldly. "And other people know where I am too."

He leaned forward and looked at her, his eyes glazing slightly from the liquor. "I think you're lying. I don't think you ever told anybody about what went on between us. You're so fucking uptight it would

horrify you to have anyone find out the kind of fun
we used to have."

Leah's blood boiled, both at the memory and the
truth that was in his mockery. "Fun?" she said, barely
containing the tears of rage.

Vince stood up, set the gun down again, and unzipped his pants. "I think you've been missing me. I
think I know exactly what you want. You need a little
refresher lesson." His voice grew more and more
angry as he went on. "You think you can fuck with
me? I'll teach you to keep your mouth shut. I'll stuff
something in there to keep it shut."

He moved forward toward her, and before she could
try to slip away he had the back of her hair in both
his hands. He pulled her face forward up against him;
his cruelty and her helplessness had excited him.

"Open your mouth," he ordered.

At first Leah resisted, pressing her lips tightly together and struggling to turn her face away, though
he held her head firmly right where he wanted it, but
she realized quickly that there was no other choice.

So she opened her mouth, he inserted himself into
it, and Leah, remembering all her rage and all her
pain, bit down as hard as she could.

Vince howled with pain, but was unable to pull
away without causing himself more damage. Leah
brought both her hands up. Grabbing his testicles hard
with one hand, she squeezed and twisted with all her
strength. The other hand she placed at the base of his
penis and twisted hard in the opposite direction.

He let go of her hair and struck hard against the
side of her head. She tasted blood as her teeth were
knocked sideways, but she held on for her life with
both hands, squishing and twisting with every ounce
of rage she possessed. Again and again Vince struck
at her head, but she took the blows. He grabbed at
her face and tried to push her away, but she dug in

her fingernails and twisted harder. Coming to her feet, she began to pull him toward the door as he began to plead with her.

"Sweet Jesus, let go. Oh, fuck me, let go, please."

Leah yanked and wrung his offensive genitalia with renewed energy as she realized he was weakening. "Call off the fucking dog," she ordered.

"Oh, please, let go."

"Call off the dog!" Leah shouted at him.

She held on, giving an additional tweak when he seemed to slow or weaken in his resolve. She forced him to unlock the door and put the dog into the garage. Then, using her reins, she made him cross to the phone and call the police. She listened to him whimper and cry his way through giving his address and telling them he had assaulted someone, and then, when he collapsed, barely conscious, onto the floor, she let him fall, and took up the gun.

Her right ear rang with a constant buzzing where he had struck her, and a tentative exploration of her face told her that her lip was split and there was a nasty lump coming up on her temple. Blood or sweat or both dripped into her right eye, and she had to squint to squeeze it away. She stood over him, panting, while hot tears ran down her injured face, the salt water stinging the abrasions.

He writhed and moaned where he lay, clutching at his injured parts.

She still didn't trust him. She'd tie him up until the police got there.

Leah looked around and spotted the closet door. She tried it; it was locked. Vince's keys were hanging loosely from his jeans, which had fallen halfway down his thighs. Carefully, keeping the gun pointed at his head, she leaned down and unclipped them from his belt loop.

Holding them under a table lamp, she matched the

brand name on the lock to the one on the key and inserted it. It tumbled with a satisfying click.

Turning the knob, Leah pulled open the door to see a row of coats hung tightly together. A shelf above held boxes, and on the floor . . . She had to take a step backward to see into the dark place shadowed by the clothes; she leaned down and peered into the small space.

There was nothing there but a neat row of cowboy boots.

Leah pulled one of the belts off a raincoat. That would have to do until the police arrived and put this fucker in handcuffs.

Chapter 63

Joy had waited until the sound of the big truck's wheels had crunched away over the gravel drive and the dog's barking had followed it to the gate. Her whole body ached from the multiple bruises she'd suffered, but for just a few seconds she forgot all of that as she raised a shaking hand to the doorknob.

"Please God, let it have worked," she prayed. She slid the screwdriver into the lock and felt it slide along the layers of packing tape she had pressed into the receiving hole for the bolt as she had fallen against the door. The metal caught on the last fraction of an inch, and in rage and frustration she jimmied the bolt, threw her shoulder against the door, and tumbled out onto the living room floor.

Struggling to her feet and ignoring the feeling of a thousand tiny pinpricks as her legs were roused from their slumber and blood began to flow into her capillaries, she moved toward the kitchen, retrieving her shirt from the floor on the way. There on the gleaming countertop was the wooden knife holder. With her wrists still bound, she reached out and grabbed at a handle with both hands, drawing out a long, slim filleting knife. She let it drop back and selected another, this time producing a shorter, serrated blade.

Sitting down on a chair, she pressed the handle of

the knife between her knees so that the blade stood straight up, and then she began to saw the rope on her hands back and forth against it. She slipped twice, nicking herself badly, but finally a strand of the hefty nylon cord was severed, and she was able to unwind the remaining loops.

She donned her shirt, then pulled up the leg of her jeans and thrust the knife into the top of her sock. The blade felt hot but reassuring against the skin of her calf. Cautiously, she moved to the kitchen door and looked out.

The dog was asleep on the deck a few feet away from the door. She knew that the animal had the run of the property within the gated area, and that no other door would offer a protected exit.

She backed away and tried to think. She felt light-headed—she'd had little to eat or drink in the last few days—and her bruised body objected at every movement. Joy went to the refrigerator and rummaged around. There wasn't much there, but she wolfed down a piece of bread and some lunch meat, drinking eagerly from the faucet. She didn't know how much time she had, but she had to assume that it was next to none.

She took everything she thought the dog might eat and went again to the door. The bolt was locked with a key she knew he had with him, but the top part of the door was made of glass slats with a screen on the inside. Grabbing a butter knife from a drawer, Joy began to turn the screws that held the screen in place.

The dog woke up, turned to investigate the sound, and launched himself at her figure in the window. She backed away a step and then returned to her work.

"It's okay, doggy from hell. I got a little treat for you." She tried to keep her voice both calm and friendly, though it seemed unlikely he could hear her over his own incessant noise.

When the screen was off, she turned the slats open and threw out a few pieces of sliced turkey. The dog stopped barking long enough to investigate and then eat them. *Good.* She went to the front door while he was busy and checked it out. There was no keyed bolt on that one. *Okay.*

Returning to the kitchen, Joy gathered up all the food items she had taken from the refrigerator and cabinets and shoved them through the window as fast as she could, trying to get them to land in different places on the deck. The dog went for them, and she ran for the other door.

There was a walking stick leaning against the wall, and as she turned the lock she grabbed it, threw the door open, and ran.

Ahead of her, dimly lit by the yellow porch light, she could see the gate that led to the road. It was thirty feet away. She had no thought of stealth or anything but reaching it as quickly as her wounded body and her fear would carry her. She had crossed the deck and started down the stairs when she heard the dog.

He'd spotted her, and with a vicious growl he took off after her. She'd made it halfway across the yard when he got hold of her right leg.

Joy screamed in pain as the long teeth pierced her jeans and entered her skin. Her forward movement was arrested and she was thrust forward onto the hard ground. Instinctively spinning to defend herself, she hit at the dog with the stick in her hand and kicked repeatedly with the other foot, but it seemed to have no effect. The dog held his grip and started to pull backward, scraping Joy's back along the rocky ground.

"Let go, you fucking monster!" Joy screamed, and grabbed out for something with which to pull herself away or to strike him. Her hand landed on a large rock, and, gripping it, she swung down and smashed it into the dog's head once, twice. The dog stopped growling but held on. Joy sat up, took the several-pound rock in both hands, and raised it up over her head. She knew that the animal wouldn't give up, that it was her or him. With a guttural howl, she launched her bludgeoning weapon downward with all the strength that her survival instinct could muster and felt it make contact with the dog's giant head.

He let go, yelped, and backed away in confusion. Joy could see blood dripping from his ear. He walked a few uneven steps and then flopped down onto his side, panting raggedly.

Her leg was a mess. The jeans were torn and wet with a dark mass of her blood and the dog's saliva. Like a crab, Joy crawled backward, still watching the wounded dog, who growled feebly, but didn't get up again.

When she felt the fence against her back, Joy used it to pull herself to her feet, felt her way to the gate, unlatched it, and slipped out. She stopped to try to examine her leg, but she couldn't see much in the dark. She took off her shirt, ripped away one of the long sleeves, and bound it tightly around the throbbing wound, then pulled the now asymmetrical garment back over her head. She tried to stand and found she could bear her weight if she favored the other foot.

Now . . . what to do? The long driveway led back to the road, but that was the way he would return. For a long section of it the road had been cut into the side of a steep incline; it dropped off sharply on one side while a sheer rock face rose on the other. If he came upon her there, she would be completely exposed with nowhere to hide. No, the road was not an option.

Only one choice left. Guessing at the right direction, she took off, limping painfully, into the dark woods.

Chapter 64

They pulled up to the Verdugo Hills Hospital emergency entrance. Greer was sitting in the backseat, still holding the ice to Jenny's head.

"I'm fine," Jenny kept insisting. "I don't need to go to the hospital."

But Sterling would have none of it. "Even a momentary loss of consciousness means that you need to get your head checked out, and we have no idea how long you were out. The fact that you are making sense now and don't seem too disoriented bodes well, but it would be stupid to take chances."

Jenny looked up at Greer. "How does he know all this?"

Greer smiled at her. "He used to work in a pub in Tooting."

"Did you lose consciousness often?" Jenny asked him.

Sterling smiled grimly. "Not very. Usually it was the other guy." As he helped her out, they were joined by Lewis. Greer had called him from the car, and he had left work to rush to meet them. He embraced his wife with tears in his eyes and then led her gently to the counter, where they took one look at her and sent her to an examining room.

Sterling and Greer settled in to wait. Greer rooted

through her wallet until she came up with the card Sheridan had given her. They'd called the police from Jenny's house and reported Leah's disappearance and the assault, but Sterling had insisted they leave for the hospital instead of waiting for the police. The operator had told Greer that an officer would meet them at the ER to take a report.

But Greer couldn't shake loose the feeling that she should talk to Detective Sheridan. She carefully dialed the cell phone number on his card and got a message. Next she tried the precinct nonemergency number, and after close to twenty rings a bored voice picked up.

"Yes, hello," Greer said. "I'm looking for Detective Sheridan."

"Hold on; I'll transfer you."

Greer nodded in response to Sterling mouthing the words, *Do you want coffee?* as she waited. After a few seconds a deep but distinctly female voice came on the line.

"Detective Arlen."

"Uh, I was holding for Detective Sheridan," Greer tried again.

"He's out. Can I take a message?"

"I guess so. This is Greer Sands. I've been talking to Detective Sheridan about the Joy Whitehorse case."

"Mm-hmm," came the noncommittal response. "Do you have some further information?"

"No . . . well, unfortunately not about Joy." Greer's heart felt as if it would break, and she had to rush on to keep herself from being overtaken by sorrow. "I'd like to speak to him about another assault that I think might be related."

"You want to report another crime?" Interest seemed to pique warily in the detective's voice, as though she spent most of her evening being teased by citizens with faux crimes and was afraid to hope that this might be an actual incident.

"Yes, I would, but I'd like to speak to Detective Sheridan as well."

"Where are you?"

"I'm at Verdugo Hills Hospital in the emergency waiting room."

"Is the victim with you?"

"Yes, but—"

"Conscious?"

"Yes, she's in with the doctor."

"There should be an officer on duty at the hospital. They'll have been alerted by the office staff. They'll give us a call if we're needed—"

"Please!" Greer cut her off. "Do you have any way of getting in touch with Detective Sheridan? It's very important that I speak with him. I'll leave you my number."

Detective Arlen let a sufficient period of silence pass to accurately depict both annoyance and disinterest. When she spoke again she sounded very put out, but she took the number and said she would pass it on.

Sterling had returned with two Styrofoam cups of weak coffee, but before she could relate the conversation, their attention was snatched away by an ambulance pulling up outside and a police car careening smoothly into the space next to it. A woman with her head partly bandaged was escorted from the back of the police car as the EMTs began to pull a stretcher from their vehicle.

Both Sterling and Greer tried to look away, to not stare intrusively at this new tragedy, at someone else's pain. Greer sipped the coffee and read the names off the magazines on the side table. But as the automatic glass doors slid open with a swish, she glanced up discreetly at the woman and got a good look at her face.

She choked and sloshed the coffee as she set it down too fast on the table, scalding her hand, but she felt nothing.

"Leah!" Greer cried, and stood with one hand clapped to her mouth. "Oh, my God! Thank God you're all right. Are you all right?"

Leah, her face swollen almost to the point of being unrecognizable, had turned at the sound of Greer's familiar voice. Until this moment she had remained stoic, hard, factual.

But as Greer came toward her with her arms outstretched, all the pretense of strength fell away. The shock and the horror that had she had lived through hit her harder than Vince's fist ever could, and she collapsed into her new friend's arms, sobbing like a broken child.

Chapter 65

The dog paced the fenced-in yard, occasionally stopping to gnaw on a large piece of rubber that looked as though it had been discarded there for that very purpose.

Sheridan didn't care much for dogs; they made his work much harder, especially stakeouts. He and the two other officers had been watching the house for about thirty minutes, during which time the dog had most definitely found them out, and made it impossible to get close enough to the windows to get a look inside. There was light behind the heavy window coverings, and there seemed to be movement, but so far there had been no one going in or out.

Sheridan glanced at his watch. Five of nine—should be any minute now.

His pager went off, causing him to jump a fraction of an inch. Damn, he hated that. He reached down and punched the button. The office—they'd have to wait. A few seconds later it buzzed him silently again; he ignored it this time.

Down the dark street came the reverberating sounds of a big truck. He drew back farther into the shadows of the bushes along the side of the road, and waited. The dog lost interest in anything except the approaching noise, getting excited and turning in circles. *The dog knows the car,* thought Sheridan. *This is it.*

The truck's big engine rumbled up to the driveway and turned in enough to have to stop at the gate. The door of the driver's side opened and a well-built man started to climb out. In the darkness Sheridan couldn't make out his face, but he was wearing shiny cowboy boots and pressed jeans, as though ready for a night out.

The detective raised his small walkie-talkie to his mouth and waited. The man walked to the gate and began to unlock it.

"Now," Sheridan whispered sharply into the transmitter, and then he moved forward. At the same time the other two officers came out of the darkness from the other side of the gate. The dog went insane, lunging and thrusting at the legs of the men just outside of his reach. The pointed ears of his breed flattened back against his head, and he bared his long teeth as he desperately tried to protect his master.

The three officers were on the unsuspecting man in seconds. Sheridan stood back with his gun drawn as the other two forced the man's hands over his head and pushed him up against the chain-link fence.

As Sheridan read him his rights, the front door of the house flew open and a young girl, maybe fourteen, peeked cautiously around the edge of the doorway.

"What going on?" she said in a high-pitched voice that was just hysterical enough to carry over the din of the dog and the men.

"Police. Can you call off the dog, please?" Sheridan's tone was much more of a command than a request.

So far the man with his face pressed against the cold metal had said nothing.

"What's going on?" The girl's voice banked steeply upward.

"Police. Call off the dog!" Sheridan barked.

"Gunner! Come!" she half cried, to no avail. She finally had to move down the steps from the porch and pull him back by the collar. She put the German shepherd in the house, where he repeatedly threw himself against the window, scrabbling up under the curtains, but the sound, at least, was now muffled.

"What's going on?" the girl asked again when she returned to the other side of the gate. She was standing directly in the headlights of the truck, and her resemblance to a deer in the same situation was marked.

"Do you know this man?" Sheridan asked. He had taken the man's wallet out of his back pocket and was searching through it.

"Yes," she said hesitantly. "Is he in some kind of trouble again?"

Sheridan raised one eyebrow at the word *again*, but other than that he didn't comment on it. "Could you identify yourself, please?" He looked at the teenager; she was blond, wearing too much makeup and a short cutoff shirt that barely covered the bottoms of her breasts. Her jeans were so low that he could see the bare skin of both her hips. If she had been his daughter he would have washed her face with a rough cloth and made her put on a sweater.

"I'm, uh, Lucy Fuller."

"Are your parents home, Lucy?"

"Uh, no, sir. This isn't my house, and anyway I live with my grandmother, but she's at work. She's a cocktail waitress at the Pine Lodge."

"I see." A cocktail waitress would mean that the woman was probably never home before at least three a.m., leaving this youngster alone until then. Sheridan wondered again that anyone could blame these kids for their moral wandering. "And do you know this man?"

"Yes, sir. He's my cousin. Our moms were sisters."

Sheridan closed his eyes and cursed softly under his breath. He needed to find Joy Whitehorse, and he needed to do it now. He rubbed his burning midsection with one hand unconsciously. What if it was too late already? "He picks you up at school sometimes?"

"Yes, sir. When my grandmother's working, he sometimes picks me up if he can get away from his work. Is he in trouble?" She sounded very afraid.

"Yesterday? Did he pick you up yesterday?"

"Yes, sir."

In response to this Sheridan gestured to the other officers, who turned the man around. He was handsome in a rough way, and his face was full of that patient, resentful hatred that came with being on the wrong side of too many law officers.

"What's your name?" Sheridan asked him.

"Army Newman," the man replied after a short hesitation that held both contempt and resignation.

"I got a couple of calls about you, Mr. Newman. It looks like maybe one of them—the one about you picking up an underage girl at the high school—was a slight misunderstanding. But in view of the fact that two girls have disappeared from that school, I'm sure you won't mind answering a few of my questions."

Army kept his eyes riveted to the ground, but he said, "I don't have anything to do with that."

Sheridan walked forward. "We'll go into that a little more later. The other call was unrelated and anonymous. It got shuffled to me because of a different ongoing investigation that happens to be in a file on my desk." Sheridan paused to burp silently, releasing some of the acrid gas from his digestive system. "You don't seem to have too many fans, Army Newman."

Again Army said nothing, just shifted his arms a little to try to ease them into a more comfortable position with the cuffs on them. His exhalations made little clouds in the harsh truck lights. He had the air of a man who was waiting to see what he was in trouble for *this* time.

"You're on parole. You've got a nine-o'clock curfew; that's how we knew when to meet you. And since you're supposed to be living clean, you wouldn't know anything about crystal methamphetamine, would you? I mean, seeing how it's illegal and would send you back to prison for a long time, you wouldn't have any on you, would you?"

The girl made a funny, impatient sound that drew Sheridan's eye. He found himself looking at someone very different from the frightened teenager he'd seen a moment ago.

"Drugs! Are you crazy?" She stomped her foot and put her hands firmly on her hips; she looked furious. "Army *never* has *anything* to do with drugs. He's a health freak. Look at him; he works out two hours a day and he drinks nonalcoholic beer. He caught me with a joint one time, and I thought he was gonna kill me. You're out of your ever-loving mind! Drugs." She said the word contemptuously. "*No way.* Let him go!"

Sheridan was so surprised by her outburst that, if he had had a sense of humor and not been in pain, he might have laughed. "Okay, okay, settle down." He pulled a sheet of paper from his breast pocket and, unfolding it, held it up for Army to read. "Search warrant. If you don't mind, we'll just have a quick look around inside and see what we see."

But Sheridan's burning stomach was telling him that a search of this house was a waste of time. Even if they found evidence of drugs, it wasn't what he needed to save the girl. He knew that, on the small chance that Joy Whitehorse was still alive, the clock was running down, and he was so far from the bomb that he couldn't even hear the ticking.

Chapter 66

"Officer Willoughby." The man in the blue uniform turned down his radio on his belt as he introduced himself. "Are you the people who called in the assault?"

Greer rose from her chair to meet the young policeman. "Yes, sir. We are."

"And are you the victim?"

Greer was sitting in the exam room holding Leah's hand, while the ER doctor carefully stitched up the cut on her lip. Sterling was squeezed into the corner; he looked as though he were trying to be as unobtrusive as possible. Leah looked up at Officer Willoughby as if he were nuts when he addressed his question to her. She could neither speak nor shake her head for fear of further injury.

"No, she's not," Greer answered for her.

Officer Willoughby's eyes rose from his clipboard with the worksheet attached and flicked from Leah to Greer. "No?" he asked incredulously.

"This is Leah Falconer. Jenny Sanchez, the woman we called about, is in radiology getting a CAT scan. She was knocked unconscious and they want to check for hemorrhaging," Greer explained. "Her husband, Lewis, is with her."

"So who is this?"

Sterling interceded. "She's a victim of a different assault, but she's already given her report to different police officers. They're in with her attacker now."

Willoughby rubbed his brow. "And where is *he*?"

The doctor spoke without ceasing his intense concentration on the minute stitches. "He's in four."

"What happened to him?" the officer asked the doctor.

"Penile abrasions, bruising, trauma to the testicles."

The officer's head had started to nod, as though he got it, even though he didn't get it. "Uh-huh. I see. Okay. So, these two, uh, three assaults are *not* related?"

Now Leah made a noise. It sounded like an angry "Uh-huh!"

"Please don't move," the doctor said with monotone calmness.

"The same man attacked both women," Greer told the young officer, taking pity on his inability to keep the disinterested face of a seasoned peace officer.

"And who attacked him?" Willoughby asked, using his pen as an accent, as though drawing his question mark in the white light of the exam room.

Another noise came from Leah, and she raised her hand, but it was Sterling who said, "She did. Well, she bit the son of a bitch when he was sexually assaulting her." He couldn't keep from smiling his pride.

Willoughby's eyebrows went up now. "Really?" He whistled softly. "Anybody else?"

Greer and Leah's eyes found each other as they both thought of Joy, and Greer had to look away. "I hope not," she said softly. She felt the pressure of Sterling's hand on her arm and smiled up at him gratefully.

"I think I'd better go and speak to the other officers. Excuse me. I'll be back in a minute."

He moved to the door and then turned and pointed the pen at Leah. "Don't leave!" he told her firmly.

A long blue suture wire was being pulled through the skin of her lip as she looked at him. Her eyes went to Greer and then rolled incredulously to the ceiling.

"Her the huk hood hi ho?" asked Leah.

Greer and Sterling looked at each other and frowned, but one corner of the doctor's mouth smiled and he spoke without breaking his gaze or ceasing his artful work. "She said, 'Where the fuck would I go?'"

Chapter 67

Sitting on his idling bike by the edge of the highway, Joshua hesitated. For the third time Sarah appeared in front of him and beckoned before flickering away. "I don't know what you want me to do." He sighed and fought back tears as he muttered, "This is crazy. I should just go back. I don't even know which direction to go."

Just behind him something fell heavily onto the dirt road. Startled, Joshua fumbled a flashlight out of his pocket and shone the beam in that direction. A rock had fallen from the steep, loose embankment onto the rutted dirt road. It wasn't impassible, but it would have been bad news if he had turned back.

All the hair on Joshua's arms prickled upright. His skin crawled as he mumbled, "Okay, but maybe you know which way to go," to the empty night. He had no idea where he was going or what he might find, but he was pretty sure that tonight wasn't going to be a ride in the park.

He had left a note on the bulletin board next to people's business cards and take-out menus, where he knew his mom would find it, that read, *Gone to look for Joy. Don't worry; Sarah is with me.* The wording was far more confident than he felt, but he hoped that his mother would understand why he had to go when she read it. He knew that no matter what he said she would worry, and that was why he had decided not to call her.

"Okay, I'm not going back. Now what?" he asked.

There was no response, but he remembered Sarah pointing up and to the left and decided to try that direction. He revved the engine and tore off, deeper into the uninhabited section of the forest, the cold stinging his unprotected face.

Chapter 68

Joy had made it only a short way up the path into the woods when she realized she was going to have to get to the highway. Her befuddled brain was telling her it would be on the other side of the crest to her left. She found after a while that she could make out the shapes of the trees and the shrubbery in the darkness. There must have been a moon behind the light cloud cover, because there was a sort of glow from the sky. Or was it just her eyes playing tricks on her?

Squinting and wiping cold sweat from her brow, she peered up the hill. She could make out no path, but there seemed to be passable open ground. She started to climb.

Each step was excruciating. Several times she lost hope and sank down, only to find herself torn awake from unconsciousness by pain—she had no idea how much later—and she forced herself to get up, to keep climbing.

It felt like an eternity of endurance. To try to keep herself awake and moving, Joy began to talk to herself.

"Maybe I'm already dead. Maybe this is hell. I'll just have to keep walking in the dark and I'll never get anywhere. Shut up—yes, you will. You can make it. Just get to the road and then someone will help you. It'll be over. You can rest."

Her breathing was so labored that the inside of her throat felt as though it were scratched raw. Her body was soaked with sweat, but she couldn't stop shaking. As she passed a hand across her face to wipe the stinging sweat from her eyes, her skin felt far too hot. But she kept on climbing.

She had no idea when she reached what appeared to be the top of the crest. All she knew was that she found herself lying on a hard dirt surface without leaves or shrubbery that seemed to her limited depth perception to continue on both sides. "It's a fire road; it must be a road," she whispered to herself, trying to clear the scum from her brain. But her thoughts were so murky that she couldn't find anything solid to hold on to. She lay on her back and watched the shapes around her spin and lurch.

"Down," she rasped. "Go down, Joy. The road will be down there."

She was so thirsty that when she tried to swallow, she called out from the burning pain. Slowly she rose to her feet. Dragging her injured leg, she crept laboriously forward. She fell onto her hands and face repeatedly, the dark shapes around her growing more and more alive as her grasp on reality flickered in and out.

There was no more breath for words; she had not one more drop of strength or courage to go on. She had to stop, to rest, to give up, even. Shivering with cold and fever, she crawled on her hands and knees to a pile of leaves under a tree and, curling up into a ball of misery, let go of the world.

Chapter 69

Sheridan strode into the ER and was greeted by Officer Willoughby.

"Thanks for calling."

"You said to let you know if I heard anything. This just seemed a little too similar for my taste, if you know what I mean." Willoughby looked slightly nervous. He wasn't a detective. He didn't have very much experience, but a vicious assault on a local woman seemed like it should be mentioned to the detective who was investigating a like crime. The truth was, the disappearances of those two girls had haunted Officer Willoughby, and he would have loved to be the one to catch the fucker responsible.

"You were right. Let's go talk to him." The two started to walk toward the hospital room. "What kind of shape is he in?"

"He's in pain. I don't think the nurses want to give him a full dose of Demerol, if you know what I'm saying. But that's good for us, because he's completely coherent."

There were two officers milling around outside the room. Both of them were veterans, older and more experienced than Willoughby. They nodded and shook hands with Sheridan, whom they knew.

"How's he doing?" Sheridan asked them.

The two men exchanged looks and then both suppressed smiles. The older of the two was chewing gum, and he rolled it around in his mouth before saying, "Not too bad, considering the victim tried to bite his dick off."

All four men grimaced, but the expression was quickly followed by chuckles of admiration.

Sheridan popped a Tums in his grinning mouth. "I can't wait to meet her," he said as he pushed the door open.

He went in alone. Vince was curled on his side, facing away from the door. Sheridan walked around and stood in front of him.

"What the fuck do you want?" Vince muttered as his eyes fluttered open.

"I want to talk to you."

"Go away."

"No." Sheridan pulled up a chair and made himself comfortable. "I need you to tell me if you know where Joy Whitehorse is."

"Never heard of her."

Sheridan sighed as though this were a big problem. "I understand you've got quite a stash of ice at your bank there. You could be going away for a long, long time. There're two women next door who have a couple of small issues with you as well." Sheridan let the burning in his stomach transfer to his eyes and made sure that Vince caught the brunt of it. "You're gonna fry."

It was with satisfaction that Sheridan watched fear enter the other man. He supposed that up until now he'd been in so much pain that he hadn't really stopped to consider the fact that life as he knew it was over. He was going to jail. Real jail.

"A nice-looking guy like you oughta do all right for a while, if you find the right boyfriend." Sheridan tilted his chair back and smiled. He had very little time. He wanted to know where that girl was and whether this bastard had her.

"All right, what if I tell you where I get the drugs from?" Vince suggested hesitantly.

Sheridan shrugged his solid shoulders. "Could help, but I'm more interested in the girl."

"I don't know anything about the girl!" Sheridan watched as Vince cringed; his voice had the cowardly ring of a man who would spill anything to save his own skin. Desperation crept into his pleading. "I'll tell you where I get the drugs from. It's a big operation. That's gotta be worth something. And this guy I get the stuff from, he's a real sick fucker. You know what I mean?"

"No." Sheridan studied the man on the bed. "Illuminate me."

"He sells the stuff to kids, you know, like at the high school. I was just the middle guy, a little bit for myself and a few other people I know. . . ."

Sheridan had straightened up. "He sells to the kids at the high school?" The methamphetamine that was allegedly Joy Whitehorse's that he had found in Joshua Sands's room. The high school from which two girls had disappeared. It clicked.

"Yeah, and he's twisted, I'm telling you. You don't want me. He's the sick fuck."

Sheridan looked down at this piece of shit who had beaten two women and sexually assaulted one of them earlier tonight. He thought, *You should know a sick fuck, you sick fuck.* But what he said was, "You got a name you can give me?"

Vince looked up at the hulking mass of detective. "I'll get a deal? You have the power to make a deal?" he asked with a whimpering, sycophantic neediness.

Sheridan hesitated and then nodded. It wasn't a lie if he didn't speak it.

"I'll do better than a name," Vince spilled. "I'll give you his address."

Chapter 70

Joshua hadn't gone too far when the image of Sarah appeared with her hand stretched out in front of her. He swerved and pulled over to the side, swearing and sweating. "Okay," he muttered, "the other way. I get it."

The image of the oak tree flashed again, and Joshua wondered how many other fire-damaged oak trees there might be in this gigantic forest. He'd already seen one, and it had revealed nothing. He turned the bike and headed the other way.

He was lost in thought about what he might find when the image of Sarah, hand raised, flashed again. This time he pulled over and turned off the bike.

"Okay," he said out loud, realizing that he was talking to himself as though that were completely normal. "It's official. I'm nuts. So. You don't want me to go left and you don't want me to go right. Should I just go home?" He looked around. With the headlamp from his bike extinguished and the closest home or streetlight half a mile away, the darkness of the cloudy night was almost total.

But Sarah, it seemed, would have none of that. Off to his right, near the trees, the image of the girl flickered, this time with her hand moving in a beckoning motion.

"Into the forest?" Joshua moaned. "Are you joking?"

He climbed off the bike and took the flashlight firmly in his right hand. Switching it on, he let the dim circle of light roam over the edge of the trees. He could make out nothing at first, and then he saw a path.

"Oh, God, help me," Joshua muttered.

But he went. He walked into the complete shadowed darkness of the trees. His cheap flashlight's batteries quickly lost power, and soon he had to shake it to get even a feeble glow to help him. Finally he turned it off and hoped that his eyes would somehow adjust to any phantom light that the sky might allow.

There was Sarah, though. She kept on appearing just up ahead and beckoning, so he followed, though it cost him to do it. His hands shook from cold, and from fear—both of the vast darkness around him and of the multitude of horrors that he might find in it. He went on in spite of those fears, motivated by the more terrible option: the unfathomable possibility that he would not find anything. That he would fail Joy, Luke, Whitney, his mother, and himself.

He had to try. What else was there? As he stumbled on, sensing rather than seeing the path, his mind filled with images of what might be happening to Joy, revolting, terrifying images of pain and abuse, of suffering, of metal burning flesh. He increased his pace and shook himself to try to empty his brain of the disturbing and distracting thoughts. He tried to force himself to keep his mind clear, to think logically. If Joy were here somewhere, the most likely explanation was that whoever had taken her had dumped her here. And that would mean that she was . . . He shivered and fought down a wave of nausea.

He realized that his eyes had somehow adjusted to the almost negligible level of light so much that he could make out the shapes of trees and the rise of the road—and it was a fire road he was on—ahead of him. Small shrubs looked deceptively like coyotes or—he pushed the thought from his mind—mountain lions, but none of them moved or turned out to be the creatures he nervously imagined them to be.

He hadn't gone far when he stopped suddenly as Sarah appeared once more, just off the road. She stood, motionless now, just below the shadow of a tree. Except for the absence of the futuristic city in the background, it was eerily like his dream.

He moved forward cautiously, pulling the flashlight from his pocket and praying that it might have recovered just enough to give him a feeble beam that would precede him under that shadowy oak.

He waited until he was just at the edge of the darkest shadow, listening intently and watching with rounded eyes for the slightest of movements.

Then he heard it: a rustle so soft that it might have been the wind moving a dry leaf. His hands trembled as he pushed the switch up on the flashlight, and a thin, weak stream of light fell on the ground.

Boots, a leg, torn and bloody, and then, just before the flashlight died again, Joshua saw Joy's face.

Throwing the flashlight aside, he rushed forward. "Oh, please, God, don't be dead," he repeated again and again as he pulled her body up against his chest. The thickness of his coat prevented him from feeling any life in her body. He braced her back with one arm and pressed his other hand to her face. It was hot, sweaty hot. Fever.

"Oh, Jesus, okay, what now?" Joshua looked around in the darkness as though he might find help there, but not even Sarah revealed herself.

"Coat, okay, coat." Joshua laid Joy gently back down and took off his coat. With some difficulty he managed to get it on her. As he struggled with the zipper by feel he heard her moan.

"Joy? Can you hear me? It's me, Joshua."

He heard her smack her lips and try to speak. He leaned near her mouth and heard the air forced through her lips to make two barely audible words. "Fucking neighbor."

He smiled. "Yeah, that's me. And right now I've got to get you back to the road. I'm going to carry you."

It was a struggle to get her up, and he had no choice but to put her over his shoulder like a sack of potatoes. She wasn't that heavy, but lifting a limp hundred and ten pounds from the ground to a standing position was no easy task without help.

She moaned with pain, and her breath came faster as he started to walk. He knew where he was now. It was the oak tree he had seen before, the one that Sarah had shown him in his dream. That meant he wasn't far from home, but home wasn't where he wanted to go. He needed to get Joy to a hospital, and fast.

With her slipping in and out of consciousness, that wasn't going to happen on the back of his little dirt bike. He would need to flag someone down on the road.

Joy grew heavier with every step, and Joshua struggled to keep his movements as steady as possible, but he winced every time his weight shifted too quickly and Joy cried out in pain.

"Hang in there. Hang in there," he whispered, once for her, and once for himself.

Chapter 71

Dario was waiting for them all with a strong pot of coffee brewed when they came through the door to Greer's kitchen. Jenny was staying overnight at the hospital, but Leah was allowed to go with them as long as she promised the doctor to stay with a friend who could keep an eye on her.

Jenny and Leah had seen each other for a brief moment as Jenny was being taken in a wheelchair to be admitted to a room. Lewis had been holding her hand as though if he let it go, it might fly away and never come back.

Leah had gone to her and knelt down. Jenny's eyes filled with tears, and then she said simply, "I knew you could do it. Good for you." The two women had embraced as firmly as their many bumps and bruises allowed, and then gone to recuperate with their separate angels watching over them.

Greer put Leah to bed in the guest room, gave her one of the pain pills the hospital had sent her home with, and told her to call if she needed anything.

Leah responded with a request that she be woken if there was any news about Joy, and then watched the light coming from under the door for a few minutes, until a deep sense of safety and completeness washed over her, bringing a sweet and dream-less sleep.

Greer returned to the kitchen and asked, "Where's Joshua?"

Dario's eyes were stern. "He's gone out. He left you a note."

Greer's heart thumped loudly in her chest. She crossed to the bulletin board and read Joshua's short note, pinned up between a pizza delivery flyer and some local business cards.

"Well," she breathed when she read it. "I suppose all we can do is wait." She felt as if her torso were being ripped in half. One part was filled with hope for Joy and pride in Joshua's acceptance of his gift; the other was steeped in horror that Joshua was out alone in the dark night.

"Doesn't he have a cell phone?" Sterling asked, as though this were so obvious. "Why don't we call him?"

Greer turned her glowing eyes toward him. "Cell phones don't work until you get a couple of miles down." She walked haltingly to the window, where, closing her eyes, she placed her palm on the cold glass.

"He's all right," she said, as though willing herself to believe it. "I would feel it if he weren't."

Softly, Sterling interjected, "I thought you couldn't see the present."

"It's different. I can sense people I'm close to. I know when Joshua is in pain or in trouble," Greer told him.

She turned and he saw the fearful tears. The green of her eyes shone like jade under sunlight on water. "He's part of me."

Without another word, Sterling moved to her and wrapped her in his arms.

Chapter 72

Pistol cursed the shocks on his truck as he rode up the small pitted street toward his house. He was eager to get back there. He had a big night planned, and now that his business was concluded, he was ready for the fun to begin.

He climbed out and opened the gate.

"Damian?" Pistol called out. "Here, boy." In response he heard muted barking from the garage. "Shit, how did you get yourself locked in the garage?" Pistol muttered, but a chilly finger ran up his spine. Hadn't he closed the garage door before he left?

Something was wrong. Pistol went back and cut the engine of the truck, then stood listening for a minute. There was nothing but the wind in the trees. He told himself he was acting paranoid. Nobody knew anything. He was fine.

He walked up the few steps onto his porch and stopped again. Someone had tampered with the slats in the window of his kitchen door. One was slightly askew. He stepped forward, squinting inside.

There was a movement, and he spun around, but dark bodies moved in from every side and he found himself pinned against the wooden deck with his hands tightly bound by a plastic ratchet behind his back.

"Stay down!" someone yelled as he struggled against the knee pressing into his spine.

There was a confused noise and then he was yanked up onto his feet and marched into his own house.

A meaty hand on his shoulder forced him into a kitchen chair, and he was read his rights.

"Good evening," said a man with a badge on his breast pocket. "I'm Detective Sheridan."

Through the open door, Pistol could see a K-9 officer with a German shepherd on a short leash being led to the back of the mail truck. *Fuck.*

"What do you want?" Pistol asked him.

"I want to know where Joy Whitehorse is."

"How would I know?"

"Because you sold her drugs at the school. We have verbal statements from two witnesses, including one other minor who also purchased from you," Sheridan said calmly. "Where is she?"

"I don't fucking know!" Pistol insisted. He tried not to look at the truck outside.

"Got it!" called out one of the officers wearing a dark blue cap as he held up a manila envelope that had been ripped open by the dog.

Pistol dropped his bearded chin onto his chest. "Shit."

Sheridan stood over Pistol and nodded sagely. "Deep shit, and you're right in the middle of it." It was all he could do to keep from striking the bastard, from shaking him until his eyes bled and everything he knew spilled out of him. "Where's the girl?"

Pistol's eyes glared back at the detective. "Where's my dog?"

"Animal control took him away."

"I heard him in the garage." But even as he said it, Pistol realized that it had been the police dog he had heard.

"He had a little accident." Sheridan looked unconcerned about it.

Pistol tried to stand up. "Sit down," Sheridan ordered, straight-arming his suspect's chest so that he was forced back down and had the breath knocked out of him by his own thrust. "He'll be fine. The officer had to tranquilize him."

Pistol stared at him.

"All right, let's try something else. Where did the meth come from?"

"I don't know."

"Where did you get the meth?"

"I'm not telling you shit."

"Where's the girl?"

"I don't know. She probably ran off with a boyfriend. She was a slut."

Sheridan breathed in sharply and then said to the two officers standing behind Pistol, "Could you please go look around in the living room?"

"We checked everything: drawers, cushions, closets. They were clean."

"Why don't you check again?" They both nodded and left without a word. Sheridan waited until they were out of sight, and then he drew back a rocklike fist and hit Pistol as hard as he could right in the face.

Chapter 73

Joshua had managed to carry Joy down to the shoulder of the road. He looked both up and down but saw and heard nothing. No oncoming lights, no distant engines. He pulled out his cell phone and turned it on.

"C'mon, work!" he told it, but it disregarded his order and obstinately read, NO SIGNAL. "Damn." Joshua turned it off to save the battery in case he needed it later and put it back in his pocket. He sat down cross-legged and cradled Joy in his lap. The clouds above him were thinning, and through a break, when the moon shone through, he could see that her eyes were open.

He stroked her hair. "Hey, neighbor."

She tried to focus, but he could see the pain on her face and the wildness of fever in her eyes.

"Just rest. Help is coming," he told her, and even as he said it, he heard the hum of an engine round the far curve of the highway. Resting Joy's head gently on the rocky ground, he stood up and moved into the middle of the road. They would stop; they would have to stop, or hit him.

The headlights rounded the far corner and slowed. Joshua waved his arms and shouted, "Hey! Help! Please, I need help!" The car braked until it was almost idling toward him, and Joshua moved from in front of the bright lights to the passenger window. The pickup truck was high, and as the window was lowered Joshua recognized it and the driver.

"Mike! Thank God. It's Joy. I found her; she's hurt bad; we've got to get her to a hospital."

Mike was out of the car and at Joy's side in a few seconds. He lifted the unconscious Joy gently and far more easily than Joshua had and laid her across the wide front seat. "Here, get in and hold her head. Don't worry, son; we'll take care of her." He climbed in and knocked the car into gear, making a wide U-turn to backtrack up the road.

"Isn't Verdugo the closest hospital?" Joshua asked.

"It's almost half an hour from here," Mike told him, looking with concern at Joy's pale face. "There's a fire station just up the road; they'll have an ambulance and EMTs. We'll go there."

"Oh, right, thanks." Joshua was infinitely relieved. Only a few more minutes and then Joy would be in the right hands.

Mike focused on his driving, but he glanced curiously at Joshua. "Where and how did you find her?" he asked.

Joshua didn't know any other answer than the truth, so he tried it. "Up the trail. I know it sounds freaky, but I get these visions, and they showed me this oak tree in the woods. I knew where it was, so I went there." Joshua deliberately left out seeing dead people and the other complications. It was close enough.

"Did you see anything else?" Mike asked, looking at him with the dubious suspicion that Joshua had expected. Right now he didn't care, or want to talk about it. He just wanted to focus on getting Joy medical attention.

"No, to tell you the truth, it just started happening. I don't really understand it myself."

"Did you tell anyone else? Call for help?" Mike asked.

"No, I couldn't. My mom wasn't home when I left, and my cell phone doesn't get any reception up here."

The huge tire of the truck hit a pothole, and the vehicle jolted a bit. Joy groaned and the heavy key chain dangling from the ignition jangled. Joshua looked over at it absentmindedly.

And then his blood froze. In the pale, luminous light from the dashboard displays, he could clearly make out the charm that hung among the many keys.

An eye. The eye. The one that Joshua had seen swinging from Joy's hand. He glanced quickly up at Mike to see if he had caught his look, but he was peering straight forward intensely.

Joshua's mind was racing, reviewing the images that Sarah had shown him. The oak tree was on the path that ran between the last place he'd seen Joy and Mike's house. The path that forked away, up and to the left from Mike's cabin. The motorcycle image that was Mike's business and his hobby. Mike had even associated himself with the image. Joshua could see clear as day the moment that the man had pointed to first himself and then his card, saying, "Mike, bike." What a fool he'd been! The charm on the key chain, which Mike wore right out in the open on his belt loop. A talisman that most people used to ward off evil, but that he had used *for* evil.

Fearfully, Joshua tried to assess his situation. He glanced sideways again at Mike. The man was much bigger than he was, powerfully built, and at the peak of his strength. Joshua would be no physical match for him. They were headed away from any other houses or streets, deeper into the open forest. They would pass few, if any, other cars this late at night.

The fire station was just up ahead on the right. Joshua could see the lights off to one side. He closed his eyes and prayed. *Please let me be wrong; please let him turn in. Please turn.*

But Mike didn't even slow down. Joshua said nothing, too mortified to speak. The stupidity of what he'd done came home to him, and with a frost that he felt to his marrow, he realized that most likely he had killed not only Joy but himself as well. With a suffocating sense of sorrow and loss for his mother, he turned and looked directly at Mike.

Mike hit the lock button on his armrest, but they were moving a good fifty miles an hour, too fast for Joshua to jump out. He seemed to relax now that they'd passed the ranger station, and he draped one hand along the back of the seat.

Joshua found his voice. "Where are we going?" he asked, but he thought he knew.

"Well, I can't very well take you home, now, can I?" Mike turned and looked at Joshua. There was a deadness in his eyes that Joshua wished he had noticed before. "Have you figured it out now?"

Joshua nodded and swallowed hard to force back down the sob that was rising in his throat.

"We'll go someplace nice and private."

Joshua stared ahead, pretending to watch the road, but his brain was working as he focused inward. *Sarah,* he was calling silently, and though he didn't know it, he was repeating his mother's words: *Sarah, help me.*

Chapter 74

Greer's head swiveled expectantly to the door before the other two heard the crunch of footsteps on the gravel outside. She rose and opened it just as Luke and Whitney started up the porch stairs.

"Have you heard anything?" she asked.

Both of them shook their heads and stepped into the kitchen. Sterling was introduced, and Greer was impressed with the gracefulness of his nonpatronizing sympathy toward them.

"Where's Joshua?" Luke asked.

There was a quiet moment, and then Dario spoke. "He's gone to look for Joy."

"What?" Whitney asked. "Where?"

"I have something to tell you," Greer began. She explained what had been happening to both her and Joshua, and apologized for not being able to tell them before. "It wasn't my place . . . if there had been anything specific or definite, I would have come to you. I told Detective Sheridan everything he saw, I just made it seem like I had seen it. Joshua's afraid of the gift. Well, he *was* afraid."

Whitney was perched on the edge of her chair, her black eyes framed by the dark circles beneath them. "Has he seen something specific now?" she asked.

"I don't know." Greer told her, taking her hand.

"He sees guides, spirit guides; it's different from the colors and emotional impressions that I get. He left us a note saying that one of the guides was with him, so we shouldn't worry." Greer tried to smile.

Dario made an attempt to shift the focus off of Joshua for Greer's sake. "Greer told me that Joy's mother had come around. Where is she?"

Luke and Whitney both looked at the floor before he answered, barely keeping the disgust out of his voice. "In the guest room, snoring like a pig."

"Oh," Dario said, "I see. Well, that explains quite a bit."

"Doesn't it, though?" Luke asked.

The sound of a car engine coming down the dirt track pulled their attention outside. They all strained to see who it was, but Sterling was the one who recognized it first. "Unmarked cop car," he said.

They watched as the door opened and Detective Sheridan got out. He paused to put something in his mouth and then proceeded toward Greer's door.

Whitney reached for Luke's hand. He took it and squeezed once, and then rose to meet the detective.

Sheridan looked slightly surprised when Luke opened Greer's door. He knew enough about the anguish parents of missing children lived through to speak directly. "Mr. Whitehorse, I'm afraid I don't have any news for you yet."

Everyone seemed to breathe at the same time.

"Is Ms. Sands in?"

"I'm here." Greer stepped up next to Luke. "Please come in. How can I help you?"

The detective came into the kitchen and regarded the faces that watched him eagerly. He felt deeply sorry that he hadn't done more, that there was nothing he could tell them to expel them from purgatory.

"You called my office earlier and left a message that you needed to speak to me. I'm assuming it was about the Vince Slater incident." He narrowed his eyes at Greer. "You seem to have found a great deal of trouble in this little community."

"Oh, no, we're not going into that again, are we?"

Sheridan managed a weak, tired smile. "Not unless you turn out to be connected to Mr. Slater."

"I happen to be friends with his ex-wife," Greer said. Then, noting the exhaustion on the detective's face, she asked, "Would you like a cup of coffee?"

Sheridan winced. "I wish I could, but I'm fighting off a bleeding ulcer."

"So did he have anything to do with Joy?" Greer asked hopefully. She sat down again, very close to Sterling. He noticed the proximity and shifted to make it even closer.

"Not directly, that we can tell. He's connected to one *major* drug operation, though—probably the one that supplied the drugs she hid in your son's room. You might like to know that we arrested your postman tonight. He's the one who was selling the methamphetamine to the kids at the high school."

Luke's hands formed into tight fists, and Whitney pulled one to her and started to loosen it finger by finger.

"We also arrested the guy you called us about." Sheridan nodded his head toward Dario. "Turns out the girl he picks up is his cousin."

"Oh," Dario said. "I'll have to apologize."

"We got another anonymous tip that the same guy was carrying meth in the saddlebags of his bike. But Leah Falconer told us later that she had seen Vince Slater plant it there. Apparently they had a little altercation at a bar over the way he was treating a girl, and framing Newman was Slater's idea of recreation. So, he's clean."

"Are we talking about Army?" Greer asked, surprised.

Dario nodded. "Pistol told me he'd seen him pick a young girl up at school, and I thought with the motorcycle and the prison record . . ."

"No, you did the right thing," Sheridan told him. "No harm done. We didn't even stick him with the drug charge; his blood was clean when we apprehended him. What's this about a motorcycle?"

Looks went all around the room. Everyone wondered who should speak or where to begin. Of course, all eyes landed on Greer.

"Detective, I have something to confess. I did have premonitions about Joy and then Leah Falconer coming to harm, but some of the images that I told you about came from my son."

Sheridan had guessed that the night they'd seen Zoe Caldwell at the hospital, but he didn't comment on his deduction. He had done the count when he came in, and he didn't need to look around now to know that Joshua wasn't there. "Where is he?" His voice was grim.

"He's gone out to look for Joy."

Sheridan sighed. "And *where* has he gone to look for her?" he asked wearily.

Dario took over. "We don't know. He left that note." He pointed behind the detective.

Sheridan turned and walked to the bulletin board. He read the note quickly. "Who's Sarah?" he asked in a voice that seemed not to really want to know, but resigned to hear the answer.

Greer explained while everyone else sat and listened to her story. "She was my friend; she was killed when we were fifteen. I asked for her help to find Joy. I was just praying, and it seems she heard me." Greer shrugged, as though apologetic that they might not be able to believe her, but it was true anyway. "She's been appearing to Joshua in dreams and waking. She keeps showing him an oak tree damaged by fire, a motorcycle, and a set of keys. We've tried to figure out what that means. Joshua's so new at this that he hasn't learned how to interpret signs. That part takes a long time. For me, the signs are personal. Colors mean something, but it took me a while to figure out which ones meant what. For instance, I might look at Sterling and see an orange glow around him. That wouldn't mean he likes citrus fruit. To me, who associates orange with health and vitality, it means that his energy and stamina are very good. Do you understand what I'm saying?"

"So, in other words," Sheridan asked, "those particular things that your son is, uh, 'seeing' might not have to do with Joy so much as with Joshua?"

"Exactly," Greer agreed.

"But it might be something to do with Joy and her kidnapper?"

Greer nodded. "That much seems certain. It's the interpretation that's difficult. It could be literal or representative. I just don't know."

Sheridan stood motionless for a moment. Finally he said, "He definitely saw an image of a motorcycle?" He was thinking of the only clue he had about the suspect at the motel. She nodded.

He turned slowly back to the bulletin board. "Like *that* motorcycle?"

He brought his hand up deliberately and pointed at the card that Mike had given Joshua what seemed like months ago, but which had really been only a few days. It had the picture of a motorcycle, and a phone number underneath it.

Greer stood up to get a better look at what he was pointing to. Luke had his back to Sheridan, and he twisted in his chair to look over his shoulder. "Yes," Greer said, "I guess so. He didn't say what kind. Only . . ."

But she let the words die. Luke was coming to his

feet. He moved to the card and ripped it off the board. "This is Mike's card," he said, staring at it.

"Yes, he gave it to Joshua and told him to call if we needed help."

"I know it's Mike's card; I've got one in my book. And that's why I didn't think anything of it when I found one in Joy's drawer."

Whitney stood up and put her hand on her husband's arm. "Honey?" she said tentatively.

His face was twisted in rage and confusion. "It was in the same drawer as the walkie-talkie," he said. "Could it be?" Luke's strong, handsome features crumbled. "Could it be him? He's our neighbor; we've known him for years."

Sheridan had already started to move toward the phone. A neighbor. Almost always someone they knew and trusted. "Where is his house?" he asked. Luke was on his feet, and Sheridan reversed his direction and stood to block the door. Sterling was next to him in a minute, and as soon as Dario understood he had placed a large hand on Luke's substantial arm.

"Hold on there." Sheridan spoke calmingly. "We're going, but let's do this right. The last thing you want now is to go barging in there, have him panic, and get her hurt. Much better to do this nice and quiet." He watched as the idea crossed over Luke's face.

With a gigantic effort of will Luke stopped himself from fighting his way through the three men and charging out the door. He forced himself to nod.

Sheridan picked up the phone and called for backup.

Please, God, the detective thought, *let her be alive.*

Chapter 75

The higher up the twisting highway they drove, the thicker the trees grew on either side. Twice now, Mike had slowed down as they came to a turnoff, and shone a flashlight around the area. Both times he had grunted and then sped on.

But now he was turning onto a small dirt track. The powerful headlights of the truck illuminated the road ahead. It curved into the trees, out of sight of the main road, and Mike drove along, the truck bouncing in and out of deep holes and pitted ruts.

About a hundred yards in, the road ended in a pile of tangled tree trunks and branches that seemed to be as far as a bulldozer had gone. They were covered with dirt and moss, obviously untouched for a long time. It seemed as though someone had started to clear a road, been suddenly called away, and then forgotten about it years ago. Mike cut the engine, turned off the lights, and sat listening. Nothing. Not a car or another living soul for miles around.

Joshua didn't know what this place was, but he had a bad feeling he knew what it was about to become: the place where he and Joy were buried.

He pulled Joy's head tighter up against his chest, and her eyes fluttered open again. "Shh," he urged.

"Just sleep; it's okay." He didn't know what else to say. Maybe she wouldn't feel anything.

Mike got out of the truck and stood looking around with his flashlight. Joshua could see only what fell into the bright circle of light from his torch. The trees, the leaf litter on the ground. The cold, hard ground.

Joshua's panic began to subside into an almost supernatural calm. So this was it. *This is where I end.* But, he decided, he wouldn't just walk out there and die. He was going to fight; at least he would struggle, maybe even inflict some pain on this bastard.

This is my life, not his! Joshua was thinking. *Who is he to say it's over?* Joy's favorite descriptive word rose in Joshua's mental monologue, and he had to laugh to himself when he recognized it. *Fuck this!* he thought. *And fuck him.*

Carefully he eased Joy's head from his lap. Mike had left his door open and walked a few feet away, where he was kicking at the ground, testing its firmness. Joshua moved himself along between the seat and the dash until he was on the driver's side. He watched tensely as Mike leaned down to move a fallen branch, and Joshua launched himself toward the big man.

Joshua kicked him hard in the back, and Mike went sprawling to the ground with a curse. The flashlight flew from his hand and landed somewhere to the right in a pile of pine needles, casting a jagged beam on the trunk of a nearby tree. Joshua jumped onto Mike's back with both knees, knocking the breath out of the other man, and tried to get his arm around his neck. Joshua knew very little about actual fighting, and it quickly became apparent to him that it was very different from what he'd seen on TV or in the movies.

With a roar of rage, Mike flipped over, sending Joshua scrambling to stay on his feet. It was dark, but there was enough light from the shrouded moon and the flashlight's residual glow for the two men to see the outline of each other. Mike moved toward Joshua, his breath coming in short bursts as he recovered from Joshua's blow. Lunging toward Mike with all his weight, Joshua caught him in the midsection with his shoulder, hoping to knock him to the ground again.

But the big man barely moved. Now he was expecting it, and he was angry. He grabbed Joshua's hair with one hand and pulled his head back far enough to hit him with the other fist. Joshua reeled from the blow, but Mike did not release him. Instead he hit Joshua in the face again, and then in the midsection so hard that Joshua was sure his stomach must be crushed against his spine.

He couldn't breathe; both his arms had stopped flailing for Mike and were now wrapped tightly around his body to try to shield himself from more pain than he had ever known. Mike hit him again, this time in the side, where he was not protected, and Joshua thought he felt a rib crack.

Mike still had hold of his hair, and with a yank he sent Joshua hurling to the ground, where Joshua lay panting and curled into a ball. Mike put his boot on Joshua's side and rolled him onto his back; then he straddled Joshua and sat on him, effectively pinning him to the ground.

Joshua felt Mike's huge hands go around his throat, and he clawed at them, trying to free himself as Mike started to squeeze. Joshua found his body separated from its ability to take in air. The pain in his body, the rocks that cut into his back, all that went away, and every fiber in Joshua's body, every cell in his brain, scrambled desperately for a solution, a way out, a chance to live. The bubbling pressure in his head and the frantic kicking of his legs intensified, and then a great weakness came over him, and he felt incapable of effort. His eyes closed and his body went limp.

The world around him vibrated distantly. He thought, *It's over.*

Mike's grunting breath suddenly stopped, his mouth opened, and his grip lessened. Joshua found one last burst of strength; he pulled the hands away from his neck and sucked hard on the frigid, welcome air, gasping and gulping the life back into his body.

Above him, Mike's hands were raised, as though in a parody of surrender, and his back was arched. Joshua struggled and kicked as he worked to get enough oxygen to clear the black fuzziness from his eyes.

Mike's body went rigid and he fell to one side, into the beam of the flashlight. The bright light directly on his face showed a look of stunned disbelief as Mike stared upward. Joshua kicked himself free and rolled away. Then he understood.

Joy was standing over Mike, hunched and breathing laboriously, a bloody knife clutched in her hand. Even as Joshua watched in amazement, she lunged at Mike again, stabbing at his hand, his arm, and then his chest. The sucking *thunk* of the knife as it plunged in up to the hilt and the click as it connected with bone jarred Joshua's ears, and bile rose in his mouth. Again and again she stabbed as the big man tried to fend her off, his face a horrified mask of incredulity, but finally, with a choking gurgle as though his throat had filled with blood, he sank down and lay still.

Joshua recovered himself enough to reenter the grisly scene. He fought his way to his feet and came around behind Joy. Her skin was burning to the touch, but he wrapped his arms around her, pinning both of hers down, and started to croak through his damaged throat, "Stop, Joy, stop. It's over; he's dead. It's over; it's okay. Stop."

He felt her go limp in his arms, and, unable to bear even his own weight, he sank down with her to the freezing ground, Joy with the blood-covered knife still in her hand, Joshua clutching her tightly against him.

For a few minutes he was aware only of the sound and feeling of his own booming heartbeat and tortured gasping. But as he settled down and both his and Joy's panting subsided, he became aware of the quiet in the clearing. All he could hear were crickets, wind, and the grateful, even breathing of two people as the warmth of their living breath mingled with the frosty air of the forest.

Chapter 76

The parking area was awash with vehicles as Joshua guided the truck down the dirt road, including—he was relieved to note—an ambulance. Joy lay with her head in his lap. He had argued that they should go straight for medical help, but she had begged pathetically to see her dad. It was only a few miles farther, and Joshua—feeling that she needed her father's support as much as a doctor's—had consented.

As he came around the last curve, he laid a palm on the horn and didn't let go until he pulled to a stop.

The doors of both Luke's and his mother's houses opened and a stream of people came out. A well of emotion surged up in Joshua, and he put the truck in park. Letting his head fall back against the headrest, he began to weep. He felt Joy's hand come up to touch his face.

"It's okay," she said weakly. "You did good."

His door was ripped open, and Joshua saw he was facing two SWAT team members and their guns. "Get your hands up where we can see them!" one of them shouted.

But another voice from behind them barked a different order: "Put your guns down; it's the kid!"

Joshua recognized Detective Sheridan as he stepped

into the light from the cab of the truck, and then he felt hands reaching in to pull him down out of the car.

"Joy, help Joy," he insisted, fighting away the hands.

"It's okay, son," the detective was saying to him. "It's okay. We've got her."

Joshua looked over to see that the passenger-side door was open and an EMT was climbing up into the cab. The man began to pull back the bloodstained coat, searching her chest for the source of the wound.

"No, that's not her blood. Her leg is bad, though, and she's really hot," Joshua mumbled.

The paramedic looked up at Joshua and smiled reassuringly. "We'll take care of her." Then he turned and spoke to his partner, who was standing just outside. "Let's get a backboard and some oxygen in here. We need to take a look at this kid's eye too."

Joshua raised his hand to his left eye. It was swollen and painful to the touch. He hadn't even thought about his own injuries. He must look horrible. He was suddenly afraid for his mother to see him this way.

"Let's go inside," said Detective Sheridan. "Your mother's here. Can you walk?"

"Yeah, I can walk," Joshua told him, but when his feet touched the ground he would have fallen if it weren't for the steady arm of the solid detective.

"Joshua, thank God you're all right!" Greer had come to support him from the other side. She would not allow herself to cry over her son when he and Joy needed help, but she had to fight for control. They started moving toward the house.

Luke and Whitney were standing nervously just behind the EMTs.

"Wait," Joshua said. And they stood and watched as Joy was carefully lifted from the car seat onto the stretcher. Whitney and Luke were beside her in a moment; her father was holding her hand and stroking her hair.

"Oh, baby." He smiled, tears streaming down his face.

Joy opened her eyes and started to cry. "I'm sorry, Daddy. I'm so sorry," she sobbed.

"Hush—there isn't anything to be sorry for. Now be quiet and save your strength."

At that moment another woman pushed Whitney aside and forced herself up against the stretcher, effectively blocking the working paramedic. "Get out of my way. I'm her mother!"

She looked down at the battered girl and then glared up at Luke. "Look at her! This is your fault; look what you've done to her!" Joy's eyes fluttered and she cringed away. "And you!" Pam said venomously to her daughter. "This is what you get for being stupid!"

It happened very fast. One minute Pam was standing, and the next minute Whitney's fist had made contact with the other woman's jaw and she had crumpled to the ground. Whitney stepped over her to resume her place next to Luke and comfort Joy, and everyone else turned their attention back to the girl as the stretcher was moved to the waiting ambulance.

Pam got up from the ground holding her jaw with a stunned expression. She looked wildly around and fixed on Detective Sheridan. "You saw that! She assaulted me! I want her arrested for attacking me!"

Detective Sheridan got a better grip on Joshua's belt loop, and he and Greer started moving forward again. "Sorry, ma'am," he said. "I didn't see anything except justifiable self-defense." They moved a few feet along, and then he stopped and turned back to the fuming woman, whose mouth was opening and closing speechlessly. "By the way," he told her, "I'd like a word with you later about using a minor to procure illegal substances."

Sheridan waited until Joshua had been examined, cleaned up, and wrapped in a warm blanket with a mug of hot chocolate in his hand before he questioned him. Joshua told him, as best he could, where the rangers could find Mike's body. He told him, in a voice that broke frequently, how he had found Joy, how Mike had picked them up, and how stupid he'd been not to have read the obvious signs before.

Sheridan could only shake his head. "You weren't stupid. You were brave, and you were smart. Hell, you told me the same signs and I didn't really even believe you, much less figure them out."

Greer was stroking her son's hair, and she looked up mischievously at the detective. "I thought you believed us at the hospital."

"No," Sheridan confessed. "As a detective I had to consider all the possibilities, including that I *might* be overly skeptical, but I still had trouble buying it."

"Then when?"

"When Mrs. Caldwell tried to kill herself."

Greer gasped, "Is she . . . ?"

Sheridan shook his head. "She's all right. We had the nurse keeping an eye on her, and she took an overdose of painkillers, but not enough to kill her."

Joshua was watching the detective, and he could see the sadness in the man's face. "Zoe didn't make it, did she?" he asked softly.

"No," said Sheridan. "She didn't."

Joshua was nodding. His mother had put her face in her hands. "It's okay, Mom. I knew she was going. Sarah was waiting to take her." He couldn't understand it, but somehow he had a calm, knowing feeling that it was all right. That nobody ever died alone.

"Well." Sheridan got to his feet and closed his notepad. "That's all I'm going to bother you with tonight. Tomorrow will be soon enough to get through the piles of paperwork." He twisted suddenly, raising a hand to his waist. "Sorry, I need to take this." He pulled out his vibrating beeper and asked, "May I?"

"Please, help yourself." Greer gestured to the phone. She and Joshua sat in grateful silence for a few moments, listening to the murmur of the detective's voice.

He came back and returned the phone to its cradle, then said, "I need to go to the hospital and have another chat with Vince Slater. Something else has come up." He didn't exactly smile, but he looked pleased.

Greer looked up at him and asked hopefully. "He won't be able to hurt Leah anymore, will he?"

"No, ma'am, he's going away for a long time. That call was from my partner, who's working with the investigation team at Mike's house. Guess what they turned up?"

Joshua and Greer waited, afraid to ask.

"The deed to a little house on Sutter Street, so he took a ride over there. Turned out to be the meth lab we've been looking for. And there was a transaction book titled, 'Slater.' Looks like Vince and Mike have had a very profitable little business going for a couple of years now."

Greer was shaking her head. "So they were connected?"

"Must have been, but they were smart enough to hide it. Funny how people find each other. I must say, it's been a productive night." Detective Sheridan's eyes crinkled at the corners and he smiled, just slightly, but he actually smiled.

And something else. Something felt different. Then he realized that, for the first time in weeks, his stomach wasn't burning.

Chapter 77

Dario and Sterling had both waited patiently in the den, and now, with the first light of day showing through the windows, they came in to see the detective off. The phone rang, and it was Whitney calling from the hospital. She told Greer that Joy was out of danger; her fever had come down, and she was sleeping peacefully. The doctors had cleaned and stitched up her leg, and, with luck, she'd be headed home in a day or two. Greer relayed the news to a round of relieved sighs and cheers.

"How about breakfast?" Sterling asked. "I'll cook."

Joshua was so tired his head was almost nodding against his chest, but he was ravenously hungry. "Yes, please!" he exclaimed. "I think I can stay awake just long enough to shovel down some eggs and bacon."

"That would be great, thanks," Greer said. She didn't want to leave her son's side yet. When he slept it would be all right, but not just yet.

"I'll help you," Dario offered, and the two of them set to work, making small talk about anything, everything, feeling the exaltation that only a sense of perspective could give.

Joshua leaned against his mom and watched the light rise outside the window. The bacon was sizzling, and everyone had fallen into a happy, quiet lull when he saw him.

It was still dark enough outside to make the window reflective, and the figure of the man was just over his mother's right shoulder. Joshua pulled away from her and turned to face her. She looked at him curiously.

"What?"

"He's here," Joshua said, smiling. "Dad. He's here."

At the sink Dario stopped and spun around. Sterling took the skillet off the flame very slowly and quietly, so as not to be distracting, and they all waited.

"Where?" Greer asked.

"Just over your right shoulder. He's holding something in his hand. It's a bird, a white bird."

Dario made a small exclamation, but said nothing further.

"He's holding it up . . . Now he's opened his hand and the bird is flying away." The figure of his father pointed first at Greer and then at Dario, and then repeated the motion of releasing the bird. "I know what he means," Joshua said, smiling. "He means that it's time for both of you to let go and move on. He's okay, he's moved on, and he wants you to be okay too."

Slowly, Joshua watched his father's face, glowing with love, pride, and a kind of indescribable joy, fade away, and he knew that that love and pride would forever remain a part of him. He felt the unbreakable connection to his father.

"He's gone," Joshua said to the three silent, amazed faces he found concentrating on him. "He's gone," he repeated. But the words didn't feel sad; they felt peaceful, okay.

Greer and Dario looked at each other. "He's right, you know," she said to him. "It's not just me; it's you too."

Dario nodded, his masculine face tight with contained emotion. "I know. I keep acting like you need to find someone else, but it's just an excuse to keep me from doing it."

Greer's eyes went shyly to Sterling, who was beaming at her. "I've got a feeling," he said, "that this is going to be a terrific Thursday."

They all laughed and eased slowly back into making breakfast, and sipping tea, and talking softly.

Dario had started to hum to himself as he made pancakes, Sterling was telling a funny story about eating eggs cooked in beer at the pub, and as Greer listened she watched her son.

His face was bruised, swollen, and lopsided. His lower lip protruded, and there were two small black cuts where his own teeth had cut into it. He wasn't a pretty sight, but Greer thought he was the most glorious thing she had ever seen. She knew that Luke and Whitney felt the same way about Joy.

It's true, she thought, *that beauty is in the eye of the beholder.*

Read ahead for a sneak peek at the next Greer Sands novel, coming in fall 2008.

The wind, hot and fierce, swept across the brown-green sage, bending the brittle branches and tugging the roots from the parched soil. It pushed ruthlessly at the skeletal leaves of the sycamores in the dry river-bed, and threw its vicious weight against the arid hills of Angeles Crest Forest.

Every year it came, sweeping the heat from the desert to Los Angeles with punishing, dehydrating gusts, and every year it came at the worst time. After almost six months without a drop of rain it came, turning the desert landscape into acres of kindling, vast swaths of dry brush leading to heartier fuel: drought-weakened trees and thousands of homes.

Greer Sands stood at the window, watching the wind blast the shriveled landscape. Behind her, a rite as old as childbirth was being played out as a community of women celebrated the expected birth of a new child; yet she felt drawn away from the women laughing and sharing their wisdom, pulled toward the unstable weather outside. It was impossible for anyone who lived in fear of fire to ignore the threat of those winds, but for Greer it was something more.

The winds strummed a melody, both forlorn and ominous, that reverberated in her marrow. It brought a feeling of being at the mercy of things greater than herself. Greer bowed her head in acknowledgment of the greatness she perceived, then exhaled the shakiness that had possessed her.

"Greer," said her friend Whitney's voice softly behind her, "are you okay?"

Greer smiled back at Whitney and hastened to reassure her. "I'm fine. It's just this wind. It's hard for me not to listen to it."

Whitney nodded, easily understanding the meaning beneath her friend's surface explanation. She moved closer and asked in a quiet voice, "Everything copacetic?"

Focusing on the question brought a quiver to Greer's breastbone. She placed a palm flat against it and half closed her eyes, letting the quiver expand until she could read it, see it as a color or a shape. It glowed, undulating in her mind's eye like a huge cloud of light, multicolored, with dark, impenetrable sections. "I don't know," Greer said slowly. "I can feel something huge. . . ."

"Oh my God, how cute is that!" came a voice from the sofa. It was accompanied by oohs and ahs in a range of soprano notes.

Happily distracted, Greer and Whitney turned to admire the blue sleeper that their friend Jenny was holding up over her swelled stomach. Even seven months pregnant, Jenny looked sexy. Her Hispanic descent was serving her well through her pregnancy: Her golden skin glowed with a sunny flush, and the extra weight added to her natural baby-fat curves in a flattering way.

"Oh." She beamed. "Louis is going to love this. He so wants it to be a boy." She smiled a little sadly. "I wish he was here."

"No boys allowed!" someone shouted.

"I just wish he could feel every kick like I do," Jenny purred.

Mindy's voice dropped to a sarcastic growl. "That

feeling gets stronger when you go into labor, except you'll wish you were the one kicking him."

The group of women shared a laugh that cut off abruptly as the kitchen door opened and a male figure entered the room. The burly man in a cowboy hat stopped when he saw the dozen women focused on him. His eyes scanned the room and then, turning his large palms up, he asked exasperatedly, "What?"

The women burst into laughter again, and Mindy got up and crossed over to her husband.

"I'm sorry, honey, it's not you; it's just your timing. I think everyone's met my husband, Reading, except you." Mindy pointed to Greer. "Reading, this is Whitney's new neighbor, Greer."

"You have a lovely home," Greer said, gesturing to the spacious vaulted ceiling of the ranch house before reaching out to shake hands. As her soft skin met his rough fingers, a distinctly unpleasant jolt went through her fingers. It didn't travel up her arm, as sometimes happened when she met a person intent on harm, but the jolt caused her to look more deeply at the man. His eyes were guarded, but she sensed nothing more.

"Nice to meet you too," Reading was saying. He released Greer's hand, and she wondered whether her reaction had been only a residual effect of her overall unease. "Well, I've got to go out and hose off a couple of the horses. They get overheated in this infernal devil wind, and it must be damned uncomfortable." Reading turned to Jenny. "You want me to give Le Roi a hose-down?"

"Yes, please." Jenny looked relieved. "I worry about him so much in this weather, but I don't know how *you* can stand to work outside in this dry heat."

Reading looked up at her with a glint of mean humor in his eyes. "It's either heatstroke out there or estrogen radiation in here. I can tell you which one will drop me faster."

With that, he waved a hand at the laughing women, kissed Mindy and headed out. Greer watched him go, then turned her attention to back to the ladies, watching as Whitney pulled out a small pink-wrapped gift.

"I'm betting it's a girl," Whitney said. And with a pleased smile, she handed over the package.

Jenny looked very touched when she removed the lid of the small white box and gazed down on a child-sized silver bracelet with a single turquoise stone banded in silver.

There were tears in Jenny's eyes as she looked up at her friend. "You made this, didn't you?"

"Yes, and I can make it bigger as she grows."

"What if it's a boy?" Mindy teased.

"I'll turn it into a tie tack," Whitney fired back.

But Jenny put her hand over her stomach with a small exclamation. "Oh my goodness, she didn't like that," she said with a smile. "I'm *sure* it's a girl. See, there's her tiara, and over here"—she prodded gently at her tummy—"that *must* be a high heel."

"I think we should ask Greer if it's a boy or a girl," Whitney said with a sly smile.

"That's right, you're psychic!" Mindy gushed. Greer squirmed slightly.

"I told you before," Greer said, "I've never done that, and please, I don't want you painting the nursery pink or blue based on a feeling I might get—"

"Please," Jenny pleaded, cutting her off. She had asked before, but Greer had flatly refused. Now Jenny had a room full of enthusiastic women on her side.

"All right," Greer agreed reluctantly. "But only if everyone in the room does the same thing and makes a guess. We can write them all down and see later who was right. You cannot take my impression as final." Greer had some feelings that were vague and some that were undeniably distinct. Then there were the visions, which were as clear as watching a moving picture, but still open to interpretation. She had no idea what this would be.

"Okay, Greer goes last. Everyone else make a line," said one of the other women, who stood up and took control. "Mindy, can you get me a pad of paper and a pencil? I'll keep the list. I'll start with me, and I say girl."

The ladies all lined up and took their time rubbing Jenny's surrendered belly as though it were a crystal ball, doing different bad impressions of stereotypical fortune-tellers. Greer pursed her full lips into a puffy moue so they resembled a round, overstuffed pink satin cushion; this was exactly why she had never advertised her ability, though she couldn't deny that this was only good-natured fun.

As Greer waited her turn, her grass green eyes floated around the handsome room. Her gaze landed on a lovely landscape painting over the stone fireplace, a peaceful mountainous view; it looked vaguely familiar.

"Mindy?" Greer addressed the smaller woman, who had just proclaimed Jenny's child a bucking-bronco-riding cowboy. "Is that a painting of one of the canyons near here?"

Mindy's eyes followed Greer's gaze. "Oh yeah, that's one of R.J.'s paintings. Local artist. Isn't it beautiful?"

"Very," Greer agreed. "Which canyon is it?"

"It's a view from up above the dam. I just love R.J.'s work. I own three of his paintings." She smiled proudly.

Rising, Greer left the group to their fun and went to stand in front of the painting to get a better look at it. It had that luminous feeling when the artist captures the light just before dusk that makes it so easy to fall into the feeling of the place. Greer relaxed her eyes and let her mind wander over the sensation of the picture rather than observing the paint and the artist's technique.

It happened before she could even sense that it was coming. Without warning, the picture before her became real: The greens and golds leaped to life and then, in a flash that Greer could actually feel on her face, they burst into flames. She stepped back suddenly from the painting, instinctively raising one hand protectively to block the imagined heat.

"Greer, your turn!" someone called from behind her. The image disappeared as suddenly as it had come.

Greer spun around; she had forgotten that she was in a room filled with women who saw only the objects struck by light in their fields of vision. She tried to smile, to recover quickly, but she saw both Jenny's and Whitney's faces tighten in concern at her own expression.

"You okay?" Jenny asked.

All the women were looking at her quizzically. Greer took a deep breath and smiled. "Oh, sure, it's just the wine. I felt a little light-headed for a minute," she lied.

Whitney frowned. She had not bought it.

Throwing Whitney a glance that she hoped would read as "I'll tell you later," Greer crossed over to where Jenny was lying back on the blue sofa with her tummy exposed. Greer sat down on the coffee table facing her and, closing her eyes, she took three deep, cleansing breaths, willing the shock that she had felt at the vision of fire to calm and leave her body so that she could get a clear reading, if one came.

Rubbing her hands together to make sure they were warm, Greer placed them flat on Jenny's belly and closed her eyes.

Immediately an image came to mind. A girl—definitely a girl, with dark hair and shining eyes—was walking toward her with sunlight glinting off her long, thick hair. The picture was so stunning and charming that Greer laughed out loud. "She's going to be a beauty," said Greer, and most of the women clapped their hands and cheered. Only Mindy and another woman who had guessed male booed. "It's funny," Greer went on when they quieted. "I see her almost grown up, about fourteen. I'd say . . ."

But Greer forgot entirely what she was about to say. Over the radiant and blissful image that she held in her mind had come another. It was Jenny's face that hovered in Greer's mind now, and her expression was as far from happy and sunny as was possible. In Greer's vision Jenny's face held a look of sheer terror. Her eyes darted everywhere as though looking for some way of escape, and over her, blotting out all else, hovered dark, black wings.

Greer had seen those wings before; she was sure of it. What did they mean to her? Where had she seen them? She forced herself to focus on the feeling they gave her and remember it. Yes! She had seen them before in a famous painting, been struck by their perfection as a metaphor. They had been on an angel. Huge black wings on an angel of terrible and final beauty.

The angel of death.

ONE COLD NIGHT

by Kate Pepper

One cold night she disappeared....

New York Police detective Dave Strauss is haunted by
the one case he couldn't solve. A schoolgirl vanished off
the streets of New York, with only a trail of blood and a
series of untraceable phone calls from "the Groom"
hinting at her fate. Now the cold dark night has
engulfed another young girl—but this time she is part of
Dave's family. He and his wife, Susan, know
fourteen-year-old Lisa has not run away, and they know
her disappearance is not just a tragic coincidence. And
once the first phone call comes, they know she's
not alone....

Also Available
Here She Lies
Seven Minutes to Noon
Five Days in Summer

**Available wherever books are sold or at
penguin.com**

HOLLY LISLE

I SEE YOU

For paramedic Dia Courvant, each day brings
the possibility of facing blood and death. But
nothing can match the horror of the day she
was dispatched to the scene of a terrible car
accident and rescued the sole survivor—only to
find her own husband dead in the wreckage.
Four years later, a series of deadly car crashes
brings handsome detective Brig Hafferty into
Dia's life. She's drawn to Brig, but can she
trust him enough to tell him of the terror that
stalks her? For Dia has received a message
warning her of danger and death—a message
that seems to have been sent to her from
beyond the grave....

Available wherever books are sold or at
penguin.com